D0053801

Praise for the Darwen Arkwright series

"Great storytelling draws you into the book just as surely as Darwen—a Lancashire lad caught in the USA—is drawn through the mirror!"
—JOSEPH DELANEY, author of *The Last Apprentice*

"Impressive feats of imagination. . . . Young readers will certainly agree with the author's supposition that some teachers are simply inhuman." —BCCB

"Hartley is most effective in creating an air of menace . . . along with an on-target satire of a school overly enamored with standardized testing."
—BOOKLIST

"A fantastic entry. . . . A. J. Hartley shows an uncanny, brilliant ability to shape the inner life of an unmoored child." —*New York Times* bestselling author ELOISA JAMES

"Jam-packed with action from the first to the last page. The characters are well drawn, the alternative world fully developed, and the situations deliciously scary. There hasn't been such a 'mirroculous' adventure since Alice climbed through the looking glass to play chess with the Red Queen. Monsters, machines, and mayhem—this imaginative story has it all, making it an enticing selection for young readers who fell in love with *The Golden Compass* and *The Chronicles of Narnia*." —NEW YORK JOURNAL OF BOOKS

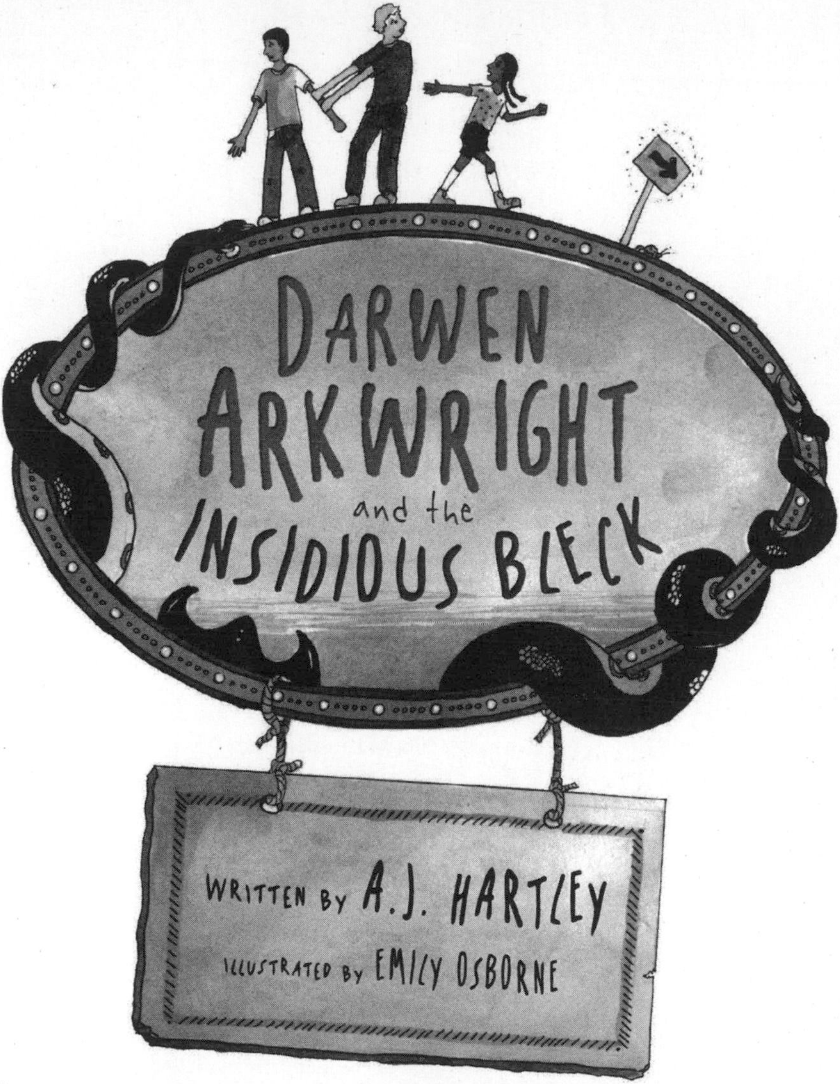

DARWEN ARKWRIGHT and the INSIDIOUS BLECK

WRITTEN BY A.J. HARTLEY

ILLUSTRATED BY EMILY OSBORNE

an Imprint of
Penguin Group (USA) Inc.

For Finie and Sebastian

Darwen Arkwright and the Insidious Bleck

RAZORBILL

Published by the Penguin Group
Penguin Young Readers Group
345 Hudson Street, New York, New York 10014, U.S.A.
Penguin Group (USA) Inc., 375 Hudson Street, New York, New York 10014, U.S.A.
Penguin Group (Canada), 90 Eglinton Avenue East, Suite 700, Toronto,
Ontario, Canada M4P 2Y3 (a division of Pearson Penguin Canada Inc.)
Penguin Books Ltd, 80 Strand, London WC2R 0RL, England
Penguin Ireland, 25 St Stephen's Green, Dublin 2, Ireland (a division of Penguin Books Ltd)
Penguin Group (Australia), 250 Camberwell Road, Camberwell, Victoria 3124, Australia
(a division of Pearson Australia Group Pty Ltd)
Penguin Books India Pvt Ltd, 11 Community Centre, Panchsheel Park,
New Delhi – 110 017, India
Penguin Group (NZ), 67 Apollo Drive, Mairangi Bay, Auckland 1311, New Zealand
(a division of Pearson New Zealand Ltd)
Penguin Books (South Africa) (Pty) Ltd, 24 Sturdee Avenue, Rosebank,

Johannesburg 2196, South Africa

Penguin Books Ltd, Registered Offices: 80 Strand, London WC2R 0RL, England

10 9 8 7 6 5 4 3 2 1

ISBN 978-1-59514-410-2

Library of Congress Cataloging-in-Publication Data is available

Printed in the United States of America

Contents

Darwen Sebastian Arkwright looked around, delighted by his first glimpse of Silbrica in weeks. He walked away from the portal, past a rainbow-colored waterfall—which strobed first turquoise, then emerald green, then a yellow as bright as liquid gold—and onto the overgrown track. He forced himself to look for signs of gnashers and listen for the roar of distant scrobbler engines, but he doubted either would be found here. It felt safe.

As Darwen pressed further into the forest, strange

lemon-colored plants with stems like columns and slick, funnel-like tops grew close around him. A startled animal no larger than a field mouse but with a snout almost as long as its body and fur that was tiger-striped green and yellow like grass looked up from drinking at the funnel flowers, then slid effortlessly down the stalk and scurried off along the path. The track wound right, then left, then right again, so that even when he turned to look back the way he had come, Darwen could see nothing but a thicket of the bizarre vase-like plants shifting fractionally in the breeze. Above these towered trees with smooth black bark and blue fringed leaves as long as coffee tables, which reduced the world below to twilight. Somewhere in the distance he heard a bird or animal call—a strange, wild sound unlike anything he had ever heard before.

I should go back, he thought, knowing he wouldn't, not after weeks without access to a mirror through which he could cross into Silbrica.

Following the greenish mouse creature, he took another few steps, and just as it looked like the track would peter out entirely, he saw something ahead: a gate made of crystalline rock, but not built from pieces fastened together or even carved. It looked like it had somehow grown out of the forest floor, eroded out of the surrounding rock by centuries of wind or rushing water. It had to be a portal to another part of Silbrica, what they called a locus. The gate was hung with twining vines, one of which held a bright white flower like an open hand, palm uppermost. Darwen peered at it and saw, just beneath, a button set into the sparkling stone. His hand reached, then hesitated.

Probably doesn't work, he thought.

It looked disused and forgotten. The stone was beautiful, veined like marble but translucent as heavy, hand-blown glass. He could see his hand through it when he reached below and—without really thinking about it—pushed the button once.

Nothing happened.

Darwen waited, but there was no sound, no rush of steam.

I knew it, he thought. *Broken*.

His sense of imminent adventure faded and the forest felt strangely dark and brooding. He turned and began cautiously retracing his steps, suddenly keen to get back into the open, alarming the tiny striped animal so that it scampered into the undergrowth and vanished. And then the plants ahead of him seemed to flicker. A yellowish light played softly over the strange leaves and his own coffee-colored skin.

Darwen turned.

The portal had come to life. It wasn't the silvery light he had seen in other Silbrican portals, but a pale gold, amber at the center. Darwen ran an unsteady hand through the tight curl of his hair. The gate would only stay open for a moment. . . .

He ran toward it, leaping in without so much as a pause.

Everything happened very fast.

He found himself sprawled in a darkness so complete that for a second he thought he had been swallowed up by the Shade monster, which surrounded its victims with empty blackness. Then there was a bright flickering light, and Darwen could see. The ground was dirt and strewn with leaves, and there was a massive contraption that looked like it had been frozen in the act of emerging from the ground. It appeared to be an armored bulldozer covered with clumsy pipes and boilers. The light came from behind it, but the machine itself was black, silent, and clearly inoperable. The air felt as humid as the jungle he had just left, and the smells were similar. But it was night, and that wasn't the only difference.

There was also the screaming.

He got to his feet, looking wildly around, trying to make sense of the flickering light that streamed around the dead bulldozer, bright as lightning in the darkness. For an instant the world became a shifting pattern of silver leaves and coal-dark shadows, and then he saw the boy.

He was the source of the screaming. He was young, about Darwen's age, wearing a T-shirt and shorts with sneakers. His dark eyes were wide with horror, and his mouth was open. Words were coming out, and though Darwen couldn't understand them, he felt the boy's terror.

The boy's legs were still, but he seemed to be moving anyway, pulling back toward the source of the light. He reached desperately out to Darwen, still screaming, and Darwen took an urgent step toward him. And that was when he saw it.

The light came from a brilliant circle on the ground behind the boy: a portal from which the bulldozer had been unable to emerge. It was flickering because something was blocking it out, something long and heavy that writhed snakelike as it reached up and through from the other side. It pulled the boy toward the gate, and Darwen saw the thick and fibrous tentacle squirming around the child's middle.

Darwen hesitated, catching the boy's terror, then he reached down to the forest floor, desperately searching for anything that could be used as a weapon. He found a ball-like stone and flung it as hard as he could at the pulsing tentacle. The stone bounced off, but the undulating movement of the snakelike arm paused for a second. Darwen stooped for another stone, but by the time he had straightened up with three more, the boy was being sucked down into the portal again, only now there were two more tentacles coming through, reaching hungrily for whatever had attacked them.

The boy shrieked again, and Darwen flung another stone, missing. In almost the same instant, the boy was pulled down and into the pool of light. Another pair of tentacles came creeping out, each one studded with suckers and ending in a set of toothlike claws. They whipped forward with horrible speed, and any thoughts of trying to rescue the boy went out of Darwen's head.

He turned back toward the amber portal he had come through, praying it would stay open a moment longer. One of the tentacles reached for him but brushed against a branch instead, seizing it for a moment, then tearing the limb free with impossible strength. Darwen surged forward, avoiding another tentacle that was snaking toward him. He risked one look back to the boy, but he was already gone. Blind with horror, Darwen leaped through the portal.

He didn't stop to look back, but he heard the tentacle follow him into the locus of the rainbow falls, heard the splintering of the crystalline rock as it tore the gateway apart from the inside. And still he kept running.

THE WORLD STUDIES TEACHER

The following day marked the end of Darwen's first semester at Hillside Academy in Atlanta, and there was an air of excitement that even the school's strictness couldn't quite stifle. One more day and they would be free for two whole weeks of vacation. With a bit of luck, it might even snow.

But Darwen's mind was elsewhere. One thought burned bright and urgent in his mind as he stared at the stone sphere he had accidentally brought back from Silbrica: he had to find that boy. He had to save him.

Madhulika "Mad" Konkani—a wild-haired girl who once caused a power outage when the kitchens couldn't produce her vegetarian meal—asked him what he was going to do over the holidays, and he didn't respond until she flicked him hard on his earlobe. The sixth graders filed into class, where the science teacher, Mr. Iverson, stood owlish at his desk in his oversized glasses and patched lab coat.

"Our last day before the winter vacation," he said, smiling. "But that doesn't mean we don't work."

A tall blond boy with perfect teeth who was draped in his chair like he owned the entire room and a black boy who was lounging like a bored cat rolled their eyes at each other: Nathan Cloten and Chip Whittley, two of the popular kids who had never taken to Darwen. Nathan yawned.

"Today you have a special challenge," said Mr. Iverson, "at the request of our new world studies teacher. Class, I would like to introduce . . . Mr. Octavius Peregrine."

"Chuffin' 'eck!" Darwen exclaimed, using one of his favorite phrases from his native Lancashire, in northern England.

"No way!" Darwen's friend Alexandra O'Connor exclaimed. "I mean . . . no way! Mr. P. is a teacher? Here?" Her mouth dropped open, her slim black hands clamped together, and her pigtails (jauntily fastened with green glow-in-the-dark plastic skulls that in no way went with her Hillside uniform) bounced as if they might fly off with the astonishment.

"Maybe it's a different Octavius Peregrine," said Darwen's other closest friend, Richard Haggerty, his face as pink as usual. Rich seemed too big for every chair he sat in and looked slightly sweaty and uncomfortable indoors, as if he should be sitting astride a tractor somewhere, chewing on a grass stalk. He had a rich Southern accent and spoke slowly, but everyone knew that he was the smartest kid in the grade, particularly when it came to science.

"Because Octavius Peregrine is such a common name, you mean?" said Alex, deadpan.

Then, as if on cue, the man they had known as a shopkeeper and one of the gatekeepers of the world beyond the mirrors entered the room. Darwen was so dumbfounded that he barely heard a word of Mr. Iverson's speech about their new teacher's impressive independent research into the "archaeology and anthropology of ritual spaces and the ancient peoples who used them." Rich, meanwhile, was gazing at the old shopkeeper with new respect.

Darwen had last seen Mr. Peregrine three days ago, but their history went much further back than that. It was Mr. Peregrine who, while masquerading as a shopkeeper, had given Darwen the portal-mirror that had led him to the magical world of Silbrica. It was because of

Mr. Peregrine that Darwen had discovered that he was a Squint, properly called a mirroculist, that rarest of people who can climb through certain darkling mirrors and can even bring along others who are touching them—humans and Silbrican creatures alike.

With his friends Rich and Alex—the Peregrine Pact—Darwen had discovered a threat to the school from a former member of Silbrica's Guardian Council. The council member, Greyling, had assembled an army of hulking, green-skinned monsters called scrobblers, creatures with huge tusklike teeth and red eyes behind brass goggles, armed with terrible energy weapons. On Halloween those monsters had broken into the human world to take children to fuel their awful power generators. Darwen and his friends had stopped them, but the mirror Mr. Peregrine had given him hadn't survived the battle. Without that mirror, Darwen couldn't travel to Silbrica—couldn't visit its enchanting creatures or see its magnificent machinery. And so Darwen was left stranded in Atlanta, an ordinary but unfamiliar city that Darwen had come to only a few months earlier, after his parents' death.

But three days ago Mr. Peregrine had produced another mirror. It had been damaged, presumably during the scrobblers' earlier attack on his shop, and the old man had warned Darwen that this one was "one use only." Once entered, it would give Darwen a few hours in Silbrica before shutting down forever. This was the mirror Darwen had used last night. And thank goodness he had, or he would not have seen the boy and the monster that had taken him.

And now, amazingly—since he had said nothing of it when Darwen had last seen him—Mr. Peregrine was their world studies teacher!

It was as if the world beyond the mirrors—a world in which Darwen had taken refuge, at least until it had been darkened by Greyling's war machine—had moved a little closer. Darwen might have no new mirror, but with Mr. Peregrine now a part of his daily life, it was only a matter of time before he could go back to Silbrica and find the missing boy.

Mr. Peregrine was dressed as if he had researched the part of a professor in movies from half a century ago. He wore a tweed suit with leather patches on the elbows, his usual gold-rimmed half-moon spectacles, and a flat-topped mortarboard cap like students wear for graduation. He was carrying a clipboard, and between his lips he held a huge and absurd-looking pipe.

"Er . . ." said Mr. Iverson. "You know you can't smoke in here, Mr. Peregrine?"

"Really?" said Mr. Peregrine, as if this was most remarkable. "Thank goodness."

He knocked the contents of the pipe into one of the

steel sinks and ran water on the burning tobacco so that for a moment the room was full of aromatic steam.

Baffled and intrigued, the students stared.

"Filthy habit," said Mr. Peregrine, smiling. "And quite horrible in the mouth. But I do like the smell. Oh," he said, turning to the class and beaming at them as if only just noticing they were there. "Good morning!"

The class responded in their usual drone ("Good morning, Mr. Peregrine"), but the chorus was ragged and uncertain. Chip and Nathan were leaning forward, their eyes narrow with attention, scouring the new teacher for every bit of information—and any possible weaknesses—they could glean. Darwen realized he was holding his breath, hoping the old shopkeeper would give him a private grin or a wink.

"Have you been discussing my little test?" asked Mr. Peregrine, nodding at Mr. Iverson's desk.

While everyone had been goggling at Mr. Peregrine, Mr. Iverson had set something beside his notebook: a small stone ball. Darwen's hand flashed to his pocket where he felt the cool and smooth surface of an identical sphere. He stared at the one on the desk.

What was he playing at? This stuff was secret!

"Your task," said Mr. Iverson, "is to determine where this object came from. At the end of the allocated time, you will present two possible answers. I want good science here, people. Not guesswork."

"Immediately after the winter break," said Mr. Peregrine, "I will be leading you all on a world studies fieldtrip overseas."

The class muttered excitedly.

"Where to, sir?" asked Rich.

Mr. Peregrine gave a saintly smile. "You tell me, Mr. . . . er . . ."

"Haggerty," said Rich, playing along. Mr. Peregrine obviously didn't want the other students suspecting he already knew Darwen and his friends. "But I don't understand, sir," Rich pressed. "How should I know where we are going?"

"I mean," said Mr. Peregrine, "that you will decide where we are going by guessing where this object came from."

"What if we're wrong?" asked Jennifer Taylor-Berry in her refined Southern drawl.

"When the class has determined its best guess," said Mr. Peregrine, "that's where we'll go, right or wrong."

There was a stunned silence. A couple of people laughed, and even Mr. Iverson smiled widely as if he thought this might be a rather odd joke, but as Mr. Peregrine continued to beam serenely, the science teacher's smile became rather fixed.

"You're not serious," Mr. Iverson said at last.

"I am most assuredly," said Mr. Peregrine. "It seems as

good a system for choosing our destination as any."

"*Choosing?*" began Mr. Iverson. "But . . . won't we be—"

"Leaving in three weeks?" Alexandra O'Connor contributed helpfully.

"Precisely so," said Mr. Peregrine. "So better get a move on."

And with another broad smile, he turned and made for the door. For a moment, Mr. Iverson seemed rooted to the spot, then he said quickly, "Okay. Get into your groups. I just want to have to have a word with . . . I won't be long." And he followed Mr. Peregrine out into the hall.

The silence lasted less than a second before the class burst into a babble of chatter.

"He's got to be kidding!" exclaimed Naia Petrakis, a girl with jet-black hair and large dark eyes.

"It's outrageous," huffed Melissa Young to her best friend, Genevieve Reddock, though she couldn't help smiling as she said it.

"I think it's kind of cool," said Carlos Garcia, and because Carlos so rarely said anything, everyone but Chip and Nathan nodded seriously.

Bobby Park, the Korean boy who Alex thought cut his own hair, gazed at the door through which the teachers had gone and muttered, "Who *is* that guy?" in an awed voice.

"He is different," said Princess Clarkson, whose mother was a famous movie star and who was thus assumed to be an authority on style of all kinds. "Classy."

Darwen and Rich exchanged looks. It was hard to believe, but the students—some of them, at least—thought Mr. Peregrine was cool.

"Oh come on. He's already booked the trip," Nathan drawled loudly. "He just wants us to think we have a hand in making the choice. Typical Hillside trying to 'empower the leaders of the future.' I, for one, won't play along. We should say the ball is from Disneyland. Call his bluff."

He pulled a comic book from his bag and started to read.

Barry Fails had left his seat and pressed his ear to the classroom door. "Shhh," he hissed. "I think they're arguing."

Half of the class immediately thundered to their feet and joined him, straining to hear through the door. Darwen didn't move. Instead he turned quickly to Rich and Alex and said, "Look." Holding his hand very close to his stomach so that no one else could see, he took the stone sphere from his pocket and showed it to them.

"He already gave you one?" whispered Rich. "The other kids won't like it if they think he's giving you preferential treatment."

"And they'll want to know why," said Alex. "I don't think we should let on that we already know him."

"He didn't give it to me," Darwen hissed back. "*I* gave the other one to *him*! I found them last night—*in Silbrica.*

And that's not all. I saw a boy. . . ."

He told them everything, and when he had finished, there was a long wide-eyed silence.

"Dang," said Rich quietly.

"A giant octopus thing with claws," Alex mused. "Doesn't Silbrica have any rabbits? Anyway, you shouldn't have gone in without us," she scolded. "We made the Peregrine Pact, remember?"

"The boy still would have been taken," said Darwen. "And if there had been three of us for it to choose from, maybe the creature would have gotten one of us too."

"You like to live on the edge, I'll give you that," said Alex, shrugging off her discontent. "'Course, it's only a matter of time before you fall *over* the edge and die horribly. You might want to keep that in mind."

"I didn't do it on purpose," said Darwen.

"Which part?" asked Alex. "Going in without us, activating the weird gate, or going through it? I'd think those things would be pretty hard to do by accident. I mean, what—you hit the button by mistake and then sort of . . . *fell* through?"

"Of course not," Darwen retorted.

"Okay," said Alex. "So when you said you didn't do it on purpose, what you mean is that you *did* do it all on purpose, but you didn't intend to nearly get killed. Uh-huh. Just so we're clear."

"The point," he said, "is that a kid was taken and I want

to know what we're going to do about it."

"You know," said Rich, "you might not have been in Silbrica."

"Of course I was," said Darwen, "I went in through a mirror, remember? And there was a scrobbler machine of some kind."

"Yeah, but you went through a second portal, right?" said Rich. "Maybe it didn't move you to another part of Silbrica. Maybe it moved you to another part of *our* world."

"Wait, what?!?" Alex gasped, slamming her hands onto the desk.

Rich shot her an impatient look.

"I suppose," said Darwen.

"The waterfall place was still light, right?" said Rich. "But the place where you saw the kid being taken was dark, so it must have been somewhere different. It could have been in Silbrica, but it could have been in our world, and in a time zone similar to ours. Western Europe is only five or six hours different, so it might still have been dark there, but the place you describe sounds tropical. Africa or Asia would have been light at that time, so I'd say you were in Central or South America."

"That's pretty smart," said Alex. "He doesn't look it, but sometimes he's positively bright."

Darwen shook his head. "It couldn't have been our world!"

"Think," said Rich. "The waterfall area was full of things you could only see in Silbrica. What about the place on the other side of the crystal portal? Was anything there unusual?"

"Other than the massive tentacled monster, you mean?" asked Alex.

"Other than the massive tentacled monster," Rich agreed.

Darwen sighed.

"I'm not sure," he said. "It were really dark. There were a lot of plants and trees, but I suppose they looked fairly ordinary. More like houseplants than wild ones, you know? My aunt has one of those umbrella plant things. I'm pretty sure I saw a plant kind of like that."

"Tropical, then," said Rich. "And it was hot and humid, right?"

"Yes."

"What language was the kid shouting in?" asked Alex.

"Not sure," said Darwen. "But now that you mention it, I think it sounded familiar."

"Like Spanish?" Alex suggested.

"Could have been," said Darwen.

"One of the many languages you don't speak," mused Alex. "Too bad I wasn't there to translate. This kid, did he look Latino?" asked Alex. "Like Carlos?"

Darwen shrugged. "I suppose," he said. "I didn't really

get a good look at him, and as I said—"

"*It 'were' dark*. Yeah, we got that," Alex concluded.

"And the stone balls?" asked Rich. "You said you threw a few at the monster?"

"Yeah, I found them on the jungle floor. There were at least five of them. Different sizes. I still had two in my hand when I ran for it."

"And Mr. Peregrine clearly thinks a bunch of random kids can figure out where they came from," Rich whispered. "There's no question: you were in our world, Darwen. And if we can find out where the stone spheres originate—"

"We can find out where the boy came from," Darwen concluded.

"He's coming back!" yelled Barry Fails. The students scattered like cockroaches caught in a flashlight beam. They fought for their seats, pretending they'd been sitting quietly the whole time, as Mr. Iverson—who wasn't fooled for a second—returned.

"Well?" he said. "Have you formed your groups?"

There was a grumbling negative murmur throughout the room, but Rich nodded vigorously, indicating Darwen and Alex with his big pale hands.

"First come, first served," said Mr. Iverson, snatching up the rock and setting it on the desk in front of Rich. "Have a good look, Mr. Haggerty. In five minutes, I'll be passing it on to the next group. Everyone," he said, raising his voice, "gets the same access to microscopes and chemicals so you can try to identify what it is. Do not damage the object in the process of your analysis!"

"Where's Mr. . . . *Peregrine*, sir?" asked Darwen, trying to sound like he was unsure of the name.

"He went to speak to the principal about his trip," said Mr. Iverson, his voice carefully neutral. "I expect he may be there awhile."

Rich lowered his face to the rock. Alex nudged it and it rolled to the edge of the desk, so that Rich had to catch it. Darwen, clutching the other sphere carefully under the desk, scowled.

"It's a ball," Alex said. "So someone made it, right?"

"Probably," said Rich. "But hailstones are round and no one makes them."

"Really?" said Alex. "I thought hailstones were individually shaped by the great sky god Xanthor and his magic colander."

"Maybe if it started really high up in a molten state," said Rich, ignoring her, "like if it was shot from a volcano, it would cool evenly as it fell and come down perfectly round?"

He looked at Darwen as if he might have an answer.

"Don't look at me," said Darwen. "You're the science guy. You want to know about British birds, I'm your man. Otherwise . . ."

"He's got nothing," said Alex.

"Which looks about the same as what you've got," said Darwen.

"Yeah?" said Alex, cocking her head. "How about this? It looks like a miniature version of Stone Mountain. Only darker."

"Stone Mountain?" parroted Darwen.

"Huge granite outcrop just outside the 285 Loop Road," said Rich absently. "East side of the city. You're right, Alex. Granite contains quartz, feldspar, microline, and muscovite, and this looks basically the same, but it's darker."

Darwen gazed at Rich, impressed. Rich was the president of Hillside's archaeology club, and he was sixth grade's most enthusiastic amateur scientist, but he got a lot of his knowledge of Georgia rock from puttering about on his dad's tiny farm.

"Wait," Rich said suddenly. "*Darker than granite*. I know this. It's granodiorite. It's like granite but has more plagioclase feldspar than orthoclase feldspar."

"Great," said Alex. "I'm really glad it's got more plagioclase feldspar as opposed to, I don't know, *arcansparklebargle*. Anytime you feel like speaking English, you let us know."

"It's the same stuff that the Rosetta Stone is made of," said Rich. "You know, the tablet they used to figure out ancient Egyptian hieroglyphs."

"We're going to Egypt?" said Alex. "Cool."

"Not so fast," said Rich. "Granodiorite is found all over the world, so this could come from anywhere. We'll need something else to nail down its origin, like maybe a mass spectrometer."

"Let me check my bag," said Alex, staring fixedly at him. "Oh dear. I seem to have left all my multimillion-dollar science equipment at home."

Rich's scowl deepened over the next five minutes, and when Mr. Iverson swooped in and took the stone ball from him, he exclaimed, "It's not fair! How are we supposed to figure out where it comes from? If it had unusual plant matter stuck to it, maybe—"

"Sorry, Mr. Haggerty," said the science teacher. "You've had your look."

Rich sulked as the rest of the class got their turn.

Eventually, Mr. Peregrine returned.

Mr. Iverson was quick to meet him at the door, and Darwen sat up, straining to hear.

"So?" said the science teacher, under his breath.

"So . . . what?" asked Mr. Peregrine, smiling his most serene smile.

"How did your chat with the principal go?" asked Mr. Iverson, glancing over his shoulder at the class so that Darwen had to look down quickly. "About the trip, I mean?"

"Oh!" said Mr. Peregrine, as if this hadn't been mentioned for weeks. "Oh, that. Yes, he seemed most enthusiastic. *Cutting edge*, he called it, though I'm not entirely sure what that means."

"*Cutting edge?*"

"Yes, my idea of letting my scholarly investigation drive the trip so that the students are, as it were, on the ground doing firsthand research. Seemed most gratified. Charming man, the principal. Charming."

"Indeed," said Mr. Iverson, with a slightly fixed smile. "Well, wonderful. That sounds . . . wonderful." He turned quickly to the class and raised his voice. "Okay, which group wants to make the first argument as to the stone sphere's origins?"

Darwen shifted, trying to attract Mr. Peregrine's attention, but the old man ignored him.

"Costa Rica," said Barry.

Darwen and Rich stared at him. Barry Fails—known, not terribly kindly, as Barry "Usually" Fails—had never answered a question in Mr. Iverson's class before.

"Specifically," said Nathan. "A small area close to the border with Panama on the Pacific coast. Possibly a tiny island just offshore called Caño."

"And your second guess?" said Mr. Iverson.

"We don't have one," said Chip with supreme confidence, "and it's not a guess. It's from Costa Rica."

"And how did you reach your conclusion?" asked Mr. Iverson, a skeptical expression on his face.

"Googled 'stone ball,'" said Barry, brandishing an expensive-looking smart phone and grinning.

Darwen and Alex exchanged outraged looks.

"Can I see that?" said Mr. Peregrine. He was peering at the phone, fascinated. Barry handed it to him, and he turned it over in his hands, gazing at the screen and smiling, rapt.

"What an extraordinary thing!" he whispered.

"It's just a phone," said Barry.

"And I think we should talk about scientific process," inserted Mr. Iverson. "Looking something up on Wikipedia hardly constitutes rigorous analytical—"

"So are they right?" Rich cut in.

"What?" said Mr. Peregrine. "Oh, I see. Well, let me think. Costa Rica . . ." Everyone looked at Mr. Peregrine, who seemed to hesitate before suddenly clapping his hands together. "Is correct!" he exclaimed, apparently writing it down on his clipboard before returning the phone to Barry. "And that's where we will be going. We'll begin classes on . . . er . . . "—he checked the clipboard—"*Costa Rica* after the holidays."

Nathan and his friends punched the air in victory, and Barry did a little dance directed at Rich, who was red-faced with fury.

"That's totally unfair," he muttered through gritted teeth.

"Look on the bright side," Alex cut in. "Nobody cares."

Rich couldn't argue with that. The students were too thrilled by the idea of visiting a country about which none of them knew anything to worry about how the location had been selected. Darwen couldn't share Rich's gloom either. The stone balls had come from Costa Rica, and that meant the boy who had been taken by the monster had been there too. Knowing that meant they were one step closer to saving him. The thought almost made up for Mr. Peregrine behaving as if Darwen was just another nameless student.

Darwen hadn't expected snow in Atlanta. He had assumed that the South was always hot, as it had been when he'd first arrived in September, but December proved as cold a month as he had ever known in northern England. Even so, the snow had been a surprise, and for a moment, a brief but shining moment, it had almost been like home.

At school they had studied Hanukkah and Kwanza—his teachers constantly looked hopefully for insight from

Darwen (whose mother had been black), but he had never heard of it, and details of the holiday had to be offered by Alex and Chip Whittley. The teachers had called the upcoming vacation "winter holidays," but to Darwen it would always be Christmas. Except that it wasn't, not without his parents, not in this still strange and vast city so different from the little Lancashire town where he had been raised.

Darwen had not lived in Lancashire since the summer when his parents had died in a car accident and he had been transported to Atlanta to live with his slightly stiff but well-meaning aunt, Honoria Vanderstay. Four months later, they were still getting to know each other, and she was fighting to get Darwen through his lowest point since arriving in the States. That low point began long before the frustration of not being able to find the captured Costa Rican boy took hold.

Two weeks earlier, a series of boxes containing things that had belonged to his parents had arrived. Darwen and his aunt avoided them for a few days, but eventually she opened them, always watching to see how he was reacting to what was inside. It wasn't easy. Even the most ordinary things were charged with memories. There was a china rabbit his mother had glued back together after Darwen had knocked it off the mantelpiece and a cookbook whose stained pages were covered in scrawled notes added by his father.

"Dad's hot-pot recipe," said Darwen, staring at the book so as to avoid his aunt's watchful gaze. "You're supposed to use lamb and kidney and stuff, but Dad had this really great way of making it by just stewing beef and potatoes and onions. Mum put the crust on. We had it with piccalilli and red cabbage on Saturdays in front of the telly. Could we try to make it?"

But Honoria didn't cook.

"I'm sorry, Darwen," she said. "Every time I turn on the stove, there's a good chance I'll smoke the building out. Maybe we can get it at a restaurant."

They looked but, unsurprisingly, couldn't find it.

Cooking aside, his aunt had tried almost painfully hard as the holidays approached. She bought and wrapped a mountain of presents, got a real Christmas tree delivered to their spotless apartment, and swept up its fallen needles only when he wasn't looking. She made a list of everything Darwen wanted for Christmas dinner, including chipolata sausages, which he couldn't describe properly, and the paper crackers with novelty gifts inside, which she hadn't been able to find until Christmas Eve. She had revealed them with a delighted "Ta da!" when she got home, and Darwen hadn't the heart to say that they looked much smaller and fancier than the ones he was used to. He had thanked her for her efforts and returned to his bedroom while she paid Eileen, the dreaded babysitter, singing along with manic determination to the endlessly repeated songs on a twenty-four-hour Christmas-music station.

Darwen closed the door behind him and slumped onto the bed. On his bedside cabinet was a photo album: the blurred and random pictures he had gotten together before leaving England. He had spent more time in the last few days going through them, staring at the images of his parents, than ever before, but the warm feelings he had gotten from the photos when he needed them at Halloween were gone, and they merely left him feeling lost and alone. Two nights before, his aunt had taken him to a place called Calloway Gardens to see a huge display of Christmas lights, and though they had been beautiful—magical, even—he had found himself thinking back to when his parents had driven him to the Blackpool seafront to look at what they called the Illuminations. The lights at that brassy Lancashire resort town were, he knew, pretty tasteless compared with Calloway's elegantly lit trees, but he would have given anything to see them again, to be there in the backseat, laughing and pointing as his dad drove and his mum glanced back at him, smiling.

But that was all in the past. That portion of his life was over, and Darwen found that all he really wanted right now was to escape the apartment and his aunt's frenetically perfect Christmas into Silbrica. He gazed at the replacement mirror through which he had crossed over into that strange jungle locus, but Mr. Peregrine had been right. It had worked once, and now it was just a cracked and battered mirror. He couldn't get inside, couldn't even see anything more than his own frustrated and miserable reflection. He pictured the nameless boy he had seen pulled from his Costa Rican home by a monster, torn away from his family and everything he knew, isolated and thrust into a new and terrifying reality.

Darwen had to find him. That meant talking to Mr. Peregrine, whose planned trip to Costa Rica clearly meant that he was working on the problem, though in ways Darwen didn't fully understand. They hadn't seen each other since school finished for the semester, and Darwen—if he was honest—felt badly out of the loop.

He had Christmas dinner with his aunt, "Jingle Bell Rock" playing incessantly as she processed in with course after course, all supplied by a local restaurant and kept warm in her sleek, stainless steel oven. They pulled their crackers filled with absurdly expensive trinkets—including pieces of real silver and gold jewelry—and Darwen listened as his aunt sang the praises of the turkey, "which is usually so dry." He said nothing about his father's famously perfect roast turkey or his mother's sherry trifle, though he could almost taste them in his mind, and his heart wept silent tears when he thought that he would never taste them again. His aunt gave him a half glass of wine with water in it "since it's Christmas," while he played conspicuously with everything she had bought him. And when he did cry, which was only for a moment, he managed to slip into the bathroom before she noticed.

As soon as Darwen heard the door buzzer and saw Aunt Honoria's feigned surprise at who could *possibly* be visiting today, he knew she had one more desperate trick up her sleeve. For a moment he was terrified that it would be some department-store Santa come to pay him a special visit, but it wasn't.

It was Rich and Alex, and—knowing that his aunt had arranged the visit because nothing she could do alone would be enough—he sidled up to her and whispered "thank you" into her ear.

The trio was clearly conscious of Aunt Honoria's watchful presence and all they couldn't discuss with her around, so they babbled happily about the weather, their faces flushed, stomping their feet as they slipped out of their snow-spotted coats. Darwen announced that he was "right chuffed" to see them, which Alex translated as "very pleased." Rich had bought Darwen a guide to American birds, and Alex had framed a photograph of the three of them on a school trip to the zoo. But they had one more package, and it took both of them to lug it into the apartment.

"Did you bring that with you?" asked Aunt Honoria.

"It was in the hallway," said Alex. "But it's addressed to Darwen."

She indicated a faded slip of paper tied with twine to the brown-paper package, on which was written in spidery and unsteady cursive:

For Darwen.

O. P.

Rich mouthed the initials, and Alex rolled her eyes.

"Mr. Peregrine," she said. "I wouldn't advertize that our new world studies teacher is sending you a Christmas present, Darwen. Favoritism. Conflict of interests. Bad for both of you."

Unable to contain his excitement, Darwen pulled at the string, feeling the weight of the thing and its curious shape. It was much too heavy to be a mirror, and he had to lay it on the floor and peel the wrapping paper away. He did so, and they all stared.

"It's an oven door," said Rich, bewildered.

"From a junkyard," added Alex.

It had once been white with a chrome handle and a heavy glass window in the center, but it was now faded, chipped, rusted, stained, and dented.

"Just what you always wanted, right, Darwen?" said Alex.

"How . . . interesting," said Aunt Honoria, with slow

caution, "only our oven already has a door. See?" She pointed into the kitchen with its matching stainless steel appliances.

"You could drill through the corners and bolt this one right on top of yours," Rich suggested.

Aunt Honoria's mouth opened, and her head cocked slowly, as if she couldn't find the right words.

"The window in the middle is nice and shiny, though, huh, Darwen?" said Alex with a significant look. "Reflective, almost."

She was right. Darwen shifted in his seat, watching his face in the clouded glass of the door. It was a portal. It had to be. And it meant that Mr. Peregrine hadn't forgotten him, however much he pretended not to know him in class.

"And this Mr. Peregrine is your new world studies teacher," Aunt Honoria mused.

"Tough to believe, huh?" said Alex. "And he's leading a trip to Costa Rica as soon as we go back to school. Our survival chances don't look good, do they?"

"He's actually a sort of anthropologist," Rich inserted, leaping to the former shopkeeper's defense. "He's published and everything."

"He's a what?" asked Darwen.

"An anthropologist," said Alex, ever the wordsmith. "Someone who studies people, their origins, culture, social structure. In his case, he has sort of an outsider's perspective."

"Outsider?" said Aunt Honoria. "In what sense?"

"Oh, she just means that he's not from around here, right, Alex?" Darwen inserted.

"And he's leading us overseas," Rich mused.

"Why do you keep saying that?" said Alex.

Rich was pink—pinker than usual—and he looked unnerved.

"What's the big deal?" asked Darwen, feeling a rush of loyalty for the former shopkeeper. "Mr. P. will get it together."

Rich nodded, but he looked quickly away.

"You've never been out of the country before, have you?" said Alex, peering at him.

Rich sighed and shook his head. "I went to Chattanooga once," he muttered.

"That's in Tennessee," said Alex.

"I was six," Rich explained.

"And that's the only time you've been out of the *state*?" said Alex.

"I like Georgia," said Rich weakly.

"And I like SpaghettiOs," said Alex, "but I don't eat them at every meal."

As soon as his aunt went back to the kitchen to clean up, Rich nodded at the oven door.

"You know what that is, right?" asked Rich.

"I hope so," said Darwen, wishing he could test the idea right there and then.

"When can we try it?" asked Alex. "We should see if we can get close to the place the boy was taken from."

"Might be good reconnaissance for our rescue mission," said Rich.

"Our *mission*?" Alex repeated. "What are you now, GI Joe?"

"That's what it is," said Darwen, "a rescue mission."

"Does it have to be the whole grade?" said Alex. "Does everyone have to come? I mean, this was *our* thing. We're the ones who stopped Greyling's invasion. Us! Not Naia or Barry or Chip Whittley."

"It's the only way we can get there while school is in session," Rich said, shrugging his broad shoulders.

"Costa Rica," Darwen mused. "You think it will be expensive?"

"You can bet on it," said Alex.

Darwen's face fell. His family in England had never had much money, and though his aunt seemed to be doing quite well for herself, he hated costing her more than was really necessary.

"I'm hoping my scholarship will cover it," said Rich. "If not, then I'm out. There's no way my dad could get the money together with the way his work has been lately. What about you, Alex?"

"I'll be okay," she said. "A present from Dad."

"That's nice of him," said Darwen.

"Oh, he doesn't know about it yet," said Alex. "But Mom says that if he hesitates for a second when I call him about it, I'm allowed to ask how much he spent on his girlfriend's Christmas gifts."

Darwen wasn't sure how to react to this, but Alex gave an expansive shrug and grinned brightly.

Aunt Honoria returned, and Darwen quickly started to talk about what great Christmas gifts she had given him.

"I got a puppy!" Alex inserted delightedly. "I got to go down to the pound and pick her out myself. She's half husky, half shepherd, and half something else with floppy ears."

"You got one-and-a-half dogs?" asked Rich.

Alex gave him a blank look.

"Three halves," said Rich, "husky, shepherd, floppy-eared thing. That's one-and-a-half dogs."

"I also got a dictionary," said Alex, "and I'll be learning a new word every day. Here's one I already got down. *Pedantic*. It means nitpicky and too smart by half. And when you look it up, there's a picture of Rich Haggerty."

Rich rolled his eyes at Darwen.

"Anyway," said Alex, "she's called Sasha, which is like a Russian version of my name, and she's gorgeous, and loyal, and huge, and fierce, and someone gave her away, if you can believe that. She's not even a year old and some old lady said, 'I'm bored with you now, so you can go to the pound.' And you know what they do with dogs if no one adopts them there?" Alex's eyes grew wide.

Fearing Alex was about to rant at them for other people's bad behavior, Darwen tried to redirect the conversation. "Well, you brought her home, so that's good. She'll like that."

"Yeah," said Rich. "A year or so with you and she'll probably learn to talk."

"I wish she *could* talk," said Alex. "'Cause then she could tell me the name of the lady who abandoned her. I've got some things I'd like to say to her. When I grow up, I'm going to set up an animal shelter where pets that don't get adopted can live forever."

"I thought you were going to be a singer," said Rich, grinning.

"Or a dancer," added Darwen.

"I can be those things as well," said Alex. "Oh yeah, I'm going to be an actor too. Strictly theater—no movies, unless they pay me so much that I'd be crazy not to do it."

"Four careers is a lot for one person," Aunt Honoria observed. "How will you find time for cooking and cleaning?"

"I'll pay people to do that for me, like you do," she said. Aunt Honoria flushed and looked out of the window, but Alex just kept talking. "My mom used to do that. When I was a baby, we had a nanny called Consuela. Why do you think my Spanish is so awesome? 'Course, we don't have a nanny now. Mom insists on looking after Kaitlin all by herself. But yeah, when we had more money—before my dad left—we had maids and gardeners and who knows what else. That's how I'm gonna live—with *staff*."

She paused to consider this, and a new idea dawned.

"Heck, I could pay you two," she exclaimed. "Rich, do the yard. Darwen, make me supper. Something with a bit of spice: some blackened catfish, maybe, with a bowl of gumbo on the side. Or some Brunswick stew. The good kind, not that dog-food-in-water mess they serve at school with leaves sprinkled on it, like *that* will make it good. *Garnish*, they call it. Serve up any old slop with a few cilantro leaves on top and they think it's high class. Hockey-puck steak cooked for about four hours until you can carve glass with it? No problem, we'll put a sprig of parsley on it, and everyone will think they're in some restaurant in Paris, France, because of the *garnish*."

Darwen grinned at Rich. Same old Alex.

"I thought the meals at Hillside were good," said Aunt Honoria, a familiar note of anxiety creeping into her voice.

"They are," replied Darwen quickly. "Kind of fancy, but good. Right, Rich?"

Rich, who would probably eat pulled pork and chicken wings at every meal given the chance, met Darwen's eyes and got the message. "Sure," he said. "They're great."

Alex rolled her eyes. "You just don't have my delicate palate," she said. "I have very sensitive taste buds."

"Sensitive as a battering ram," muttered Rich.

"I heard that," she said, unoffended. She gazed around the apartment. "Nice tree," she said to Aunt Honoria. "Could use more lights, though."

"Oh yeah," said Rich. "Real sensitive."

After they had gone, Darwen sat beside his aunt on the couch in front of the gas fire, watching the snow fall on Atlanta's towers of offices and condos.

"Good Christmas, Darwen?" she asked.

"Good Christmas," he said.

Clearly relieved, his aunt patted him on the head awkwardly and then got ready for bed. It had been a long day. Darwen said good night, then spent a minute gazing into the fire, listening to the sounds of his aunt preparing for bed. The moment things went quiet, he dragged the battered old oven door into his room, careful not to make too much noise. He was propping it up against the back wall of his closet when his fingers found something taped to the back: a scrap of paper. On it were numbers inked in Mr. Peregrine's untidy hand and a thumbprint, not in ink but in a dark brownish red.

Blood?

Darwen frowned, but then he noticed the image that had appeared in the glass pane of the oven door. He had known that it would be a portal by now, since the sun had been down for hours, but it wasn't at all what he'd expected.

It was dark inside the oven-door portal, a tight, square tunnel made of metal. In fact, it looked a lot like the inside of an oven except that it kept going back as far as Darwen could see. Darwen reached in tentatively, and the surface rippled where the glass should be, just as his old mirror had. Still, this wasn't the beautiful forest he had been looking forward to, and he wasn't sure he wanted to get into that cramped passage, no matter where it might lead him.

Come on, he thought. *Don't chicken out now. Mr.*

Peregrine sent the portal for a reason, probably something to do with the missing boy. And if the blood was anything to go by, it had cost him something in the process.

With that, Darwen lay down on the carpet, pushed his arms in, and then crawled through the oven door headfirst.

It was no better inside. Darwen could smell the metal in the air, and his hands and knees were quickly coated with dust. The only light came from Darwen's bedroom, and his body was blocking most of that out. Darwen tried to adjust his position but only succeeded in whacking his head on the side, which rang like a gong. He considered climbing back out, but he pushed the thought away and started to crawl forward, half on his hands and knees, half slithering on his belly.

The darkness thickened, and after a few yards Darwen could see nothing in front of him at all. He glanced backward through his legs and saw the little square of light that was his bedroom glowing like a distant television in the night. He continued on, slower now, feeling in front of him, his heart beginning to pound. He wasn't sure how much more of this he could take.

And then, without warning, the floor of the passage sloped steeply down, and he began to slide. For a second he tried to stop himself, but it was no good, and he was soon hurtling down.

Faster and faster he went. The chute banked suddenly

to the right, then to the left. It leveled out for a moment and then dropped more steeply than ever, so that Darwen cried out as he careened through the pipe. He rolled, felt the metal wall burn his elbow, and tucked his arms in tight, shutting his eyes. Twice more the tube switched direction, turned him over, and gave a burst of head-spinning speed. Then the roof was gone, and he could feel light and air as he shot across a polished metal platform on his back, slowed, rotating, and stopped.

Darwen opened his eyes and looked up.

Above him was a sparkling dome of brass inlaid with copper and braced with polished chestnut-colored wood. From the center of the dome ran a glass tube filled with pulsing golden light flecked with amber and pinpricks of white, like stars or diamonds. The tube came down into the heart of a vast and elegant machine, and, recalling things Mr. Peregrine had told him before, Darwen knew where he was: inside the Great Apparatus.

Above him the tube ran up to the heart of the hall where Silbrica's Guardians sat in perpetual council. It had been dying the last time Darwen had seen it—the energy purplish with spots of crimson, whole areas burned black like spent embers. But this was how it should be: bright, like sunrise, but soft and full of life.

Despite the discomfort of his journey, Darwen found himself basking in the glow from above and smiling. It was like being inside a thousand clocks. All around the chamber were brass cogs and dials, some small as watch parts, some big as houses. Some spun freely, others seemed quite still, and all were linked so that however different they were, they were clearly parts of a whole. There were flywheels and sprockets, levels and ratchets, levers, switches, springs, cranks, and a hundred other machine parts for which he had no name. Everything shone, and the air was full of a soft but steady ticking under which was a distant hum, like wordless notes sung in harmony.

The room was circular with the golden energy from above flowing down into the machine at its center. From there a hundred pipes ran like the spokes of a great wheel to a rim composed entirely and unmistakably of portals, all framed in varnished wood and set with controls like those Darwen had first seen on the wooded hill where the fairylike dellfey Moth lived. They had the same elegance but were all slightly different in shape and in the pattern of their wood grain, and as Darwen studied their bases, which were swollen and fluted like something between a column and a tree, an idea struck him.

They're growing, he thought.

Their roots spread beneath his feet. The machine fueled the gates, but the gates were also alive, drawing sustenance from Silbrica itself.

They were numbered simply from one to one hundred.

Darwen checked the paper—the one Mr. Peregrine had given him—in his pocket and walked around the outside until he came to number sixty-four. Then, just to be sure he would be able to get back out, he revisited the chute. He discovered that the entire pipe rotated and that the top side had steps built into it. Satisfied, he returned to the portal and began the process of opening the gate. First he pulled a lever, then he turned a dial, and finally he pushed a button and waited as, with a great pneumatic hiss, the empty frame of the gateway shimmered into pearly brilliance.

Darwen paused, enjoying the moment. Then he stepped in.

On the other side of the gate, Darwen stood and stared. He had expected that Mr. Peregrine's instructions would have brought him back to the crystal waterfall where he had seen that monstrous tentacled creature grab the boy, but this was somewhere entirely different. Why had Mr. Peregrine brought him here? He was in a forest of what he thought was a kind of bamboo, though it was taller than any he had ever seen, its stems as thick as tree trunks, its tops reaching forty or fifty feet into the night sky. Every trunk was smooth and slender, like a tall gray column, and overhead each sprouted slim, silvery leaves that rustled like foil in the breeze. The gate he had come through was fashioned out of the same bamboo, and all around him was more of the same. There was a clearing that housed a familiar, ornate fountain containing what looked like tiny birdhouses in which greenish lights glowed and flickered. One of the lights was coming toward him.

"Moth!" exclaimed Darwen.

And so it was.

If the dellfey hadn't been so small, he would have hugged her. She looked healthy, her mechanical wings immaculately reforged, showing no trace of the scorching and oil stains that had been there when he had last seen her. Her face was a mask of delight.

"You found me!" she exclaimed. "The dellfeys feared we would not see you again after all the terrible things that Greyling did. We thought you would never return to Silbrica!"

"I was always going to come back," said Darwen. "I just couldn't find a way."

"Do you like my new home?" she said.

"It's beautiful," Darwen said. "Yes. You won't go back to the old forest?"

"That locus has to grow," she said, shaking her head.

"So?"

"If we went there," she said, "we would grow too."

"You mean we'd get taller?"

"No," she said, her face a mixture of exasperation and dread, "we would get old."

"What?" said Darwen. "Why?"

"Remember the damage the scrobblers did, the trees they killed? A new forest has to grow."

"I don't understand," said Darwen. "So it's growing. Why would that make us get older?"

"Because that locus has been reset," Moth exclaimed. "The Great Apparatus has been adjusted so the forest can regrow."

"That was the machine with all the gates that I just came through?" said Darwen. "It can control the passage of time?"

Moth frowned and tipped her head to one side. "In a way," she said. "They can make it run faster in some loci. Time is passing quickly in the forest now so that the trees can reclaim the locus." Moth made a bobbing motion in the air, and her wings flickered with coppery light. "You look like you have something to ask me?" she asked.

"Yes," said Darwen. "I was in another locus. But then I found a way back into my world, and there was a boy, and then . . . I don't know, something took him, right in front of me. I was just standing there and this huge tentacle thing had a hold of him and it dragged him through a portal and I threw stones but there was nothing I could do to stop it and then it came after me and all I could do was run and . . . I left him."

As Darwen spoke, he felt his skin prickle. His eyes were wide, and his heart was racing.

"I just left him," he said again, horrified. "He was alone but I couldn't do anything." He blinked and cleared his throat. "So now I have to find him."

"No," she said, and she had become quite still. "You must leave."

"What do you think it was?" Darwen asked. There was something about the dellfey's manner that spoke of things she didn't want to say.

"I don't know," she said. "There are many strange beasts in Silbrica's wilder places."

"Yeah, you said. Scrobblers and flittercrakes and shades and gnashers. I know. This wasn't like any of them. It was huge and—"

"There are hobstrils, Darwen Arkwright," said Moth, "and drifters and other monsters whose names I have not told you before, some so terrible that we do not speak of them."

"Come on, Moth," begged Darwen. "You know something." He had seen a look of horrified recognition in her face when he had said "tentacles," a flicker of terror in her eyes as clear and desperate as a scream, which she had then banished completely.

"I cannot talk about that which you wish to know," the dellfey insisted, and her tiny hands shook. "You must go. Now."

PLANS and PREPARATIONS

With Moth being so pointedly unhelpful, Darwen felt an even greater need to get Mr. Peregrine, Alex, and Rich in the same room together. But Christmas was a tough time to get people to drop their plans, and it wasn't until the following Saturday that they were able to meet at a local bowling alley, which was almost as odd to Darwen as Silbrican bamboo forests.

"We have to rent shoes?" he asked, pulling a sour face.

"Hey, when you have a puppy eating her way through

your wardrobe, renting shoes looks like a pretty good option." Alex shrugged. "Anyway, it was your idea."

"I wanted somewhere we could get away from my aunt and meet with Mr. Peregrine," said Darwen. "She thinks it's odd that he's friends with us."

"Ohhhh," said Alex wisely, watching Mr. Peregrine as he inspected a selection of bowling balls a few lanes away. "Gotcha. Still, at least he's a teacher now and not just some guy who sent you an oven door."

"Are you sure these are right?" Mr. Peregrine demanded of one of the attendants. "They seem very heavy."

Alex met Darwen's anxious eyes and smirked.

Rich was a superb bowler, throwing strike after strike, much to Alex's irritation. Having never bowled in England, Darwen was hopeless, but Mr. Peregrine was worse, cheerfully throwing one gutter ball after another and then watching keenly as if they might just pop out at the last second and hit all the pins. After a couple of games in which Rich systematically wiped the floor with them, Darwen gave up.

"So, Mr. Peregrine," he said, grinning. "You're a teacher."

"Astonishing, isn't it?" said Mr. Peregrine, beaming. "I have always rather liked the idea of being a teacher, but having to actually *know things* is proving more of a challenge than I had anticipated. And that school! So strange that some of the teachers seem determined to crush the spirits of those placed in their charge, don't you think?"

Darwen thought of Mr. Sumners, the math teacher, and nodded his agreement. For a silent moment he stood next to Mr. Peregrine, watching Alex abandon the bowling with a shout of frustration, and he couldn't help smiling. Whatever difficulties lay ahead, he would be with his friends and with Mr. Peregrine. It was going to be a good semester.

"So we're going to Costa Rica to find the boy I saw kidnapped," Darwen said as Rich and Alex joined them. "Somehow, and it looks like we'll be doing this without Moth's help, we need to find where he was taken from, then we can cross over to Silbrica using whatever portal that thing pulled him through."

"And into its tentacled embrace," said Alex, dropping her bowling ball so heavily onto the floor that a big man with tattoos shot her an accusatory look. Alex turned to him and said, "Hey, how ya doing?"—holding his gaze until he shrugged and looked away.

"We may not need to actually *follow* the boy to the other side," said Mr. Peregrine delicately. "Our primary goal is not so much to bring him back as to identify his point of entry."

"What do you mean?" asked Darwen.

"There are ancient creatures in Silbrica, and there are points, as you know," said Mr. Peregrine, "where the fabric separating their world from ours is fragile. Sometimes hunting beasts stray through the barrier. I was able to pass along what you saw, so the Guardians are now aware of the breach. They want us to find it and close it. That is our mission."

"But we have to get him back!" said Darwen.

"If the creature that you saw is, as I suspect, merely an animal," said Mr. Peregrine, "albeit a large and powerful one, I'm afraid it will be too late to save the boy. The incident took place two weeks ago. If a child was taken by a bear or a lion, you would not expect to find the child alive after that time. In all likelihood—"

"No," said Darwen, cutting him off. "That's not good enough. I'll go through the oven door tonight and see if I can find Moth again. I might be able to persuade her to—"

"Oven door?" Mr. Peregrine echoed vaguely.

"The portal you sent me. Thanks for that, by the way. Too bad it's too big to take with us."

"Ah," said Mr. Peregrine. His face was blank, as if he had forgotten what they were talking about. Then he cleared his throat and said, "Yes, of course. You are most welcome. Now . . . where are we going again?"

"Costa Rica," said Rich, flashing Darwen a pained look.

"Quite," said Mr. Peregrine. "I keep wanting to say Ecuador or Paraguay, but I think that's just because I like the sound of the names." He patted Darwen on the shoulder. "Well," he concluded, "it is time I should be going.

Classes to prepare!"

He winked. When the old man had left them, Darwen turned to the others, frowning.

"Is it just me, or does it sound like the Guardians aren't completely grasping the situation?"

"Enter the Peregrine Pact," said Rich.

"Right," said Darwen. "Alex, you should poke around online. See if you can find anything about kids going missing in Costa Rica on the day I was there, December 14."

"Why me?"

"Your Spanish is better than mine," he said.

"There are mollusks whose Spanish is better than yours," she said.

"And Rich?" said Darwen.

"Boss?"

"Go into research mode," said Darwen. "The more we know about the stone spheres and about plants and animals that live in Costa Rica, the better chance we have of tracking things that don't belong."

"And what are you going to be doing, oh great commander?" asked Alex.

"I'm going to see what I can find out from the other side," he said. "Moth knows something, and even if she won't tell me, I can use the Great Apparatus to get me to every corner of Silbrica. If that kid is being held somewhere, I'll find him."

"When do we get to visit Silbrica again?" asked Rich.

"Soon," said Darwen. "I promise."

"Your job sounds a lot cooler than ours," Rich grumbled.

"That's 'cause he's the mirroculist," said Alex.

Darwen gave her a quick look, but she just shrugged.

"Okay," she said, standing and gathering together four heavily loaded bags. "I'm outta here. Got some gifts to return. I can't decide if my mother doesn't know me at all or if she does and wishes I was someone else."

For the next three nights, Darwen returned to Silbrica through the oven door and traced his way back to the rainbow falls, but he found only the shattered remains of the crystal gate. Worse, the gate that connected him to Moth's bamboo grove wasn't working. He pulled the lever, turned the dial, and pushed the button repeatedly, but nothing happened. It worried him.

Feeling slightly guilty about not bringing Rich and Alex along, Darwen sampled portal after portal looking for anything that might lead to the missing boy. He appeared among palm tree hedges in deserts of curiously red sand. He explored meadows of pink flowers that closed up, as if embarrassed, as he came near them. He trekked across great green ice flows that sparkled like emeralds, and he watched a shaggy yak-like beast using its spiral horn to forage for roots. Only once did he find a locus resembling a jungle, a place the tentacled monster might call home, but it was so dark there, the air so thick with strange scents and noises, that he made it only a few yards from the portal before deciding that unless he returned home, he was going to wind up lost or eaten.

There were, of course, things other than Silbrica to worry about. The holidays were ending, and school was around the corner. From time to time the weather threatened to delay the start of classes, and while there was no more snow, they did get a significant ice storm, something Darwen had never seen before. Trees and power lines looked encased in glass, and everything strained under the weight of all that frozen water. They were without power for an afternoon, but then—just when it seemed that the first school day would have to be cancelled—the sun came out, and Atlanta's beleaguered road crews and utility workers got a break.

"I've checked all the hotlines," said Honoria brightly, "and we're all systems go for school tomorrow. Make sure you get a good night's sleep."

"Great," said Darwen, meaning it. He wasn't looking forward to classes or to dealing with the likes of Nathan Cloten, but delaying the start of school could jeopardize the trip, and that just wasn't acceptable. Darwen had a mission.

That night he crawled through the oven door and shot down the chute to the Great Apparatus. Mr. Peregrine hadn't had an answer for him about how they would get into Silbrica from Costa Rica. What if they never found a working portal? This might be one of the last chances he would have to explore the problem of the kidnapped boy from the Silbrican side. Steeling himself, Darwen returned to the only jungle locus he had been able to find.

It was extremely dark; the canopy of leaves overhead shut out all but the softest starlight. Darwen took a small flashlight from his pocket and shone it around so that the colors leaped into sudden focus. The beam was narrow and seemed to emphasize the darkness around it. He moved cautiously away from the portal—its glass-fronted dials and brass controls hung with the twining vines that grew up from the jungle floor—and found what looked to be a path. The air was thick with a warm, sweet-smelling fog that hugged the ground and pooled wherever the earth sank away. Darwen, imagining the missing boy calling for help, took two careful steps and fought back the certainty that this method of investigation was hopelessly random and probably dangerous. Who knew what lived in such a place?

The thought had just registered when something moved a little ways off the track. He stared into the shadows of a plant whose leaves were as big as rhubarb. It flickered with a bluish glow like that of the tiny sea creatures Darwen had seen in nature documentaries. As he tried to catch the creature—if that was what it was—in the flashlight's beam, it flicked out of sight, leaving only an eddying swirl in the ground mist.

Darwen became very still, his light trained on the spot where he had seen—or half seen—the movement under the huge and softly pulsing leaves, certain that something—or someone—was watching him.

It surfaced on the other side of the path like a warrior stepping out from cover to make his attack. Darwen swung the light toward it, and its eyes tightened in the glare. It looked a little like an otter or a mongoose, but it stood on its hind legs, its fierce little eyes and whiskery snout only inches above the undulating fog.

Darwen laughed—it was just a harmless rodent! "You scared me!" he remarked at the little animal. "You want to be more careful where you pop up."

"The same could be said of you," snapped the creature, waving a paw at the flashlight.

Darwen jumped and nearly lost his footing on the soft ground. "You can talk!" he said.

The animal's eyes hardened.

"Did you think only you could talk?" it said. Its voice was rough—a snarl with words in it—and would have been funny in someone so small, except that its black eyes promised a nasty bite if you so much as snickered.

"Sorry," said Darwen. "I'm not used to talking animals."

This too, it seemed, was the wrong thing to say.

"Talking *what*?" rasped the otter-like creature. As it

spoke, one tiny claw rose above the mist, and Darwen could see that it cradled a brass implement with a long barrel and a broad, slotted muzzle. The animal pointed it menacingly in Darwen's direction.

Darwen began, "Is that some kind of—"

Zap!

The little brass weapon kicked in the animal's paws, and a bolt of orange flashed inches from Darwen's head and exploded against a tree like a firecracker.

"Oy!" Darwen shouted, angry. "Watch what you're doing with that thing!"

He swung for the animal as he spoke, his fingers reaching to grab the creature by the scruff of its neck. It ducked and weaved with remarkable speed, vanishing again into the ground fog. As Darwen pounced on the spot where the creature had been, it popped up again like a gopher from a hole three feet away, its gun—or whatever it was—aimed squarely at the side of Darwen's head.

"I told you to watch where you point that!" Darwen whispered, keeping very still.

For a long moment the animal did nothing but watch him shrewdly, then it lowered the weapon.

Darwen turned very slowly and then snatched like lightning, catching the animal around the midriff with one hand while twisting the little gun away with the other. The creature sank its claws into Darwen's wrist and leaned in toward his face, its tiny, pointed teeth bared so that Darwen had to hold the thrashing beast at arm's length.

"Put me down!" it rasped.

"When you put down that gun," said Darwen.

"Put me down first, and I will," said the otter thing, suddenly sly and still.

"Oh, right," said Darwen. He tried to wrench the weapon from its grasp, and it yelped with genuine distress.

"You'll break it!" it said.

"I won't break it," said Darwen. "But you have to turn it off, or I won't put you down."

The creature hissed like a cat, then its features sank into a comical sulk.

"Fine," it spit. "Fine. Look, see? I turned it off."

The creature took its free paw from the mechanism of the weapon, and Darwen saw that a tiny bulb that had been glowing with amber light faded out. Very carefully, Darwen turned and set the now limp body of the animal on a tree stump that rose out of the mist.

"There," he said.

The animal did not respond.

"Come on," said Darwen. "I put you down. There's nothing wrong with you."

The otter thing opened a baleful eye and glared sorrowfully at Darwen.

"What?" demanded Darwen.

"I let you do that," said the creature. "If I'd really wanted to fight you . . ." The animal considered Darwen carefully, and something registered in its head. Its body flexed so that what had looked like someone's discarded fur hat became lithe and supple again, rippling with life and strength, and it sat up, its eyes focused and hard.

"You," it said thoughtfully, "are a child. A human child. And you are here alone, which means . . . which can *only* mean . . . that you are . . . the mirroculist!"

As it said this last word, a transformation came over the creature. All trace of brooding or irritation vanished. It became alert, excited, and, as Darwen watched, it began to skip on the spot, the brass muzzle of its weapon waggling about, forgotten.

"You," it announced with a thrill of delight that rippled through its fur from head to foot, "are Darwen Arkwright!"

And it bowed.

Now that he could see it properly, Darwen thought the creature that had ambushed him looked as much like a weasel as it did an otter, though its fur was slick and dark as a mink's, except around the eyes, so that it looked like it wore a pale mask. Its paws, however, belonged to no animal he had ever seen, because though they ended in serious-looking claws, their digits were long, like fingers, so that the paws finally looked less like paws and more like hands. Around its waist it wore a belt that housed a holster for the weapon, a power pack, and a series of loops from which hung a helmet shaped like a soup bowl with a chinstrap, a long knife in a scabbard, and a tiny buttoned satchel.

"What kind of . . ." Darwen began, but decided that *animal* was sure to cause offense.

"What is your name?" he tried.

This seemed to work. The little animal puffed up its chest and performed a species of salute.

"Call me Weazen," it announced, "Peace Hunter."

"Is that your surname or your job, Peace Hunter?"

"Both," said the creature called Weazen. "I keep the Silbrican peace by hunting out those who threaten it, don't I?"

"Like a policeman," said Darwen. "Or something," he added less certainly. It was hard to imagine Weazen, who was no more than two feet tall from snout to tail, being much of a law enforcer, even with that little brass blaster of his, but he supposed that were he a dellfey or something of similar size, he might feel differently.

"Some'at like that, yeah," said Weazen with a smirk and a sideways look. He picked at his teeth with one long claw. "Only I'm an independent contractor, aren't I?"

He started to absently groom his ears, watching Darwen.

"So," said Darwen. "How do you know who I am?"

At first Darwen thought the little creature was having a

coughing fit, but then he realized that Weazen was laughing.

"How do I know who he is, he asks!" Weazen chuckled. "The mirroculist thinks his actions are a secret in the land he saved! That's most amusing," he added, wiping his eye and forcing himself to calm down.

"Word gets about, does it?" Darwen said.

"That it does, Darwen Arkwright. That it does."

"Okay," said Darwen, who was beginning to see an upside to the chance encounter. "Well then, I'm sure you—as Peace Hunter and what have you—will have heard that a human child was taken from my world—from a place like this—by a Silbrican monster."

Weazen stopped laughing abruptly, and his face got that shrewd look again, his head tipped slightly to one side, his bright eyes narrow.

"Hmmm," he mused. "Out of my league is that. But yeah, I've heard of it. Not the same as last time, mind," he said, as if thinking the matter through, and Darwen was struck by the idea that Weazen might not be absurd as a kind of policeman after all. "Last time it was the big gates and the machines all over the place, but this time . . ." He shrugged thoughtfully. "They tried it again," he said. "But it didn't work. I saw the wreckage. Burned-out scrobbler equipment half in and half out of Silbrica, like they couldn't get it through the portal. Then things go quiet for a while. . . ."

"And then?" Darwen prompted.

"Rumors," said Weazen. "Whispers of something different, something alive and very old that no one has seen for years, centuries even."

"A thing with tentacles," said Darwen with certainty.

"Hmmm," Weazen echoed, nodding and smiling a strange, mirthless smile that showed his sharp little teeth. "Too big for the likes of Weazen," he added, "but yeah. The Guardians say nothing, but I know its name. So do the dellfeys. It's been in and out of their bedtime stories since before the Guardians came, and they call it"—Weazen hesitated and did a half check over his shoulder, as if anxious about being overheard—"they call it the Insidious Bleck."

Darwen suppressed a shiver. Moth had told him that name one of the first times they met. He still remembered her fear and guessed that that was why she didn't want to talk about it. "What is it?" he asked.

"No one knows for sure," said Weazen darkly, "because those who see it don't tend to stick around, if you catch my drift."

"Where can I find it?"

At this the little creature looked at Darwen, its face wry.

"Find it?" it said. "You don't find the Insidious Bleck. It finds you, and then you run. Very fast and as far away as possible."

"But how do you fight it?" Darwen pressed. "Surely

you, as a Peace Hunter, know. . . ."

"I know which battles can be won," said Weazen seriously, "and which give you the choice of retreat or, if you like, total destruction. Take it from Weazen, who has seen sights told only in songs: you can't win against the Bleck. If that is what is taking children, Darwen Arkwright, you will have to let them go."

"Never," said Darwen. "I won't."

"You're a tough one," Weazen said, nodding in a grandfatherly way. "But you've got to have a bit of *nouse*," he said, tapping the side of his head. "Sometimes, my lad, you have to know when to walk away. This is one of those times."

"No," said Darwen. "We could fight it together. You could come with me. . . ."

But the little creature was shaking its head sadly, and suddenly it looked old.

"You should go back to your world, Darwen Arkwright," he said. "There may be a way to fight this thing from there. Here in Silbrica, you are up the proverbial creek with nary a paddle in sight."

Darwen tried to unravel this remark.

"You can't win," said Weazen, to be clear. "Most creatures that hunt are themselves hunted by something larger or more terrible. Very few have no natural enemies, Darwen Arkwright."

"You are saying this Insidious Bleck is an apex predator?" asked Darwen, borrowing a term he had learned from Rich. "The thing that lives at the top of the food chain that everything else tries to stay away from, like tigers or great white sharks?"

"Right, and correct," said Weazen. "In the forests of Silbrica, the Insidious Bleck is your apex predator, and I'm pretty sure it would eat your tigers and sharks—whatever they are—for breakfast. So I'll say it one more time. Go home."

And so saying, he bowed once more, adjusted the settings of his weapon, and dived neatly into the carpet of fog, leaving Darwen alone.

"Wait!" Darwen called after him, but Weazen did not surface again, and after a few minutes, Darwen gave up waiting. He had already been in Silbrica too long and couldn't risk being trapped inside the oven door after the sun rose. It was time he got back.

He returned to the Great Apparatus and rotated the chute so that he could use the built-in steps up to his bedroom, then he crawled in and started to climb. It was a long, exhausting ascent. At last he could see the bright hatchway of the oven door up ahead, but then he saw something that stopped him cold.

Legs.

Long, slim legs in black slacks. Aunt Honoria was in his room.

UNDER A CLOUD

Darwen panicked. How was he going to get out without her seeing him?

He had frozen in the shaft so that she wouldn't hear the metal echoing as he moved, but then he decided that she wouldn't be able to hear him for the same reason she wouldn't see him behind the oven door: only mirroculists could see the world beyond the reflection. He slithered as close to the end of the square shaft as he could without poking his head out into the room.

The duvet had been torn from his bed, and the floor was strewn with clothes from his wardrobe. Honoria had obviously gone nuts searching the room. How long had she been there, fretting over his absence? She was sitting on the edge of the bed now, her phone clutched tightly in one hand and a hanky in the other. He could hear her sobbing.

Great, thought Darwen. *Now what?*

He had, he figured, two choices. Stay where he was until she moved far enough away that he could get out and come up with some plausible explanation about where he had been, or come right out of the oven door in front of her very eyes. Then, if she didn't have a heart attack on the spot, he would have to tell her everything.

Boy, he thought, *do I not want to do that*.

In the last few months he had grown more comfortable with his aunt, but she was a practical, no-nonsense woman. Darwen didn't think there was room in her head for Silbrica and its various monsters. At best, she'd have him seeing a psychiatrist twenty-four hours a day. At worst, she might believe him and spend the rest of her life in terror of what might be lurking behind the bathroom mirror.

No, he decided. He could not tell her.

Which meant he had to stay where he was until she left, but he couldn't wait too long, because once the sun came up, he was trapped. He sighed, shifting to find a more comfortable position in the confines of the shaft, but it wasn't possible. He lay on his back, staring at the metal inches from his face, and when he had exhausted the interest value of that, he closed his eyes.

He woke with a start, banging his forehead on the metal. For a moment he had no idea where he was, but then he was rolling, straining against his cramped and aching muscles to peer out into his room. He heard voices, but they were distant, and he couldn't see his aunt no matter how much he twisted and turned. He thought he heard the crackle of a radio like on cop shows. She was probably sitting up in the living room with the TV on. Now was as good a time as ever.

He worked his arms through the oven door, grabbed it by the rim, and pulled himself out in one smooth motion. He got to his feet hurriedly and, without thinking of what he was going to say, walked quickly into the living room.

Honoria wasn't watching a cop show. She was sitting on the couch looking teary, and with her were two police officers, one male, one female. Darwen stared at them, and as they turned to gape at him, he said the only thing he could think of:

"Hi."

It was a disaster. It was dangerously close to dawn, which meant he had been missing for at least six hours. The police had been searching the building, waking their neighbors in the process, calling his friends and teachers, and scouring the surrounding streets. Worse, Darwen could think of nothing that would explain his absence. He suggested he had fallen asleep under the bed, which sounded so deeply stupid even to his own ears that he couldn't believe he was saying it.

"But I looked there!" his aunt exclaimed.

It was awful. The cops were annoyed with both of them, uncertain whom to blame. No one was convinced by Darwen's story that he had never left his bedroom (though he was able to argue this point convincingly, since it was—in a manner of speaking—true), but they couldn't figure out how he had gotten in and out of the building unseen. The female cop insisted on going back over his room in search of a rope ladder, but since they lived on the seventeenth floor, nobody thought that was plausible either.

Worst of all, of course, was Aunt Honoria. Darwen braced himself to be yelled at, but she just cried and said, between sobs, that she was glad he was back. It didn't make him feel like he had gotten away with anything though. She looked more than humiliated that the police thought her incompetent, more than scared that he had been missing. She looked crushed, as if Darwen's acting out just proved what a failure she was as a parent and exposed all her careful Christmas planning as an empty shell, an idea of family that wasn't real.

"I thought you were doing so well," she said,

suddenly exhausted. "I thought *we* were doing well. I'm so sorry, Darwen."

Darwen had hoped that going to school would take his mind off the previous night's fiasco, but it was only when he reached Hillside that the full scale of the disaster became clear. In her panic Honoria had given the police the names of every kid in his class, and their midnight calls generated a lot of hostile looks. His classmates watched him everywhere he went, scowling and muttering. Darwen, tired beyond anything he had felt before, tried to avoid their eyes, but it was impossible.

"Bet you thought that was funny, huh, Arkwright?" remarked Chip Whittley as they filed into the assembly hall. "Waking my mother at two in the morning? Like you might be with *me*? Like we're *friends*?"

"I never told anyone you were my friend," Darwen shot back.

"Yeah, right," said Chip. "Maybe if you had friends who weren't total losers you wouldn't have to lie about it, and maybe you wouldn't be out in the streets in the middle of the night breaking store windows and selling drugs."

"What?" Darwen gasped.

Chip sauntered away.

"Ignore him," said Rich. "Nobody thinks that."

"They will now," grumbled Darwen.

Chip was high-fiving Nathan Cloten.

"I'm going to tell him," said Darwen, elbowing his way out of the line and toward Chip.

"Tell him what, Darwen?" said Rich, laying a heavy hand on his shoulder.

Darwen stood there feeling furious and powerless.

"Ahhh, Mr. Arkwright," said a sardonic voice behind him. It could only belong to Mr. Sumners, the math teacher who took delight in pointing out Darwen's failings as a student.

"I suggest you get back in line," said the teacher with a nasty smile. "Wouldn't want to have to call your, ahhh, aunt on the first day, would I? Even if it would make me feel a little better about losing an hour's sleep last night."

"They called you?" Darwen blurted, his face flushing.

"I'm sure you think that hilarious."

"No," Darwen protested, adding at the last moment, "*sir*. I don't. It was a . . . a misunderstanding."

"They seem to follow you around, don't they, Mr. Arkwright," said Mr. Sumners coolly. "I think we'll need to establish some, ahhh, very clear rules, you and I, just so we don't *misunderstand* each other."

The teacher walked away and Darwen took his place as the principal, Mr. Thompson, walked out onto the stage. Darwen noticed with a stab of guilt that even the principal looked tired, as if he might have been dragged from his bed in the wee hours by a police phone call.

A perfect start to the new year, he thought heavily.

The principal's announcements went through Darwen's head without engaging his brain. All, that is, but one: the reminder of the sixth grade trip organized by the new world studies teacher, Mr. Octavius Peregrine, whom they welcomed with the obligatory three-second burst of applause. Details of the trip, said the principal, a little uncertainly, had been mailed, though some were still being resolved. Darwen saw Alex grin at that. One of the details as yet unresolved seemed to be where, exactly, the trip would go.

"It's definitely Costa Rica," said the principal, looking far from definite, "though the precise . . . er . . . *vicinity* . . . is still being finalized so that it will coincide with our new world studies teacher's ongoing research. Hillside's involvement in such investigation will, I am sure, be another feather in our collective cap. College admission boards are surprisingly impressed by such things. I am also sure that the trip will be an innovative learning experience and that you will serve as our little school's finest cultural ambassadors. Now let us conclude with the Hillside Academy Principles of Learning."

As the rest of the students boomed them out ("Memorization, organization, and logic"), Darwen glanced over at Mr. Peregrine, who was smiling and blinking contentedly, unaware of the slightly dubious looks he was getting from some of the other faculty. Darwen wished he was closer. He had to talk to him, tell him what he had learned from Weazen about the name of the tentacled monster. But he couldn't get to him now, and besides, Mr. Peregrine was talking to an olive-skinned, skinny boy with quick, uneasy eyes whom Darwen had never seen.

"Who's that?" he asked Rich as they marched out.

"The new kid," said Rich, eyebrows raised. "Gabriel something. They just introduced him. Weren't you paying attention?"

Darwen shrugged.

"So," said Rich. "Do I need to ask where you were when the cops were calling my dad in the middle of the night?"

"No," said Darwen, lowering his voice. "I was on my way back and my aunt was in my bedroom. I waited behind the oven door, but I fell asleep."

"You fell *asleep*?" echoed Alex, who had just joined them, her face like thunder. "How nice, getting a little shut-eye while the rest of the school searched for you. You must have been *right chuffed*."

"Don't you start," said Darwen.

"That means happy, yeah? *Right chuffed?*" Alex continued, testing the phrase in her mouth in what was supposed to be a version of Darwen's accent. "*I got an oven door for Christmas. I were right chuffed.*"

They entered the homeroom classroom and moved to their desks, Darwen frowning.

"You need to put a lock on your door, man," said Rich.

"I don't think my aunt will go for that right now. She thinks I'm . . . I don't know."

"Insane?" suggested Alex. "Bonkers? Mental?"

"Sad," said Darwen. "She thinks I'm not adjusting well to being here, I suppose."

He looked down, flushing. Rich patted his shoulder awkwardly.

"I'm fine!" Darwen protested. "She's got it wrong, that's all. I just couldn't think up a good enough excuse. I'm fine."

"Fine," said Alex with her trademark skepticism. "I'm totally convinced. You hide your feelings about as well as my dog. Hey, Darwen!" she exclaimed with ridiculcus enthusiasm. "Wanna treat? Wanna go on the trip? Good boy, Darwen!"

"Funny," said Darwen.

"You wanna know the truth, Darwen Arkwright?" said Alex, leaning in close. "You wouldn't have gotten into this mess if you had taken us with you—you know, me and Rich, the people who stood by you every step of the way when the school was about to go down in a blaze of scrobbler glory—instead of going into Silbrica by yourself. So don't expect sympathy from us."

Darwen turned to Rich for understanding, but Rich looked down, his face glowing like a stoplight. His friends had clearly had this conversation before without him.

Darwen nodded once, eyes downcast.

"Okay then," said Alex, as if that closed the matter.

"Stand behind your chairs, class," said Miss Harvey. "Some of you seem to have forgotten how to conduct yourselves over the vacation. I realize this is your first day back, but I will make no further allowances. Now single file to your first class, which is, I believe—"

"Science, ma'am," Rich supplied happily.

"Quite so, Mr. Haggerty. Lead the way."

Rich marched down the hall so quickly that everyone

had to jog a little to keep up.

"It's not a race, Mr. Haggerty!" called Miss Harvey.

"He's another with Sasha's gift for self-restraint," said Alex.

"Sasha?" Miss Harvey repeated.

"My dog," said Alex. "She's half husky, half shepherd, and half floppy-eared something else while still only being one dog, not, you know, one and a half. She's very talented."

"To class, Miss O'Connor," said Miss Harvey. "In silence."

They slowed a fraction, and Darwen felt a foot come down hard on the back of his ankle. He stumbled and fell headlong on the floor, knocking Genevieve Reddock down with him. As Melissa Young shrieked unnecessarily, the class's neat line broke apart giggling, and several more people managed to fall over in the confusion, including Gabriel, the new boy. Miss Harvey came marching down the corridor shouting about discipline and "all this fooling about." Darwen rolled over and found himself gazing up into the tanned, handsome face of Nathan Cloten.

"Have a good trip, Arkwright?" he asked, grinning maliciously. Then, as the new boy accidentally bumped him in the ribs, he snapped, "Watch yourself, amigo."

Gabriel blushed and shuffled away.

Darwen got to his feet and brushed himself off, averting his eyes.

"Darwen, I'm surprised at you!" exclaimed Miss Harvey as she swooped in and started dragging people to their feet.

"It weren't me, miss," Darwen sputtered, his Lancashire accent kicking up a gear as it always did when he was flustered. "It were Nathan, right? 'E stood on ma foot and—"

"I am not interested in excuses, Mr. Arkwright," said Miss Harvey in a chill voice. "Hillside students take responsibility for their mistakes, misjudgments, and misdemeanors."

Another line from the school brochure, Darwen guessed.

"Now," said Miss Harvey, "do you think you can make it to science class without treating the other students like pins in a bowling alley?"

"Bowling would be better, miss," said Alex. "We'd still be standing, and he'd be in the gutter. Trust me. I've seen him bowl."

"That's enough, Miss O'Connor," said Miss Harvey. "Off you go. Left, right, left, right."

And so they did, though the moment they were out of the teacher's earshot, Darwen could hear Nathan behind him, whining in what he thought was a comical imitation of Darwen's accent: "*It weren't me, miss. It were Nathan, miss. Miss, will someone teach me to speak English? Please, miss. Only, I'm a complete moron, miss.*"

Darwen stared fixedly at the back of Genevieve

Reddock's head. "The sooner I can get on that plane, the better," he muttered.

"You're still allowed to go?" said Genevieve, turning, eyebrows raised.

"Of course," said Darwen, with a rush of panic. "Why wouldn't I be?"

Genevieve raised her eyebrows, but she said nothing and turned away.

Alex leaned in. "Well, the teachers—not to mention your aunt—think you've been climbing out of skyscraper windows," she said. "They might not all think you're a juvenile delinquent who breaks windows and sells drugs, but I'm not sure they see you as a cultural ambassador right now."

Darwen's heart sank. It wasn't just a trip. It was a mission. Not going was not—could not—be an option.

The rest of the week was completely dominated by the upcoming trip. Science classes focused on the Central American rainforest, Mr. Peregrine's world studies classes had turned—albeit hazily—to Costa Rican history and culture, and Spanish classes were swamped with what Nathan derisively called "tourist phrase-book stuff": "I would like some red beans and rice, please," "How many pesos does that cost?" and "Why is my luggage in Nigeria?" Everywhere Darwen turned, people seemed to be talking about the trip in excited and panicky terms.

Genevieve and Melissa seemed to have been clothes shopping all through the holidays and were keen to break down their travel wardrobes for whomever would listen.

"Of course, we won't be able to make the final choices," said Genevieve, "until we know what kind of hotel we'll be in. If we're spending most of our time by the pool, that's going to change the way I accessorize."

Darwen caught Alex's eye, and they exchanged a knowing look. If Mr. Peregrine was involved, it was unlikely they would be spending much time lounging by a hotel pool. Of course, if everyone assumed Darwen was a juvenile delinquent, the kind of accommodations Mr. Peregrine had planned would be the least of Darwen's problems. Conversely, not being there to save the boy would, naturally, rank at the top.

As if she had read his mind, Alex leaned over and whispered, "I have news, by the way. I've been reading Costa Rican newspapers online."

"And?"

"The boy you saw taken was called Luis Vasquez," she said. "He was the second to go missing."

Luis, thought Darwen. Finally he had a name.

"And that's not all," said Alex. "His brother, Eduardo, kept going into the jungle, searching for him. A week later, whatever took his brother took him too."

That evening over dinner (pasta with a green,

strong-tasting sauce his aunt told him was a "simply divine" pesto), Darwen finally raised the question.

"So, about the sixth-grade trip," he said, trying to sound casual.

"I got a letter," said his aunt, palms down on the table, face unreadable.

Darwen knew she had. He had recognized the envelope with its embossed HA emblem and had seen enough to make sure it wasn't another summons to a parent/teacher meeting about his behavior.

"It's only a week away," he said. "I should probably be packing. If I'm going, like."

He looked at his plate. His aunt wasn't speaking, but he could feel her eyes on him.

"You want to go," she said finally.

"Is it too expensive?" he asked, looking up.

"No," she said, waving the question away. "I can find the money. I may have to work longer hours while you're gone. . . ."

"So I can go?!" Darwen exclaimed. "I mean, I'm sorry you'll have to work extra hours. I didn't know you could work longer hours than you already do. I don't mean you're not around enough or anything," he blundered on, knowing he was making it worse but unable to stop, "I just mean that you work really hard, and I really appreciate it and everything—"

"Darwen," she said. Darwen stopped speaking abruptly and looked into her shrewd dark eyes. "Where did you go?"

Darwen didn't need to ask what she meant.

"I never left the apartment," he said. "I swear I didn't. I'm fine. I'm happy. I'm not homesick . . . well, not too much. Not usually. And I'm not shoplifting or dealing drugs. . . ."

"Who said you were dealing drugs?" Honoria gasped.

"Just some kids at school," said Darwen, wishing he hadn't said it, "trying to get me in trouble."

"Do you have enemies at school, Darwen?"

Darwen's brow furrowed. He really wasn't sure. There were kids like Nathan and Chip who didn't like him much, but enemies? No. He met her concerned, watchful gaze and shook his head.

"Just, you know, kid stuff," he said. "Nothing bad. Nothing I can't handle."

"And you really want to go on this trip?"

"Yeah! Rich and Alex are going, and there'll be loads of teachers there too. They're basically shutting down a bunch of classes for the older kids so enough faculty can go."

"They do say they have a very high teacher-to-student ratio," said Honoria approvingly.

"There you go then," said Darwen. "That's good, isn't it? And it's 'innovative and experiential learning.'" Honoria nodded sagely, as if she thought this—whatever it was—was a good thing. "And," Darwen concluded, "Mr. Peregrine is leading the whole thing so . . ."

"So?"

"Well," Darwen finished lamely, wishing he hadn't brought the ex-shopkeeper into it at all. "He's nice, isn't he?"

"Darwen," said Honoria very seriously, "he gave you an oven door for Christmas."

"Right," said Darwen. "Yes. He's got a . . . you know . . . quirky sense of humor."

He tried to smile in an upbeat kind of way. His aunt laid down her knife and fork and sat back, blowing out her breath in a long rush that took her eyes up to the ceiling. At last, she shrugged.

"Okay," she said. "The books say I'm supposed to let you find yourself so . . . okay."

"I can go?"

"You can go," she breathed, swallowing back what Darwen felt sure was a sob. "But keep your nose clean or I'll cancel, and if I hear so much as a rumor of you wandering off while you're there, you'll be on the next flight home, you hear me?"

"Yes, ma'am," said Darwen, gripping the stone sphere in his pocket.

Darwen had been trying to catch Mr. Peregrine alone for days, but he always seemed to be dashing off, his arms laden with maps and travel documents. At last he found him behind a stack of books in the world studies classroom.

"What's the Insidious Bleck?" Darwen asked. He had wanted to ask Moth the same question last night but, once more, had not been able to enter her locus.

"Nothing," said Mr. Peregrine, without looking up from his book. "A fairytale monster. Where did you—"

"Didn't you say that about the Shade?" asked Darwen.

"Hmm?" said Mr. Peregrine. "Oh yes. You saw one, didn't you? Well done!"

"I think the Insidious Bleck is the thing I saw," Darwen persisted.

"Really? Well, you have been right before. And besides, whatever we call it, it's still just a lost and hungry animal."

"All the more reason to find Luis as quickly as possible," answered Darwen.

"Who?" asked Mr. Peregrine.

"Luis Vasquez," said Darwen. "The boy who was taken."

"You know his name?" asked Mr. Peregrine.

"Alex found it online," said Darwen.

"Online?" Mr. Peregrine echoed.

"It doesn't matter," said Darwen, grinning. "How are we going to find him?"

"Well," said the teacher, "I suppose we'll have to figure that out when we get there. Our first priority is plugging the breach between worlds."

"We still need some way of getting to Silbrica while we're there."

"Darwen," said Mr. Peregrine, rubbing his temple like he was developing a headache, "I'm sorry, but I really must get on."

Darwen turned to go but caught himself.

"Mr. Peregrine," he said.

"Yes, Darwen?"

"You do believe me about Luis, don't you?" Darwen said. "About the monster pulling him into a portal, I mean."

"My dear boy," said Mr. Peregrine, "of course I believe you. Did you doubt that?"

Darwen blushed and looked down, but he felt better.

"Now, I'm sorry," said Mr. Peregrine, "but . . . these little countries in the middle," he said, peering at a map of Central America, "are very confusing. I keep forgetting which one we're going to. Wait, I think I have the map upside down. . . ."

"Right," said Darwen, with another twinge of anxiety. "I'll leave you to it."

Darwen had assumed that the air of mystery and strangeness that hung around Mr. Peregrine would go away once the students started having classes with him. He even feared that the former shopkeeper would turn out to be incompetent in the classroom and would become a bit of a joke. He couldn't have been more wrong.

For one thing, there were rumors about him. Several of the students thought they recognized Mr. Peregrine, and one of them, Carlos Garcia, remembered that he had seen him three months before on that most famous night in Hillside's history, Halloween. There had been a party at school, the Halloween Hop, that had ended with power outages and explosions and policemen running about trying to establish order. People saw strange things that night, and though most of it was chalked up to costumes and fireworks, the students still talked about it in hushed and excited tones. Now they remembered that this strange new teacher had been on campus that night, that he had somehow taken charge, consulting with the police and EMTs and telling the teachers what to do. Parents had been overheard saying that they thought he had saved student lives.

"He just took over," Carlos murmured to Gabriel and a rapt audience of sixth graders, "ordering people around and everything, but he wasn't even a teacher! So who was he? And what happened to him afterward? At the end of that night, he just walks away, and no one sees him until the last day of term, when he's suddenly the world studies teacher?"

Darwen, Alex, and Rich avoided each other's eyes, and Darwen found himself irritated that Carlos—who was usually so quiet—should pick this moment to come out of his shell.

"I heard he's a kind of shadow principal," said Jennifer Taylor-Berry in her rich Southern drawl. "That he comes in when the school is in trouble."

"I heard he works for the government," said Simon Agu, whose father was a diplomat at the Nigerian consulate on Roswell Road. "Some kind of secret agency connected to paranormal activity. I mean, there was stuff that happened at the Halloween Hop that no one has ever explained properly."

"Yeah," said Alex. "Because what's going on in an Atlanta middle school is a matter of national security. And you say *I* have a vivid imagination!"

"Nice one," said Darwen as soon as the others had traipsed off looking shamefaced.

"Maybe, but these kids aren't utterly stupid," said Alex. "Mr. P is going to have to watch himself or even Barry Fails will start putting two and two together." Barry "Usually" Fails was, as Darwen sometimes said, as thick as two short planks.

"Anyway, the Peregrine Pact is supposed to be us," Alex concluded, "you, me, and Rich, not the entire school."

Mr. Peregrine's demeanor in class didn't help the situation. He did a lot of smiling, as if he had secret knowledge that amused him, and he taught by asking questions, frequently waiting for minutes at a time until someone came up with the right answer. Darwen suspected that the teacher didn't actually know a lot of what he was teaching, but the others took these long silences as a clever strategy to make them learn for themselves.

"Best teacher we've had," said Bobby Park, "at least for this subject."

"I wonder who he is, though," said Melissa Young to Genevieve Reddock conspiratorially. "I mean who he *really* is. He's obviously not from around here and has lived in all sorts of places. You can hear it in his voice, see it in his eyes. He knows things the other teachers don't."

Darwen, Rich, and Alex made eye contact again, then—as they seemed to be doing a lot lately—looked hurriedly away.

The night before they left, Darwen went over his luggage with his aunt twice. It seemed that the only thing he wasn't packing was the stone sphere, and that was only because Aunt Honoria had yet to learn of its existence. "Are you sure you won't need warmer clothing?" she said, considering a T-shirt skeptically.

Darwen consulted the list that had been sent from the school again.

"Says warm-weather clothes," he said. "Costa Rica is in the Northern Hemisphere but only just, and it's actually summer there now."

"But wait, it also says long pants and sturdy walking shoes," replied Aunt Honoria, horror dawning. "You'll be burning up!"

"I'll be fine," said Darwen, smiling and patting her hand. She returned his smile with an effort, and her eyes welled up.

"Oh, insect repellant!"

"What?" exclaimed Aunt Honoria, the shock of their having possibly forgotten something nearly causing her to swoon.

"The list says I need insect repellant for mosquitoes and stuff," said Darwen.

"There's a pharmacy on the corner," she said, quickly composing herself. "Get your coat on, and we'll walk down together."

By the time they were back, weighed down by the medical supplies with which Aunt Honoria planned to pack his suitcase, it was after sundown. Darwen waited patiently, trying to look appreciative as his aunt doubled the weight of his luggage with boxes of pills and bottles of sprays and ointments.

"That's to keep the bugs off," she said. "That's to put on the bites if they get you. This is if you can't go to the bathroom, and this one is if you're going too much. Don't mix them up, or it could get ugly."

"I get it," said Darwen. "Thanks."

She paused and took a breath, as if resigned that there was nothing more she could do. "Okay," she said. "Let's get some rest. I'm sorry I can't come to the airport with you. I have to—"

"Work," said Darwen smiling. "I know. It's fine."

She hesitated at the bedroom door, then turned meaningfully back to Darwen. "I'll miss you, you know."

"I'll miss you too," Darwen answered, surprised that it was true.

"And please, Darwen . . ." she began.

"What?"

"Be careful."

His aunt had no idea just how careful Darwen *wasn't* being. That night, he traveled through the oven door one last time in the hopes of finding any information that could help in their search for Luis and his brother, anything that would make their mission in Costa Rica easier. But the gateway to Moth's bamboo grove remained troublingly sealed, and though Darwen retraced his steps to the crystal waterfall, he found nothing helpful. He had hoped for another glimpse of Weazen the Peace Hunter or some clue that would make his mission clearer, but no new evidence revealed itself.

At last, Darwen returned to his room. He put on his pajamas and snuck into bed. And though he remained frustrated by his lack of progress, he stared up at his featureless ceiling safe in the knowledge that for once the morning would bring something almost as exciting as Silbrica. The prospect of being away from home with his friends for a whole week thrilled him, but when he finally fell asleep, he dreamed he was searching for a boy called Luis among jungle vines that turned into tentacles.

The Atlanta airport was vast and crowded, and though Darwen had been through it once before, he found it all very intimidating. Mr. Peregrine bustled about looking dazed, so it was Miss Harvey and Mr. Sumners who ultimately had to engineer the logistics of gathering the students and marching them en masse to the departure gate.

"What's Sumners coming for?" asked Darwen wearily. "He's a math teacher."

"High teacher-to-student ratio, remember?" said Rich.

"Maybe we can push him out halfway there," said Alex. "He can swim to Miami. It would be a shame if the sharks got him, though. I hate sharks, but they *are* endangered, and eating math teachers can't be good for them."

Besides Mr. Peregrine, Miss Harvey, and Mr. Sumners, the sixteen sixth graders were accompanied by Mr. Iverson and the foreign-language teacher, Miss Martinez.

"We need to make sure we're always with Mr. P," said Alex.

"Or Mr. Iverson," said Rich.

"So long as we stay away from Sumners, I don't care," said Darwen.

Their flight would take them south over Florida and out into the Atlantic, then between Cuba and the coast of Mexico, before dropping further south past Belize, Guatemala, Honduras, and Nicaragua. They were to land in San José, Costa Rica, and then get a local connection still further south to Drake Bay, which sat on the Pacific side, almost on the border with Panama. The names meant almost nothing to Darwen. They were faraway places as strange as anything in Silbrica, and he sympathized with Mr. Peregrine, who was as unfamiliar with them as he was. At least Darwen didn't have to pretend he was an expert on world studies.

Once they had waved off their families and trundled

through security, the excitement started to mount, and by the time they were on the plane, it was like someone had turned a volume control up on the students. They were laughing and gossiping, flicking excitedly through Rich's brand-new *Field Guide to Costa Rican Wildlife*, planning and speculating, squabbling, and—in the case of Alex—singing very loudly.

"We are not the only people on this aircraft," said Miss Harvey. "Miss O'Connor? Miss—will someone please tell her to take those earbuds out?"

Alex continued to croon at the top of her lungs, her eyes shut. She didn't respond when Rich, who was getting fidgety, tapped her on the shoulder, so Darwen leaned over and pulled the earbuds right out of her ears.

"Hey!" she roared. "You could just ask, you know."

"That is what we have been trying to do," said Miss Harvey icily.

The group quieted but a few moments later produced a great cheer as they felt the aircraft tip up and away from the runway. Mr. Peregrine, who seemed to be having the time of his life, cheered loudest of all, so that Mr. Sumners shot him the kind of look he normally reserved for Darwen's homework. Darwen found himself grinning widely at Rich, unexpectedly delighted that they were in the air at last and a huge step closer to starting their mission. In the next row, Gabriel, the new boy, was looking blank-faced beside Melissa Young, who was ignoring him and leaning over to whisper to Genevieve Reddock.

"First flight?" asked Darwen, turning all the way around.

"Second," said Gabriel.

"Mine too," said Darwen. "I think it's brilliant."

"Hey, Darwen," said Genevieve. "Is this Mr. Peregrine the weirdest teacher you've ever had or what?"

It wasn't a criticism. Darwen peered over to where Mr. P was sitting, collecting all the tiny bags of mini pretzels no one wanted and piling them up in front of him gleefully like they were treasure.

"Pretty weird," agreed Darwen, grinning.

They landed in San José and emerged from the plane pointing at the mountains, which surrounded the town. The warm, muggy air hit them, so everyone shrugged themselves out of their winter jackets.

"Northern Hemisphere geography, Southern Hemisphere seasons," Rich muttered.

Darwen and Alex exchanged knowing looks. They had been told this a dozen times so that they wouldn't stuff their luggage with winter clothes.

"You okay?" asked Darwen.

"Fine," said Rich. "Why wouldn't I be? It's just a regular town, right?"

Except that it wasn't a regular town—not by Georgia standards, at least, and not only because all the signs were in Spanish. It was bustling with pedestrians, for one thing. Also, while there were cars and traffic lights and shops that might just have passed unnoticed in parts of Atlanta (though Darwen doubted his babysitter Eileen would have found the kinds of stores she liked), the whole still felt different, if only because of the wooded mountains that loomed in every direction. They made everything feel just a little strange and unfamiliar.

"I like it," Alex pronounced as they took the shuttle bus across town to a smaller airport. "It's like Silbrica without the monsters."

"Let's hope so," muttered Darwen.

The students were glued to the bus windows, all except Nathan and his friends, who played cards at the back, but even they took notice of the rush of mingled concern and excitement when everyone saw the planes they were to board next. There were two, each one built to carry no more than a dozen passengers.

"We're flying in those?" gasped Barry Fails.

"Propeller planes are perfectly reliable," said Mr. Iverson, considering the slightly battered aircraft. "Even . . . er . . . older models like this."

Rich, who had stopped dead to stare wide-eyed at the antiquated-looking planes, had to be virtually shoved into the tiny airport. Darwen gave him an encouraging smile as they checked in, but it didn't seem to help.

"Isn't this a treat!" exclaimed Mr. Peregrine as he gazed at the antique planes.

"Everyone stand on the scales with your luggage," called Miss Harvey, who seemed rather less enthusiastic. "Ladies first, single file and with dignity."

An official from the airline checked the weight of each student and their bags, then told Princess Clarkson she was twenty pounds overweight. Princess looked scandalized, then brandished a credit card and announced she would just pay the overage.

"I'm afraid not," said the official, shaking his head and smiling. "Each passenger is allowed twenty-five pounds of luggage. No more."

"Then I'll just buy another seat," said Princess.

Darwen and Rich gaped at her.

"No," said the official, still smiling as if he was used to this. "The plane is full. If you need the bag, we can fly it down tomorrow, for a charge. If you can manage without it, you should leave it here and collect it on your way back."

Princess sighed theatrically.

"Fine," she snapped. "Bring it tomorrow."

She waggled the credit card.

"What is in the bag," said Mr. Peregrine, "that you cannot manage without, Miss . . ."

"Clarkson," prompted Miss Harvey.

"Stuff," said Princess. A huddle of students had gathered around, and more were pricking up their ears.

"Of what kind?" pressed Mr. Peregrine.

"Personal stuff," said Princess with a haughty glare.

"Could you be more specific?"

"Er, Mr. Peregrine?" inserted Miss Harvey. "I don't think we need to know precisely what Miss Clarkson is carrying. In fact, I'm not sure we are allowed to ask."

"Getting another bag to us tomorrow is going to be extremely inconvenient for whoever has to actually bring it," said Mr. Peregrine. "I want to be sure we are not wasting anyone's time, as well as this young lady's money."

Miss Harvey frowned, but before she could say anything, Princess muttered, "Fine," and unzipped her bag with a flourish.

"Happy?" she said.

"This," said Mr. Peregrine, peering into the pink suitcase, "is a device for drying hair? And this entire container is full of makeup. These," he said, holding up dresses of shimmering, lustrous fabric studded with sequins, "are evening gowns?"

"Gotta have something to wear for dinner, don't I?" said Princess, as if she had made her point.

"Where we are going, these . . ." said Mr. Peregrine, searching for the right words, "aren't going to work."

Princess opened her mouth to protest, then closed it

just as quickly. Mr. Peregrine's kindly face spoke volumes about where they were going.

As Princess, dumbstruck, watched her pink suitcase get carted into storage, Genevieve Reddock put a supportive arm around her shoulders, and Alex turned to Darwen. "That," she said, "was pretty cool. Did you see the designer label on that dress? Sell a case full of those and you could probably buy Rich's house."

"Thanks," snapped Rich.

"What?" said Alex. "I'm just saying."

They squabbled as they walked across the runway and up the narrow metal stairs into the plane. Inside they had to bend over, squeezing into their tight little plastic seats and strapping themselves in with considerably more care than they had on the jet from Atlanta. Darwen's tiny window gave him an unnervingly good view of one wing and an engine, and if he looked ahead he could see right into the cockpit, where the two pilots were flicking instruments to make sure they were working.

The engines were loud, starting deep and low like the revving of a scrobbler motorbike, then growing higher and more nasal as they approached takeoff. The students, who had been so excited before, were now edgy and quiet, avoiding each other's eyes. Instead of the long, slow taxi the jet had made, the tiny plane reached its bumpy, rattling takeoff speed alarmingly quickly, and in seconds they were up and banking hard as they climbed.

Darwen waited for the engines to stall and for the plane to drop out of the sky like a rock, but when time passed and nothing of the kind happened, he began to relax. The plane stayed below the cloud level, so he could see the city fall quickly behind them, instantly replaced by densely forested hills on which, it seemed, no one lived. He thought *forested* because that was what the proper name—rainforest—suggested, but the word that more firmly pressed itself into his mind was one that had popped out of *Treasure Island*. The word was *jungle*.

The land below was a thick green carpet, but these were not fields, they were treetops, the canopy of a rich ecosystem positively throbbing with life. Darwen stole a look at Rich and was pleased to see that he sensed it too. Rich's anxiety had melted away once they got airborne, and there was a hungry excitement as he gazed at the jungle below.

And somewhere down there, thought Darwen, *is a creature that doesn't belong, and it's taking kids.*

"Good thing Princess dumped her evening gowns, huh?" said Alex.

They landed less than an hour later on a grassy strip of land cleared of trees with what looked like a bus shelter next to it. It was so hot when Darwen climbed out that he thought he was too close to the plane's engine, but as he walked away and the temperature didn't change, he tugged at his tie and unfastened his collar button. Then someone screamed.

Darwen spun around and saw Barry Fails, one hand clasped over his mouth, the other pointing at something long and green in the grass: it was four feet from head to tail and covered with spines like something out of one of Darwen's old dinosaur books. Several people jumped and took hurried steps away.

"Chuffin' 'eck!" Darwen gasped.

"It's a dragon!" Barry exclaimed.

"Probably," said Rich, taking a step toward it. "Or, since dragons don't actually exist, it's an iguana."

He said it casually, but he shot Darwen a look, and there was a flicker of uncertainty in his eyes that Darwen immediately understood. They had, after all, seen plenty of things that shouldn't exist: flittercrakes, scrobblers, gnashers, shades, and other things for which they had no names. They had come here searching for a monster called the Insidious Bleck. Were there dragons in Silbrica? Darwen had no idea, but if there were, it was at least possible that they might be here too.

Rich got a little closer to the iguana and squatted beside it. The massive lizard took a few slow, lumbering steps away, then settled again, watching him. Rich was sweating heavily but looked as happy as Darwen had ever seen him.

"Man," Rich muttered, almost to himself, "this is going to be a great trip."

The other students didn't look so sure.

They were loaded into dirty jeeps and pickup trucks and driven along a narrow winding road through the jungle, occasionally passing clusters of ramshackle houses. At one point they forded a swollen river, and the water rose alarmingly above the wheels, though the drivers seemed unconcerned, laughing and calling to each other in Spanish as if nothing could have been more normal.

Alex, who was riding up front, leaned toward their driver, a small man with a deep tan and a faded baseball cap, and said something in Spanish. When the driver nodded and muttered a few words, Alex began looking around at the river with new urgency.

"What did you ask him?" said Darwen.

"If there were crocodiles in this river," said Alex, without taking her eyes from the brown, sluggish water.

"And?" Darwen pressed, staring.

"There are," said Alex. "Lots. And sharks."

"Sharks?" said Rich. "But sharks don't live in rivers. They live in the ocean."

"You'd think," said Alex, still scanning the water uneasily.

Darwen wanted to think the driver was pulling her leg, but he wasn't so sure, and it took the edge off his enthusiasm. In his mind he saw the slobbering shark mouths of the gnashers from Silbrica and, imagining them swimming up and down the river, he gripped the armrest a little tighter.

They disembarked on a stony beach lined with coconut palm trees, where a single vulture sat tearing at a stinking fish the size of a sheep.

"Gross," said Genevieve Reddock, stepping hurriedly away, as if she might throw up.

Though it was hot, it was also overcast, and the sky promised rain. Darwen moved down toward the shore, picking his way between the hundreds of tiny hermit crabs that seemed to be everywhere. Mr. Peregrine came waddling down the beach, looking like some kind of robot penguin: he had changed into the kind of rubber overalls that fishermen use for deep wading. Barry Fails pointed and laughed, but the other students took this to be an ominous development.

"Why is he dressed like that?" asked Rich, looking alarmed. After all the talk of sharks and crocodiles, Darwen couldn't blame him.

Moments later, Rich got his answer. The students were loaded onto motorboats, which meant having to wade knee-deep into the ocean and clamber on board, assisted by a pair of strong local men.

"My shoes are ruined!" exclaimed Princess Clarkson,

sitting miserably on the side of the tossing boat.

No one said anything. Even the teachers were silent and watchful. It was becoming clear that Mr. Peregrine's idea of a school trip was not what they had had in mind, and some of them were starting to worry about far more than their shoes.

"We take the boats around the coast," Mr. Peregrine announced happily. "Just twenty minutes or so. The camp can only be reached by water."

"Camp?" Mr. Sumners repeated in a stony voice.

"That's right," said Mr. Peregrine, apparently oblivious to the fact that everyone except Rich was starting to look genuinely panicked. "You can't experience the jungle from outside, can you? Got to get right into it. Live in it. Sleep in it."

There was a rumble of thunder and the first steady pattering of rain. Somewhere from the tree-lined shore something started to call, a wild, whooping shout that might have been a bird or something else Darwen couldn't begin to name. Maybe it was the call of whatever had taken Luis. It was a sound that would have been quite at home in the strange and unpredictable world beyond the mirror, but this time, Darwen thought with an unsettled feeling in the pit of his stomach, he couldn't just climb back into a safer and more familiar reality. Here, the weirdness and danger were everywhere.

The tent camp redefined the term *basic*. There was a long tin-roofed shelter open on one side, where meals would be served at wooden tables with benches. There was a makeshift building that constituted office, kitchen, and storage unit. At the back of the camp, at the end of a path that wound through heavy vegetation, there was a complex of toilets, washrooms, and showers made of concrete blocks. Darwen peered in and saw, squatting beside one of the toilets, a brown toad the size of a volleyball.

There was no hot water, and the electricity was powered by a generator that ran for only two hours each evening. Darwen eyed it warily, half expecting to find little seats with wires running to great Silbrican batteries, but the generator looked quite harmless. There was no computer, no fridge, no phone, and the students who had brought cell phones quickly discovered that they were miles from any service. Sleeping accommodations were in a series of yellow tents on wooden platforms, each tent just big enough for three students and their luggage. The tents, they were told, should be kept zipped up at all times to keep the snakes out, and no one was to move around at night without a flashlight.

"Can I share with you?" asked Gabriel.

Darwen gave Rich a shrug and said, "Sure. Come on in."

Alex was sharing with Naia and Mad.

"Thanks," said Gabriel half-apologetically. He was olive-skinned and dark-haired, and his voice—on the rare occasions that Darwen had heard him speak—had a lilt to it that sounded like Carlos's.

"So . . . where are you from?" asked Darwen.

"Florida," said the new boy, his eyes down.

"This is gonna be way more fun than anything in Florida," said Rich, slapping Gabriel heartily on the back so that he almost fell over. "A bit, you know, *exotic*, but fun nonetheless."

"Tell Alex," said Darwen, rummaging through his backpack. "She didn't sound too thrilled about the crocodiles and sharks."

"Alex is a city girl," said Rich sagely. "Me, I'm a country boy at heart. Living in the rainforest for a week?"

"Jungle," said Darwen.

"Rainforest," said Rich. "Surrounded by the kind of nature most people never get to see? Trust me, this is going to be a blast. I read there are jaguars around here."

Gabriel looked like he was going to say something skeptical, but he caught Darwen rolling his eyes at Rich's enthusiasm and just grinned.

"Come on," said Rich, checking his watch. "We have a meeting."

"Do I have to go?" asked Gabriel. "I would prefer to stay here and read."

"Wouldn't risk it if I were you," said Darwen. "I'm sure Sumners is looking for an opportunity to remind everyone that Hillside rules still apply."

They crawled out and put their shoes back on.

"Don't forget to zip the tent," said Rich. "All the way. There's a bit still open."

"Nothing could get through," began Darwen, but Rich pushed him aside and carefully zipped up the last half inch. "Better to be safe," he said breezily, as if he didn't really care one way or the other.

The camp was only yards from the ocean, and the sandy dirt swarmed with even more hermit crabs than before. The three boys followed the path up to the dining shelter. It was late afternoon, and the light was already softening. Halfway up, Rich paused, gazing through the heavy branches toward one of the other tents where an old man in shorts and a screamingly loud Hawaiian shirt was snoozing in a hammock tied between two palm trees.

"Is that . . ." he began. "It can't be . . . Mr. Peregrine?"

It could and it was. The former shopkeeper clambered awkwardly from the hammock as they watched and checked his gold pocket watch on its chain, which he had fastened to the belt of his shorts.

"Oh, that's just wrong," said Alex, who had appeared behind them and was gazing at the spindly old man in his shorts and sandals. "That man needs a suit. I don't care if we're in the jungle. He needs a suit."

Mr. Peregrine beamed at them as he sauntered over, gazing up at the once again threatening sky. A vivid, green bird—some form of parakeet, Darwen guessed in amazement—soared overhead, and Mr. Peregrine pointed at it, smiling proudly, as if he had arranged for it to be there.

"What a delightful place," he said. "Quite remarkable."

The students made uncertain noises in response, so Rich swooped in with, "It's fantastic," as if he was their elected representative. Alex raised her eyebrow.

"And it's just starting!" said Mr. Peregrine.

"I'll bet," said Alex darkly.

"First, dinner," said Mr. Peregrine, unabashed, "and then we meet our guide. You're going to like him. He's a real expert on the area."

"Pretty cool, huh, Darwen?" said Rich.

"What?" Darwen replied vaguely. He had been gazing off into the trees, which marked the beginning of the jungle proper.

"You okay?" asked Alex.

"Just, you know," said Darwen. "Keen to get started. The mission, I mean."

"Cut yourself a little slack," said Alex. "We just got here."

"We don't even know where to start looking for the boy, man," said Rich.

"Luis," Darwen shot back. "His name is Luis. And if we don't know where to look, then we had better get on that, don't you think?"

"We will," said Alex, her tone rising to match his. "But we just got off the plane, Darwen, and we can't just wander off into the jungle without any idea where we're going! Sheesh."

"Someone needs to be looking for him *now*!" Darwen returned. "Don't you get it? His parents have been taken away from him, and he's been alone for weeks now."

"You mean he's been taken away from his parents," said Alex.

Darwen blinked.

"What did I say?" he said.

"That his parents have been taken away from him."

"Oh," said Darwen, flushing. "Same difference."

Dinner was served on the uneven wooden tables of the long shelter. From their seats there, the students of Hillside Academy could look out over the camp's gardens to the Pacific beyond, where the sunset was painting the clouds with a blaze of color. They ate red beans and rice on tin plates, followed by a selection of extraordinary local fruit—mango, banana, and pineapple—all of which tasted so much like it had been picked only minutes earlier that the students' moods improved significantly.

"That wasn't bad," said Alex. "Could have used some hot sauce, but yeah, not bad. Tasty. Scrumptious, even. Healthy too. And fresh. A hearty meal—"

"Okay, Alex," said Rich, shooting Darwen and Gabriel a knowing look. "You liked the food."

Not everyone did. Princess Clarkson had refused to touch anything but a few pieces of fruit, and Barry Fails had complained loudly that there was no meat.

"I could have brought some if I'd known we were coming to, like, the third world," he said.

"And stored it where?" asked Nathan Cloten lazily.

"There's no fridge."

"If I'd brought some, you'd want to share it," Barry persisted.

"Oh yes," said Nathan. "Rancid hamburger à la Usually. Sounds delicious."

Chip Whittley gave his woodpecker laugh, and Miss Harvey told him to be quiet.

"We are still to behave like young ladies and gentlemen," she said, "even if the surroundings are a little . . ."

"Rustic?" Alex offered. "Rural? Woodsy?"

"Oh, I'm so glad," said Nathan, "that despite all the luggage restrictions we were able to find room for O'Connor, the Incredible Talking Thesaurus."

"Thesaurus?" said Barry. "Right. 'Cause she looks like a dinosaur."

"Thank you, Barry," said Miss Harvey with tired finality. "Always helpful. Now simmer down, Hillside. It's time to meet our guide, and I want you to make a good impression. Remember, 'Manners maketh man' and 'Learning is the path to self-improvement.'"

Alex rolled her eyes, but a hush had descended on the students, who were craning to see who was striding up the path from the camp below.

The man who was coming toward them through the gardens might have stepped out of a movie screen. He was perhaps thirty, tanned, athletic, with jet-black wavy hair and large dark eyes. He wore a short-sleeved safari shirt and rugged-looking shorts with hiking boots. He also had a sizable snake draped over his shoulders, and, judging by the way he was holding its head, it was alive and irritated.

"This," said Miss Harvey, her voice carefully neutral, "must be Jorge."

There was an uneven attempt at the typical Hillside greeting ("Good afternoon, Jorge"), but too many of the girls were nudging each other and giggling, while the rest were trying to get either as close to or as far from the snake as possible. One person in the latter group was Rich.

"I thought you liked animals," said Darwen.

"I do," said Rich through tight lips. "Just not . . . those."

"Hi," said Jorge simply, smiling to show white, even teeth, a gesture that was met with even more giggling from the girls. "My name is Jorge, and I will be your guide."

"What's the snake called?" asked Carlos.

"He is not a pet," said the guide. "I found him in the kitchens and thought I would show him to you before I released him back into the forest. Normally I would not handle him, but today I make an exception so that you can see one of the beautiful creatures who is sharing the camp with us."

This last remark did not get quite the response Jorge seemed to want.

"Do not be scared," he said. "He is a boa constrictor. Not poisonous."

"Couldn't he, you know, squeeze you to death?" asked Bobby Park, looking alarmed.

"No!" Jorge laughed. "He is only a baby. It will be many years before he can kill you." He paused. "I am joking, of course. He will probably only reach about ten feet long. Here in Costa Rica, it is the venomous snakes that we need to watch out for."

Bobby didn't look entirely comforted.

"And are there poisonous snakes here?" asked Darwen.

"Oh yes," said Jorge cheerfully. "I saw an eyelash viper on the flowers by the showers"—he paused to consider—"four days ago. It is not there now. When you walk past the bushes, even here in the camp, you should always keep your arms close to your body. Snakes sometimes coil around branches with flowers," he said, curling one hand around the other, "and wait for birds or other prey. Some of them are very aggressive and quite dangerous, so please be very careful. Also, *pay attentions* to the ground, especially where there are a lot of fallen leaves, and never put your hands where you cannot see. Two weeks ago—no, one week ago—wait, what day is it?"

"Monday," said Mr. Sumners. He was watching Jorge carefully, apparently unsure of whether the man was stupid, dangerous, or both.

"Really?" said Jorge. "Huh. In the jungle, all days are the same. So, one week ago I saw a bushmaster on the trail we will be walking tomorrow."

Rich went pale. Jorge noticed.

"Yes, this is a very dangerous snake. This and the fer-de-lance. We have both here." He sounded quite proud. "So it is very important that you are always on the alert."

"Do you have antivenom?" asked Nathan, shifting in his seat.

"We do," said Jorge. "But it will take a long time to reach a hospital from here, and *antiveneno* is . . ." He waggled his hand to indicate *shaky*, *unreliable*. "It will be much better if you do not get bitten."

The students exchanged wary looks, and Jorge started to speak again with more urgency.

"You need to understand that this is a very wild place," he said. "People are used to thinking of the land around them as theirs, the places where they live and work and sleep. Animals in such places are pets or have strayed in from outside. But here in the jungle it is the other way around. It is people who do not belong here. You are in the world of the animals, and some of them can be quite—what is the word?—*lethal*. Yes. So please *pay attentions*."

The students had gone quiet again, some of them thrilled, others clearly terrified. The teachers were quiet too.

"It's because of stuff like this," whispered Mad to Naia,

"that my parents left India." Darwen, who had grown up in a little town where there were no dangerous animals of any kind, tried to give her an encouraging smile, but his heart wasn't in it.

"Tomorrow we will go on our first hike in the jungle," said Jorge. "We will not disturb the forest. Take only pictures and leave only footprints. It is very important that you dress appropriately and do exactly as I say."

No one said a word, and for a moment there was no sound but the noise of the distant surf on the beach.

"I have posted a list of what you should wear tomorrow on the notice board, and you should study that before you go to bed. There is a battery-operated lantern for each tent. Turn it on by twisting this part," he said, demonstrating on a small handheld lamp that produced a bluish glow. "We recharge them during the day. Breakfast is at five thirty. We leave at six—without you, if you are not ready. Get a good night's sleep. Tomorrow will be . . . quite strenuous."

Barry Fails turned, muttering to Chip.

"It means hard, Usually," said Chip. "He's saying tomorrow is going to suck."

"No," said Jorge, beaming. "Tomorrow will be glorious: a day to remember for the rest of your lives. I can't promise we will see any wildlife, because this is a jungle, not a zoo, but I think it will be a very special day for all of you."

And with that he bade them good night. The students

broke into huddling groups, some of which went immediately to consult the notice board. There was an air of quiet panic, touched here and there with excitement.

"No flip-flops!" wailed Melissa Young, studying the notice in disbelief. "What am I going to wear?!"

"Time for bed, I guess," said Rich.

"In a moment," said Mr. Peregrine, who had appeared beside them with a mug of what looked like tea. "I'd like a quick word."

"Good," said Darwen, who wasn't remotely sleepy, "I wanted to ask where—"

"I'll check the notice," said Rich. "Come on, Gabriel," he added, giving Darwen a significant look. Darwen nodded gratefully, then turned to the teacher.

"So," he said, "where do I start?"

"Tonight," said Mr. Peregrine, "you don't. You rest. Tomorrow—"

"Tomorrow?!" Darwen exclaimed. "I've come all this way. Luis was taken weeks ago. . . ."

"Darwen," said Mr. Peregrine, his voice gentle, "your mission is to find the tear in the barrier between worlds so that we can mend it. If we chance to find the missing child in the process, of course we will try to rescue him, but we have only one week, much of it taken up with schoolwork and excursions. You need to make progress quickly."

"But how?" asked Darwen. "How am I supposed to

find a patch of jungle I saw for a few seconds weeks ago?"

"The Guardians trust your gifts as a mirroculist," said Mr. Peregrine, lowering his voice as he turned to face him. "Tomorrow's hike will take you through part of the region where we think breaches have opened."

"Portals," Darwen said.

"'Portals' suggests someone is controlling them," said Mr. Peregrine. "This is just a tear in the fabric separating us from Silbrica. Tomorrow during the day you can do little more than observe, but in the evening you will cross over."

Darwen's heart leaped.

"You know where there's a portal?!" he exclaimed.

"Let's just say that I think I can get you in," he said, winking. "Come to my tent first thing in the morning. I have something for you."

"What is it?" asked Darwen.

"Patience, my boy, patience," said Mr. Peregrine with a chuckle. "Trust me: you are going to like it."

Darwen nodded, then asked the question that had been nagging at him ever since he and his classmates had begun trudging through the jungle: "So we really are all here because of me—the whole class, I mean—so that I can wander around the jungle looking for holes in the fabric of reality?"

"And," said Mr. Peregrine with a twinkle in his eye, "for the excellent pineapple."

With that he left Darwen to his thoughts, but as he rose, Darwen's gaze flashed across the dining shelter and settled on Nathan Cloten, who was watching him with a suspicious look on his face. Darwen turned hurriedly away. He had felt responsible for saving Luis and his brother before, but as he scanned the dark ground for venomous snakes and who knew what else, he felt a burden as heavy as all of Princess Clarkson's excess luggage strapped to his back.

We're here because of me, he thought. *So anything that happens from here on out is . . . my fault.*

"Ready to head back?" said Rich, interrupting Darwen's realization. He nodded in Gabriel's direction to indicate that they weren't yet alone. The skinny boy was loitering behind Rich, looking lost.

"Uh, sure," Darwen muttered.

"Not sure about these lanterns," said Rich, peering at the one in his hand. "We'll have to stick pretty close together."

"What does the list say?"

"Pretty much what you would expect," said Rich. "Strong shoes or boots that you don't mind getting wet and muddy. Actually the main gist is that you should expect everything you wear to get wet and muddy."

"Perfect," said Darwen. "How's Gabriel?"

"Okay, I guess," said Rich. "Doesn't say much. Probably a bit freaked out by all this."

"Imagine that," said Darwen dryly.

The three boys wandered down toward the tents, got their toiletries, and came back up past the dining shelter to the washrooms. The toad that Darwen had seen earlier was still there, squatting fat and watchful by one of the toilets, his presence ensuring that his stall stayed off-limits to the students from Hillside.

Darwen was brushing his teeth when an immense and shiny brown cockroach scurried across the floor. One of the girls screamed.

"Just like back home," said Rich. "Outside, I mean. Not in the house. Not usually."

Darwen grinned and went back to cleaning his teeth, but as he did so he caught a flash of color in the mirror and a face over his shoulder—and a strange one at that. He spun around.

There was no one there.

"What?" said Rich.

"Nothing," said Darwen instinctively. He had imagined it. Still, it was a strange thing to have imagined.

The face had been pink and shiny, like a mask or a doll. It was tipped at an odd angle, like the person was leaning back and to the side. Its eyes were round, bulging, and glassy, and its mouth was wide open and dark inside, as if frozen midway through a wild and maniacal laugh. Darwen wasn't sure why, but he knew the laugh would be terrible, as if he had heard it before.

He shuddered, staring at his expression in the mirror.

"You look like you've seen a ghost," Rich remarked, toothbrush held perfectly still in one hand.

"Thought something was behind me," said Darwen, checking again. "Must have been a trick of the light."

"But"—Rich looked around and then whispered—"the sun has just gone down. Maybe the mirror is . . ."

"I don't think so," said Darwen, studying it. "It's just a regular mirror. Or it is now."

By the time they were done, it was truly dark, the kind of darkness Darwen had rarely experienced, having spent his life in cities and densely populated towns. It reminded him of being inside the Shade: a thick, almost liquid blackness that obliterated everything outside the meager glow of the lantern. Darwen, Rich, and Gabriel squeezed inside the tiny circle of bluish light and inched their way back along the path toward their tent. Rich kept his arms rigidly at his sides, so that he wouldn't accidentally brush against any of the vegetation, which seemed to breathe musky perfumes at them from the hot night. All around them insects chirped and frogs called with strange, unearthly voices.

The boys took their shoes off on the little platform outside the tent proper and then crawled into bed, saying nothing, oppressed by the darkness and the sounds of the jungle. Darwen lay there, eyes open, listening for whatever might be moving close by, wondering if he would dare to go back out into the darkness if he needed to pee. He thought of the washrooms and the mirror, the laughing face. He rolled over, trying to push the idea away and focus instead on getting some rest so he would be ready to begin their mission. It was hours before he got to sleep.

The sound that woke him could only come from Silbrica: a repeated roaring bark, as deep and potent as a lion's roar and so terrifyingly loud that it sounded like it was right next to the tent. Darwen sat up, but it was still dark, and he could see nothing.

"What the chuff is that?" he hissed.

The sound paused for a second, then rolled up again, swelling in volume.

URRRR . . . RAGH! AGH! AGH! AGH!

"We gotta get out of here!" muttered Rich. "Whatever it is, it's right outside."

"So you wanna go out there and meet it?" Darwen shot back. "Where's the lantern?"

"Here, but all that will do is give it light to eat by," said Rich. "Try this."

Darwen felt something digging him in the ribs. He took it. It was a heavy flashlight at least eighteen inches long.

"What are you giving it to me for?" hissed Darwen.

"So you can see what it is when you go outside!"

"You're the one who wanted to go out!"

"Shhh," said Gabriel suddenly. "I think it's gone."

The three boys grew very still, listening hard. Darwen thought he could hear sobbing from one of the other tents. Then, just as the night seemed to have quieted at last, it began again.

URRRR . . . RAGH! AGH! AGH! AGH!

And this time there were more answering cries from all over the camp. Whatever was making the noise, there were several of them. Darwen's eyes were wide, though he could see nothing, and suddenly he had to know. He threw off the single sheet he was lying under and blundered out into the night, snapping on the flashlight as he slipped into his shoes. The deafening cry came again. He shone the beam of the flashlight around a tree until he located the source.

Something was crouching in the branches, a squat, heavy body and long powerful limbs covered with hair. He adjusted the beam and found a small black face with deep brown eyes and a heavy pouch-like wattle around its neck. He remembered the pictures in Rich's wildlife field guide and found himself laughing, first with relief, then with a kind of delighted joy.

It was a howler monkey. The trees above the dining shelter were full of them, and their great booming chorus rang out like an artillery bombardment.

Well, thought Darwen, *fat chance of going back to sleep now*.

He yawned and stretched, then stuck his head back into the tent to grab his toiletries.

"Is it a jaguar?" whispered Rich.

"Three of them," said Darwen. "And they look really hungry."

As Darwen walked away, he heard Rich sigh, "Hilarious," through the tent. Amazingly, Gabriel was already snoring.

The darkness had softened fractionally, and out over the ocean Darwen could see the pink of dawn, but he still couldn't follow the path up to the washrooms without the flashlight. Bugs scattered as the beam advanced, some of them huge, not just roaches, but grasshoppers and mantises and centipedes with six-inch segmented bodies that shone hard in the flashlight. Twice Darwen stopped to give the insects a chance to get out of the way, and he started to wonder if he should have stayed in the tent until sunup.

The howler monkeys had gone quiet, but from time to time Darwen heard a soft *thunk*. Scanning the trees with his flashlight, he saw that the monkeys were nibbling on small round fruit and dropping the cores onto the shelter's tin roof as they finished eating. He grinned to himself as he watched them, fastening the beam of his flashlight on one and watching as it ate nonchalantly, looking around like a man finishing breakfast and considering what kind of weather the day would bring. And then, quite suddenly, there was something else up there in the tree, a large cat-like face that flashed into view, fangs bared.

The monkey dropped from its perch, swinging and barking at the top of its considerable voice, setting the other howlers off so that in a second the entire camp area was alive with their booming calls. But this was no monkey dawn chorus. It was full of fear and panic. If these were cattle or horses, thought Darwen, they would be stampeding.

Something was after them, something Darwen had caught in his flashlight just before it could pounce. He swept the flashlight beam over the tree and caught a flash of movement, of something larger than the howlers, almost as big as Darwen, but moving as the monkeys did, loping from branch to branch on long arms. He tried to follow it, but it was too agile, too fast, and in a moment it had gone completely.

What on earth . . . ?

He thought of the face he had seen, which he had thought was dark and catlike, but that couldn't be right, not considering the way it had moved. He stood quite still as the howlers fled into the forest inland, their cries fading with them, and he realized he didn't want to go up to the dark washrooms alone. He turned and headed back to the tent.

"Rich," said Darwen as he stuck his head inside. "Wake up."

"Wha'?" groaned Rich, rubbing his eyes. "Dude, it's still dark."

"It's dawn," said Darwen. "We have to go see Mr. Peregrine."

Rich grumbled, but he came out onto the platform, peering carefully into his shoes before putting them on.

"You know what time I got to sleep?" he said gruffly.

"No," said Darwen.

"Neither do I, but it was late. I kept thinking there was something alive in the tent with me."

"There was," said Darwen. "Me and Gabriel."

"I mean bugs or . . ." he faltered.

"Snakes?"

Rich shrugged and looked away.

Darwen told him everything he had seen: the monkeys'

terrified flight and the curious creature stalking them in the trees. Rich was impressed, but not in the way Darwen had hoped.

"Man, you are so lucky!" said Rich. "I wonder what it was. A jaguarondi, maybe, or a margay. There are six different cat species in Costa Rica, you know. I am *so* jealous. First day and you've already seen a wild cat."

"But it moved like a monkey."

"That must have been something different. Probably one of the howlers."

"It was bigger than the howlers," said Darwen. "I'm sure."

"Well," said Rich, shrugging. "You'll have to ask Jorge on the walk. He probably sees them all the time." Then he added wistfully, "I hope the howlers come every morning. I'd love to get a good look at them."

"I might prefer an extra hour's sleep," said Darwen, rubbing his eyes. "I'm barely awake enough to stand. I hope this hike isn't hard work."

"Well, way to jinx it," said Rich as they reached Mr. Peregrine's tent.

"Sleep well?" asked Mr. Peregrine brightly.

"Not really," said Darwen, sniffing the air. The tent smelled slightly sour, like spilled vinegar.

"Oh dear," said Mr. Peregrine without a trace of remorse. "I slept like a top. Good morning, Richard. Now it goes without saying that what I am about to give you must remain strictly secret."

"What about Alex?" asked Darwen.

Mr. Peregrine blinked, then smoothed his hair with the back of his wrist like a cat grooming itself.

"Of course, you can take Miss O'Connor into your confidence," said Mr. Peregrine, as if this was a given, "but no one else, yes?"

He produced a tubular leather case about two feet long and fastened with buckled straps. Smiling, he presented it to Darwen and inclined his head as if he was bowing.

"What is it?" asked Darwen.

"Open the carrier and see."

Darwen undid the straps, popped the cap off the tube, and slid out four telescopic brass rods, like the parts of a tripod or the poles of a tent. They were designed to snap together to form a square, which could then be pressed into soft ground so it would stand upright. Two small devices were clamped to the uprights. One was a contraption of cogs and sprockets not unlike the screen device Darwen had used to protect himself from the eyes of the gnashers and scrobblers until it had been broken during their attempted invasion on Halloween. The other was a glass-fronted gauge displaying five numbers, with brass wheels on the side by which those numbers might be adjusted.

"It's already been set," said Mr. Peregrine, "so don't alter the dial."

"It's a gate," said Rich.

"Precisely so, Mr. Haggerty," said Mr. Peregrine, clapping with boyish delight. "A portable portal, and one that can be set to connect with a number of different Silbrican loci. Very rare and very expensive. You must be careful with it."

"And it will get me to Luis?" gasped Darwen, not bothering to conceal his excitement.

"Ah, the missing boy," he said. "Well, it will get you to Silbrica, indubitably. But it must be used in secret, and that means where no one will stumble upon it while you are inside, not just when you are coming and going. If the gate were interfered with while you were in Silbrica, you might not be able to use it to return. And, of course," Mr. Peregrine concluded, "it can only be used after sundown."

"And what do I do when I'm in?" asked Darwen.

"We," Rich prompted.

"What?" said Darwen. "Oh. Right. What do we do when we're in?"

"Investigate!" said Mr. Peregrine airily. "Ask around. Put your ear to the ground. Play the gumshoe, the detective. Find out where the weak points are in the barrier between Silbrica and this place."

Moments later, as the two boys walked away, Rich grumbled, "Not very specific, is he? Investigate? How? I mean, where do we start once we're through?"

Darwen glanced down at his shoes, then shrugged, his eyes lighting up. "We look for Luis."

Ten minutes later they were eating breakfast with the rest of the students: yogurt, cereal, and fruit with juice and coffee. Half of the students had had a lousy night's sleep, and Jennifer Taylor-Berry swore that she had seen a bat the size of a chicken flying around the washrooms. This, of course, made Darwen think of the strange cat-faced creature he had seen in the trees, while it prompted everyone else into an animated discussion of the howlers.

"I thought it was a tiger!" yammered Barry Fails to anyone who would listen.

"That had swum over from Asia," said Rich.

Barry didn't get it.

"I thought we were dead, man," he said. "Totally."

He wasn't the only one who felt they had had near-death experiences over the last few hours, but the mood was generally upbeat, and whatever had terrified the students at night seemed quite exciting now that they could actually see where they were going.

"I hope we see something cool today," Barry added, and with this even Rich couldn't disagree.

The only people who didn't seem caught up in it all were Chip and Nathan, both of whom seemed quiet and a little surly, as if resenting how much everyone else was enjoying the prospect of their first hike. Princess didn't seem too pleased either, but that was because, as Alex was quick to point out, she had brought absolutely nothing suitable to wear. Jorge took one look at the spangled sandals she wore to the beach and sent her slouching back to her tent.

"We have some boots you can borrow," he said.

Princess wrinkled her nose as he produced them, though whether that was because of what the boots looked like (knee-high and rubbery—what Darwen called Wellingtons) or because they had been worn by other people, she didn't say.

Darwen was delighted to see that Mr. Sumners looked absurd in wide, flapping shorts and a cowboy hat shading his pink face. Their tight-laced homeroom teacher, Miss Harvey, was wearing carefully ironed pants, long boots, and a blousy shirt tucked meticulously in at her waist, but her normally well-coiffed hair looked wild and frizzy no matter how much she fiddled with it. The boys stared at her, blinking, as if unsure who she was, and she gave them a hard look, practically daring them to speak.

"All aboard!" called Jorge, striding down the shingle with a backpack and water bottle slung over his shoulder.

There were three small powerboats that had to be maneuvered into position with their sterns toward the beach. The sixth graders squealed and shrieked as they waded out into the surf and were hoisted into the boats by the shirtless local boys who doubled as drivers. The faculty divided themselves and clambered awkwardly into the boats one at a time. They all looked very self-conscious, though Darwen thought that Miss Martinez was having more fun than she wanted to let on. Mr. Peregrine, clad once more in his rubbery waders, just smiled and gazed out over the open water as everyone got into their life jackets. The oddest looking of the group was Gabriel, who had rigged an Atlanta Braves baseball cap with a kind of veil made out of fishing net.

"Keep the bugs off," he said.

Darwen, who couldn't see Gabriel's face properly, just shrugged and grinned in a way he hoped was encouraging.

It was going to be a hot and humid day. Beyond the thin line of beach, the world was the green of the jungle on one side and the blues of ocean and sky on the other, and if the boat would stop tossing long enough for him to enjoy it, Darwen thought it would look like paradise. But the boat did not stop, and as it hit full speed, Darwen's stomach started to squirm with each slap of the boat's keel. After half an hour, he was feeling queasy, and after an hour he was miserably nauseated. The boat bounced from side to side, sending Darwen's head flopping as if he were a rag doll. He gripped his knees and stared at the boat's wet plastic floor.

"How much farther?" he called over the engine noise, without looking up.

"One more hour," said Jorge brightly.

Another hour?

Ten minutes later the roar of the boat's engine cut out, and they drifted to an uneasy, sloshing stop. Darwen looked up, praying they were at the shore, but the boats were still out in open water, and all the students were gazing in the direction Jorge was pointing. Holding his stomach, Darwen peered out and saw something large and dark surface briefly, its sides flashing in the sun. Then another appeared close by, and a moment later another puffed a cloud of water only feet from the boat.

For a split second Darwen thought, *It's the Insidious Bleck!* but then the students *oohed* and *aahed* as Jorge proclaimed the shapes in the water to be pilot whales. The cloud they had blown out dispersed around the boat, and several students groaned and winced away. Darwen got a lungful of the stinking rancid-fish-and-ancient-garbage substance, so that for a second he had to hold on to the side of the boat, certain he was going to throw up. As he did so he realized he was not alone. Someone else was staring green-faced into the water. It was Sumners. For a moment their eyes met, and a kind of desperate understanding passed between them. But then the math teacher vomited for real into the ocean, and Darwen turned quickly away as the boat restarted.

They were heading roughly south along the Pacific

coast, always in sight of the shore a mile or so to their left. To their right a strangely flat-topped island loomed.

"That is Caño Island," said Jorge. "Some of the best snorkeling in Costa Rica. We will do that tomorrow."

"In the boat again?" asked Darwen, a little desperate.

"There is no other way to get there," said Jorge cheerily.

And then, at last, the boat was slowing and pulling in toward a stretch of beach not clearly different from what they had been passing for the past two hours.

Two hours, he thought. *And no way back but the same lousy boat ride.*

Amazingly, he and Sumners seemed to be the only ones stricken with seasickness. Rich was trying to be sympathetic, but he was clearly having a wonderful time and couldn't wait to start the hike proper. As the boat coasted through a placid and reedy river estuary, Darwen inched himself toward the back so that he could be first off. As the pilot reversed the boat up to the shore, Jorge leaped out and manhandled the stern end in the sloshing waves before extending a strong brown hand to Darwen.

He didn't need to be asked twice.

He leaped down, splashed his way up the shore, and collapsed onto a fallen tree trunk, his eyes shut, reveling in the sudden stillness of the world. When he opened his eyes again, he was surprised to find that he had been joined not by Rich but by Mr. Sumners.

"Boats," muttered the math teacher. "I'll kill Peregrine."

Darwen laughed in spite of himself, but that made him feel worse, so he went back to sitting very still and quiet until everyone was ashore. Mr. Peregrine came well up the beach before climbing carefully out of his rubber waders and directing the students along a path.

"You don't look too chuffed," said Alex as the group began to walk inland. "Can you be *unchuffed* or only *right chuffed*? I want to be able to use it correctly."

"I'm not too chuffed with you right now," Darwen muttered.

"I see you were bonding with Sumners," said Alex, pretending to be offended. "You *must* be sick. I had no idea seasickness affected the mind."

"Hilarious as ever, Alex," said Rich. "Feeling better?"

"Yeah," said Darwen. "I'll be okay in a few minutes, once the ground stops moving."

Rich grinned.

"What, no 'hilarious as ever' for Darwen?" said Alex, punching Rich on the shoulder as they set off after the others.

"He's an invalid," said Rich. "Be nice."

"Let's hope it's nothing serious," replied Alex. "If you need to go to a hospital, you can forget it. We are in the middle of nowhere."

She was right, of course, but Darwen knew that whatever

the place looked like, it was exactly where he needed to be, and that thought focused his mind on something other than his seasickness. They had passed Caño Island, and that meant they were in the region known for the strange stone spheres, the place from which Luis had been taken.

"*Nowhere*," Alex repeated. "Officially. Find Nowhere on a map, and we are in the middle of it. Nowhereville. Population: us."

"Okay, Alex," said Rich.

"I'm just saying that if anything terrible happened and we needed serious medical attention," she went on, "you know, like, if we got bitten by a massive bushmaster snake—like that one right there!" She screamed, pointing into the undergrowth beside Rich, who bolted away, white- faced, just as she started to roar with laughter. There was, of course, no snake.

"Man!" she exclaimed. "You *really* don't like snakes, huh? I mean, *really*. You bolted like a jackrabbit from a cougar."

"Dag gum it, Alex!" Rich shouted.

"What is the matter?" exclaimed Jorge, running back toward them.

"Nothing," said Rich, reclaiming his dignity as best he could. "Alex's sense of humor . . ."

Jorge glared at them. "We do *not* make false alarms here," the guide said fiercely, "and we do not make more noise than is necessary. Remember. *Pay attentions!*" He tapped the side of his head, staring at each of them, and then marched away.

"Nice going," said Rich.

Alex raised her eyebrow. "Whatever, snake boy."

The vegetation tightened as soon as they left the beach, and soon they were following a narrow trail through hot, dense forest of the kinds of plants Darwen had only seen in greenhouses. Occasionally the group would stop and Jorge would talk about the trees, the ecosystem, or some particular creature, like the leaf-cutter ants whose parade lines crossed the path from time to time, each tiny orange insect bearing a piece of bright green leaf several times its own size so that the forest floor seemed to run in emerald rivers. They also paused at the actual rivers, and Jorge scanned the water carefully before instructing everyone to wade across.

"Looking for crocodiles," said Alex to Rich. "And sharks."

"Sharks live in the ocean," said Rich dismissively. "The driver was just trying to freak you out."

"Actually, she's right," said Jorge, who seemed to have gotten over his initial irritation with them. "These rivers are brackish—part freshwater, part salt. When the tide is high and the rivers rise, sharks swim up from the coast to hunt. Bull sharks, mainly. Much more dangerous than crocodiles. Sometimes tourists go missing and then, a few days later, we find their clothes beside one of the rivers where they decided to swim."

He shrugged and smiled at the silliness of the visitors, apparently not noticing that all the students—and Mr. Iverson—were now moving twice as quickly across the shallow river.

But, to the students' relief, they saw no sharks and only one small crocodile sunning itself on a sandbank. What they did see was a variety of monkeys, an anteater, a motionless, greenish sloth, and a dozen exotic birds including a massive scarlet macaw that flew overhead, the sun flashing on its brilliant plumage. To Darwen's eyes it was nearly as exotic and remarkable as anything he had seen in Silbrica. It wasn't until they had paused for a packed lunch that they saw the tapir.

In appearance, tapirs are somewhere between very large black pigs and small hornless rhinos. They are rare and endangered, and Rich had expressed a great deal of excitement about the possibility of seeing one. So when Jorge became very still and raised his hand in the air to silence the students, it was Rich who had craned to get a better look, Rich who had first whispered that he thought the great beast was sleeping, and Rich who had quickly amended that verdict when he saw the blood.

"It's dead," he said, his voice heavy with shock. "Something killed it."

He was right. Though Jorge and the teachers tried to shield the mutilated carcass from the students' eyes, they saw enough, and while some of them became subdued and even a little weepy, Barry led a gleeful discussion about what could have brought the big animal down.

"Got to be a jaguar," he said. "Look for tracks!"

There weren't any, but close to the tapir's body there were a lot of smaller paw prints, each about the size of Darwen's fist. Miss Martinez had pressed a handkerchief to her mouth at the sight of the dead creature. As she looked away, Darwen slipped past her to get a better look.

He was glad his stomach had had time to settle since the boat ride. The tapir had been half-eaten, though the sight was more sad than it was horrific, and Darwen was able to take it all in without flinching. The wounds on the body matched the odd little paw prints they had seen in the muddy earth: four short talon marks, one of which extended backward like the claw of a bird, while one at the front was two or three times the length of the others. Darwen turned to find Rich at his shoulder, and their eyes met.

"No cat would leave marks like that," Rich whispered.

"And the tracks don't extend onto the trail," said Darwen.

"So they attacked from the trees," Rich agreed.

"They're a lot smaller than the tapir, but there are several of them."

"A pack, working together," Rich mused. "Each one bigger than a monkey."

Darwen was watching Jorge. The guide was pacing around the carcass, studying the tracks and the wounds, then looking up into the forest canopy, his face baffled and concerned.

"Move back there," said Mr. Sumners, bustling over and spreading his arms like a cop on a TV show steering people away from a crime scene.

Darwen rejoined the group in silence, thinking of the strange creature that had spooked the howler monkeys that morning, the creature that did not show up in Rich's field guide.

"Still," said Rich, "it's not what you saw when you went into that jungle locus, is it? You saw a huge tentacle. These things are more like apes."

"So things are worse than we thought," said Darwen. "There's a breach in the barrier between worlds, and the Bleck is leading things through. Dangerous things."

"What's that?" called Barry.

He was pointing through the trees to where something dark and hulking leaned out of the ground. The students peered through the trees.

"It's just some old bulldozer," said Nathan Cloten. "Looks like it's been there a hundred years."

In fact, of course, it didn't. It looked part steam train, part tank. It was a massive, clumsy machine spouting pistons and flywheels and a pair of grotesque chimneys, and sticking out in front of its massive, tracked wheels was a huge plow-like blade, big enough to handle the oldest trees. It looked antiquated, but it had only just begun to rust, and Darwen was prepared to bet that it had been there no more than a few months.

"Looks like it was burrowing up out of the ground when it stopped," said Barry.

"You are such an idiot, Usually," said Nathan casually.

Darwen looked at Rich and Alex, but they were watching Jorge, who had suddenly started directing everyone's attention to another column of leaf-cutter ants that were marching across the trail.

"They do not eat the leaves," he was saying. "They are farmers, and they use the leaves to fertilize a kind of mushroom that they eat."

Darwen wondered if it was his imagination or if the guide was deliberately distracting the group from the spectacle of the paralyzed bulldozer, a device that had clearly originated in another world entirely.

It was mid-afternoon, and Darwen was sitting on the damp edge of the tent platform he shared with Rich and Gabriel while he recovered from the return boat ride. It had rained twice already today, long heavy showers that began and finished abruptly, but that pounded the ground until it swam. The sky was clear again now, but the air felt thick and heavy. Alex swung lazily in a hammock fastened between two trees, watching as a pair of white-faced capuchin monkeys browsed in the branches only feet above her.

"In mourning for the dead pig, Arkwright?" called a jeering voice. It was Nathan, with Chip and Barry in tow.

"Yeah," Chip added, "Redneck Rich was crying his eyes out."

"Nobody cried," said Darwen, shielding his eyes with his hand.

"Yeah, right," said Nathan.

"Another devastating Cloten riposte," said Alex. "You

must be on the debate team."

"I can't believe they didn't let us bring it back and roast it up for dinner," said Chip. "A nice bit of steak. Way better than that slop they served yesterday."

"That was a very nutritious meal," said Alex, wiggling out of the hammock as if her family's honor had been called into question.

"Probably the best food you've ever had, right, O'Connor?" said Nathan, putting on a rustic Southern accent quite unlike his usual precise tone. "You head on over to Haggerty's for chitlins and gravy?"

"What's chitlins?" asked Barry.

"Cheap, nasty stuff," said Chip. "I'd rather eat that dead tapir right where it was."

"Yeah!" Barry agreed stupidly.

"I told that guide—" began Nathan.

"Jorge," Alex inserted.

"Whatever," said Nathan. "I told him to cut a piece off that hadn't been damaged and we could barbecue it, but he was like, 'We must *pay attentions* to the world of the forest. We take only pictures and leave only footprints.' And dead animals, apparently. I mean, what's the point of the stupid, useless tapir if we can't even eat the ugly thing when it's—"

Bonk.

"Hey!" said Nathan, grabbing the back of his head and ducking. "What the—?"

Chip stooped and picked up the object that was still rolling at his feet: it was a piece of fruit about the size and shape of a lime.

"Who threw that?" Nathan demanded, spinning.

Standing a little way up the path to the dining shelter was Mr. Peregrine.

"Perhaps," said the teacher, "it was one of the monkeys or another of the wonderful creatures that live in this place, offended by your heartless remarks about the tapir."

There was a shocked pause.

"*You* threw it?" said Nathan, aghast.

"You did not listen to what I said," said Mr. Peregrine, smiling benignly and waving at a fly that was buzzing around his head. "You might consider using your ears as well as your mouth."

"Whoa!" said Alex.

The others just stared at the teacher, who had started to gaze up into the trees.

"There is no way that was a monkey," said Nathan, half to himself, as if not quite able to believe the alternative.

"I, alas, did not see the incident," said Mr. Peregrine. "But I would advise you to show a little respect to the creatures we encounter."

"The stupid monkey couldn't understand what I said," sneered Nathan.

"Really?" said Mr. Peregrine. "Such certainty in one so

young. I find that if I assume less about the world around me, I learn considerably more. Now," he said, producing a bag of shiny green-and-gold sports jerseys, "if you would put these on, I believe that Miss Martinez and Miss Harvey are organizing a soccer match with some of the village children."

There was so much strange news in this seemingly casual remark that everyone forgot what Nathan was so upset about. There was a village? There was going to be a soccer match? Involving *Miss Harvey*?

For a moment Darwen thought that Mr. Peregrine was making the whole thing up to distract them from what Alex was soon calling the Mystery of the Flying Fruit, but it turned out—bizarrely—to be true. At the southern end of the beach was a horse trail that skirted the forest and, between a cluster of ramshackle, single-story wooden buildings, an area of cleared grass just large enough for a soccer field. A dozen local kids, some the children of people who worked at the tent camp, others who had come over from Drake Bay, were kicking a ball around. They wore faded and stained cotton T-shirts and shorts with either ratty sneakers or nothing at all on their feet. By comparison, the Hillside kids looked like world champions in their official green-and-gold uniforms.

They just didn't play like them.

True, the Hillsiders hadn't brought their cleats—but

since the opposition was largely barefoot, this wasn't much of an argument—and true, they weren't used to playing together as a team, and true, many of them didn't have much experience playing soccer, and true, Gabriel, who said he played a lot in Florida, didn't show up, but none of that could explain away how utterly they got crushed. After ten minutes the locals were leading by four goals to nothing, and after half an hour it was 7–1, the lone Hillsider goal coming when Darwen had run half the length of the field and slotted the ball into the center, where Nathan tapped it home. Their eyes met briefly, but Nathan didn't thank him for what was, Darwen felt, a gift. Other than that one high point, the game was a disaster.

Rich, who was looking more than usually huge, lumbering, and pink, was sweating heavily as the local kids zipped around him. Alex had been running madly around the field, but Darwen didn't think she had touched the ball once—she seemed more interested in practicing her Spanish on the opposition.

"Miss O'Connor," called Miss Harvey, "if you are not going to play, kindly leave the field."

Alex shrugged and walked off, and the local girl she was chatting to went with her to keep the sides even, at least numerically. They sat on the edge of the field where some of the adults—both teachers and a few of the men and women who worked at the camp—had gathered to watch.

When Miss Harvey blew the final whistle, Darwen, Carlos, and Simon shook hands with the other team, while the rest of the Hillsiders skulked away looking exhausted and surly in their now soiled green-and-gold jerseys.

"You lot are really good," said Darwen to a boy who had scored a spectacular volley. Carlos translated, and the boy shrugged, smiling.

"Thanks, Carlos," Darwen said. Then he turned toward the field's edge. "Alex," he called, "come here a minute."

"What am I, your servant?" shouted Alex, stomping across the grass. "Your majesty called?"

"What is it?" asked Carlos. "What do you want to know that you need Alex O'Connor for?"

"It's nothing, Carlos," said Darwen. "Just . . . I was curious where he learned to play like that."

"I can ask him," said Carlos, pleased with the opportunity to be useful. "His name is Felippe, by the way."

"Hi," said Darwen.

The boy nodded. Carlos started speaking in rapid Spanish.

Darwen glowered at Alex.

"Don't look at me," she whispered. "Anyway, I already know."

"What?"

"While you were kicking that ball around like the

future of civilization depended on it, I was making friends. And gathering news."

Darwen stared at her, but Carlos was already giving the other boy's answer about where he learned to play, which amounted to "here." Darwen nodded and made impressed-sounding noises while trying to suggest that he now needed to be somewhere else.

"Wow," he said again. "That's great. Well, maybe we can play again. Bye!"

He waved vaguely and walked away, leaving Carlos and Felippe looking slightly confused.

"Well?" he said as soon he and Alex were out of earshot.

"I met this girl called Sarita. That one there." She waved, and a slim girl a year or two younger than they with shoulder-length hair waved back. "I used my natural charm and started by telling her how much I missed my dog. Which is true, by the way. Anyway, we talked for a while, and she said that very odd things have been going on."

"Luis," said Darwen. "He was from here?"

"He and four others," said Alex. "Two more have disappeared since Luis and his brother."

Darwen stopped walking and stared at her.

"Five?" he said.

"Over the last six weeks."

"What do they think is happening?" he asked.

Alex shrugged.

"Some of them are saying it's a jaguar," she said. "But jaguars never hunt people."

"Why do they think it's a jaguar then?"

"Well, I don't think the possibility of abduction from another world accessed only through mirrors has been seriously considered," said Alex. "Some pieces of odd machinery have appeared in the jungle—like that bulldozer thing we saw this morning—but they clearly don't work and look abandoned. No one is connecting a few old-fashioned engines to the missing kids."

"So what have they done about it?"

"Same thing we would," said Alex. "They called the police."

Darwen was amazed that the idea had not occurred to him. They might be in a remote part of the jungle, but that didn't mean there was no law enforcement.

"So there's an investigation?"

"I guess, though they don't seem to be making much progress."

"If what is attacking them is taking them out of this world entirely," said Darwen, "that's hardly surprising, is it? What did you learn about Luis?"

"Our age," she said, "smart, good soccer player. Ordinary, except that he and his brother were inseparable, closer than twins, though they didn't look alike. Sarita said that when Luis went missing, Eduardo searched the jungle for three days and nights by himself. His parents had to force him to go to bed because he collapsed miles away and had to be brought back by boat. The following night he was out again. They figure he stumbled on whatever took his brother a couple of nights after that. No one has seen him since."

Darwen stared at the ground, suddenly overcome by a tide of anger and sadness. He had no brother, but he knew what it was like to lose your family, the people who knew and loved you best.

Alex had opened her mouth to say something else, but stopped. There was a distinctive thrumming sound getting louder each moment: a helicopter, approaching from inland and traveling very low. The kids who were still on the soccer field scattered to the edges, grinning expectantly. When the helicopter came into view and slowed, hovering briefly before descending, several of them clapped and waved. The grass flattened and the trees swayed in the wind of the rotor, and then the chopper was sitting in the middle of the field where they had been playing only minutes before, as out of place as a bulldozer in the jungle.

Darwen's first thought was that it was a police helicopter, but then the door on the side of the cockpit opened, and he knew it wasn't the police.

A long, slender woman's leg reached down, a leg ending in a bright red shoe with a high pointed heel. The heel sank into the grass, but the woman wrenched it free and stalked away from the chopper smiling.

She was, Darwen supposed, beautiful in the way that movie stars are beautiful: perfect, regular features, flowing blond hair, and an air of polish about her that—in this rough-and-ready setting—made her seem unearthly, as if she had strode out of the pages of a magazine. She wore a crimson jacket and skirt that matched her shoes, and her long fingernails were the same vivid color. She reached into a spangled handbag and pulled out what Darwen thought was candy, which she proceeded to distribute among the clamoring local children, walking among them like a princess. It took a moment for him to realize that it wasn't candy at all.

"She's giving out money!" Alex exclaimed.

Sure enough, she was handing out large yellow coins quite unlike anything Darwen had seen since arriving in Costa Rica.

"Maybe it's chocolate," he said, thinking of the foil-covered candy coins he used to get in his Christmas stocking in England.

"If it is," said Alex, "no one's eating it. It looks like gold. It can't be though, right? 'Cause that would be, you know, nuts. . . ."

The kids danced around and shook the woman's hand and then scampered off, some to the little houses where their parents were emerging, others to the camp. They looked more than happy. They looked delighted, like the answer to their prayers had just drifted down from the heavens.

Not everyone was pleased to see the woman and her helicopter. Jorge came running from the tent camp, shouting and exclaiming in a mixture of English and Spanish as the noise of the chopper's slowing blades finally died away.

"Who are you?" he demanded. "This is a protected environment. You cannot land here."

She turned and looked him up and down coolly, the tip of her tongue moving between her shining ruby lips.

"You must be the jungle guide," she said in a voice that was much lower than Darwen had expected but still reminded him of slowly dripping honey. She sounded pleased, and one corner of her mouth twitched in a half smile. "Jorge," she said. "I seem to keep missing you. So glad we will finally have the chance to chat a little."

Jorge's eyes seemed to lose a little of their fire for a moment, but, as the students began to gather silently around, he came back at her with a new surge of anger.

"I demand to know who you are and what you are doing here," he said.

"Demand?" she said with a throaty chuckle. "Let us not get above our station, Jorge. There is no need to demand what will be given to you freely. My name is Scarlett Oppertune, and I'm here to give the people who live here a chance at a real life."

"What are you talking about?" said Jorge. "They have real lives."

"Living in the woods?" she returned with amused condescension. "Making a few pesos bringing milk and cheese in for the tourists? Miles from decent hospitals, schools, and law enforcement? With no opportunity for advancement or profit and surrounded by dangerous animals?"

"This is their home!" exclaimed Jorge.

"For now," said Scarlett smoothly. "But everyone is free to make their own choices—at least they are where I come from."

"Which is where?" said Jorge.

"I represent Sunbelt Vacation Properties," she answered, flashing a brilliant, toothy smile. "We build hotel chains."

Jorge's eyes widened.

"You want to build a hotel? Here?!" he said. "We're on the edge of a nature reserve! This is one of the most biodiverse regions in the world."

"I know!" said Scarlett Oppertune, her eyes bright, "and think of how many tourists will want to see it if they don't have to sleep in tents! It's time all this 'nature' was shared with the world, don't you think, Jorge?"

The guide looked at a loss for words, like the air had been driven from his body, but Rich stepped up.

"If you develop the area," he said, "you wipe out the environment that makes it worth visiting!"

"Not at all," Scarlett said, smiling. "You know how big these woods are? We won't get rid of all of it. And if we make it smaller, that will make it so much easier for people to find the fuzzier, less dangerous birds and animals, now won't it? Once we've got the park boundaries redrawn so that we can get some decent roads through here, an airport, a mall or two—"

"A mall?" gasped Jorge.

"Tourists have to shop," she said, winking and smiling. She seemed completely unaware of Jorge's outrage. "Maybe a hunting lodge . . ."

"You'll never get the government to approve," said Rich, his face pinker than usual.

Scarlett's gaze lingered on him, and her right eyebrow twitched with something like amusement. "You don't think a government will give up a patch of land covered with trees that generates next to no income," she said, smiling at Rich, "for a sack full of cash up front and the promise of more once the tourist jets start landing? Please."

"But it's . . ." Rich fumbled for a word.

"Illegal?" Alex cut in. "Immoral? Unethical? Exploitative?"

"All of those," said Rich, as red now as Scarlett's shoes.

"It seems that way to you," said Scarlett, "because you are"—she settled on the last word with her sweetest smile yet—"a child."

She smiled again, this time in a pitying sort of way, and Rich glared at her, furious and embarrassed, as she took the brown hand of one of the smallest local kids and said, "Okeydokey. Let's have a chat with your mom and dad, shall we? I expect *they* might be interested in freedom and the pursuit of happiness."

She turned in the direction of the little cinder-block houses.

"I don't trust people who use words like that," said Alex.

"Like what?" asked Darwen.

"Like they're flags that you wave to get people cheering."

They watched Scarlett walk away. Several of the local kids had flocked to her, touching her fancy suit and gazing happily up at her, though Sarita and Felippe kept their distance, muttering to each other. Scarlett moved slowly, beaming down at the smaller kids who were holding her hands, and Darwen was reminded of an old science-fiction movie he had seen on TV with his dad in which a man moved up a ramp into a spaceship surrounded by fascinated little aliens.

Jorge watched her go, speechless, then turned and stomped back toward the tent camp. Rich was muttering furiously.

"Come on," said Darwen bracingly. "Nearly time for dinner, and then we get to try out Mr. Peregrine's portable portal."

"Did you hear what she said?" Rich demanded, rounding on him.

"Yes," said Darwen, "but—"

"Doesn't it matter to you?" Rich said. "That we've come all this way to see this amazing place and the things that live here, and she's going to tear it down to make a few bucks?"

"Well," said Darwen, who had never seen Rich so angry, "not *all* of it."

"Oh, not all of it?" repeated Rich, his voice loud and heavy with sarcasm. "That's all right then. I was worried they were going to bulldoze all the region's endangered species into the sea, but so long as they're leaving a few trees for the tourists to look at over their TVs, that's okay. A coconut palm or two, yeah? Tourists like coconuts. Hang a plastic monkey on one of them and no one will know the difference, right, Darwen?"

"Hey, don't blame me," said Darwen. "I'm just saying it might not be as bad as it sounds."

"You know what, Darwen?" said Rich. "You're right. It won't be as bad as it sounds. It will be worse. Trust me: I've seen it back home. Once the forest goes, it doesn't come back, and everything in it goes away. Forever."

Darwen, unable to think of anything to say, looked down, and Rich stalked off after Jorge.

For a long moment, no one said anything, then Darwen heard Alex's voice.

"Anyone ever told you that you're a huge comfort to your friends when they're upset?" she said, adding before he could respond, "Ever wonder why not?"

Dinner that night was tense. Rich didn't speak to anyone, but he glowered at Princess Clarkson when she made the mistake of saying that she thought a hotel would be an improvement on the tent camp. The other students were quiet, and though some of them were sympathetic to Rich, there were others who thought Princess had a point. The generator wasn't working properly, which meant that the water was cold and they had to go to bed as soon as the sun went down since they couldn't see their hands in front of their faces. To make matters worse, it began to rain again, a drenching downpour that turned the paths to streams and sent the students running for their tents, where they sat, steaming and damp, listening to the drumming of the rain on the nylon. The humidity was so high that even when the rain stopped, nothing dried out, and their wet clothes began to smell sourly of mildew.

"Well?" said Rich. It was the first word he had said all evening, and Darwen and Alex just stared at him. They were sitting at the long tables in the shelter, watching the other kids as they filed back and forth from the washrooms and headed to bed.

"Well what?" said Darwen.

"Don't we have something to do?" said Rich in a low voice, his eyes loaded with meaning.

"You mean . . . where Mr. Peregrine said we should go?" said Darwen.

"Obviously," said Rich.

"We thought you . . ." Darwen couldn't think of how to end the sentence.

"He thought you were mad at everyone and wouldn't want to go," said Alex in a matter-of-fact voice.

"What?" said Rich. "Darwen, you aren't the only one who wants to save Luis, you know. I was upset about . . . It has nothing to do with this. So. Now?"

"Er . . . great," said Darwen. "Yes. We can set the portal up in the trees behind the dining shelter. No one will see it there."

Rich nodded.

"You want me to get it from the tent?" he said.

"Sure," Darwen said. "Meet us by the sinks in ten minutes. We'll wait for everyone else to go to bed and then sneak around the back and into the woods. Bring your flashlight."

"Okay," said Rich, and for a moment he looked cheerful again, but as he half turned to leave, he seemed to think better of it and stopped. "Were you two going to go without me?" he asked.

"No," they both said at once.

"We hadn't even talked about it," said Darwen, conscious that while that was true, he and Alex might well have gone to Silbrica by themselves had Rich not spoken up.

Rich nodded but looked unconvinced.

As he walked away, Alex shrugged.

"Come on," she said. "Sumners is giving us the stink eye."

It was true. They were the last students still sitting at the tables, and the math teacher was watching them suspiciously. They got up and made their way to the bathrooms, Alex pausing to smile at Mr. Sumners and wish him "a very good night's sleep" along the way.

Sumners watched their backs as they walked away, but then said something that stopped them in their tracks. "What on earth, Mr. Haggerty, are you carrying?"

Darwen and Alex wheeled around to see Rich carrying the long leather tube containing the portable portal. He was staring at the math teacher, pale, his eyes wide open in what Alex called his "deer in the headlights" look. They were about to go back toward him when he spoke.

"Toiletries, sir," he said.

"In that thing?" said Sumners with undisguised disbelief.

"Special travel pouch, sir," said Rich, improvising. "Toothbrush, soap rod, vacuum-packed towel, all in a handy space-saving container. My dad got it from a late-night TV ad."

"Did he indeed?" said Mr. Sumners, peering at the leather case. "There's a towel in there?"

"Not a hand towel," said Rich. "A bath towel. There's a plunger on the bottom that sucks all the air out."

"Huh," said Sumners, who looked like someone had

sucked all the air out of him. "Well, get a move on, boy. Everyone else is already in bed."

"Yes, sir," said Rich. "Thank you, sir."

He came up the path grinning.

"Not bad," muttered Alex. "I'm not sure about 'soap rod,' but the plunger-on-the-bottom thing was a nice touch."

"It's a good thing he didn't ask to see it," said Rich.

"Oh, come on," said Alex. "If there's no risk, there's no fun. Meet me here in five minutes. Gotta pee."

Rich's eyes met Darwen's, and they grinned at each other. Darwen found himself looking at one of the mirrors over the sink and, remembering the unsettling impression of the laughing face over his shoulder, looked quickly away.

"I wish Mr. Peregrine had some more specific plans," he muttered. "I mean whatever killed that tapir—"

"Hey, guys, whatcha doin'?"

It was Gabriel, still in his cap with the veil.

"Oh," said Darwen. "Hi, Gabriel. We're just . . . you know . . . getting ready for bed."

"Where are your toothbrushes?"

"Already cleaned our teeth," said Darwen, smiling awkwardly. "We're just . . ."

"Going to sneak out to see the stars," said Rich. "I'm a bit of an amateur astronomer."

"Oh," said Gabriel. "Cool. Is that your telescope?"

"Yeah," said Rich.

"Can I have a look?"

"Well, it's kind of . . . expensive and I don't really . . ."

"Please," said Gabriel. "I won't break it. Promise."

"Sorry," Darwen said. "Astronomy club rules. Members only."

"And the members are you two and Alex O'Connor, right?" said Gabriel, looking crestfallen.

"No," said Rich. But at that moment Alex emerged from the washrooms, and Gabriel's expression hardened.

"Oh, *Alex*," said Rich. "I thought you said, er, Melissa."

"If you don't want to be my friend," said Gabriel, "you could just say so. There's no need to lie."

"It's not that, Gabriel, really," Rich protested, but the skinny boy was already walking away.

"Nice save," said Alex. "*I thought you said Melissa*. Very convincing."

"Oh, shut up," said Rich.

"Well," said Darwen as Gabriel disappeared. "We'd better get on with it. Has Sumners gone?"

"Looks like," said Alex.

They set off around the back of the washrooms and into the trees behind the dining shelter, following Rich's flashlight.

"Do we really need that?" whispered Darwen. "Someone might see."

"I'll take getting caught over stepping on a bushmaster, thanks," said Rich.

They inched further into the woods.

"Gotta say," said Alex. "Not a fan of those washrooms. I don't know if it's the lizards and toads, but I always feel like I'm being watched. Naia and Mad think they're haunted."

"By what?" said Rich. "The ghost of a howler monkey?"

Darwen stopped walking.

"How about here?" he said.

Rich handed him the leather package, and they set about snapping the brass frame together. Though the rods did extend some, the portal was still only about a yard square.

"We'll have to go through one at a time," said Darwen as he snapped the dial with the locus number to one upright and pushed it into the soft earth.

"How?" asked Alex. "We won't even be able to see through if we're not touching you."

"I'll reach back through for you," said Darwen. He was winding the watch-like device on the other upright. "Ready?" he said. When they nodded, he pressed the button on the side.

There was a soft whoosh and a crackle, then the air framed by the portal flickered before stabilizing into the tiny window of a brick building.

"Weird," said Darwen.

"What's weird?" said Alex, who couldn't see. She snatched at his hand.

"Oh," said Darwen. "Sorry."

He took Rich's hand too, and the three of them stared through the portal in amazement. It had to be one of the strangest things Darwen had ever seen: a cracked and dirty window frame with a brick surround sitting in a dark Costa Rican jungle.

"Maybe it connects to that central machine you told

us about," said Alex.

"Only one way to find out," Darwen answered. "I'll have to let go of your hands while I get the window open, but I'll stick my hand back out for you, so don't go anywhere."

"And don't you go on without us," said Alex. "The Peregrine Pact, remember? It's not just you."

"I know," Darwen answered, irritable.

He released them, stepped up to the slender brass frame, and reached in. The air buckled slightly, but then his fingertips found the hard surface of the window glass. He pushed, but nothing happened, so he reached for the wooden frame and lifted. The window slid up easily, though the opening was still only about a foot and a half wide.

Darwen grabbed the ledge and pulled himself in, realizing as he did so that the window was several feet up. Below him was a cracked porcelain sink marked with brown water stains. He climbed down headfirst, bracing himself against a brass tap, crawling into the sink itself, and finally jumping onto an uneven tiled floor.

It was a bathroom. Old and badly in need of repair and redecoration, but a bathroom nonetheless.

"Weird," he said again.

He used a wooden laundry hamper to climb back onto the sink, and from there he reached through. He felt Alex grab his hand, and he pulled until her head was through and she could see what she was doing. Then he did the same for Rich.

"Hey," said Alex. "Our very own bathroom! And not a lizard in sight."

The house—if that was what it was—felt cool and smelled musty. One thing was certain: they weren't in the jungle anymore.

"This is awesome," said Alex. "Before, we went into Silbrica to see exotic, weird stuff, right? To get a break from boring old reality. Now we go to Silbrica to use a decent bathroom, maybe watch some television, and generally get away from the weird, exotic stuff all around us!"

Darwen opened the bathroom door and stepped out onto a narrow landing. It *was* a house, and a small one at that. There were wall-mounted gas lamps that glowed bluish, though several of them didn't work. What light there was showed peeling textured wallpaper spotted with mold and a carpet gray with dust. Darwen doubted they'd be sneaking in here to watch television.

They were, apparently, upstairs. There were two scratched doors on one side of the hallway—bedrooms, presumably—and a narrow staircase to their left, which went down in three angular turns.

"This place feels . . . I don't know," said Alex. "Familiar. Like I've been here before, or dreamed about it."

Darwen felt the same way, but he couldn't think of when he might have been here. It reminded Darwen of the old terraced houses in Lancashire, but one that had been derelict for years. There were no signs of portals or the elegant machinery he was used to in Silbrica.

He pushed open the closest door and saw what he had almost expected: a dim room with a bay window, a moldy-looking bed, and a wardrobe with its doors hanging open. He stepped inside, and the floor creaked beneath him. He pulled the curtains open. Outside he saw trees, their branches brushing up against the house, and again he had that odd feeling that this wasn't the first time he had been there. He rejoined the others.

"Downstairs, I suppose," he said, leading the way. There was something about the stair carpet that seemed familiar too, as did the wallpaper at the bottom. He frowned and looked at Alex, who had the same expression on her face. Rich, by contrast, looked merely interested.

"What?" he said.

"This place doesn't ring any bells?" asked Alex.

"Nope," said Rich. "Never been anywhere like it in my life."

"Shhh," said Alex. "Listen."

They all became still, and Darwen could hear it too, a faint clicking and chittering that seemed to be coming from somewhere down the hall.

Machinery?

It was possible, he supposed, but it didn't sound quite

right somehow, and he could feel the hairs on his arms and neck starting to stand up, like his body remembered something his brain didn't.

Alex pushed past him, down the hall and into a kitchen. Darwen followed with Rich trailing behind him, but then Alex became quite still, blocking the door. Darwen gave her a shove, and she turned. Her expression stopped the two boys cold.

"I know where we are!" she hissed.

Darwen had never seen her look so scared.

The chittering had grown louder. Darwen turned toward it and saw another half-open doorway into a tiny lounge with a fireplace and a table with the shattered remains of an old tea set . . . and a floor littered with pale balloon-like objects that Darwen instantly knew were eggs. Maggots, three feet long, milky white but with black pincer mouths, covered the rotting furniture, and over in the corner were five huge, shiny insects, all as big as he was.

The Jenkinses.

That was what they had been called when Darwen had last seen them: huge, horrible insect creatures disguised as an elderly couple whose bodies they wore like flesh suits. But it couldn't be. At least one of the Jenkinses had been killed by the train months ago. But there they were, and now Darwen knew why the house had seemed both familiar and unfamiliar. He had, after all, not been upstairs last time.

They looked like giant mantises, though they were the hard and shiny black of beetles, and they had large, compound eyes like flies. They were, perhaps, a little smaller than the two that had disguised themselves as the Jenkinses, but that made them no less repulsive or dangerous—and last time Darwen and his friends had only escaped because of the screen device he had broken at Halloween.

His first instinct was to make for the front door, but that wouldn't get them back to the jungle camp. "Back upstairs!" he gasped.

The insects responded as if they hadn't known he was there. Their whip-like antennae flicked toward him, and their mouthparts opened, drooling. Then they moved, a sudden scuttling, one across the egg-strewn floor, one up and over the ceiling, a third diagonally across the wall.

They were fast. Much faster than the Jenkinses had been.

Rich cried out. Alex just stared, hands clasped over her mouth. Darwen pushed both of them back into the kitchen. As he did so, Rich slipped on some nameless slime on the tiles, knocking Alex onto her back. He slumped heavily against the wall, splitting the rotten plaster open, and out of the wall cavity fell two huge pale maggots, both at least a yard long, one landing wetly in Alex's lap.

She screamed, thrusting it wildly from her, eyes shut against the horror of it. Rich rolled to one side as the other one arched its back and pulsed toward him, its black horny lips gaping.

Darwen looked wildly around for a weapon and, finding a heavy saucepan, he snatched it up and flung it at the maggot. The pan bounced off the creature's rubbery body, went straight up into the air, and came down handle first. With a soft *splosh*, it impaled the maggot, and the creature began to whip back and forth, emitting a thin and awful scream.

For a moment Darwen was frozen with horror—aware that two of the mantis creatures were approaching fast but somehow unable to run away. One of them glared at him, its mouthparts uncoiling, and then it sprang. It shot through the air with astonishing speed, its clawed feet splayed, and then something happened. There was a flash and a pop like a firework, and the insect fell heavily, smoking as it slid lifeless across the floor. Darwen turned back toward the front of the house. Silhouetted in the open doorway like an Old West gunfighter was a tiny animal cradling a smoking weapon on which glowed a pinprick of amber light. It stepped into the light of the hallway, and Darwen recognized the dark, stoat-like form.

Weazen!

"Evening," he growled as he fired at the other mantis, which ducked and weaved as a cabinet of moldy crockery exploded behind it. He spit to the side, then fired again. "Can't hold 'em off for long. I suggest you do a runner, mate."

Darwen dragged Alex to her feet as Rich ran back through to the staircase. Behind him, he could hear the click of insect feet and the crack of Weazen's blaster. As they got into the hallway, Darwen glanced back through the kitchen door. At first there was nothing, and then the head of the first creature appeared upside down on the door's lintel above him. He ran, and it came after him, scrabbling across the ceiling.

Rich and Alex pounded up the stairs. Darwen was momentarily sure that the steps would be rotten too, that they would fall through into some appalling maggoty nest, but they managed to successfully reach the top and bolt across the landing to the bathroom. Darwen gave chase and was almost at the top of the stairs when he felt something snag in his hair.

His hand brushed at it automatically, but he felt the stick-like insect leg, and his revulsion gave him a new burst of speed, breaking the connection. He flew up the last three steps and down to the bathroom, slamming the door behind him on the first of the three insects.

"Lock it!" Alex screamed.

Darwen snapped the little brass bolt home, but he knew that wouldn't hold them. Through the door, he could hear the sounds of their clicking beaks and scratching claws as they groped and fumbled, desperate to gain entry. "Curtain rod!" he yelled, putting his shoulder against the door as it shuddered under the weight of the insect assault.

Rich climbed onto the edge of the bath and lifted the brass shower rod down. Together they tried to brace it between the foot of the toilet and the handle of the door. The insects were pushing harder, and one of the door's thin panels had started to bulge and crack around the edges. Darwen heard the distant zap and crack of Weazen's weapon, but he knew there were too many of the insect monsters for the Peace Hunter to handle alone. For a moment he hesitated, wondering if he should head back.

"Help Alex!" shouted Rich, taking up position with Darwen at the door. "She can't get out without you. Now, Darwen!"

Darwen stepped away, and the door quivered for a terrible second until Rich could take his place. Darwen took Alex's hand, helped her onto the sink, and kept hold until she was up and through the window.

"Now you," he said to Rich.

"The door's not going to hold," Rich answered.

As if to punctuate the point, the loose panel in the top left-hand side popped right out, and something long and clawed reached in.

There was a cabinet under the sink. Darwen dropped

and opened it, hoping vaguely for bug spray. There wasn't any. There was, however, a glass bottle of bath salts. He grabbed it, swinging it hard at the insect leg that was reaching for Rich. The leg was snatched back, and in that instant Rich made a run for it, Darwen seizing his hand as he clambered onto the sink.

Darwen vaulted up after him, pushing him through the window as the bathroom door flew open and crashed against the wall. One of the shiny bugs skittered in on the tiled floor, another on the ceiling.

Darwen shoved Rich through and leaped for the window frame, grabbing and pulling in one motion. Something snatched at his feet and he kicked wildly, connecting with what he thought was a giant insect head, propelling himself the rest of the way through.

Rich and Alex grabbed his arms and pulled him through into the dark of the jungle. For a moment he felt the sudden warmth of the night, and then Alex was screaming, and he turned to see the first of the insects clambering through after him. Rich leaped backward, but Alex picked up a rock and smacked the windup contraption on the side.

The first insect was halfway through when she hit the device a second time. There was a shrill scream as the portal failed and the mantis's head was lopped neatly off. Alex hit the gate once more for good measure, and the slim brass frame buckled and snapped.

She turned on Darwen, and her face was wild, her breath coming in great surging gasps.

"Let's NEVER go there again," she shouted. "Okay?"

Darwen sank to the moist earth, panting.

"It may be the blind, screaming terror of the giant homicidal bugs talking," said Rich in a dazed voice, "but were our lives just saved by a ferret with a rocket launcher?"

Mr. Peregrine flexed the bent and ruined remains of the portable portal in the morning sun. Repair was, quite clearly, out of the question.

"Couldn't you have just dismantled it?" he asked, sounding forlorn.

"There wasn't time," said Alex.

Rich and Darwen eyed each other sheepishly. Taking the gate apart now seemed the obvious thing to have done.

"Right," said Mr. Peregrine, weighing the shattered

remains like they had been a family heirloom. "Well, this presents a difficulty," he said. "Unless we can find the original breach, we have no way of getting into Silbrica from here."

"That's your concern?" said Alex. "Do I have to point out that this is the second time you've sent me to that house and its charming inhabitants?"

"Yes," said Mr. Peregrine, thoughtful. "Terribly sorry. You are sure these creatures were the same as the Jenkinses?"

"Er . . . yeah," said Alex. "Giant man-eating bugs in people suits tend to stick in your mind like they're tattooed on the back of your eyelids, so yeah, I'm pretty sure."

"Quite," said Mr. Peregrine, and for a moment he looked miles away, but not vague, as he often looked. His brain was working a mile a minute, and his eyes had a narrow, fixed quality.

"Still here," said Alex.

"What?" said Mr. Peregrine, coming out of his reverie with a start. "Yes. Well, as I say, sorry about that. I suppose the equipment malfunctioned. Most unusual."

"Malfunctioned?" said Darwen. "It was tampered with. Someone changed the setting to send us there."

"No one has had access to it except us," said Mr. Peregrine.

"It was in the tent all day yesterday," said Rich. "Anyone

could have gone in and messed with it."

"A person?" said Alex. "You know, Nathan Cloten and Chip Whittley act like they didn't see anything unusual back at Halloween, but what if they did? What if they are spying on us?"

"What about this Peace Hunter?" said Mr. Peregrine. "His arrival sounds most suspicious."

"Weazen helped us escape," said Darwen. He didn't know for sure if the little creature had made it out alive, and the sense of responsibility weighed on him like cold, wet clothes.

"Or he came to catch you and found you already in a fight," the teacher mused.

"No way," said Alex. "I only got a glimpse of him, but he's way too cute and fuzzy to be working for the Bleck. I hope he got out okay."

"No one," said Mr. Peregrine, "is working for the Bleck! It is an animal. Nothing more. You must not invent things to worry about. You have classes to focus on as well as the breaches."

"But what about Luis?" Darwen sputtered.

"I don't see what you can do to help him." Mr. Peregrine sighed. "For now, keep your eyes open and do try to enjoy yourselves. This is a once-in-a-lifetime experience."

Darwen looked away, but Alex nodded for him.

And, as it turned out, they did enjoy the day.

For one thing, the boat ride was better—most of the way, at least. They followed the same course as they had the previous day, but the water was calmer, and Darwen's nausea didn't kick in until they started veering out toward the flat-topped island. He, Alex, and Rich had agreed that their top priority now was finding another way back into Silbrica. Darwen didn't know how they were going to do it, but knowing that his friends agreed with him made him feel better.

They pulled into a rocky bay, and Jorge talked about safety issues while the driver handed out snorkels, masks, fins, and life vests. "We stay in this area here," said Jorge, pointing. "The current will push you, but if you drift too far, we will come get you in the boat. The rocks are sharp, so *pay attentions*, and be alert. If you see a shark bigger than this"—he held his hands about three feet apart—"shout."

"Are we likely to?" asked Simon Agu, staring.

Jorge shrugged. "Probably not, but if you do, they will most likely be white-tipped reef sharks. Not dangerous." He looked at the sky. "Not at this time of day."

Darwen watched the students exchanging the now familiar mixture of uneasy glances and thrills of excitement. Gabriel was first in, casting aside his cap with the absurd veil and looking more at home than they had ever seen him. He dove straight down, blew out a fountain of seawater from his mouth, and laughed out loud.

"Wow!" said Alex, climbing awkwardly over the side. "He's coming out of his shell."

Only Mr. Peregrine, still clad in his chest-high waders, showed no sign of actually getting ready to swim.

"You're not going in?" Rich asked him.

Mr. Peregrine shook his head. "Not much of a swimmer," he said.

"You can just float about," said Rich. "See? We've got life jackets and everything. It's quite safe. I'll keep an eye on you."

Mr. Peregrine shook his head again. His usual pallor had developed a greenish tinge. "I don't like water," he whispered, wincing away from a few drops on the side of the boat like they were acid.

"I thought only Darwen and Mr. Sumners got seasick," Rich answered.

"I don't mind being *on* it," said Mr. Peregrine, regarding the water carefully. "I just don't like being *in* it." Then, gathering some semblance of composure, he added, "Wasn't exactly much opportunity to practice my swimming while I was running the shop, unfortunately."

"Oh," said Rich. He gave an apologetic shrug, put on his mask, and tipped awkwardly backward out of the boat. He hit the water with a loud, slapping splash, but came up grinning, both thumbs up. Darwen met Mr. Peregrine's anxious eyes. They were alone except for Jorge, who had extended his hand toward Darwen.

"You sure you won't come?" said Darwen to Mr. Peregrine.

"You go ahead," said the teacher. "Maybe I'll come in later."

They both knew this wasn't true, but Darwen nodded anyway, then inched into position, arms outstretched for balance.

Jorge sat him on the edge of the boat, back to the water, and checked his mask. "Ready?" said the guide.

Darwen nodded, and Jorge gave him a gentle nudge backward.

Darwen hit the water with his shoulders, but it didn't hurt, and though the life jacket felt hot and constraining, he was glad to get out of the bobbing boat. As the others started to swim about, he took a moment to float quietly by himself, fiddling with his mask, while his seasickness passed. He was still waiting when Rich burst from the surface.

"Hot dang!" he shouted. "I saw a parrot fish. Right in front of my face! I could have touched it. A real wild parrot fish!"

Soon everyone but Darwen was popping up laughing and whooping with delight, swapping tales of what they were seeing under the bright blue water. Hating to feel so left out, Darwen bit down on the snorkel's mouthpiece and dove.

His queasiness was forgotten the moment he went

under. The world beneath the water was glorious. He was surrounded by schools of exotic fish so brilliantly colored that it was like being inside an aquarium. The rocks below him gathered and thrust in strange swollen formations like the landscape of an alien planet. Delicate corals of white and pink bloomed in shafts of bluish light.

And among it all moved the fish. Darwen saw dozens, perhaps hundreds, right away, silver shoals moving as one and bright, beautiful individuals for which he had no name. He gasped in wonder at it and found himself, like the others, laughing privately with delight as something roughly the size and shape of an American football idled past—a puffer fish, he thought it was called. For a moment he understood perfectly Rich's outrage at Scarlett and anything she might do to destroy the beauty of this place.

He broke the surface and found Jorge floating close by.

"Good?" said the guide.

"Chuffin' brilliant!" said Darwen, and he went back under, taking a deep breath this time so that he could dive. He swam deep into a rock crevice alive with orange fish, swimming down until the pressure in his ears began to hurt. He rolled easily onto his back and floated to the surface, past what he took to be an angelfish with a long dorsal fin that trailed after it like a ribbon of white and gold. At the surface, he blew the water from his snorkel and whooped with delight.

It was a perfect morning. Apart from Mr. Peregrine, who never made it into the water, the mood at the ranger station on the beach where they landed for lunch was exuberant. Even Nathan and Chip had forgotten to be sour about the "nature" for which they were generally so disdainful, and Princess Clarkson had stopped whining about the conditions of their accommodations. She ran her fingers through her golden hair and blithely declared that it would dry in the sun "just fine."

They ate peanut butter sandwiches at wooden tables under the shade of the cliffs that lined the beach and watched a huge and spiny black iguana scaling the rocks.

"It's like something out of *Jurassic Park*!" exclaimed Barry, and, for once, Darwen thought he was right. It was odd, he thought, that after all the strange things he had seen on the other side of the mirror, a part of the real world could only be compared to movies.

The sandwiches were dry, but no one complained, engrossed as they were in swapping tales of what they had seen in the water. Simon and Carlos had seen a sea turtle, while Melissa and Genevieve had spotted a jellyfish, and Chip had seen what he claimed was a moray eel.

"It was green," he said, "with these little beady eyes, and it had its mouth open so you could see its teeth, like little knives in a row."

Each story produced another rush of excitement and

pleasure.

"So," said Mr. Peregrine, now out of his waders, as they packed their trash to take back in the boats, "how am I doing?"

"Great," said Darwen. "Best school trip ever."

"This afternoon I fancy you might learn something more directly connected to your mission," said the old man in a low voice. "I am confident that you and Mr. Haggerty will find it especially compelling."

Darwen felt his pulse quicken. It was about time.

"Students!" called Miss Harvey. "Everyone with their walking shoes on in single file in front of me in two minutes."

"We're not going back into the ocean?" called Naia with cartoon dismay.

"Not just yet. Mr. Peregrine and Mr. Iverson have something to show us before we do any more snorkeling."

Someone groaned.

"This is not a holiday," Miss Harvey reminded them. "It is a school outing. We are here to learn, to immerse ourselves in that which we do not know in order to emerge enriched by the experience. Now, Hillside. Quick march."

And they began to trudge up the winding slope that climbed inland from the beach, wending their way through cactus scrub and heavy-leafed rainforest shrubs. Lizards skittered in the underbrush, and Jorge gave another of his favorite warnings to *pay attentions to the nature*, if only because some of it might kill them if they didn't.

The trail was easy to follow, and in ten minutes they reached a partially open area in the woods where the leaf litter had been swept and a square of topsoil carefully removed.

"It's a dig!" exclaimed Rich, picking up a trowel from a box of tools.

"The Caño Island archaeological site," agreed Mr. Iverson, beaming at Rich. "Right up your alley, I think, Mr. Haggerty."

"Archaeology?" groaned Mad. "I wanna go back and see the fish."

"Hey, check it out," called Barry. "Cannonballs."

For the briefest of moments, Darwen thought he was right. The forest floor and the area around the dig itself was scattered with stone balls of varying sizes, several of them as big as large pumpkins. Darwen's gaze moved from them to Rich, but his friend's eyes were fixed on Mr. Iverson, who had crouched to consider one of the spheres. It was about the size of a baseball, and though it was greenish with lichen, it was clearly identical to those Darwen had thrown at the monster that took Luis. The science teacher turned quickly and gave Mr. Peregrine a probing look.

"These are the famous stone spheres," said Miss Martinez. "They are found only here and on the mainland close by. They are about a thousand years old, perhaps more, carved by the ancient people who lived here long before

Columbus came. Their precise function is uncertain, but they seem to have been used to mark special places and events in the ritual life of the tribe. This is a graveyard."

"Cool," said Carlos.

And if this wasn't the exact spot from which Luis was taken, thought Darwen, then it was somewhere very like this and very close. There was a portal to Silbrica around here. There had to be.

"Since he has been assisting the archaeologists, Jorge will explain the excavation," continued Miss Martinez. "Afterward, he will answer questions, so start to think about what you'd like to know. Quietly, Mr. Fails."

As Chip and Barry elbowed each other, the guide began to talk. "The Caño Island site where you stand has been used by people for many centuries, though we do not believe they lived here," he said. "Perhaps they came here only to bury their dead."

"Is the island haunted?" asked Barry.

"Questions later, Mr. Fails," said Miss Martinez firmly.

"I am sure that the people who used to come here thought the place special," said Jorge, by way of an answer, "and, yes, I'm sure they had all kinds of stories about the island's function as a cemetery. Recently a discovery was made here at Caño. In addition to the stone balls, we found metates—a kind of stone slab for grinding corn—and several of these."

From his pocket he drew a clear plastic box with something yellow inside. It looked like a tiny figure, strangely shaped but roughly apelike.

"Is that gold?" exclaimed Princess Clarkson.

"Yes," said Jorge, shifting as the students crowded in closer. "I will pass it around, but handle it carefully, and do not open the box."

As the students cooed over the gold figurine, Darwen turned his attention back to Mr. Iverson, who had moved quietly over to Mr. Peregrine and had started to speak in a low, urgent voice touched with something—accusation or suspicion—that Darwen had never heard from him before.

"That sphere is like the one you brought to class," he hissed. "No. Not *like*. It's the same. Identical. Where did you get it?"

"Oh, you know," said Mr. Peregrine airily. "You tend to acquire things in your travels."

"*You tend to acquire things?*" whispered Mr. Iverson, so that Darwen had to strain to hear over the babble of questions being directed at Jorge. "How do you acquire an ancient and valuable artifact like this and then toss it around at school like it's no more than a punctured soccer ball? Did you know what it was? Is there something about this trip that you haven't told the other staff?"

Before Mr. Peregrine could answer, Mr. Iverson caught sight of Darwen watching him. Listening. The science teacher gave Darwen a long, level stare. Flushing, Darwen turned quickly away. At the same moment, Rich nudged him. It was his turn to look at the gold figurine.

Darwen considered it carefully through the magnifying glass that came with it, at first just so that he wouldn't have to look at Mr. Iverson, who he sensed was still watching him, but then with real interest. The tiny statue was indeed apelike, long limbed and hunched, but the head was that of a jaguar, and the paws showed long, savage-looking claws. Though the figurine was only a couple of inches long, its feet were finely modeled and showed birdlike talons, one extending backward, three more going forward, the middle one of which was considerably longer than the others.

"Do these things have a name?" Rich asked.

Jorge smiled and shook his head.

"The ancient peoples of this region made images of many animals and the gods or spirits associated with them," he said. "Sometimes they created hybrids: different animals combined. This is one of those. I call them *pouncels*," he added, shrugging and smiling apologetically, "but that is just me."

"You should call them, like, killer death monkeys," said Barry.

"Pouncels," Alex echoed musingly. "Yeah. I like that."

"Or jungle monsters of death," Barry continued.

"Or tapir killers?" whispered Darwen to Rich.

Their eyes met.

"The claws?" said Rich.

"Exactly like whatever left the tracks in the woods," said Darwen as soon as the group spread out to consider the stone spheres around the site.

"But if these pouncel things are from Silbrica, then they didn't just start coming through recently," said Rich. "Those gold figurines are a thousand years old. If the people who made them knew what the pouncels looked like—"

"Then there has been a tear in the barrier between the two worlds for a long time," Darwen agreed. "It was probably sealed up years ago—"

"But has come open again," Rich concluded.

"Come open," said Darwen, "or been ripped open on purpose."

"By what?"

"By the Insidious Bleck," said Darwen.

"But Mr. Peregrine keeps saying the Bleck is just an animal," said Rich, sounding worried.

"Aye," said Darwen, half turning to look at the former shopkeeper. "He does. But at least we know that one of the breaches or portals is on this island. And if the pouncels can get through from Silbrica, then we can go there from here. We just have to figure out how."

As soon as Darwen recovered from the boat ride back to the tent camp, he joined the line of students progressing up to the dining shelter, as ordered by Mr. Sumners.

"It will be Jorge talking about animals," said Chip with a showy yawn. "Something seriously lame."

It wasn't, but the student response was unanimously unenthusiastic. The tables were spread with notepads, pens, books, and charts.

"We're not having classes here?!" exclaimed Mad.

"This is a fieldtrip, Miss, ahhh, Konkani," said Mr. Sumners, "not a holiday. You are here to learn, and learning takes work. Take a seat, and I want at least, ahhh, eighteen inches between each student. This place has enough distractions as it is."

The rest of the day was given over to forty-five-minute science lectures (botany, zoology, and marine biology) from Mr. Iverson, Spanish from Miss Martinez, history from Miss Harvey, and world studies from Mr. Peregrine, with each subject tailored to Costa Rica. As they worked Mr. Sumners hovered, watching, listening.

"What's he even here for?" asked Darwen again.

"He's the senior faculty member," said Rich. "Genevieve overheard him saying that he calls the principal from Drake Bay every evening to report on how the trip is going. Apparently Principal Thompson wouldn't have let Mr. Peregrine bring us otherwise. He has to take the boat," he added, grinning. "Not his favorite part of the day."

Mr. Peregrine ended the session by talking about the hunting techniques of the people who lived in the forest before the Europeans arrived. "Tomorrow," he announced, "we will be making bows and arrows in the traditional style, and Mr. Iverson will explain the physics of how they work."

Mr. Iverson sat up abruptly, and from the upward motion of his tufty eyebrows, Darwen felt sure this was the first he had heard of Mr. Peregrine's lesson plan. He shrugged his acceptance but watched the world studies teacher with his head slightly to one side.

"Sit down, Mr., ahhh, Fails," roared Mr. Sumners.

Barry had leaped to his feet and started shooting imaginary arrows at everyone in sight.

Darwen turned to look and saw Carlos and Alex apparently arguing.

"He said so," said Alex. "You saying he's a liar?"

"You must have misunderstood," said Carlos.

"What?" asked Darwen.

"Oh, nothing," said Alex. "Our friend Carlos here is saying that our school-appointed guide is a liar, that's all."

"I didn't say that," said Carlos. "I just said that he's not from around here."

"I asked him," said Alex, "and he said he was from San José."

"No way," said Carlos. "Ask Miss Martinez. Listen to him, Alex. He's not from anywhere in the Americas. He's a European, from Spain. He may have lived here awhile, but you can hear it."

Alex opened her mouth to protest, but at that moment a great *ooh* went up from the students.

Darwen turned and saw, fluttering haphazardly through the shrubs of the gardens beside the dining shelter, a huge butterfly. It must have been six inches across, its wings flashing with turquoise and aqua and a deep blue vibrant as the summer sky and gleaming like metal. It wove in and out of the bushes and then flew gracefully into the shelter itself, weaving and bobbing as if borne on an invisible breeze, and then, astonishingly, it settled on one of the long wooden tables.

"A blue morpho!" exclaimed Rich, fumbling for his camera.

The students flocked to the table to consider the massive and dazzling creature as it rested.

"Give it some room," said Mr. Iverson. "Butterflies are very fragile."

"It's gorgeous!" exclaimed Naia.

WHAM.

A heavy book slammed down onto the butterfly. The leg and fragment of wing that stuck out never even moved.

Chip Whittley looked at what he'd done and, in the momentary shocked silence, shrugged. "What?" he said, the hint of a smirk fluttering at the corner of his mouth. "It was only a bug."

There was an explosion of outrage from the other students, and Alex flew at him, fists balled.

Chip's composure evaporated, but he moved too slowly to dodge her first punch. He stumbled back against one of the tables, and she was on him, arms flailing. Chip cried out in shock, and within moments Mr. Sumners was dragging Alex away, giving her a warning stare when she looked poised to attack again. For once, she didn't speak, but her eyes were bright with angry tears.

"Don't move," said Mr. Sumners, pointing squarely into her face, "or I'll have you on the next plane home."

"And him?" said Mr. Iverson.

The science teacher's face was white and hard, quite unlike his usual expression. He was furious.

"What about him?" asked Mr. Sumners.

"What do you propose we do with this boy?" said Mr. Iverson, his voice trembling with the effort of not shouting.

Chip looked hot in the face, and he was watching Alex warily, but a hint of the smirk remained. He shot Nathan a glance.

"What Mr. Whittley did is no excuse for such an assault."

"No excuse?" repeated Mr. Iverson, his voice colder than ever. "I think Miss O'Connor's anger perfectly understandable. If I were not a man of considerable self-control—"

"You'd do what?" asked Mr. Sumners, pouncing on the remark.

There was a sudden, tense silence. Mr. Iverson lowered his eyes and said nothing. The students watched, riveted. Taking the silence for a kind of apology, Mr. Sumners nodded, smiling mirthlessly.

"I think what Mr. Iverson meant to say," said Mr. Peregrine, stepping forward suddenly, "is that people of violence, people who have no appreciation for life or beauty, people who think the destruction of what others value is a source of amusement, cannot be reasoned with. They can, perhaps, be taught, but they do not want to be. They are the worst kind of thugs and will grow up—if they show such tendencies as children—to be the worst kind of adults."

This extraordinary speech produced almost as much shock and bewilderment as Chip's destruction of the butterfly had, but from the looks being leveled at Chip by the other students, there weren't many who disagreed with it, and Darwen felt a rush of pride in Mr. Peregrine.

"If Hillside stands for anything," he continued, "it is that such behavior cannot be permitted. I recommend in the strongest possible terms that this matter be raised with Principal Thompson so that he may determine if Mr. Whittley should be allowed to remain on the trip."

For a moment Mr. Sumners said nothing, just looked from Mr. Iverson to Mr. Peregrine and back as if they had started speaking Swahili, then he curtly nodded and turned to Chip. "Clean it up," he said, nodding at the table.

Chip sighed and reached for the book, but Alex stepped forward again.

"No," she said.

Sumners tensed, poised to block her if she attacked again, but she just said, "I don't want him to touch it." Sumners hesitated, then nodded slowly. Chip shrugged and turned his back to them, shooting a grin at Nathan as he did so. Alex moved slowly forward, took the book in both hands, and lifted it carefully. She set it down, and for a moment everyone but Chip looked at the broken remains of the once magnificent butterfly. Naia turned quickly away, her face in her hands, and Genevieve Reddock muttered, "Oh no."

Saying nothing, Alex tentatively lifted the butterfly by its wings, then, cradling it in her open hands, walked toward the bushes over which it had flown. She held it in front of her chest as if she was part of a ceremony, and wordlessly the students followed her.

She moved down into the tent camp, selected a sunny spot beneath a tall palm, and dropped to a crouch. She seemed uncertain where to lay the insect down, and Darwen hurried forward. He brushed some stones away from the surface of the ground and then dug his fingers into the dirt as she sat quite still beside him, hands outstretched. Darwen scooped a shallow grave out of the soft earth and waited as Alex laid the butterfly inside it. Between them they covered the vivid blue with the dirt and stood up.

The other students had been clustered around them in

silence, but once the butterfly was buried, the spell broke almost immediately. They looked suddenly embarrassed and uncertain of what they were doing, and seconds later they dispersed. Chip, Nathan, and Barry had not come down but were watching, blank-faced, from the dining shelter where the teachers also stood, saying nothing.

"Come on," said Darwen.

Alex, who had been staring up at Chip, her face expressionless, nodded. Rich glowered at the ground and muttered as they walked down to the shore, where they sat in silence, watching the sky soften as the afternoon turned to evening. Darwen wanted to talk about the gold figurine and its links to the creatures that he was sure had brought down the tapir, but the time didn't feel right.

At dinner they sat as far from Nathan, Chip, and Barry as was possible and avoided their eyes. Once Barry waggled his arms in what was clearly supposed to be an impression of a wounded butterfly, but no one laughed, and Rich shot him such a murderous look that he abandoned the joke and went back to his food, grumbling.

As darkness fell and the students picked their way to the bathrooms in a trail of bobbing flashlights, Darwen, Rich, and Alex sat alone in the dining shelter listening to the sounds of the waves below and looking at the stars. Rich was telling them about the constellations.

"But there's still a polestar, see?" he was saying,

"because we're just north of the equator and—"

"I miss my dog," said Alex.

"Excuse me?" said Rich.

"I'm just saying," said Alex. "I miss Sasha."

Darwen reached over and put a hand on her shoulder, and Rich, who had been about to say something, nodded sympathetically.

"How am I supposed to go after Luis if we can't find the portals?" said Darwen suddenly.

"I was talking about the stars," said Rich, miffed.

"I know," said Darwen, who had been watching a pair of hermit crabs scurrying softly through the grass. "Sorry. But I know the portals are here. I can almost feel them. There has to be one on the island, but where? We've been to the dig site, and we've trekked through the jungle—"

"Rainforest," corrected Rich.

"Rainforest," said Darwen, "and I thought we'd see a big iron gateway like the one Greyling built at Hillside last year. Or we'd see something like that little stove in the janitor's basement, you know? The one that was a tiny portal that they used for passing all the stuff they stole from us. But we've seen nothing, and so far as we can tell, neither has anybody else."

"It's a big jungle," said Alex.

"Rainforest," said Rich.

"Whatever," said Alex and Darwen together.

"It can't be random," said Darwen, shaking his head. "If those gold figurines are the same as the things that are wandering the jungle—*rainforest*," he corrected himself before Rich could get the word out, "then they've been coming here for centuries. But if it's just a tear in the barrier between worlds, why doesn't the council know exactly where it is?"

He moved his foot toward a rock that hopped slowly into the darkness. It was another of the large brownish toads that cropped up all over the camp. Darwen winced.

"I know that building a hotel here would be bad," he said, a little defensively, "destructive to the environment and, you know . . ."

"Exploitative," suggested Alex.

"All that," said Darwen. "But it would be really nice to be able to go to bed for a night—just one night—without worrying what might already be in the tent when we get there."

Rich was about to respond when they heard the first shot.

There was no question that the bang that had suddenly torn through the jungle night, sending the birds squawking and the monkeys howling, was anything other than a gunshot. There were no cars to backfire, no construction workers with heavy equipment, nothing else that could create the hard, short crack and the two others that followed.

Somebody was shooting.

Darwen had never heard a real gunshot before. It wasn't quite what he had expected—it was tighter and flatter than the booming cannon he had heard in movies and without the electric fizz and roar of Weazen's blaster. Still, he ducked instinctively.

A fourth shot.

Then silence.

Moments later, the camp was a chaos of flashlights, whirling and stabbing into the night around the tents. The quiet was rent by a confusion of voices: teachers, guides, and camp workers, but mostly the Hillside students.

"What was that?" shouted Carlos.

"Is someone hurt?" faltered Genevieve.

"That was a shotgun!" called Barry gleefully.

"No, it wasn't," said Rich quietly, almost to himself. "It was a rifle."

"You can tell the difference?" asked Darwen.

"I live on a farm," he replied absently, listening to the night, eyes closed as if he was trying to strain out the babbling excitement around him.

"Oh yeah," said Alex, appearing on the path beside them. "This is exactly what my mom had in mind when she agreed to this trip. Snakes and toads and getting shot at. Awesome. But at least we'll be safe in our hotel rooms—oh wait, no, we're in tents, which means we're all gonna die horribly—"

"Hillside students!" bellowed a voice.

It was Mr. Sumners in striped pajamas and a belted

bathrobe with what looked like a shower cap on his head.

"Students, make your way up to the dining shelter. Quickly and quietly, please. Don't run, Mr. Fails!"

"What do they want us up there for?" asked Darwen.

"To make sure we're all still alive," said Rich.

"Oh yeah," Alex mused. "When my mom gets my first postcard, they're gonna need to sedate her until I get home. *Dear Mom, didn't get eaten by sharks today, but did get shot at. Wish you were here. With a house. And a tank. Yours, Alex.*"

"Quiet, everyone," said Mr. Iverson, who was still dressed. "Sit at the tables so we can do a head count."

Miss Harvey bustled among them, pointing as she counted.

"Thirteen, fourteen," she muttered. "Fourteen. We're missing two."

Simon Agu emerged from under the table grinning broadly.

"Fifteen," she said. "Sit down properly, Mr. Agu. This is no time for jokes. Who else is missing?"

The students looked around.

"No one, ma'am," said Rich. "You must have miscounted."

She started again but came to the same number. "Fifteen," she said. "Who is not here?"

"I think you counted me twice," said Barry Fails.

"No, Barry, I didn't," said Miss Harvey crisply, "and if

I had, we'd be missing two people, wouldn't we?"

"Oh," said Barry. "Right."

"Where is Mr. Cabrera?" said Mr. Iverson, peering around the tables.

"Who?" asked Barry.

"Gabriel!" Rich exclaimed, aghast, turning to Darwen. "He just . . . slipped my mind. We're sharing a tent, and we completely forgot him."

In the awkward silence that ensued, the students shone their flashlights into the gardens below.

"We should check the tent," said Darwen to Rich.

"Us?" said Rich, looking apprehensively into the darkness.

"Us," said Darwen with a finality he didn't really feel. "Miss Harvey, we'll be right back."

"What?" said Miss Harvey. "I would really prefer that you stay—"

"I will go with them," said Mr. Peregrine, appearing from the kitchen end of the dining shelter in a bathrobe so long it looked like a cloak. He was holding one of the battery-powered lanterns above his head, and his gray hair shone softly in the light so that he looked for a moment like a figure from a stained-glass window, saintly and powerful.

"Very well," said Miss Harvey.

Rich and Darwen set off at a run, not bothering to wait for Mr. Peregrine.

Darwen felt suddenly responsible for Gabriel, to whom he had been—it was suddenly clear—a lousy friend. The kid knew no one, had been tacked onto a group who had been together for one semester already, a group that had proceeded to ignore him almost completely. Darwen and Rich had let him share a tent with them, and they had thought they were doing him a huge favor, but instead of keeping an eye on him, helping him make friends, they had neglected him entirely.

There was a flash of movement in front of them. Darwen shone his flashlight ahead and caught a streak of motion, then another, then several all together.

He gasped and took a step backward.

The cat-headed monkey-like creatures that Jorge had called pouncels—a pack of them, maybe ten or fifteen, all about the size of German shepherds. One of them stopped with uncanny control and turned to face him, snarling. Its head was smaller than a jaguar's, but not by much, and its bared teeth were long and sharp. It had glassy yellow eyes with vertical black pupils. The creature spread its clawed paws, each with one overlarge and deadly looking talon, and lowered its head as if about to spring. It put out its tongue and hissed, a long, slow rasping sound that raised the hair on the back of Darwen's neck.

And then, as Darwen stood rooted to the spot, it took off, racing after the others in a long bound that took it out of Darwen's flashlight beam and into the night. In no more than a second, they had gone.

"Whoa," said Rich. He looked pale in the lamplight and badly scared.

"Still think they're too small to bring down a tapir?" asked Darwen.

Rich shook his head briskly, mouth closed and eyes wide. Mr. Peregrine was coming down the path behind them.

"Slow down," he said. "I'm supposed to be escorting you."

"Did you see them?" Darwen demanded.

"See what?"

"The pouncels!" said Rich and Darwen at the same time.

"The what?"

"Pouncels," said Darwen. "Like the figurines Jorge showed us! There was a pack of them right here in the camp. They must be working for the Bleck."

Mr. Peregrine shushed them, hurriedly looking over his shoulder.

"Show a little discretion," he said in a whisper. "We came looking for Mr. Cabrera. And here he is."

Dazed and bleary-eyed, Gabriel was emerging from their tent. He looked tired but also embarrassed and alarmed. "What's going on?" he asked. "Where is everyone?"

"Didn't you hear the shots?" asked Darwen.

"Shots? What shots?" said Gabriel. "I was asleep, I think."

"In your clothes?" said Rich.

"I was tired," said Gabriel. He sounded weary, and Darwen thought he was on the verge of tears. It all seemed quite clear to him now. The boy felt abandoned and alone. He'd probably been in the tent for ages, miserable and homesick. Getting to sleep would have been a relief.

"Come on," Darwen said as kindly as he could. "We'll get you up to the dining shelter. Let me get my pack of cards, and we can play until they figure out what happened."

He put an arm around the boy's shoulders, but Gabriel flinched, and Darwen let him be. Darwen knew what it was like to feel different, an outsider, and he also knew that a sudden outpouring of pity wasn't the answer. Instead he stuck his head in the tent, grabbed the playing cards from his bag, and zipped the tent closed.

They moved up to the dining shelter, and there was a rush of noise as the others saw them approach.

"Why didn't you come when you were called?" Miss Harvey wanted to know.

Alex looked ready to scold Gabriel, but Darwen caught her eye, and, for once, she thought better of it. Darwen fished his cards from his back pocket and prepared to deal.

"Okay, Gabriel," he said. "What can you play? Blackjack? War? Whist?"

But Gabriel didn't answer. Jorge had appeared with two of the local men who worked at the camp, one of whom had been watching the soccer match the day before. It was this heavyset man with a thin black mustache who was cradling the rifle. Jorge was talking quickly to Miss Martinez, who was looking serious, and the man with the rifle was nodding and gesturing. Miss Martinez seemed doubtful. She leaned in, and Darwen thought he caught a word repeated back to the man with the rifle: *demonio*?

The man nodded emphatically. Jorge shook his head and waved the word away, but the man with the gun rattled off a stream of irritated Spanish. Darwen turned to ask Gabriel what they were talking about, but the boy had slipped silently into a dark corner and was watching the debate closely.

"I don't care if he was attacked by a fire-breathing T. Rex," Mr. Sumners roared, "shooting those stone balls you are all so fond of out of its nose: he cannot discharge a firearm this close to a camp full of children! Tell him."

The squabble escalated. Miss Martinez shepherded the man with the gun away from the crimson-faced Mr. Sumners and spoke in soothing tones as Mr. Iverson tried to convince the students that the danger had been dealt with.

"But what did he shoot at?" Mad wanted to know.

"Probably a margay or an ocelot," said Jorge. "He was protecting his livestock, but he should not shoot such creatures. I am sure the sound scared them off, and they will not return."

"Them?" said Rich. "You said a margay or an ocelot."

"He thinks he saw more than one," said Jorge, gesturing hopelessly.

"Both of those are solitary hunters," said Rich. "They wouldn't attack in a group."

"I think he was mistaken," said Jorge.

"What does *demonio* mean?" asked Darwen.

"What?" said Jorge, clearly dodging the question. "I don't think that's what he meant."

"It means *demon*," said Carlos. Everyone went quiet. "Mr. Delgado—the man with the gun—said a pack of demons came out of the jungle and attacked his chickens. He shot at them, but they escaped."

"Rainforest," said Rich grudgingly. "A pack of demons came out of the *rainforest*."

"Thanks," said Nathan. "That makes much more sense."

"All right, that's enough," said Miss Harvey. "Time for bed."

There was a general sputter of exasperation, but several voices rang out louder than the rest.

"You think that Scarlett woman has already built any hotels around here?" said Princess Clarkson. "'Cause I've about had it with this place."

"No way am I going to bed after all this," called Melissa Young, who looked quite terrified.

"Bed?!" shouted Bobby Park. "With demons on the loose?"

"Mr. Park," said Miss Harvey, very stern, "I personally give you my word that you will not be attacked by any mythical monsters in the night. You too, Miss Young. Bed. Quick march."

Protests turned to groans, but several students were genuinely frightened. Miss Harvey relented a little and spent a few moments huddled with those who seemed least sure of returning to their tents. Only Darwen, Alex, and Rich held back, keen to learn what else they could overhear.

"Mr. Arkwright," said Mr. Sumners. "You are, ahhh, still here. Why is that?"

"Waiting to go to the bathroom," said Darwen.

"I can't be sure from here," said Mr. Sumners, smiling mirthlessly toward where Carlos was coming back down the trail, towel and toothbrush in hand, "but they seem to be vacant."

"Only the ones with the toads, sir," said Darwen, improvising. "I don't like toads."

"No," said Mr. Sumners, bending and peering into his face with careful emphasis. "Neither do I." He checked his watch. "Very well. I want you in bed in four minutes and not a second more. And walk!"

"Come on," said Darwen to Rich, trudging up toward the bathrooms, casting one last look back to where Miss

Martinez, Jorge, and the man with the rifle—now joined by Mr. Peregrine—continued to chatter in rapid Spanish.

"And you, Miss O'Connor," said Mr. Sumners. "Or are you afraid of toads as well?"

"I never said I was afraid of 'em," muttered Darwen as Alex fell into step beside him.

"Just his lucky guess then," said Alex.

"What happened to Gabriel?" asked Rich, looking around. "One minute he was over there, the next . . ."

"He likes to keep to himself," said Alex. "Didn't even join in the soccer match. You didn't notice?"

Darwen and Rich exchanged shamefaced looks.

Moments later they were brushing their teeth. Alex had been right. None of the students much liked the washrooms. They tended to go in groups and to get out as quickly as they could. It was only a matter of time, Melissa Young had said, before someone peed in their tent, because you'd have to be crazy to go up to the haunted washrooms alone at night. Darwen figured their fear had more to do with snakes than ghosts, but still . . . he understood their concern. He bent over the sink to spit. As he straightened up, it happened again.

It lasted only a second, but there, quite clearly, over his shoulder, as if standing right behind him . . .

The laughing face.

As before, it didn't look quite real. More like a model,

its eyes glassy and dead, its mouth gaping, showing white, even teeth.

Darwen spun around, and though there was nothing there, he was sure he could hear the wild laughter trailing away. And once more, in its wake, came the nudge of a memory that was just out of reach. That thing, whatever it was, he had seen it before, heard its laughter before, long ago.

"What?" asked Rich. He was looking at Darwen closely, and his voice was low.

"Nothing." Darwen shrugged. "Just . . . I don't know. Nothing."

"Okay," said Rich. "Fine."

Rich thought he was keeping secrets. Remembering how put out they had been about him visiting Silbrica without them, Darwen relented.

"It's stupid," he said, putting his toothbrush away.

"Go on."

"Well, it was only there for a second," said Darwen. "Less. But it looked, sort of like . . . a clown."

"A what?" said Rich. "Like a circus clown? Red nose and all that?"

"No," Darwen answered, trying to fix on the details. "The face wasn't made up or anything. And it wasn't a real person. More like a model or a doll. Laughing."

"Okay . . ." said Rich, looking uneasily at the mirror.

"I told you it was nothing," said Darwen.

"A happy clown?" asked Rich hopefully.

"Kind of," said Darwen apologetically. "More manic."

Rich frowned.

"That's gonna give me nightmares," he said. "Not a big fan of clowns."

"Me neither," said Darwen, shuddering. "Let's just . . . forget it, okay?"

"Fine by me," said Rich.

Darwen splashed water on his face and, when he straightened up, managed not to look back into the mirror.

"What was all that about?" said Alex.

"Darwen thinks he saw—" Rich began.

"Nothing," said Darwen. "I didn't see anything."

"If you're keeping secrets from me . . ." Alex began.

Darwen turned to say something but stopped. There was confused movement down in the tent camp: running people, some of them shouting. Even from here Darwen could sense their panic, their fear.

Something had happened. Something new.

"Quick!" said Darwen, snatching up his things and hurrying down toward the commotion.

"You've got to hand it to Mr. P," said Alex as the three of them hurried back the way they had come to see what was going on. "His trips are never dull."

There were four of them: a young man, two teenage boys, and a girl. Darwen recognized the kids from the soccer game. One of them was Felippe, the boy who had scored the spectacular volley. He looked quite different now: urgent and anxious, and he was looking around like something might attack him at any minute. The young man was carrying a small ax. They made for the man with the rifle—Mr. Delgado—who was with Jorge and the teachers in the yellowish light of the generator lamp, and began speaking all at once.

There was a moment's silence. Then the rifle slipped from Mr. Delgado's grasp. It clattered to the ground, and for a moment he stood there, his hands clamped over his nose and mouth, frozen in some terrible rush of emotion.

They hadn't seen Darwen, who had stuttered to a halt in the shadows behind the dining shelter. He pulled Alex and Rich in beside him. "What are they saying?" he asked.

"I'm *trying* to listen," said Alex, shrugging out of Darwen's grasp and pressing her head to the wooden upright.

The young man picked up the fallen rifle and started moving back the way they had come. The boys and the girl dragged Mr. Delgado after them, though he still seemed to be in a kind of daze.

"What's wrong with him?" asked Rich.

"Quiet," said Alex, her voice low, her face serious.

The teachers were muttering among themselves, then they broke hurriedly apart. Jorge went after the locals. Miss Harvey, Miss Martinez, and Mr. Iverson all went down to the tents. Mr. Sumners went into the makeshift office by the kitchen, and Mr. Peregrine sat at one of the tables, as if waiting.

"Well?" said Rich. "What's going on?"

"Another kid has been taken," said Alex. "A girl called Calida. Felippe's sister. Right from her bed. They're going there now."

For a long moment no one spoke.

"It can't be the pouncels," said Rich. "We saw what they did to the tapir. They attack. They feed. They leave. They don't kidnap."

"Nice," said Alex.

"Rich is right," whispered Darwen. "The pouncels behave like . . . well, like animals. The thing I saw in Silbrica was different. It thinks. Maybe the Bleck is just using them to wreak havoc or drum up fear."

"I don't like the sound of that," said Alex.

"We should go the village," said Darwen, ignoring her. "Look for tracks."

"We're supposed to be in bed," said Rich.

"Yeah, sneaking around tonight of all nights seems like a really bad idea," Alex agreed.

"Sumners has gone," said Darwen. "I say we follow. Quietly."

"No way," said Rich.

"Come on," said Darwen. "This is what we came for!"

"What is?" asked Alex.

"To learn what is happening here," Darwen replied. "Another kid has been taken. We have to follow while the trail is fresh."

"What trail?" asked Alex.

"We won't know unless we look, will we?" Darwen shot back.

"I don't know, Darwen . . ." Rich began.

"Look," said Darwen, taking charge. "I'm going to follow them. You can come with me, or I can go alone. Your choice. But we're supposed to be the Peregrine Pact, remember?"

Rich and Alex looked at each other, then shrugged their halfhearted agreement.

"Okay," said Darwen. "And no lights."

"What?" hissed Rich. "Are you serious? There are snakes and God knows what else out here."

"And if we run around with flashlights, they'll catch us and send us back to bed before we've seen anything," said Darwen. "Come on."

Darwen knew that Rich and Alex were looking at each other, trying to decide whether to protest, but he went anyway, slipping into the darkness of the grounds. He could see Mr. Sumners sitting inside the little office, tapping anxiously on a desk, but he was sure they were invisible outside. He used the glow from the window to find the path and padded cautiously along it. As long as they were out in the open, there was enough light from the moon and stars to just about make out the way, but once they were under the trees, traipsing toward the tiny village, they really were in the dark.

"This is a bad idea, Darwen," Rich muttered.

"Okay," said Darwen. "One flashlight between us,

pointed straight down. Keep close together."

He snapped on the beam and aimed it at the leaf-strewn ground. Something skittered into the underbrush unseen.

"Okay," said Alex. "Walk. Slowly."

They moved cautiously through the forest, the warm air humming with insect noises and the otherworldly calls of frogs. Somewhere far off, something shrieked, but whether the creature that made the sound was human, animal, or bird, was from their world or the one beyond the mirrors, Darwen could not say. Rich could correct him as many times as he liked, but to Darwen this was and always would be the jungle.

"Just keep the light steady," said Alex. "I saw something move over there."

She tucked in her arms, and Darwen felt her shudder as a moth the size of his hand—so big he could actually hear the beating of its wings—fluttered inches past their heads, swooping at the flashlight. For a moment he thought of his dellfey friend, feeling a twinge of anxiety about why he had not been able to get back to her bamboo grove. He was considering this uneasily when he noticed horse hoofprints in the rain-softened earth of the trail. There was nothing else to suggest anyone ever came this way except for the creatures that called the place home. To his right, Darwen could hear the waves breaking on the rocky portion of the shore and see the glow of the moon through the trees, but to his left, the jungle stretched for miles.

They heard voices. Darwen looked directly ahead and saw a space where the deep shade of the trees stopped. It was the soccer field and the cluster of tiny houses. He snapped the flashlight off, then closed his eyes tight to get them used to the dark. Alex and Rich both groaned, but he shushed them.

"If I get eaten by something in these woods, Darwen Arkwright," hissed Alex, "I'm going to have something to say about it."

Darwen pressed on, feeling the ground carefully with his feet with each step. The voices were getting louder. A woman was crying. A man was shouting angrily, and someone else was responding in a placating tone, which was not helping the situation at all: Jorge.

Darwen veered inland across the moonlit field, moving toward the lights of the houses, and nearly stepped on a large iguana, which hissed at him. Under a great, spreading tree was a roughly timbered shack with an open veranda hung with hammocks. There were people there. Darwen could make out Felippe sitting on the deck, his head in his hands. Jorge was standing, murmuring, continually lowering his palms as if urging calm and then looking up into the branches that hung over the house.

Darwen, Rich, and Alex hugged the tree line and moved slowly closer, certain they would not be seen unless someone shone a light right at them. It was Mr. Delgado who was doing the shouting. Darwen was glad to see that someone else had the gun now, because his fury was frightening. He kept pointing at Jorge and shouting, cursing, spitting at the ground, and calling "Calida," until he finally collapsed beside the hammocks, weeping uncontrollably.

"Her father," whispered Alex.

Darwen said nothing, but he suddenly felt embarrassed, even ashamed, that they had come skulking around these people's grief. What had he been thinking intruding like this, sniffing for clues while a family mourned its lost child? Shouldn't he of all people know that this wasn't the stuff of adventure? He turned around, pulling at the others wordlessly, determined to get out of there before they were caught spying.

Alex shot him a look, and as their eyes met, he stumbled on something at his feet and fell sprawling to the ground with a dull *splat*. The next thing he knew he was lying on the forest floor, up to his elbows in a slippery and foul-smelling mud. Though the area around them was quite dry, Darwen had somehow managed to find a round, saucer-like depression that must have been holding rainwater for days. The brown goop was everywhere, all over his face, hands, and clothes. He had even managed to splash some of it onto the others, and they glared at him with disbelief and annoyance. Darwen tried to get to his feet, slipped in the forest slime, and landed on his back.

Alex gave him a look of withering contempt, as if he was being stupid on purpose, but she didn't get a chance to say anything. A flashlight from where the adults were talking came lancing through the darkness toward them. Then another. Voices called, and Darwen heard the distinct and terrifying snap of a rifle being cocked to fire.

"Run!" he yelled. Darwen scrambled, sliding in the mud, gripping the stone over which he had tripped in the first place, realizing even as he got to his feet and began to sprint that it was perfectly round and was not the only one on the ground there. There was a ring of them—about ten—circling the muddy depression in which he had just been lying.

He dashed blindly along the path after the others, feeling the light vanish as soon as they reached the tree line.

"I can't see!" sputtered Rich.

"Just keep moving," said Darwen, catching up with them.

"Do they think we might be the missing kid," asked Rich, "or the things that took her?"

"Well," said Alex, "there's three of us, and Darwen currently looks like the creature from the black lagoon, so I don't think they're looking to take us home and feed us empanadas."

"Good point," said Rich. "Shine the light on the ground."

"And Darwen," Alex added, considering the mud on her shirt, "don't touch me, okay? This stuff stinks."

"Just *move*!" hissed Rich, exasperated.

They jogged along the trail, eyes glued to the shifting pool of light at their feet. From time to time they glanced backward into the darkness, but if the villagers had seen enough of them to give chase, they were a long way back. They slowed, getting their breath back, but as soon as they did, they heard something new above the constant hum of the jungle and the surf: a steady, rhythmic pounding.

Horses.

Darwen, Alex, and Rich began to run again, harder now, all wondering the same thing: could they get back to the tent camp before the horsemen caught up, or did they have to hide in the jungle? If they waved the horsemen down, would they get a chance to explain themselves before someone took a shot at what they assumed to be a pack of ravening pouncels?

Darwen turned to see how close the horsemen were, so he was the last to see the flashlight coming toward them from the tent camp, the last to realize that they had nowhere to go, the last to learn that they had already been seen, and the last to recognize that the man in front of them was the one person they wouldn't have wanted to catch them out of bed at night.

"What in the name of all that's holy are you doing out here at this time?"

Darwen spun around. Rich had raised the flashlight slightly, and in its beam he saw the pink and furious face of Mr. Sumners, the math teacher.

"Could have been worse," said Alex. "We could have been shot."

Darwen couldn't argue with that, but it didn't help. Sumners had flagged the horsemen down and sent them back to the huddle of forlorn little houses looking disappointed and angry, then marched Darwen, Rich, and Alex back to the camp and bed, refusing Darwen permission to shower and wash his clothes.

"But I'm filthy," Darwen had protested. "The tent will stink."

"You should have thought of that before you, ahhh, decided to poke your nose into other people's business," said Sumners, "risking death and dismemberment in the process for your friends. And you, Haggerty," he had said, glaring at Rich. "You're supposed to be smart. I would have thought you of all people would know the dangers of wandering around in a place like this at night."

They walked back to the tents in silence, Alex clearly peeved that she wasn't the one whom Sumners recognized as the clever member of their little group. "That was a bad idea," she finally said. "Following them to the village. Terrible idea."

"What are you looking at me for?" said Darwen.

"Because it was *your* bad idea," she said. "We told you."

"It was your choice," Darwen muttered.

"Yeah?" said Rich. "What about 'We're supposed to be the Peregrine Pact, remember?'"

"Hey," said Darwen, defiant, "you didn't have to come."

"Next time," said Alex, "maybe we won't. You might be the mirroculist, Darwen, but that doesn't mean you get to make all the decisions."

She stalked off.

"I just thought . . ." Darwen began.

"Save it," said Rich. "I'm beat."

They didn't speak as they walked the rest of the way. Darwen was annoyed, so he just muttered a goodnight to Gabriel, who had sat up as soon as they unzipped the tent.

"A kid has gone missing?" Gabriel asked, his meek voice suggesting that he already knew the answer.

Darwen paused. "How did you know?"

"I heard them shouting," said Gabriel, his face unreadable in the dark. "Which one is it?"

"A girl called Calida," he said. "Felippe Delgado's sister. He was the one who . . . but you weren't at the game, were you?"

"No," said Gabriel. "I, uh . . . don't know them. I was just curious."

He didn't sound curious. He sounded upset, as though he had spoken through gritted teeth, trying to get a hold of himself. Darwen asked him if he was okay, but the boy didn't respond.

Darwen lay there in the dark, exhausted. Moments later, he was asleep. He dreamed of the jungle and of huge, brightly colored snakes that hung from the trees and slithered across the path in front of him. For some reason they didn't bother him, but the further he moved into the trees, the more of them there were, and soon it was difficult to walk without stepping on them. They were also getting bigger, and some of them now were marked with a black zigzag pattern down their backs. These, Darwen knew, were very dangerous, and the dream quickly turned to nightmare as they multiplied, emerging from the underbrush on all sides and approaching him with implausible deliberation. As the largest one reached him, mouth gaping to reveal a swelling tentacle where its tongue should be, he heard wild, maniacal laughter. He turned, and there between the trees was a seated figure, rocking back and forth with odd jerky motions, its head tilted backward and its mouth open. It had red curly hair and wore the garish, oversized clothes of a clown.

Darwen woke with a start.

It was hot and muggy in the dark tent, and Darwen felt himself sweating, even though he was only covered by a single cotton sheet. He pushed it back and then kept quite still, listening, waiting for his heart to slow as his memory of the dream faded. He could hear Rich snoring softly. And then, just as he was about to drift off again, he heard the unmistakable sound of the tent flap being slowly, carefully unzipped.

For a moment he lay quite still, staring into the blackness. The sound came again. Someone was coming in.

Darwen sat up, one hand reaching desperately for the flashlight under the bed. He groped along the plastic floor and found it, swinging it up and turning it on.

The tent entrance was half-open, the zipper moving down, gripped by a spindly black claw. Another was pushing the flap wide, and through the gap the swinging beam of the flashlight found a cluster of black eyes and hard, shiny mouthparts.

Darwen shrieked, scrambling backward on his bed, the light lurching around the tent as the flashlight slipped from his hands. He had the impression of something large stepping quickly inside, and he held his hands out in front of him, terrified that the thing would touch him. He could hear skittering movement inside the tent.

Rich grunted and woke. Darwen's fingers groped for

the flashlight again, finding it and directing it once more toward the tent door.

"What?" gasped Rich. "What is it?"

The flap was still unzipped, but there were only the three boys inside. Darwen swung the light around, and Gabriel sat up, rubbing his eyes and looking scared.

"Something came in," Darwen gasped. "I heard it."

Rich snapped on the rechargeable lantern and held it up.

"Check under the beds," he said grimly. "On three. One. Two. Three."

The three boys thrust their heads under the beds, turning from side to side but finding nothing more than half-open luggage and their own anxious faces.

"You must have dreamed it," said Rich.

"No way," said Darwen. "Someone opened the tent."

"Have you been out, Gabriel?" asked Rich. "To go to the bathroom or something?"

The skinny boy shook his head fervently, but his eyes were cautious, watchful.

"There's nothing here, Darwen," said Rich. "Maybe someone got the wrong tent by mistake."

"Maybe someone was trying to go through our luggage while we slept," suggested Gabriel.

"Maybe it was nothing," Rich replied. He sounded irritable, as if he thought Darwen was being dramatic to attract attention to himself. "Can we *please* try to get some sleep?"

Darwen said nothing. He couldn't be sure what he had seen by the flickering light of his erratic flashlight, and he *had* been having a nightmare. But he saw in his mind's eye the rail-thin leg with the little black claw, the clustered hard-candy eyes, and the beak-like mouth with the pulsing black feelers beside it.

A name came to mind: a stupid, ridiculous name that made the tropical night feel as cold as November in Lancashire.

Mr. Jenkins.

IN TROUBLE AGAIN

The next morning Rich still looked crestfallen and surly. Sumners had taken the night to think of a suitable punishment and had come up with something that hit Rich particularly hard. After breakfast, while the other students worked on their bows and arrows and then went on another jungle hike, Rich, Darwen, and Alex were to stay behind with Miss Martinez and help the cleaning staff.

"What's the point of coming here if we're not allowed

to look around?" he sputtered to the others. When they didn't respond, he added, with less anger and more sadness, "The hikes are the best part."

Rich didn't speak again until the rest of the students were in the motorboats, Nathan, Chip, and Barry waving and laughing as they pulled away. He didn't even look up as a pair of white-faced capuchin monkeys started dropping half-eaten bits of fruit onto the roof of the tent.

"I hear you had a nocturnal visitor," said Alex as Rich stomped off to start work.

"Mr. Jenkins," said Darwen. "Or something like him."

"Can't have been," said Alex. "We smashed the gate that led to their charming cottage. How could one of them be here?"

"Same way I was here, or hereabouts, weeks before ever getting on the plane," said Darwen. "I came through a portal."

They were sitting on the platform outside Alex's tent.

"That *particular* monster finds a way through to this *particular* spot in the jungle and then finds your *particular* tent?" Alex replied. "It's too much of a coincidence."

"It's not a coincidence at all," said Darwen. "It's all connected. The thing that once called itself Mr. Jenkins was looking for me. I'm sure of it."

"I'm surprised it could fit in the tent with your giant ego."

"I'm not saying I'm special," said Darwen. "I'm just . . .

I don't know. Involved. Central to this whole Silbrica thing."

"So long as you're not saying you're special," said Alex wryly.

"It's because of what I saw that we're here at all," said Darwen.

"So the rest of us are what? Your sidekicks? Your helpers?"

"You remember the Halloween Hop, Alex?" said Darwen, suddenly fierce. "I didn't want to go. I wanted to sit in my room. You made me go because you thought I was important. I was the mirroculist. I still am. That makes me special. I didn't ask to be. I'm not even sure I want to be. But I am. That's all there is to it."

Alex considered him for a long moment, then nodded seriously. "Okay," she said, looking up toward the dining shelter. "Miss Martinez is coming. Better get your stuff together, Captain Special, you've got some scrubbing to do. Too bad being a mirroculist doesn't get you out of cleaning."

Darwen glowered at her, but she grinned, and eventually he did too.

"There you are," said Miss Martinez. "Come on, there's work to be done. Mr. Haggerty is helping Señor Torres bring the supplies up from the beach to the kitchen. Miss O'Connor, you can help Juanita replace the bed linens in the tents. Mr. Arkwright, you have to go to the village and apologize for the confusion you caused last night. You will need to extend your sympathy to the Delgado family. And quick march."

Darwen's heart sank. "Can't Rich and Alex come with me?" he said.

"They are busy with other tasks," the Spanish teacher answered brusquely. "Tasks that will be assigned to you also when you return. And take a shower. *Rapido.*"

Darwen showered in the only stall without a lizard, toad, or insect more than two inches long. He put on shorts and a T-shirt, sprayed himself with mosquito repellant, and set off to the village along the coastal track, wondering what on earth he was supposed to say in his idiot-level Spanish. How was he supposed to convey his feelings about the loss of their daughter and his ridiculous behavior, which had made the situation worse, when his language skills hadn't gotten beyond "Is this a banana? No, it is a pineapple."

Who dreams this stuff up? he wondered. *"Is this a banana? No, it is a pineapple." Seriously? Who would ever say that? I mean, my Spanish might be rubbish, but I'm not a complete moron. I can tell the difference between a banana and—*

The thought died as he spotted the muddy depression into which he had fallen. The stone spheres that had ringed the damp hole last night were gone. He gazed at the little hollow, wondering why it was the only piece of ground that still looked wet.

"Are you lost, little boy?"

Darwen looked up. It was a bit like looking at a picture of a shopping cart in the middle of the desert or a fussily upholstered couch on the edge of a cliff, so clearly did Scarlett Oppertune not belong in this place. She was dressed today in an electric-blue suit with padded shoulders, matching high heels, and an elegant little purse. Her watch, ring, and designer spectacles were all studded with diamonds. Her perfectly made-up lips were wide and smiling, her eyes were bright, and her head was cocked slightly to one side in an expression of welcoming interest, which Darwen did not trust for a second.

"No," said Darwen. "I'm going to the houses."

"*Houses*," she repeated with a still broader smile that suggested he was stretching the definition of the word. "Get a good look," she said. "After what happened last night, I don't think they'll be here much longer."

She was still smiling, still looking perfectly cheerful, so Darwen was at a loss to explain why he felt cold and uneasy, as if he was alone with one of the pouncel creatures he had seen the night before.

Scarlett's eyes narrowed thoughtfully, but the smile didn't alter, as if it was held in place by wires. "So," she said. "What are you doing out here at this time? Shouldn't you be out looking at birds or something with your little friends?"

"I've come to talk to Mr. Delgado," said Darwen, wondering what business it was of hers. "What are *you* doing?"

"Talk to him about what?" she asked, ignoring his question, and it was there again, that watchful curiosity beneath a catlike smile.

"I . . . I just need to find them," he said. It was going to be hard enough talking to the Delgado family. He saw no reason to explain himself to this woman first.

She looked at him, and for a moment Darwen thought she might try to stop him, but then she shrugged, and the smile buckled at one side so that it looked more like a smirk. "Better hurry then," she said. "I'm not sure how much longer they'll be here."

"They're moving out?" asked Darwen, aghast.

"I paid them the first installment this morning," she answered. "I think Mr. Delgado will be hunting the jaguar that took his daughter first, which is understandable. But once that is dead, they'll be on the next boat out of here."

"To where?" Darwen demanded. "To do what? This is their home. Their life."

"Not anymore," said Scarlett, still smiling that wide, bland smile. "They've suffered a deep and touching loss here. Hardly surprising that they want to put it behind them. As for what they will do, well, Mr. . . . whatever your name is, it's not good to look after people too much.

Better that they make their own way in the world. If they don't have the knowledge or the skills to do that," she concluded, still smiling, "well, that's what you environmentalist types call *natural selection*, isn't it? The survival of the fittest. Well, run along. You might be able to catch them before they go shoot themselves a kitty."

She didn't actually clap in girlish delight, but it was a near thing. She beamed, like she was saying they were going to roast marshmallows or something, and Darwen felt the kind of revulsion he had experienced when he first saw the toad in the shower stall. He stepped deliberately around her and started to run toward the buildings at the edge of the soccer field.

Whatever else she was, Scarlett was telling the truth about the Delgado family. As Darwen got close to the house beneath the great tree, he could see a woman—the woman he had seen crying the night before—loading cardboard boxes onto the porch outside. The door was wide open, and the place looked deserted already. Darwen watched her work for a moment, feeling stupid and ashamed, then said, "*Hola*." She looked up but did not seem to recognize him, and for a long moment Darwen just stood there, clasping and unclasping his hands.

"*Pesarosa*," he said. *Sorry*.

And since he didn't know whether that was the right word exactly, he added the only other word he could think of and the girl's name: "*Excusa. Por Calida.*"

He knew he wasn't making any real sense.

Mrs. Delgado was a strong-looking woman, but her face looked weary beyond measure. She considered him, smiling sadly, then took a few steps toward him and sat on the edge of the porch. Beside her, as if forgotten, was a bag spilling gold coins: Scarlett's payoff.

"Señor Delgado?" Darwen asked.

Mrs. Delgado gave a long, slow shrug that somehow said that she didn't know where her husband was or what he was doing. Darwen tentatively raised his hands, miming someone shooting a rifle. She nodded and shrugged again, a gesture that was both knowing and hopeless, and then motioned for Darwen to approach her. Uneasily, he did so. She reached up and touched his face, looking into his eyes. The woman's hand was rough, but the touch held an almost painful tenderness, and her shining eyes suddenly brimmed over so that tears flowed silently down her cheeks.

"I'm sorry," said Darwen in English. "If there is anything I can do to bring your daughter back, I will. I promise."

Mrs. Delgado nodded once, though Darwen doubted she had understood what he had said, then she reached absently into the bag of coins and pressed one into his hand.

"No!" he exclaimed. "This is yours. Please."

But she waved his protests away, patted his hand, and then hauled herself laboriously to her feet. Without another glance, she returned to work. Darwen looked at the coin in his hand, felt its curiously rough surface, and took a last look at the porch where the child's hammock had been hanging until a few hours ago. He scanned the wooden deck for anything that might resemble the tracks of a pouncel. The creature's long claws would surely have left nicks and gouges in the soft wood.

There was nothing.

He looked up at the tree, but that seemed unmarked as well, though the act of looking up reminded him that Jorge had done the same. He gazed out toward the rest of what they called a village, though it was really only five little houses. The most distant looked the newest, a tidy log structure with a porch where one of the local girls was sweeping, a bucket of cleaning supplies at the foot of its steps. The girl's incongruous pink jacket was hanging on a hook by the door, and even at this distance its brass buttons sparkled in the sun.

As he took one last look at the Delgado house, Darwen saw that it was not completely deserted after all. Felippe was standing at the window, watching him, his face blank. Darwen raised a hand in greeting, feeling foolish and awkward, and the boy inclined his head in acknowledgment.

He walked back to the camp, his mind full of questions. There was no sign of Scarlett, so he had been able to study the muddy depression in the earth and make sure that the stone spheres were indeed gone. Could that be why Scarlett was so keen to get her hands on this piece of land—because she planned to sell its archaeological treasures? The stone spheres must be worth a lot of money to collectors, but if she was able to take them so easily while the villagers were distracted by the hunt for a missing child, why bother buying the land? And who was Scarlett anyway? She had gone out of her way to talk to him. She had even called him "Mr. . . . whatever your name is," as if she knew him and had remembered at the last minute to pretend otherwise.

It made no sense. Neither did the coins. Why was an American developer paying for land with gold? He looked at the coin. It didn't have the smooth surfaces of worn metal, and when he ran his fingertips lightly around the edge, he could feel tiny points and angles, some of them quite sharp. He held it up to the light and saw that it had no visible design. It wasn't so much a coin as a gold disc, and the metal was oddly marbled and uneven.

Darwen trudged through the humming jungle, watching the trail for snakes, feeling hot and damp and exhausted. Two days ago it had all seemed so exciting, but he was tired of the smelly tent and of not knowing what was going on. He felt no closer to rescuing Luis or his brother, Eduardo, and with another child gone, who knew how long they would be allowed to stay?

Miss Martinez spotted him the moment he returned to the camp.

"Where do you think you're going, Mr. Arkwright?"

"To my tent, Miss," said Darwen.

"Go and help Mr. Haggerty in the kitchen."

"Yes, Miss."

Rich's mood hadn't improved, and it wasn't hard to see why. Lugging plastic boxes and crates of canned food and other supplies up from the beach was no picnic, and the camp's pantry was so small that everything had to be carefully stacked.

"What's this?" asked Darwen, hoisting two plastic bins full of white powder.

"Nondairy creamer," said Rich. "There's no fridge, so everything has to survive at room temperature. Which would be fine if that didn't mean, like, a hundred degrees."

"One only," said the athletic-looking kitchen helper they called simply Torres. As usual, he was wearing jean shorts and no shirt. "One box for here, the other to go out to the ranger station on Caño Island."

"So I've got to take it back to the beach?" grumbled Rich.

"Not until the boat is ready," said Torres. "Tomorrow. Put it there."

As soon as the local went out, Darwen relayed the story of his trip and his encounter with Scarlett. He handed Rich the coin Mrs. Delgado had given him.

"Is this money?" said Rich. "It has no numbers on it. Can I show it to Mr. Iverson?"

"What for?"

"To see if we can do some tests on it or something," said Rich, holding it up to the light and squinting at it. "Does that look like pure gold to you? If it's not, maybe the villagers aren't getting what they think they're getting. Not sure we could do much in the way of real tests out here, but it's worth a look."

"There's something about that Oppertune woman," said Darwen. "I don't know what it is, but I think she's connected to the missing kids."

"How?" asked Rich.

"No idea," Darwen answered. "It's just a hunch." He looked out of the window and saw Alex walking down from the trees behind the dining shelter. She was moving quickly and looking nervously about. Darwen called her name.

She jumped, thought for a moment, and then walked over to the kitchen. "What?" she said, poking her head around the door.

"Aren't you done cleaning the tents out yet?" asked Darwen.

"No, I'm not. That's it? You wanted to see how far

behind I was while making me more behind?"

"Keep your hair on," said Darwen.

"I don't know what that even means," she rejoined, walking off and letting the door snap shut behind her.

"What's eating her?" asked Rich.

"Got me," said Darwen. "What was she doing up in the jungle back there if she's not done cleaning?"

"Rainforest," supplied Rich automatically. "Probably just taking a break. Getting a little air. If the other tents smell as bad as ours, I couldn't blame her."

"It's not my fault," said Darwen. "If Sumners had let me take a shower last night . . ."

"Yeah, yeah," muttered Rich, "it's Sumners's fault that our tent smells like a possum's armpit."

"All right," said Darwen, "It's my fault. Happy?"

"If I still have to sleep in there, then no, not particularly, but it's cool. What did you tell Gabriel?"

"Not much," said Darwen. "He didn't seem to mind."

Rich stared. "Did he still have a nose?"

"He spends so much time in there I expect he's forgotten what clean air smells like," he said. "He did care about Calida, though. Have you seen him with the local kids at all?"

"No," said Rich. "I know he's shy and all, but he really won't talk to them. Sarita came into the camp yesterday, and he bolted for the tent the moment he saw her. Kind of rude, I thought."

"Are we done?" asked Darwen.

"Just about. I guess we're supposed to help Alex now. If we're quick, maybe we can do some work on our bows and arrows."

Alex, it turned out, had made very little progress at all.

"How can you have only done one?" asked Rich. "You've had hours."

"One hour," said Alex. "And it's hard work. Let's see how fast you clean the next one, and I'll go hang out in the kitchen with Torres."

"That's what you think I've been doing?" said Rich. "Hanging out?"

"Oh, I'm sorry," said Alex. "No doubt you've been scrubbing the beach or rescuing stranded whales or—"

"Will you two give it a rest?" said Darwen.

The three of them fell into a sulky silence that lasted until lunchtime, when the hikers returned full of tales of the birds and other animals they had seen. Rich's mood darkened still further, and when Darwen asked why the Hillside kids weren't all talking about Calida's disappearance, he gave a nasty laugh.

"She's not one of them, is she?" said Rich, eying Nathan across the dining shelter.

Darwen was shocked. "You think they don't care?" he said. "Even the worst of them aren't that bad, Rich."

"Yeah?" said Rich. "Nathan Cloten's a big fan of poor

people, is he? Thinks we're all the same whether we wear Hillside's glorious green and gold or not? I hope you're right. I'm going to get some more fruit."

Darwen thought of Scarlett with her little coins and her big plans, and he thought of Luis and Calida and Eduardo and the monster that had taken them, and he knew, just *knew*, there was a connection that he had to make if he was to do any good at all.

The afternoon was to be spent in group study. Darwen, who couldn't face the prospect of working with Rich and Alex without something to distract them from their current moods, seized the opportunity to talk privately with Mr. Iverson as soon as the science teacher arrived. "Show him the coin, Rich," he said.

Rich's face brightened immediately.

"Wait," said Alex. "If this is Peregrine Pact stuff, you shouldn't be telling a teacher."

But Rich already had his arm in the air. "Sir?" he said. "Could you help us try to figure out what this is made of?"

As Alex glared at him, Mr. Iverson considered the coin.

"Where did you get this?" he asked, his face hawkish.

"Found it," said Darwen, ignoring Alex's told-you-so stare. "That woman—Scarlett Oppertune—was giving them out to the kids on the soccer field. She says they're gold."

Mr. Iverson looked at him. "You found it?"

Darwen blushed. "Kind of," he said. "One of them gave it to me."

He didn't know why, but he didn't want to discuss Mrs. Delgado or her missing daughter. Mr. Iverson returned his attention to the coin and nodded.

"I'm not sure we'll be able to do much," he said, "but there are some fairly simple tests used in archaeology to see if something is gold. Let me get everyone else started, and I'll come find you."

"I'll go get my field guide," said Rich.

"The birds and animals thing?" said Alex vaguely. She was fidgeting and glancing around as if looking for an opportunity to sneak off.

"No," said Rich, as if she was being unusually dull-witted, "the archaeology one."

"That got destroyed last year," said Alex.

"I got a new one," said Rich. "You didn't think I'd come to a place like this without it, did you?"

"How silly of me," muttered Alex as Rich headed down to the tent. "I know if I had a book about archaeology, I'd take it just about everywhere—to church, into the shower. Maybe he needs to feed it or it dies."

"What is it with you at the moment?" Darwen demanded.

"He shouldn't have told Iverson," she said. "We should be keeping this stuff to ourselves, not sharing it with the whole school."

"But there was something on your mind before that happened," Darwen pressed. "What?"

"Nothing," she said, looking away.

"Yes, there was," said Darwen. "You've been biting everyone's head off as soon as they speak to you, and you're twitchy all the time."

"Twitchy?"

"Yeah, like you want to be somewhere else."

"Somewhere I can take a bath, maybe, somewhere there isn't something lethal hiding under every bush?"

"No," said Darwen, "it's more than that. Ever since last night, you've been jumpy, impatient, like you're waiting to do something by yourself."

"A girl went missing last night, Darwen, or don't you remember? Taken right from her bed. And everything just goes on as normal, like nothing happened. Hikes and classes and stuff. I think Rich is right. It's not a Hillside kid, so no one cares."

"I don't think that's fair," said Darwen.

"And what about you, Darwen? All you're thinking about is your Silbrican mystery, like it's just an adventure."

"It's not an adventure; it's a *mission*."

"And while you're having fun with that, people are dying."

"We don't know that," said Darwen. "She might be okay. Somewhere."

"Well, animals then."

"Animals are dying? What do you mean?"

Alex hesitated, and as she looked away, the color rose in her cheeks. "Oh, you know, shrinking environments and Scarlett's plans for a hotel. And Chip Whittley killing that butterfly. And the entire village hunting a jaguar even though there were no paw prints anywhere near the house. It's stupid. And typical. If in doubt, kill something."

She sounded genuinely angry, but Darwen was sure there was something she was not saying, and when he continued to look skeptical, she turned back toward the tents.

"Here's Rich," she said. "Hi, Rich. Let's hear about those tests Mr. Iverson was talking about."

Rich was surprised, but only for a moment. He was too pleased by the idea of sharing the wonders of his field archaeology book with them. Darwen continued to watch Alex, and as she avoided his eyes, he became surer than ever that she was hiding something.

"Okay," said Rich. "So there are three tests we can do without any special equipment and a fourth we can do if we can get hold of some acid."

"Not sure I want to be handling acid even if we can find some," said Alex, all business now. "What are the other three?"

"We need an unglazed porcelain tile, a magnet, and a piece of glass," said Rich. "I have a magnet on the end of my flashlight, so I brought that too. It's pretty powerful."

"I'll get a glass from the kitchen," said Alex brightly. "They might have some unglazed ceramic as well. I'll take a look."

"Thanks!" said Rich. "She cheered up," he observed as Alex walked away.

"Didn't she just."

"What?"

"Don't know," said Darwen. "As usual, I have no clue what is going on."

"You think she's hiding something? From us? You're imagining it."

Darwen watched Alex positively prancing back up the path toward them, a water glass in one hand and a ceramic jug in the other, grinning like the cat that got the nondairy creamer.

"I hope you're right," he said.

Because if there was one thing he was sure about in the baffling haze that hung over this trip like the mist clinging to the jungle, it was that he needed his friends. Last night after they had squabbled, he had tossed and turned for hours. Some of it was the mystery and their lack of progress toward finding Luis and his brother, but some of it was just the tension he felt with Rich and Alex and knowing that they were right. It *had* been his fault. He had taken over, ignored their advice, and gotten them in trouble. He needed to be careful about that. Danger he could stand, but not loneliness. Not now.

"Okay," said Rich. "Pass me the jug, will you? Right, now run the coin against it."

"Done," said Alex.

"Did it leave a black mark on the ceramic?" asked Rich, head in his book.

"Nope," said Alex.

"Okay, so it's not pyrite—fool's gold. Could be the real thing. Now try the magnet."

Darwen took Rich's heavy flashlight and put it up against the coin.

"Anything?" said Rich.

Darwen pulled the flashlight slowly away.

"No," said Alex. "Wait. Try that again."

Darwen repeated the action, and this time it seemed like the coin stuck to the magnet for a moment.

"Maybe a tiny bit," said Alex.

"Hmmm," said Rich. "Pure gold should show no magnetic properties at all. Try the glass."

Alex took the glass. Gabriel was hovering at the edge of the table, watching closely, and a couple of the other students were craning to get a better look from their seats.

"Can you scratch the glass with the coin?" asked Rich.

Alex tried.

"Nothing," said Alex.

"Which means what?" said Darwen.

"All minerals have a measurement of hardness from one to ten," said Rich. "It's called the Mohs' scale. Glass has a hardness of 5.5, gold of 2.5 to 3. So true gold shouldn't scratch glass."

"And this didn't," said Alex. "So it's gold?"

"Not necessarily," said Rich. "It could be, or it could be made of something else with a similar hardness, like copper."

"So we don't know anything," said Darwen.

"If it's magnetic, then there's something other than pure gold mixed in, at the very least," said Rich. "Copper isn't magnetic either, so it can't be that, or not purely that."

Mr. Iverson returned with a box. "Oh, I see you found your book, Mr. Haggerty. Any progress?"

Rich repeated the results of the experiments so far and then summarized his instinct. "I'd say it is gold, but there are other minerals blended with the metal, so it's probably cheap."

"Which would suggest that the villagers are being ripped off," said Darwen.

"No surprises there," Alex remarked, shaking her head.

"Try this," said Mr. Iverson, setting the box on the table and opening it. Inside was a potent-looking microscope. "I hoped it might come in handy."

"Cool," said Rich.

As they set the microscope up, the crowd of students watching got larger, despite Alex's advice that they should all mind their own business. Rich turned on a light at the instrument's base, positioned the coin, and peered into the eyepiece. He adjusted the focus and magnification, and, for a long moment, no one spoke. Rich eventually sat back, but his face was confused, even shocked.

Mr. Iverson looked in, and his body suddenly became quite still and tense.

"What is it?" said Alex. "Here, let me see."

At last it was Darwen's turn, and at first he thought he'd made a mistake. The surface of the coin didn't look regular or solid at all. It was pocked with little holes and irregular shapes. He adjusted the focus and saw why the metal felt so uneven, even sharp to the touch. It looked like the surface of the little balls he sometimes made by combining the tinfoil wrappers off candy. If this was a coin, it was one unlike any he had ever seen before.

But why?

"What am I looking at?" he asked, still staring into the eyepiece. He rotated the coin slightly. As he did so, a tiny feature of the metal caught his attention. It looked oddly familiar. He stared at it, trying to remember where he had seen that precise shape before.

"I said the gold was probably very cheap," said Rich. "But that's not the only explanation. It could also be very old."

"How old?" asked Alex.

"Hundreds of years," said Rich. "Maybe more."

"It can't be," said Mr. Iverson.

"It would make sense," said Rich. "The impurities in the metal, copper and other minerals including trace elements of iron, which give it a slight magnetic quality."

Mr. Iverson began, "Are you suggesting—"

"What?" asked Alex, exasperated. "What do you think it is?"

And then Darwen remembered. At the heart of the coin, he could make out a tiny hook that had not been completely flattened into the surface, and now he could also see the way that the metal's marbled surface laid out the outline of a strange leg—a leg with talons on the end.

He sat up and gaped at the others.

"It's a pouncel," he said. "These coins have been stamped from the figurines they found on Caño Island."

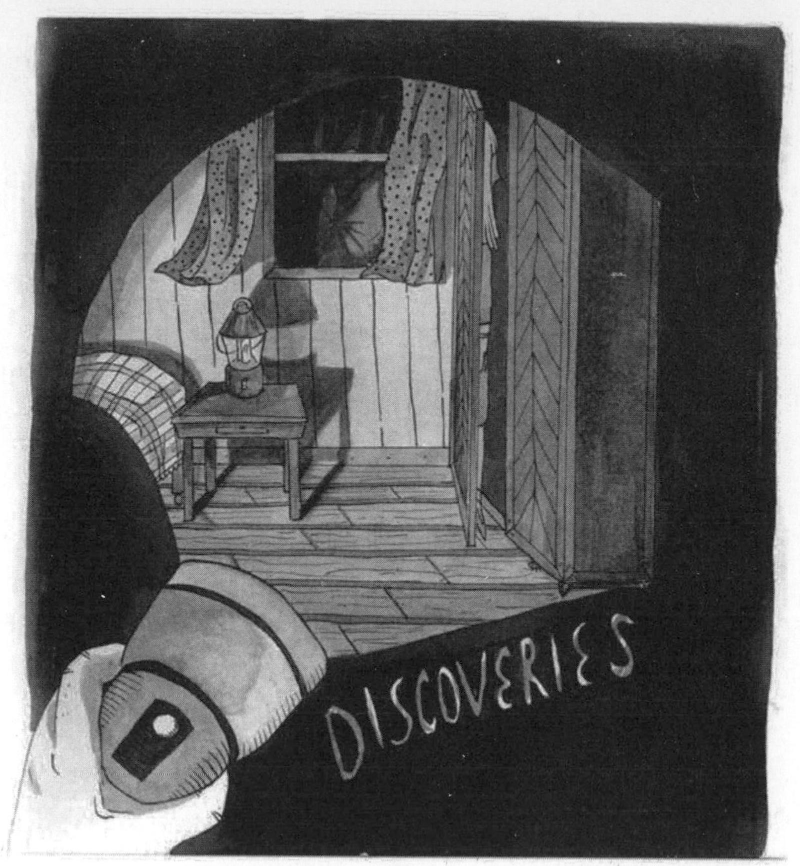

There were more red beans and rice for dinner, something even Alex couldn't get enthusiastic about. "Once or twice is fine," she exclaimed, exasperated. "Great, even. But every night? How about some jambalaya with jalapeño cornbread?"

"We eat what they eat," said Rich, nodding to the staff. "It's local stuff. That's why the fruit is so good. Anything else has to be imported, and that's expensive. In case you hadn't noticed, these people don't have a lot of money."

"Fair enough," said Alex, resolving to eat with greater enthusiasm. "And it is pretty good, really."

"What do they have," said Rich, putting his knife and fork down suddenly, "except their history and their life in the rainforest? Nothing. And Scarlett is taking those things away from them, paying them off with gold that is nothing more than the mangled remains of their own past."

Darwen and Alex stared at him, surprised as much by his passion as by his expression.

"The mangled remains of their own past," Alex echoed. "That's good. I'm gonna write that down. *Remnants* is better, though. The mangled remnants of their noble history."

"*Contempt* is what it is," said Rich, ignoring Alex's editorializing. "Scarlett is rubbing their noses in their own desperation. She comes in her helicopter and her fancy business suits, and she tells them they're poor and reminds them of how dangerous their life here is."

"Kind of is," said Alex.

"And then—just to show how little she respects them and their culture—she buys them off with—"

"The mangled remnants of a once noble past."

Rich turned to yell at her, but changed his mind. "Yes," he said. "Exactly."

Alex nodded thoughtfully.

"You're right," she said at last. "It's terrible. We should stop her."

"Could Scarlett know anything about the pouncels?" asked Darwen. "The real pouncels, I mean, not just the figurines."

"I don't see how," said Rich. "Why?"

Darwen scowled. "I don't know." He shrugged. "It just feels . . . weird. An odd coincidence."

"That's what coincidences are," said Alex. "They feel weird."

"Scrobbler technology in the jungle," said Darwen. "Missing kids. Creatures crossing over from Silbrica. I feel like I'm missing something."

"Like what?" asked Rich.

Darwen just shook his head and shrugged again.

"And we still don't know how to get back into Silbrica," said Alex. "Fat lot of good having your own pet mirroculist if there are no portals for him to open for you."

She was, annoyingly, maddeningly, right.

They cleared their dinner things away, played a casual game of darts during which everyone stood a long way from the board every time it was Alex's turn, and then went up to the washrooms to get ready for bed.

Darwen moved to turn on the tap, and it was there again in the mirror.

The laughing face.

He froze, looking at it from the corner of his eyes, terrified that if he moved a muscle, it would vanish. It was just as before, pink and shiny, the hard eyes with their manic glare and the gaping mouth. Then he heard it, the laughter cycling around and around through his head, and this time he saw the head jerk back once into blackness, then come back, as if yanked into place by a wire.

And suddenly he knew what it was.

The memory he had almost been able to taste came back to him clear and whole. He was, perhaps, seven. His family had taken a trip to the seaside in Blackpool, an old Lancashire resort town. They had gone to the fairground there, the theme park called the Pleasure Beach, which had been built for all those Victorian holidaymakers who had come by train over a century ago.

Inside the park, over by one of the rides, there had been a glass case containing a life-sized figure dressed as a clown, with a smaller clown on its lap. The sign above had indicated that it was Blackpool's "World-Famous Laughing Man." Darwen's dad had told him it hadn't always been dressed as it was now, but it had been there for decades, since before the war, he thought. It was mechanical. One minute it was sitting still and dead-looking, the next it would start rocking backward and forward in its chair, its head thrown back and this awful laughter coming from it. It never stopped. Just went on and on laughing and laughing all day. His mum had hated it, and it had given Darwen nightmares for weeks. Even now, the memory made him shiver. But if he was right, and that's what the image in the mirror was, then what was that flash of Darwen's past doing in a Costa Rican jungle camp?

That night Darwen lay awake, listening to the sounds of the forest, trying to make sense of all he had learned and trying just as hard to shut out the memory of the mechanical clown's hysterical laughter. Everything but the clown pointed back to Scarlett: her plans to get rid of the village, her money, which wasn't real money at all but a kind of ancient echo of Silbrica. Even the disappearance of the children seemed to be helping her get rid of the village. Could she be working for the Bleck?

Rich and Gabriel were both asleep, or seemed to be. Rich snored like a donkey, but Gabriel never made a sound, so that more than once Darwen shone his flashlight over to Gabriel's bed to make sure the boy was still there. Darwen felt sorry for him—and had since he'd arrived, though he knew he hadn't really helped make him feel welcome.

Maybe you should tell him why you're really here, he thought.

No, said Alex's voice in his head. *Bad idea. The kid is scared of his own shadow now; what would he be like knowing that the woods are full of monsters waiting to grab him?*

Darwen grinned in spite of himself. That was exactly what she would say, and he suspected she would be right. And then a word came to him, a word that didn't seem to belong in this set of ideas at all, but that somehow slotted itself in perfectly. The word was *helicopter*.

He breathed it aloud, then sat up, shrugging off the sheet and reaching for the flashlight. "Rich," he whispered. "Rich!"

But Rich didn't wake, and Darwen hesitated before poking him. He didn't want more bickering, he didn't want to get Rich into trouble again, and he certainly didn't want to wake Gabriel. For a moment his hand stayed where it was, index finger extended and ready to jab Rich in the shoulder.

But then he withdrew it and slid quietly out of bed. As he got dressed in the dark, he noted that the night was hot and heavy with the promise of more rain, so the tent felt clammy and oppressive. It wasn't much better outside, but there was a faint breeze coming in off the ocean. He shone his flashlight into his shoes to make sure nothing had crawled inside, then put them on, sitting on the edge of the platform and wondering how bad it would be if he was caught out of bed at night again.

The word *helicopter* hovered in his mind like the object itself had done the first time he'd seen it coming in low over the trees. That was how Scarlett had first arrived.

It had been dramatic and, most importantly, it had been loud. But since that first day, he had not heard it again. Which meant one of two things. Either Scarlett had another way of getting to and from the village—though there was no way she was hopping out of a boat and wading up through the surf in those immaculate high heels of hers—or she hadn't left. She could have come and gone by helicopter while Darwen had been hiking or out at Caño Island, but he had not left the camp since seeing her this morning, and there was no way that helicopter could have come and gone without him noticing it.

So where was she? Not here in the camp, surely. So she must be staying in the village. But where? Someone like her would loathe the living conditions in this place.

The answer came immediately. In his mind's eye he saw the carefully maintained hut set back from the others, the pink jacket with the brass buttons. How could he have thought a jacket like that would be worn by one of the local girls? The one he had seen sweeping the porch had left a bucket of cleaning supplies at the foot of the stairs just the way the maids he saw in his aunt's building did when they were going from one apartment to the next. There was no doubt that was Scarlett's place, and if she was spending whole nights in conditions she would surely despise, she must have a reason for it.

Maybe she knew where the tear in the barrier between

worlds was. Maybe it wasn't just a tear. Maybe it was a portal after all, a way into Silbrica that could be opened and closed on command. . . .

Darwen turned his flashlight to the path and set off along the coast and into the jungle. He moved quickly and quietly, keeping his eyes on the track and avoiding the leaf litter in which snakes might nestle. Once as he turned to look toward the ocean, he caught sight of what he first thought was a flittercrake—the strange flying creature he had once glimpsed in an Atlanta mall—but as the animal flew back and forth, he realized it was some kind of large bat that was fishing from the air with its hind feet. He shuddered and started walking again. He didn't mind bats on television, but the thought of those long, drooping legs tangling in his hair gave him the screaming creeps.

He hurried on through the steamy darkness and at last felt the relief of open sky as he got out from under the trees. There was the soccer field and, just beyond it, the huddle of buildings where the camp workers lived. There were no lights, no signs of movement, and the hammocks on the porches were all deserted. No one wanted to risk being outdoors at night.

Darwen turned off his flashlight and moved carefully between the buildings along the closest thing to a street, though it was little more than a path from which the tiny houses were set back, looking at each other. He walked past the oldest four, two on each side, moving toward the new one, which sat silent by itself, its back right against the tree line. As he got close, he could smell its fresh-cut timber, but that only made it feel out of place and a little sinister.

He had no idea what to do next.

He put one hand on the stair rail, then tested the first step with his foot. It creaked, and he adjusted, suddenly aware of his heart thudding in his chest. There was a window beside the door. It had mosquito netting tacked around it and curtains inside, but Darwen thought there was a gap between them. If he could get up there, he might be able to get a look in.

He tried the second step and, when it made no sound at all, the third. One more and he was up on the porch decking, only a few feet from the door. He lifted his right foot, spreading his arms for balancc, and took another step, listening hard.

Nothing.

One more step and he was touching the wall. He shifted, and the planking groaned loudly beneath him.

He froze, breath held, eyes wide and staring at the wall, terrified that even looking around would make more noise.

Seconds passed. Ten? Thirty? He wasn't sure.

At last he took the final step to the window and peered in through the two-inch gap in the curtains. There was only darkness.

Now what?

He considered shining the light in through the crack, but he knew that would just alert anyone inside to his presence. He had come this far. There was only one choice.

He took two quick, quiet steps, avoiding the plank that had creaked, and put his trembling fingers on the door handle. He grasped it, feeling the sweat on his palm, listening for any sign of movement beyond the constant hum of the jungle, and then, with infinite care, he turned it.

There was a tiny snap, and Darwen felt the weight of the door in his hand as it swung free. He pushed it carefully, and it made no sound as it opened.

Several things struck Darwen at once. First, he sensed the darkness inside soften a little, though he could still barely make anything out beyond hulking black outlines. There was a scent too, sweet like perfume but with something a little sour under it, masked like the persistent edge of vomit after a bathroom has been disinfected. He knew that if someone was lying awake, they would see him standing there in the doorway, but he needed the light, so he stayed where he was and waited.

Still, incredibly, nothing happened. No movement, no breathing. Nothing.

He took a step inside, hands outstretched in front of him, but he knew he would find nothing without light. His body was tense, and he felt cold, though sweat was running in his eyes. Carefully he turned and pushed the door silently so that it almost closed, then he dropped slowly to a crouch, put the flashlight down headfirst on the floor, and turned it on.

He paused and raised it just a crack off the floor. Thin, yellow light rippled around the room casting long, flat shadows all around. There was a wardrobe, a door to what was probably a tiny bathroom, a bedside table with a battery-operated lantern, another window looking down toward the sea, and . . . a bed. Darwen stared at it, trying to make sense of its lumps and creases. He raised the flashlight a fraction more, and now he could see.

There was no one there.

He released his breath in a long sigh that contained a laugh. He put one hand to his chest as if to calm his racing heart and then played a little more light about the room.

There was no gate to Silbrica here. No mirror, no oven door, nothing that might provide a portal for the pouncels.

He considered the carefully made-up bed. It hadn't been slept in. He shone the light underneath it, checked the bathroom—which also was mirrorless—and then opened the wardrobe. It was full of brightly colored suits on hangers. Darwen pushed a garish pink one aside and staggered back in horror.

Hanging on the rail, wearing the blue suit he had seen her in that morning, was Scarlett Oppertune.

It was Scarlett Oppertune, or something very like her. In fact, it looked like a Scarlett Oppertune *suit*, a costume that went beyond clothes and had some kind of mask built in. And skin-colored gloves. They hung there, limp and rubbery, but when Darwen plucked up the courage to touch them, they felt horribly like flesh. He shone the light on the thing's face and knew immediately that this was no mask. The detail was extraordinary, the tiny wrinkles, the eyelashes, the smear of makeup on the cheeks.

He forced himself to touch the face, to lift one drooping eyelid, and was repulsed to find a staring, if faded, eye glaring back at him.

His first thought was that Scarlett was dead, drained somehow, her skeleton removed so that she just hung there, but then he remembered that awful night when he and Alex had encountered the people who had called themselves the Jenkinses. What had seemed to be a kindly old grandmother and her husband had turned out to be little more than suits like this one, the true inhabitants being the giant insect-like creatures he had seen again only a couple of nights ago.

Darwen closed the wardrobc door so he wouldn't have to look at it anymore. He turned toward the bed, and, for the first time, his eyes strayed to the window. Feeling the air move fractionally, he realized it was open. He snapped off the light. Something was moving outside.

It was too dark to see clearly, but it seemed to Darwen that there was something like a gargantuan snake out there, yards long and as thick as an anaconda. He dropped to a crouch, hands gripping the window ledge, as he stared in fascinated horror.

The creature was moving. One end stayed almost still, while the other end—which Darwen thought was the head—rotated like the hand of a clock. As he watched, he saw it complete one cycle and then begin again. It traced one more circle, then started doing something else, pushing objects into place around the rim. In the dim light, Darwen thought that they rolled as the monster moved them.

The stone spheres, he thought. *And what the thing has just made is like the muddy hole I fell into.*

The thought was incomplete in his head when he realized that the creature outside had stopped what it was doing and was moving quickly across the ground toward the open window. Toward him.

Darwen gasped. He turned toward the door before realizing that he was on the wrong side of the bed.

The monster was almost at the house. He had no choice. He dropped to the floor and rolled under the bed just as the snake thing slid up the wall and in through the window. He felt the weight of it on the bed above him, saw the shadows leap as the lantern clicked on a soft, bluish glow, but it didn't pause, sliding over and down with a soft slap as it hit the floor inches from his head.

He lay absolutely still, stiff with fear and revulsion. The creature slithered heavily to the wardrobe, and Darwen couldn't help himself. He had to see. He angled his head back and watched as the creature reared up and wrenched the wardrobe open with its teeth. Its tail flexed, flicking a hair's breadth from Darwen's face, and then it slipped into the wardrobe among the hanging suits. Darwen gaped as the thing forced Scarlett Oppertune's slack jaws wide open and then eased itself nose first into her mouth. The long slow body followed, yard by terrible yard, and the Scarlett suit inflated unevenly, squirming, shuddering, filling. There was a series of metallic snaps, and with each one a flabby limb became firm and straight like the fabric of an umbrella tautening as it goes up. The new weight of the thing brought it down from the rack of hangers, but Scarlett Oppertune, high heels and all, stepped out of the wardrobe as if nothing could be more normal.

Darwen just stared, knowing that if she looked down, she would see him.

She didn't. She stalked back to the table and turned off the lantern, then climbed onto the bed and lay there. Darwen was motionless, wondering if she might hear his galloping heart no more than a foot away from hers, assuming the creature inhabiting her body had anything as ordinary as a heart.

He didn't know what the creature was, not really, but he had seen something very like it before. It had been the true shape of whatever lived inside Miss Murray, his former world studies teacher, whom Rich had called—with uncanny perception—Murray the Moray, like the eel with the razor-sharp teeth. She had led Greyling's attack on Hillside. Could that be why he had felt like Scarlett knew him, like she had almost called him by name? Could it really be Miss Murray? And if it was, what could that possibly mean beyond the fact that, if she got the chance, she would surely kill him?

He lay very still on his stomach, wondering how long it would take her to get to sleep, wondering if she would sleep at all, and what would happen if she suddenly got up and saw him lying there. He had to get out.

He had been able to get the front door open silently when he came in, and he hadn't re-latched it behind him. If he could crawl quietly across the floor, he might be able to slink out. He spread his fingers on the wooden floor and felt his muscles tighten as he prepared to move. He eased himself out a fraction, then paused, waiting. He could see the faintest graying of the blackness around the edge of the door, and he focused on that as he inched his way out from under the bed.

Slowly, so slowly it felt like hours, he raised himself onto his hands and knees, one tiny motion at a time. Keeping the toes of his shoes and the barrel of his flashlight off the floor, he began to creep toward the door: hand, then knee, then the other knee, then the other hand—four movements, each one a risk, to advance eight inches.

Then something touched his left hand.

A cockroach the size of a cell phone.

Darwen forced himself to stay still and silent as it climbed up his left arm and over his back. He fought the impulse to cry out, and he crawled another eight inches.

The roach rattled across the floor, and Darwen froze, sure that Scarlett would put the lamp on to see what was making the sound. The noise changed, and Darwen risked a look back into the darkness.

He thought he could just make out the shape of the bug moving up the leg of the bed and onto the thin covers, black against the pale sheet. It wandered up toward the pillows, and then, without warning, the figure in the bed, whose shape he had not been able to see properly, shifted suddenly. A pale hand snatched at the roach and lifted it wriggling up toward the head.

Darwen turned away as he heard the unmistakable crunch of teeth.

Then he was moving again, reckless in his desire to get out. He didn't look back, but he heard the slow chewing, felt the presence of the creature in the bed behind him like a nightmare he couldn't shake.

One more hand-knee "step" and he felt the door against his head. He moved, shifting the door fractionally, and, before he could stop it, it closed with an audible click that sounded like a gunshot in the silent hut.

There was a noise like a breath from the bed, and Darwen got clumsily to his feet, fumbling for the door handle as he turned to see if Scarlett was coming for him. From where he was, he couldn't see anything, wouldn't see her until she was virtually on top of him. The latch clicked again as he worked the handle, and this time he couldn't wait, couldn't be careful or slow. He snatched the door open and stepped hurriedly out, only just resisting the urge to sprint off the deck and down through the village.

He knew he was making noise, but fear drove the concern away. There was a flash of light, and he winced, sure it was Scarlett's lamp, sure that the creature inside her was coming after him, but then there was a crash of thunder overhead, and he realized it had just been lightning. By the time he reached the stairs, it was raining. He risked a look back, and as another ripple of lightning creased the sky, he saw that the door had swung softly shut. There was no sign of pursuit.

He wanted to get as far from this place as possible, but there was one more thing he had to see. Keeping a safe distance from the open window, he ran silently through the rain around the side of the house to the spot where he had seen the thing like Miss Murray—or Scarlett, or whatever he was supposed to call her now—in her eel shape scooping out the saucer-like depression in the ground.

He found it easily and without needing the flashlight. It was exactly as the other had been, and he had been right: she had circled the shallow hole with a dozen of the ancient stone spheres.

But why? She could easily have been seen doing it, so why take the risk?

Darwen crouched on the edge of the circle, looking back up to the isolated hut. The rain was getting heavier by the moment, and little rivulets were forming in the village and rushing down toward the beach at his back. The circle itself was starting to fill with water. It was time for Darwen to get back.

He got up to leave, and the shift in his perspective coupled with a timely sheet of lightning overhead revealed something new: his own reflection. As the shallow depression filled with water, it was turning into a great mirror!

Darwen stared, his mind racing, oblivious to the driving, hammering rain. Then the pool was full to the rim of stone spheres, and something happened.

There was another flicker of energy, but it wasn't lightning. It was soft and greenish, and it ran around the mirror-like pool, leaping from stone to stone as the circuit completed. And then the surface of the water was buckling and sloshing not because of the raindrops hurtling into it but because something was coming through, something far too big to be contained in that shallow puddle.

It was long and thick and studded with suckers, purplish and black on the top, but pale beneath, and though it looked snakelike, Darwen knew instantly what it was. The tentacle reached its pointed tip into the sky as if tasting the air, and then it surged through, yards at a time, and behind it came more, filling the pool as the monster squeezed in through the portal.

Darwen's terror finally broke out. He gave first one cry and then another, shouting to the villagers to wake up, to defend themselves before the thing in the pool took their children.

Lights came on, and he saw the pale face of Scarlett Oppertune in her window. But he did not run. Instead he kicked at the stone spheres, pushing them away from the circle. The greenish light around the pool flickered and stalled. The great tentacles seemed to hesitate, hanging suspended in the air with a strange and sudden stillness, and then they and the Insidious Bleck to which they belonged were sucked back into the pool with a splash and were gone.

No one believed Darwen. He had no hope of persuading the adults about what he had really seen, so he made up some half-baked story about sleepwalking. He didn't care if the villagers thought him stupid or blamed him for interrupting their night's sleep. It didn't matter to him whether or not they knew that he had probably just saved another of their children from the monster in the pool. He had just found himself out here, he said, woken by the thunder, and then he thought he had seen something, but it had turned out to be a trick of the light.

But if he thought that he would be allowed to get away with merely looking foolish, Darwen had another think coming. One of the men sleeping in the village was Jorge, and he was instantly suspicious. He insisted on personally escorting Darwen back to the camp, where he was handed over to the teachers to repeat his sleepwalking yarn.

"And you do this a lot, do you?" said a bleary-eyed Mr. Sumners. "I don't recall your aunt referring to your, ahhh, somnambulant strolls on your medical form."

"My what?" said Darwen.

"Your sleepwalking," said Sumners, his patience strained to the breaking point. "You'd think she would have mentioned something like that, considering where we were going."

"Oh," said Darwen. "No, I've never done it before."

"Is that right?" said Sumners. "Next time do us all a favor and sleepwalk into the ocean, Arkwright, okay?"

"Yes, sir," said Darwen.

"Looks like you're on tent-cleaning duty again tomorrow," he said.

"But sir—"

"Good night, Mr. Arkwright. Try to make it back to your tent without dropping off. I'd hate for you to step on something deadly."

"Yes, sir. Right, sir. Good night, sir."

Darwen trudged back toward his tent with his flashlight trained disconsolately on the ground, so he didn't see Mr. Peregrine until he almost bumped into him.

"Want to tell me what really happened?" asked the teacher.

They walked down to the beach, where they wouldn't be overheard, and sat on a fallen palm trunk facing the black ocean. The torrential rain had stopped as suddenly as it had started, and the sky was already clear enough to see stars.

Darwen told Mr. Peregrine everything: Scarlett's sinister transformation, the part played by the stone spheres in the creation of the portal, and the terrible thing that had started coming through it, a creature Darwen was now prepared to name aloud. "It was the Insidious Bleck," he said. "I'm sure of it."

"Well," said Mr. Peregrine, "let's not get ahead of ourselves. I think you are right that the stone spheres are somehow connected to the portals—that would explain why the ancient peoples who lived here treated them with such reverence—but what you saw coming through could have been any number of Silbrican beasts. As to the nature of Miss Oppertune . . ." He hesitated thoughtfully, and Darwen felt his doubt.

"What?" said Darwen. "I saw the suit thing the creature inside her used. I saw her out there making the portal."

"Well, it was very dark, Darwen," said Mr. Peregrine, "and you were—understandably—scared. There's no shame in admitting that. You need not invent—"

"I'm not *inventing* anything," said Darwen, his confusion turning to anger. "I know what I saw."

Mr. Peregrine held up his hands in surrender and smiled. "Darwen, you have done what you came here to do," he said, "and it is a remarkable achievement of which you should be very proud. You have solved the mystery of how Silbrican creatures are coming through, and this will undoubtedly save lives. But your suspicion of Miss Oppertune, unpleasant though her plans may be, seems to me beside the point."

"No," said Darwen, standing up, his face dark with fury. "The children haven't been taken by Silbrican animals hunting at random. It's the Insidious Bleck, and it's being brought through on purpose by the thing we used to call Miss Murray. I don't know why, but that is what's happening."

"If that were the case," said Mr. Peregrine reasonably, "why would Miss Oppertune be trying to drive the villagers away? She would want the children here."

"I don't know," said Darwen. "You tell me. You're supposed to be the one who helps me figure this stuff out, aren't you?"

"Yes," said Mr. Peregrine, "I am. And I am telling you that your work is done, and well done. I will pass the information about the stone spheres along to the council, and they will seal the breaches by their own means. You have completed the task assigned to you and can now concentrate on enjoying the rest of the trip with your friends."

"What about Luis?" asked Darwen, his voice a little high.

"It's over, Darwen," said Mr. Peregrine. "You have a busy and fun-filled day tomorrow. You'll need your strength to enjoy it. Bedtime."

He spoke with such finality that Darwen didn't bother protesting. He turned, leaving the old man sitting in the dark, and made for the tent camp, dazed and struck by the special pain that comes from feeling totally powerless.

"Been out for a stroll?"

It was Rich. He was sitting in the dark in his pajamas on the platform outside the tent. He snapped his flashlight on and shone it in Darwen's face.

"Not now, Rich," said Darwen. "I'll tell you all about it in the morning."

"Why bother?" said Rich. "You obviously didn't think I was worth taking along wherever you've been."

"What?" said Darwen. "Rich, seriously, this isn't the time."

"Sure," said Rich, whose face was pink with anger, "why tell me? It's your business, right? Private mirroculist work?"

"Shhh," said Darwen, glancing at the tent. "Gabriel might hear."

"Yeah," said Rich, getting up and turning back toward the tent. "Wouldn't want anyone to know what's going on. You're big on secrets, aren't you, Darwen?"

"It's not like that!" Darwen hissed.

"Really?" said Rich, bitter and unconvinced. "How many times have you been through to Silbrica since Halloween by yourself, when you knew Alex and me were dying to go in with you?"

"You weren't there!" Darwen exclaimed. "It was Christmas. You were at home."

"You could have invited us for a sleepover," said Rich, even redder now as he revealed a hurt he knew sounded petty and stupid.

"A sleepover?" exclaimed Darwen, who couldn't believe he was having this conversation after everything that had happened over the last couple of hours.

"A sleepover," Rich snapped. "It's something friends do."

"Silbrica is dangerous, Rich! Don't you get it? It's not a holiday resort where you go to look at neat animals like they're in a zoo. Half of those animals would take your head off as soon as look at you."

"So you're protecting us?" Rich shot back. "Is that it?"

"Yes!" said Darwen, realizing for the first time that this was true. "You know how many times I've gone over what happened at Halloween and thought about how badly it might have ended? If something had happened to you or Alex? You know how I would have felt about that?"

"Because it's all about how you feel, right, Darwen?"

"That's not what I meant."

"You didn't even tell us about Weazen until after we saw him," said Rich, furious now. "How is that protecting us?"

"I just didn't think you needed to know!" Darwen roared back.

Immediately, he wished he hadn't said it.

"And there it is," Rich said, quieter now. "You thought you knew best. Again. Okay. Now we know. Well, Darwen, thanks for your protection, but for future reference, we don't need it. We don't want it."

"Fine!" yelled Darwen.

"Fine!" shouted Rich.

"Wait," said Darwen, but Rich was already unzipping the tent and crawling in.

Darwen sat outside in the dark for another five minutes before following him. He didn't think Rich was asleep, but when Darwen whispered his name, he didn't respond. It was some time before Darwen climbed into bed, longer still before he fell asleep, and his dreams were full of the mechanical clown lurching in its chair, roaring with laughter, while great snakes with Scarlett Oppertune's face coiled around it.

Darwen got up when the howler monkeys started calling. He took a cold shower, dressed, and ate alone as soon as Torres had laid out the breakfast buffet. He reported to the kitchens and told the staff he was to help with cleaning again. As the other students came up to breakfast, he went from tent to tent with a bucket of cleaning supplies. When he came to Mr. Peregrine's tent, he waited to be sure the ex-shopkeeper wasn't inside before going in to clean. The vinegary scent was stronger now, but Darwen didn't try that hard to get rid of it. Serve the old man right for betraying him.

He knew he was overreacting, but that was what it felt like to Darwen. Mr. Peregrine had not believed him about Scarlett and had ordered him to abandon his search for Luis and the others. Either on his own authority or on the Guardians' orders, the old shopkeeper had betrayed him.

When Darwen emerged, Alex was waiting for him, eating fruit from a bowl.

"This cleaning thing wasn't supposed to be a career choice," she said. "The word is that you decided to wake the entire village in the middle of the night. Sleepwalking, supposedly, which is about the dumbest excuse I ever heard. Rich doesn't know any different and 'would prefer not to discuss it, if you don't mind,' so I'm assuming you two had one of those he-broke-my-toy-tractor fights that boys have. Wanna give me your version?"

Darwen sighed and sat on the edge of the platform beside his bucket. He told her the same story he had told Mr. Peregrine, this time including an account of that conversation and the one he had had with Rich.

"Wow," she said. "You are making yourself popular. Thought about running for class president?"

"We don't have a class president," said Darwen.

"Sure we do, Darwen. You're the very first. And it's all because we love you."

"Were you planning on saying anything helpful, or are you just here to take the mickey?"

"See, why couldn't you have fallen back on a colorful British expression like that last night? No one would have understood a word you said, which would have been better than that sleepwalking hogwash. Honestly, that's the best you could come up with? That's just sad."

"You believe me?"

"About Scarlett the snake woman and the Insidious child-nabbing tentacled whosit?" she said. "Sure. You're dumb, but I can always tell when you're lying."

"Thanks a lot," said Darwen.

"You're welcome. Anyway, you need to finish up. We're going zip-lining, whatever that is. Meet on the beach in"—she checked her watch—"half an hour. Get your bug repellant, camera, strong shoes, blah, blah, blah. The usual surviving-in-the-wilderness stuff."

"I'm ready," said Darwen. "Why don't you hang out with me for a while? I've been trying to think through why Scarlett might want the land the village is on if it's not just about building a hotel."

"Not now," said Alex. "I've got to get ready."

"I'll come with you," said Darwen.

Alex hesitated. "I have to . . . do private stuff," she said. "Pee and what have you."

Darwen considered her. She was being evasive. Maybe she was going to report back to Rich. "Come on, Alex," he began, but she cut him off.

"It's not just Rich who's mad at you, Darwen, okay?" she said. "You did it again, going off by yourself, figuring you'd just report your adventures to us afterward. We're not your fans, Darwen. We're supposed to be friends. More than that. We're the Peregrine Pact."

"I'm not sure I want to have much to do with Mr. Peregrine, if you want to know the truth," said Darwen.

"So you really are alone," she said. "I hope that makes you happy."

And with that she stalked off.

With nothing better to do, Darwen went down to the beach early and sat on the same palm trunk where he had talked to Mr. Peregrine the night before. Gabriel was already there, alone and wearing the ridiculous cap with the veil again.

"Cleaned our tent out," said Darwen.

"Good," said Gabriel, adjusting the veil so that Darwen could see his face.

"You should get out more," said Darwen. "Get some air and sunshine. Maybe we could organize another football—I mean, soccer—game with the kids from the village."

Gabriel's eyes flickered, and Darwen thought he looked pained.

"Tough here, isn't it?" said Darwen. "I mean, exciting and full of neat stuff, of course, but still . . . tough. And then these kids going missing . . ."

Gabriel looked down, but Darwen caught that flash of anguish in his face again.

"Listen," he said. "If you need someone to chat to, you know, since you're new and all, Rich and I are—"

"What?" said Gabriel, looking up again, his face now blank. "Sounded like you were yelling at each other last night."

Darwen said nothing, relieved to see Genevieve Reddock leading a gaggle of girls down from the camp, looking excited and—as always seemed to be the case on this trip—a little uneasy.

"What's zip-lining?" said Darwen, changing the subject as the girls splashed noisily past them and climbed into the first boat.

Gabriel shrugged. "I guess we have to get there by boat," he said.

"Always," said Darwen miserably.

They waded out and climbed aboard next to Genevieve, Naia, and Mad. Mr. Peregrine was already on board, clad again in those ridiculous rubber waders. Darwen said nothing and avoided his eyes. There was no sign of Rich. They were pulling away from shore before Darwen saw him, walking down to one of the other boats with Alex.

"How long will we be in the boat?" he asked Jorge.

"Ten minutes," said the guide. "We're just going around to Drake Bay."

Darwen breathed a sigh of relief.

"Is it true that you sleepwalk?" asked Naia Petrakis.

"Not usually," said Darwen.

"Rough place to start," supplied Mad.

"Yeah," said Darwen, turning away in the hope they would drop the subject. He seemed to be doing a lot of that lately. The thought made him feel more alone than he had since coming to Hillside. He thought of Lancashire, which felt so very far away now, and a wish rose in his mind, clear and sharp and fully formed, an image of him returning to his parents and telling them about all the amazing things he had seen in Costa Rica. They would sit with plates of steaming hotpot and talk about everything that had happened since he left England, since they had died. He stared at the water as the boat bounced over its surface, turning away so that no one could see his face.

Since he and Gabriel had been the first to get aboard and had taken seats by Mr. Peregrine in the prow, they were the last to get out, by which time the boat was rocking and sliding in the surf. Darwen went first, but the boat pitched suddenly. He stumbled, but Mr. Peregrine came off worse. As the old man slipped backward, his hand reached for the prow and caught on a rusted rivet, which stood proud and sharp.

"Mr. Peregrine!" Darwen shouted. "Are you okay?"

"What?" said the teacher, his face blank.

"Your hand," said Darwen.

"Let me see," said Jorge, scrambling over.

"It's fine," said Mr. Peregrine.

Jorge didn't listen, but turned the teacher's hand over. He winced, sucking the air in between his lips, and for a moment Darwen's head swam. There was a deep gash running across Mr. Peregrine's palm, deep enough that Darwen could see what looked like muscle inside, though the cut beneath the flap of skin was bloodless.

Jorge exclaimed in Spanish, then helped Mr. Peregrine up and over the side, though the water was waist deep. He hurried Mr. Peregrine up the beach to where a cooler of supplies had been unloaded and took out a first aid kit. Darwen and Gabriel splashed after him, laboring in the surf, feeling the shingle beneath their feet sucking away with each out-rushing wave. By the time the boys reached Jorge, Mr. Peregrine's hand had already been smeared with ointment and bandaged. The teacher looked calm, but Jorge and Gabriel were both anxious.

"You want to go back to the camp?" asked Jorge.

"No," said the teacher. "I need to supervise the excursion."

"It must hurt," said Jorge.

"Not as much as you would think," said Mr. Peregrine, climbing carefully out of his waders and smiling, "and I'm tougher than I look."

Darwen watched them as the girls crowded around, and there was something odd about the way Gabriel looked at Mr. Peregrine. The boy's eyes were hard and focused.

Mr. Peregrine, for his part, merely shrugged and smiled blithely. "See," he said. "It has already stopped bleeding. Let's not overreact. Very well," he added, turning to the gathering students, "this way, everyone."

Darwen glanced at Gabriel, but whatever he thought he had seen in the boy's face before was gone, so that he wondered if he had imagined it.

Once the other boat had arrived, a pair of rickety jeeps, a pickup truck, and an ancient minibus ferried the students up through Drake Bay and into the heavily wooded hills above the village. Darwen made the journey in the open back of the pickup, which would have been fun if he had had someone to share it with. Rich had deliberately hung back to travel in the minibus with Alex.

The zip line turned out to be what Darwen called an aerial runway: a cable strung between poles down which you slid. Darwen had seen them on playgrounds and campsites, but nothing could have prepared him for the length and height of this particular specimen. It was made up of twenty stages, some of them hundreds of meters long, designed to take them through the very canopy of the rainforest and back to the campsite. They hiked up to the starting point—a wooden platform built around a massive tree that had to be accessed by ladders—wearing helmets and a complex system of straps and carabineers.

"It's perfectly safe," said Jorge, smiling.

It didn't feel it. The first platform was a hundred feet in the air, and the cable extended out over a valley that fell sharply away. The greenery below didn't seem too distant, but Darwen knew they were looking at the tops of trees, some of which were very tall. It was a long way to fall if something went wrong.

"Who is going to go first?" asked Jorge.

Everyone looked around, some uncertain, some clearly afraid. Darwen's eyes met Rich's, and for a second he thought there would be a shared comment or joke, but Rich scowled and looked away.

"I'll go first," volunteered Darwen.

He had come all this way. He wasn't about to let Rich spoil it.

Jorge and the pickup driver checked his harness, snapped a new cable in place, and told him how to control the speed of his descent.

"Put your right hand up here," instructed Jorge. "If you are going too fast, lean back and pull down on this leather part. This is your brake."

Darwen couldn't see the "brake" making much difference, but he could feel everyone watching him and was determined not to show his fear.

"Have fun, Arkwright," called Nathan. "Try not to fall hundreds of feet to your messy death."

"Ready?" said Jorge, swinging him into position.

"Ready," Darwen lied.

And then he was off.

For a split second he thought he had come unlatched, that the cable had broken and he was just falling, but the sensation passed, and he was soon arcing out over the treetops, speeding faster and faster, the drone of the pulley wheels rising in pitch as he hurtled along. Trees whipped past in a flash of green, and then he was out in the blue air, looking down on the jungle canopy, swooping birdlike toward the next station, where one of the jeep drivers was waiting, braced for impact. For a moment all the tension, problems, and anxieties of the trip fell away, and Darwen was just a boy flying above the treetops and feeling the wind on his face.

He whooped with delight, and an unmistakable bird called back at him before taking flight, a bird with a beak as long and heavy as its body.

"A toucan," he exclaimed as he barreled into the pickup driver. "I saw a toucan!"

His fear was gone, as were all his concerns about Silbrica and Rich. He led the way, stage by exhilarating stage. The zip line led them steadily back down toward the tent camp, and two hours later they were trekking along a path that emerged behind the bathrooms.

Darwen's uncomplicated happiness at the thrill of it all was disturbed only once, a little over halfway down, when he realized that the towering trees around him showed signs of considerable damage, as if something large had been moving through the canopy, snapping heavy branches as it went. He might not have thought much of it, except that he caught Jorge studying the damage with the same look of concern that he exhibited on the night the village girl had gone missing. It wasn't over, no matter what Mr. Peregrine said. Somehow he would find those kids and bring them home again.

And now he knew how to do it.

The stone spheres could be made into a portal with

nothing more than water and his mirroculist talents. He just had to gather some together, get away from everyone else, and cross over to Silbrica. He even knew where he could find the stone balls, and just as he was trying to figure out how to get back to them, he had a stroke of luck. It came in the form of an announcement from Mr. Iverson over lunch.

"Those who wish to stay in the camp this afternoon can do so," he said, "but we will be taking two boats out to Caño Island again, one for those who wish to do some more snorkeling, the other for any who want to return to the archaeological site."

That was it. Finally, after weeks of frustration, Darwen was going to be able to do something. He was going to Silbrica, and he was sure that on the other side he would find Luis, Eduardo, Calida, and the others. He didn't need Mr. Peregrine. He was going to complete his mission—his real mission—by himself.

But even as he thought this, he found himself looking around for Rich and Alex. They were huddled together, talking earnestly as they sipped from straws stuck in green coconuts. Even as he watched, Alex got up and came over. "Mr. Richard Haggerty requests the pleasure of your company at the Caño Island dig site," she said.

"I'll bet that's not the way he said it," said Darwen.

"Not exactly," said Alex. "He thinks you ought to go

there. See if there's anything you can learn about the pouncels."

"And you?" said Darwen, suddenly hopeful that Alex would come too. He needed a buffer between himself and Rich right now.

"He thinks I should come too," said Alex, "but I'm not gonna."

"Come on, Alex," said Darwen. "He won't even talk to me if you aren't there."

"Oh, I see," said Alex. "So you don't want me there because I'm your friend and the only person who doesn't think you are a lying snake, but because you want me to run interference for you with Rich."

"Run interference?" said Darwen.

"It's a football term," Alex snapped. "American football. You might wanna bone up on the culture that you, ya know, *live in*. Anyway, what I'm saying is that I'm not going to be your translator or your nursemaid or the padding that stops you from knocking each other's corners off."

"Is that another football phrase?"

"No, that's just me."

"But Alex . . ." Darwen implored.

"I have spoken," Alex announced, drawing herself up to her full height. "Do not ask me again."

"Fine," said Darwen. "Don't help."

"Oh, I'm helping," she said. "I'm helping you both to

grow as people. Uncle Bob says that to me a lot. I think he got it from daytime TV. It's what he says when he knows I'm not happy with him, which is pretty much always, but this time I think it's actually on the money. Patch up your own squabbles, Darwen. You'll grow as a person."

And with that, she stalked off, not toward the tents but back to her table. She glanced quickly around and took a bowl of grilled chicken, then headed swiftly back toward the showers.

Darwen frowned. He didn't like being lectured by Alex, even when she was right. He considered going to find Rich, but decided he would yell at her instead.

He ambled up the track to the bathrooms, but there was no sign of Alex. He called her name and walked around the block twice, then followed the path into the woods, the one that led to the last stage of the zip line. He walked a few hundred yards into the forest, climbing steeply all the way, but there was still no sign of her, and his anger turned into confusion. Where had she gone? He paused, and through the perpetual hum of the jungle came the sound of voices.

Or, rather, the sound of *a* voice: Alex.

She was burbling in a low, musical tone, like she was talking to a baby.

The sound came from some distance off the path to his left, but he couldn't see far enough through the trees to pinpoint the spot. He stepped carefully into the leaf litter, watching for signs of movement underfoot, and took a few stealthy paces. The sound of the voice went away and then came back, nearer now. Darwen walked a little further, and as he emerged from behind a massive tree whose trunk seemed composed of several plants that had grown into a single mass, he saw her.

She was sitting on the ground, cooing over something, and, as Darwen watched, her hand reached into the bowl of chicken and dropped some of it. Something on the ground reached up and snatched at the meat. Something apelike but with the distinctive head of a large cat.

Darwen gasped, and as he did so, his weight shifted. A twig snapped underfoot, and Alex's head spun around. Her eyes found him, and she leaped to her feet, her face a mask of rage.

"You *followed* me?" she bellowed.

"What are you doing?" Darwen roared back. "You're feeding one of those things?"

"It's hurt, okay? It got shot, and I've been looking after it. So now you know. Now you can take off, Darwen Arkwright!"

"Are you nuts?" said Darwen, closing on her. "Those things are dangerous!"

"You sound like Scarlett."

"You saw what they did to the tapir."

"*They*, Darwen, *plural*. This is *one*. It's young and it's hurt."

"And what if the others come looking for it?"

"They haven't so far."

"How long have you been doing this? Were you ever going to tell us?"

"What, only you are allowed to have secrets, Mr. Mirroculist?"

"That is so not fair," said Darwen.

"I told Sarita," said Alex. "She helped me get food for it from the kitchens."

"You told *Sarita*?!" Darwen exclaimed. "Are you out of your tree? We have a mission, Alex! We're supposed to be finding the missing kids." He took a furious step toward her.

The motion spooked the pouncel, which got awkwardly to its feet and limped a few paces away, where it sat, baring its fangs and hissing.

"Don't scare it!" yelled Alex, though the creature seemed as alarmed by her voice as by his.

"That thing could take your hand off, and you're feeding it like it's a pet rabbit?" Darwen shouted. "That is so stupid."

"Stupid?" roared Alex, rising and squaring up to him as if ready to throw a punch. "You calling me stupid?"

Darwen braced himself, but before she could come at

him, the pouncel took another shrinking step away.

"Wait," said Alex, taking a step toward it, but the movement only made it break into a run. Alex blundered after it, but the pouncel sped up, springing unevenly on its injured hind leg. In a moment, it was gone.

"Look what you did!" yelled Alex, rounding on Darwen, her eyes bright. "It's gone, and something will get it or someone will shoot it, and it's your fault."

"I didn't mean to!" said Darwen. "I just wanted to talk."

"Well, I don't want to talk, Darwen, okay? Not now, not ever. Just go away."

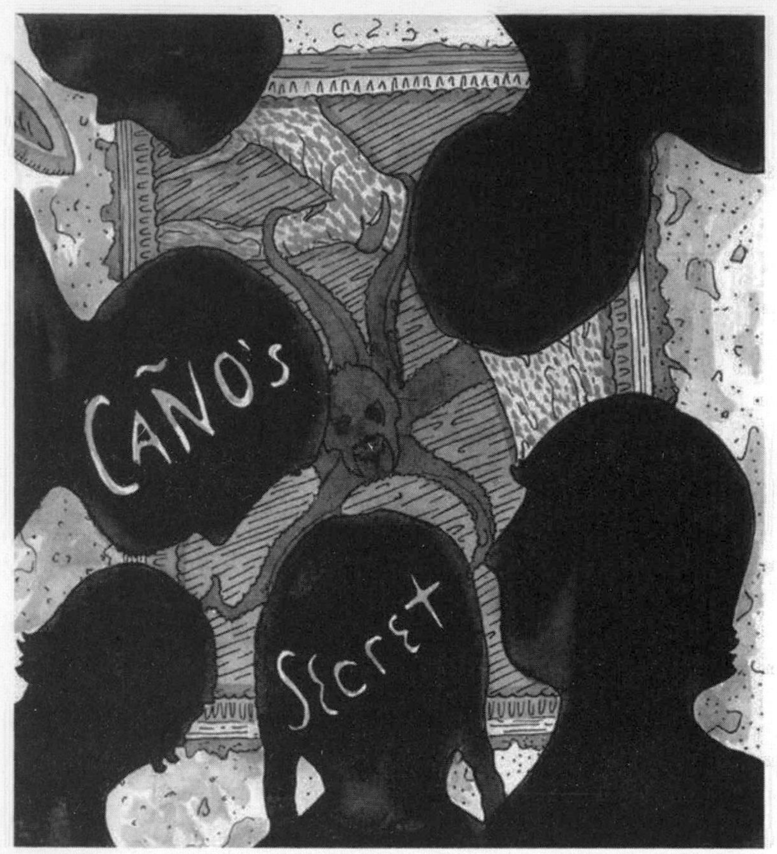

Darwen had never seen Alex so angry. He left her but did not know where to go. Rich was in the tent, but Rich wasn't talking to him either, and Mr. Peregrine was now, as far as Darwen was concerned, just another teacher. So he sat alone at one of the dining-shelter tables, which was piled with bundles of sticks and lengths of string, and looked out upon what had turned into a hot and glorious day feeling utterly miserable.

"Homesick, Arkwright?" called Nathan Cloten. He

was playing darts with Chip Whittley in a recess at the back of the shelter.

"Not now, Nathan," said Darwen, wishing he'd spotted them before sitting down.

"Probably not homesick anyway," Chip observed. "For him and Haggerty this is probably paradise. Haggerty lives in a barn with no roof, and Arkwright doesn't have a real home, do you, Arkwright?"

Darwen's hands recognized the sticks for what they were before his conscious mind did. He whirled around, fluidly fitting an arrow into one of the few finished bows and aiming it first at Nathan, then at Chip.

They ducked comically, but they were both holding the darts they had been playing with. Darwen glanced at the arrow he had loaded. It was just a stick: straight, but without a tip of any kind. Their darts, on the other hand, had sharp metal points.

He put the bow down as quickly as he had snatched it up.

But if he thought that would end the matter, he was sorely mistaken. The two boys approached his table and stood looming over him. Chip snatched the bow and arrow off the table.

"Gonna shoot us, Arkwright, like some Indian savage?" asked Nathan.

"Leave me alone, Nathan," said Darwen.

"Or what?" taunted Chip. He had unscrewed the head of one of the darts and was trying to fit it to the arrow shaft.

"Fine," said Darwen, standing up. He just couldn't be bothered with this, and the students and teachers were already starting to gather in the camp below for the afternoon excursions. "You want to hang out here by yourselves? Fine by me."

He started to walk away.

"Hey," yelled Chip, "we didn't give you permission to leave!"

"Whatever," Darwen answered.

He didn't hear the creak of the bow or the thrum of its string. He didn't hear the whoosh of the arrow through the air. He didn't know Chip had shot at him until he felt the arrow's two inches of needle-sharp steel slam into his shoulder blade.

The pain was sudden and intense. He cried out and reached behind him in disbelief, half turning in the process. He saw Chip, his face a mask of calm, smiling slightly, but Nathan looked horrified. Darwen stumbled against one of the dining shelter's roof supports, conscious that the dart-tipped arrow waggled and slid out as he fell.

"Whittley!" someone bellowed.

Darwen was sprawled across a bench, but he thought the voice was Mr. Iverson's. There were more shouts, and he felt hands on him.

"Get Jorge and the first aid kit," said Mr. Iverson. "Put that down, Whittley!"

"I'm fine," said Darwen, sitting up. "I just lost my balance."

He turned around and saw Naia, her face pale and scared, holding the arrow with the dart tip, its point smeared with blood.

"What do you think you're doing, Whittley?" said Mr. Iverson. "This is barbaric! You could have caused serious injury. I've never seen such stupidity from a Hillside student. At home, this would be a matter for the police."

That last phrase wiped the smirk off Chip's face. His haughty self-confidence fell away completely, and he looked suddenly young and scared. "Sorry, sir," he said, his eyes cast down.

"Apologize to Mr. Arkwright," said Mr. Iverson, glaring at him.

"Sorry, Darwen," said Chip quickly. "I didn't mean to."

"It's okay," said Darwen. "It doesn't hurt that much."

This was a lie, but by the time Jorge had finished cleaning and patching it, it was barely even noticeable. "Change the Band-Aid every few hours," said the guide, "and keep it clean. If it swells or gets red, let me know."

"Well," said Darwen, twisting his head over his shoulder, "I can't really see it."

"Mr. Haggerty," said Mr. Iverson. "You are sharing a

tent with Mr. Arkwright, yes?"

Rich nodded but said nothing.

"Then you will keep an eye on his injury."

Rich's eyes met Darwen's, and he nodded. Chip was looking at the floor while Miss Harvey berated him further. Everyone was staring at Chip with undisguised bitterness, and his eyes shone with tears. Darwen even felt a little sorry for him. Even Nathan had backed away from his friend, as if he had something infectious.

Darwen walked down to the beach, conscious that Rich was shadowing him, looking anxious, even a little guilty.

"I'm fine," Darwen repeated.

"When we get back from the dig, I'll take the Band-Aid off and check it," said Rich. "We should wash it with drinking water."

"It's okay, really," said Darwen. As they walked away from the others, he looked at his friend and took a breath. "There's something I need to tell you," he said. "Several things, actually. First, you'll never believe why Alex has been sneaking off to the woods. She's been looking after one of the pouncels."

"What?" exclaimed Rich, stopping in his tracks.

"It got shot and couldn't walk properly, so she's been feeding it."

"Feeding it what, her fingers?" said Rich. "Is she insane?"

"No more than usual," said Darwen.

It was terrible. They were discussing something awful, something that had left Alex hurt and furious, and they were doing it moments after Darwen had taken an arrow in the shoulder, but he couldn't help grinning. They were, after all, talking again.

"I don't know if we have to wait until sundown with these portals," Darwen was saying, "but we can use the stone spheres on Caño to cross over."

He couldn't help the tremor of excitement in his voice.

They climbed into the boat. Other than Jorge and Mr. Iverson, who were sitting all the way in the prow and out of earshot, the students were jockeying for places aboard the other boat. Snorkeling was still a lot more popular than archaeology. Darwen noticed that there was no sign of Chip or Nathan and thought, with a flash of grim amusement, that at very least they would be spending the afternoon cleaning tents. Only Gabriel joined Darwen's group.

"You wouldn't prefer to go swimming?" asked Rich.

"Not today," said Gabriel, adjusting his veil. "I thought the archaeology thing sounded interesting."

Darwen wasn't convinced.

"Probably just wants to stick with us," said Rich after Gabriel was out of earshot.

"Yeah," said Darwen.

"Look," said Rich, "I'm sorry about before. I just didn't like being left out."

"I should have taken you with me," said Darwen. "It was my fault. I'm an idiot."

Rich grinned at him. "Not compared to Alex," he said. "She was feeding one of those things? Seriously?"

"Seriously. And she told that girl from the village, Sarita, about it."

Rich gaped. "What happened to keeping things within the Peregrine Pact?" he exclaimed. "Who else knows?"

Darwen shrugged. "I think she wanted a secret of her own. That's why she didn't tell us. Because she felt we—well, *I*—had been holding out on her."

But before they could discuss the matter further, they saw her stomping stony-faced down the beach and into the water.

"You are coming to the island?" said Jorge.

"Apparently," said Alex.

Jorge reached for her hand and hauled her in. She avoided everyone's eyes and stared haughtily out to sea.

"I'm glad you came," Darwen ventured.

"You think I'd let you two bond over how stupid you think I am?" she said, watching a tern skimming the waves off to the starboard side of the boat.

"I guess not," said Darwen.

"So," she stated. "I hear you got shot."

"Yes," said Darwen. "In the shoulder, look."

"Fantastic," she replied. "I hope it hurt."

There was an awkward pause.

"We good now?" said Rich.

"Sure," said Alex, finally turning to look at them. "Why wouldn't we be?"

Darwen grinned, and the others joined him.

"Okay," said Rich as the boat roared out of the bay and around the coast. "So now that we're talking again, I've got a few things to say, and most of them are about the stupidity of trying to hand-raise wild carnivores."

And they were off. Alex called Rich an unfeeling monster, and Rich said that he lived on a farm and knew animals.

"It's not like Bambi, you know, Alex," he said. "The birds don't come and lay the table for you while the rabbits sing songs about how pretty you are. Animals act on instinct: fight or flight, kill or be killed. The pouncels are predators. I can't believe you!"

"Whatever," said Alex. Then, turning to Darwen, she added, "Before he bursts into a chorus of 'Thank God I'm a Country Boy,' can we at least acknowledge that he said I was pretty?"

"I did not!" yelled Rich, flushing pink. "I said the rabbits thought you were. If you were in a movie. And they were cartoons."

"I know what I heard," said Alex, smiling.

Darwen laughed, and soon they joined him. It seemed

like they hadn't laughed together for a very long time. It was a good feeling, good enough to mute the unease Darwen felt every time his eyes fell on Gabriel, who was sitting very still, his head turned slightly toward them, as if he was listening very carefully to everything they said.

Darwen didn't know if he was becoming a better sailor or if he was just relieved to have Rich and Alex to talk to again, but the journey to Caño Island passed without the usual nausea. Rich had brought his pocketknife with the bundles of wood and string from the dining shelter, and they used the journey to catch up on their bow making. By the time they reached the island, they all had bows, though only Rich's looked like it might actually shoot, and Alex's arrows were all wonky.

"Doesn't matter," she said with a pointed look at Rich. "I won't be using it to hunt defenseless animals."

"If you did," said Rich, eying her bow critically, "they'd be quite safe. It's not straight."

"Straight!" said Alex. "Straight is overrated. Straight is stiff, inflexible, square. I'm a free spirit, and my bow should match."

"So long as you don't mind putting your own eye out," said Rich.

They beached the boat. Jorge left the yellow plastic fuel cans by the ranger station and headed up the trail to the dig site, chatting to Gabriel. From the shore they had been able to see the other boat unloading the students with their masks and snorkels into the water, but once they turned inland, they were completely alone.

As they walked through the jungle, Darwen told Alex and Rich about his realization that the clown he had glimpsed in the mirror was Blackpool's World-Famous Laughing Man.

"How can it be?" said Rich.

"Must be one of those psychology thingies," said Alex. "Repressed memory or something."

"What?" asked Darwen.

"You know," said Alex airily, "in the movies there's always someone who saw something that they almost remember but can't quite because it was something really awful, like a murder. But their unconscious mind holds on to a bit of it, and it keeps coming up, and eventually the character faces up to the terrible thing they've managed to forget, and that helps the police catch the killer, and everything works out."

"I don't think that's it," said Darwen.

"I don't think it's anything," said Rich.

"I know I was scared of the Blackpool clown," said Darwen. "And there were all kinds of weird stories about it. Some people said it was inside the fun house during a fire that destroyed the building, but the clown was untouched by the blaze. And some people said that the laugh was actually recorded in an insane asylum. And some people—"

"I think that's more than enough information, thank you," said Alex.

Darwen looked up the trail. Jorge, Gabriel, and Mr. Iverson were waiting for them.

"Mr. Iverson tells me you are keen archaeologists," Jorge said, smiling.

"They are," said Alex. "I'd rather be swimming with the fishies."

"We have our own club," said Rich, eager to show that he would not rather be swimming with the fishies.

"Have you found anything interesting?" asked Jorge.

Rich couldn't resist a sideways grin at Darwen.

Well, Darwen thought, *last year we found a scrobbler that had been shot two hundred years ago. That was fairly interesting.*

"Certainly they have," said Mr. Iverson. "Rich has developed a whole theory about our school having been built on sacred Indian land."

"Really," said Jorge, his voice neutral. Gabriel was listening closely.

"Just a theory, right, Rich?" said Darwen, wanting to steer the subject elsewhere. "It's not like we've found any real evidence."

"Well," said Jorge, "I hope we'll find something interesting today."

"At least there won't be bottle caps out here," said Alex.

Rich frowned at her. He had often been accused of digging up nothing more than twenty-first-century trash.

The group rounded the last bend in the path together and stuttered to a halt, staring at the site.

The central dig square was just as it had been before, except for one thing. Beside one of the larger stone spheres embedded in the ground was something new, something between a backpack and a kitchen appliance. It was studded with dials and switches and linked by a piece of hose to something with a nozzle and a trigger that looked like a flamethrower.

Darwen gasped. It was an energy weapon of the kind carried by scrobblers. He flashed a look at Rich and Alex.

"What's that?" said Mr. Iverson, stooping to it.

"Don't touch it!" exclaimed Rich, so that Mr. Iverson jumped and took a step back.

"Mr. Haggerty, you startled me!" he said.

"Sorry," said Rich. "I thought it looked . . . I don't know. Dangerous."

In fact, it didn't. As Darwen got closer he could see that the pack was blackened and the glass over its various controls was broken. He cautiously flipped a few switches, but nothing happened. It was quite dead.

"Whatever it is, it should not have been left here," said Jorge. "Maybe one of the archaeologists brought it to use on the site, but"—he frowned—"I have never seen anything like it before."

Darwen didn't know why, but he wasn't sure that he believed the guide.

"Even archaeological work should leave no trash behind," he said. "The island's environment must be preserved."

Jorge removed the tarp from the site and distributed the trowels that were stored in a box just outside the square.

Darwen took one last look at the burned-out energy weapon and found himself wondering why all the scrobbler equipment they had found in Costa Rica was clearly broken. He pictured the armored bulldozer, which seemed to have died the very moment it crossed over from Silbrica. What had Weazen said? Something about the old gates not working this time?

Burned-out scrobbler equipment half in and half out of Silbrica, like they couldn't get it through the portal . . .

But animals like the pouncels could get through. There had to be a reason.

"We work slowly," said Jorge. "I have strict orders from the excavation leader. One inch at a time. If you find anything at all, tell me."

It was hot work, made doubly so by the cramped conditions of the square. They couldn't all fit in at once, so they developed a rotation with two resting at a time. Twice Darwen thought he had found something only to discover that it was just a perfectly normal piece of rock, and after half an hour, he began to wish the grown-ups would leave them to it so that they could set to arranging the stone spheres in a circle.

"Huh," said Alex.

"What?" said Mr. Iverson, who was standing to the side, wiping the sweat from his face with a muddy hand.

"I hit something," she said, and tapped the tip of her trowel against it to make the point. It chinked. "Stone, it looks like, but big and flat. And there are lines on it, like it's been carved. Is that good?"

The others stared at her for a moment, and then Rich was pushing closer to see, and Jorge was calling for brushes from the box. They worked around the edges with the trowels and swept the surface of the stone slab clean until they could see the design etched into its surface.

The carving showed a swirl of lines beside what looked like a pole.

"It's an octopus," said Gabriel.

"But this," said Mr. Iverson, perplexed, indicating the vertical line, "looks like a tree. An octopus that lives in trees?"

Darwen said nothing. He stared at the carving, and when he looked up, Rich and Alex were both looking at him. He nodded fractionally.

It was the thing that had taken Luis. The Insidious Bleck.

So it too had been here long ago. The Guardians had been able to seal off Silbrica and its monsters from this place. But now the beasts were back, they had a purpose, and they had at least one "person" on their side—Scarlett Oppertune. Darwen didn't know how he was going to stop them, but his eyes slid over to the stone spheres half-buried in the hard ground, and he knew he was ready to try.

Jorge couldn't sit still. He kept pacing around the excavated square taking pictures of the carving with a little digital camera and muttering to himself. Finally he couldn't wait any longer. "We should go back to the mainland," he said. "I need to get to a computer and consult with my colleagues."

"Your colleagues?" said Mr. Iverson.

"The archaeologists," said Jorge. "I must send these pictures to San José."

"I promised the students a whole afternoon of research on the island," said Mr. Iverson. "Can't it wait a few hours?"

"No," snapped Jorge. "This is important."

"So is the education of my students," said Mr. Iverson carefully.

"We'll be fine by ourselves if you want to head back," Darwen tried.

"I can't leave you here alone, even with your teacher," said Jorge. "And you can't drive the boat."

"I'll take the pictures," said Gabriel in a sudden and unexpected burst of enthusiasm. "I've had enough of archaeology anyway. I could swim across to the boat where the others are snorkeling."

Jorge considered him and checked his watch. "The reef sharks will be starting to hunt soon, so the snorkelers will be getting ready to go."

He said this like Gabriel was merely booking a slightly earlier flight.

"Are you a strong swimmer?" asked Jorge, slipping the camera's memory stick into a ziplock bag he had in his pocket.

"Yes," said Gabriel

Jorge hesitated, thinking, then nodded.

"Okay," he said. For a moment he stood, as if still undecided, then he took out a pen and wrote on a piece of paper. Gabriel read it, and something came into his face, a hesitancy that might have been fear. Jorge met his eyes and nodded once before handing him the plastic bag. "Send this to my colleagues when you get back to the camp," he said. "Mr. Peregrine will know how to reach them."

Darwen was not the only one who looked surprised that Jorge had such confidence in the world studies teacher. Mr. Iverson's face was carefully blank, but Alex's eyebrows were about as high as they could go. Gabriel just nodded, then set off at a run. In seconds he had disappeared from view.

Jorge turned to find everyone looking at him. Something odd had just happened, Darwen felt sure of it, and even Mr. Iverson seemed cautious, watchful.

"Water break," Jorge said. "And snacks. But we should eat back at the ranger station. We must not contaminate the environment. Let us cover the dig site and put our tools away. There is no one on the island now but us."

Darwen felt a shiver of excitement at the idea: just the five of them on a deserted patch of jungle ten miles out into the Pacific. It was like something out of *Treasure Island*. If only Jorge and Mr. Iverson had opted to go with Gabriel so that he could have gotten that portal working . . .

"Caño Island has been completely cut off from the rest of the peninsula," said Jorge, returning to tour-guide mode as they finished cleaning up and began the walk down to the beach, "so it has far fewer bird and animal species than on the mainland. Only one percent of the insects that live there"—he stopped midsentence, seeming to forget everyone around him. He was staring at a patch of dried mud by the trail.

"What?" asked Rich. "What do you see?"

"Nothing," said Jorge, and he kicked at the earth with his boot, scuffing the dirt.

Rich gave him a hard look.

Jorge's face was expressionless, but when Mr. Iverson gave him an inquiring look, he just shrugged and smiled and moved off along the path. Darwen was about to go after the adults when Alex tugged his shirt.

"Look," she whispered.

A few feet from where Jorge had been standing, there were tracks in the now hard ground, tracks showing claws and a central talon much longer than the rest.

"You know what that means?" said Alex.

"That there are pouncels on the island," said Darwen, frowning, "and Jorge doesn't want us to know."

"And they didn't swim ten miles to get here," said Alex. "So the stone spheres back there are an active portal."

"But someone has to arrange them into a circle," said Darwen. "You don't think Jorge is working with Scarlett? They hate each other!"

"People lie, Darwen," said Alex.

Darwen hung back as she followed the others.

He had liked the guide, and he still did. If Jorge was

working with Scarlett, if he was involved in any way with the disappearance of Luis, Eduardo, and Calida, then the world was a little less pleasant, less trustworthy, less good. But why would he be? Why would anyone be abducting children?

The question brought a name they had barely spoken in weeks to Darwen's mind: *Greyling*.

Last time, it had been Greyling who had been directing Miss Murray to power his machines, and though Darwen was able to tell himself that they had not seen any direct signs of him yet—no gnashers or scrobblers, no kid-sized generators—he knew that if Greyling was somehow behind everything, behind the Insidious Bleck, things would be far worse than he imagined.

Darwen's unease deepened as he reached the beach. A strange scene was playing out there. Mr. Iverson was standing on the shore gesturing wildly with both hands toward the distant snorkelers, whose boat was speeding away with Gabriel—presumably—on board. Jorge was kneeling beside their own boat looking serious.

Darwen broke into a run. "What's going on?" he shouted.

"Him!" yelled Rich. "It was him!"

"What are you talking about?"

"Jorge," said Rich, turning fiercely. "He did it."

"It wasn't him, Rich," said Mr. Iverson, splashing his way to the shore. "It was like this when we got here."

"Like what?" asked Darwen. "Will someone please tell me what is going on?"

Rich pointed at a patch of wet sand by the boat where Jorge was squatting. Darwen took a step toward it and was immediately overwhelmed by a familiar and powerful smell.

Petrol—or, as he had gotten used to calling it over the last few months, *gasoline*.

The yellow plastic cans were uncapped and on their sides. Someone had dumped their fuel. They were stranded.

"Maybe the wind blew them over," said Mr. Iverson.

"And unscrewed the tops?" said Rich.

Jorge stood up. He met Rich's hostile gaze, then began walking down the beach toward the ranger station.

"So we're stuck here?" said Alex. "Until when? Not overnight, right? Someone will come for us before dark, yeah?"

"Mr. Iverson," called Jorge as he walked away, "could we talk for a moment?"

Mr. Iverson, looking bewildered, hurried after him.

The students watched them go.

"It was Gabriel," said Darwen, stunned. "It had to be. That explains why he wanted to leave so quickly. But what would make him do it in the first place?"

"Because Jorge told him to," said Rich. "I've been

saying it all along: we can't trust that guy."

"He expects something to happen tonight," said Darwen. It was a guess, but it felt right. "Something is going to happen, and he wants to be here to see it."

"I knew we couldn't trust him," spluttered Rich.

"Rich," said Alex in her no-nonsense voice. "Stop talking."

Rich opened his mouth to argue, but she stared him down as only she could, and he turned sullenly away.

"So now what?" asked Darwen. "There's no cell phone signal out here. What about a radio?"

"Yes," said Rich. "I saw one on the shelf back there with the food supplies. It's pretty old and has a hand crank. They may be using it right now."

"Come on," said Darwen.

They ran over to the shelter and found Jorge sitting at the ancient radio. He avoided their eyes and cranked the handle vigorously, then flipped switches, crammed a battered headset on, and adjusted a dial, talking. Alex listened closely, but her face showed no sign of doubt or alarm. After a few moments, he sat back and slammed the headset to the desktop, uttering a single shouted syllable that Miss Martinez was unlikely to ever teach them.

"That was a bad word," said Alex, in case they hadn't guessed. "He seems pretty upset."

"No one said he wasn't a good actor," whispered Rich.

"*Nada*," said Jorge. "Nothing. Probably no one is near the radio. They won't be until the other boat gets back. If we cannot reach them soon, it will be too dark for them to come in to shore. The rocks are very dangerous, and there are no lights out here."

"If they could get close to the island," said Darwen, acting as neutrally as possible toward Jorge, "could we swim out to meet them?"

Jorge shook his head. "Sharks," he said. "I will keep trying," he added, "but we should prepare to be here overnight. We should camp on the beach. It will be safer than in the rainforest."

"I thought there were no large predators on the island," said Rich, barely keeping the skepticism out of his voice.

"There are some snakes," said Jorge without looking at them directly. Darwen knew the guide was thinking about the pouncels whose tracks he had tried to hide. "Why don't you gather some wood for a fire?"

"Er . . . because it's, like, a hundred degrees," said Alex.

"For safety," said Jorge.

"Ah," said Alex. "Wood it is. Coming right up. Lumber. Logs. Kindling—"

"Okay, Alex," said Rich, fishing in a box of supplies and emerging with a cigarette lighter. "We'll get the wood. Mr. Iverson can stay here with Jorge," he added, with a meaningful look at Darwen and Alex.

"What?" said Mr. Iverson, who seemed to be lost in his own thoughts. "Sure. That's fine."

As soon as they were out of earshot of the shelter, Rich said, "Someone has to keep an eye on Jorge. How's Mr. I's Spanish?"

Alex waggled her hand and made a noncommittal noise: not bad, not great.

Rich raised his eyebrow.

"Good enough to tell if he's ordering Silbrican monster attacks, I guess." Alex shrugged.

"You know," said Darwen, "this is actually perfect."

"Being stranded on an island with monsters on it?" said Alex. "Yeah, it's a dream come true. No, wait. It's a *nightmare* come true."

"I mean we can activate the portal by the dig site tonight," said Darwen. "We wait for the adults to go to sleep, and then we sneak up there, make a circle with the loose spheres, pour some water in—unless it rains, which it probably will—and we're in."

They looked at each other, and the excitement passed through them like the electricity they were about to stimulate.

"Let's do it," said Rich.

"Agreed," said Alex, taking their hands. "But until then we let Mr. Iverson and Jorge think they're running the show. Let's get that wood."

They worked for an hour, gathering fallen timbers and branches and dragging them onto the sand where the gas had been spilled.

"Might make it easier to light, at least," Rich shrugged. "And it's a good distance from the forest. Wouldn't want to accidentally devastate the environment, would we?"

"No," said Darwen. "That's Scarlett's job, though I still don't know why."

"Maybe she doesn't need a reason," said Alex. "Maybe she just wants to destroy what other people value. Some people are like that. Ask that ignoranus Chip Whittley why he killed that butterfly."

"You mean *ignoramus*," said Rich.

"I know what I mean," said Alex.

Back at the ranger station, Jorge had laid out food rations from the plastic storage bins and made coffee on a tiny propane stove. "Cream and sugar?" he asked as he handed out chipped enamel mugs.

"Cream?" said Alex. "We have a fridge?"

Jorge laughed, pushing one of the big Tupperware boxes. "Just the powdered kind," he said. "It lasts forever." He looked out toward the ocean. "The sun is going down. Even if I reach the tent camp now on the radio, no one will come until morning. You should decide where you are going to sleep."

"What about you?" asked Darwen.

"I am not tired," said the guide, "and someone should *pay attentions* for a while."

"Why?" said Rich.

"No reason," said Jorge, though his eyes had that evasive look again. "Just to be safe. You can take your bows."

Darwen doubted their homemade bows and arrows would be of much use if the pouncels—or worse—attacked, but since he had nothing better to offer, he just shrugged. Even Alex brought hers, though Rich gave her a you-can't-be-serious look.

"Don't be making fun of my bow," she said warningly.

"Oh, it's a bow," said Rich. "I thought it was a rare one-stringed harp."

"How about I use my one-stringed harp to put an arrow in your butt?" Alex responded.

"You couldn't hit the ocean with that thing," said Rich.

"From where?" asked Alex.

"From the edge of the ocean," said Rich.

Darwen laughed.

"We'll see about that," said Alex, looking affronted. "We're going to have a little competition, you and me, Rich Haggerty."

"Let's get sorted out first," said Darwen. "Then you can test whose bow is the worst."

"You mean the best," said Alex.

"I know what I mean," said Darwen, who didn't think

either bow looked too impressive.

Clouds were sweeping in from the sea, promising rain, but they set up camp on the beach by the fire anyway, lugging some of the supply boxes out there to sit on. It was quieter on the island than on the mainland, and the muted jungle buzz was without the sudden calls of birds and monkeys, which they had grown used to at the camp.

"So if Gabriel marooned us here," Darwen said, thinking aloud, "because Jorge told him to, what's going on?"

"He obviously wanted to get word to his *colleagues*, whoever they really are," said Alex, "but he didn't want to leave the island. Mr. Iverson wouldn't let us go back to the mainland, so he decided to maroon us all here."

"Or he always planned for us to get stuck on this island," said Rich. "Maybe we're about to be the first Hillsiders taken by the Insidious Bleck."

It began to rain almost as soon as they had lit the fire.

"Great," said Alex. "We'll have to sleep in the shelter."

They returned to the ranger station, cleared the wooden floor, took off their shoes, and lay there in their clothes, watching the rain by the light of the fire on the beach, waiting for the adults to fall asleep.

"This trip just keeps on getting better," said Alex. Without warning she started to sing, rocking back and forth in time to the music.

"What are you doing?" asked Rich.

"Helps me get to sleep," she said.

"It's not doing much for me," said Rich.

"Just a few minutes," she said, "and I'll drop right off. Promise. Got any requests?"

"'The Sound of Silence,'" Rich deadpanned.

"Hilarious," said Alex. "What's that anyway, some moldy old song your dad listens to? You need to get with the times. Try this on for size."

She started madly warbling, "Baby! Baby! Baby!"

"You do this in your tent with Naia and Mad?" Rich cut in.

"Every night," she said. "Sometimes they join in."

"And I thought sleeping in a stinky tent was bad," said Rich.

"You know whose tent is worse than yours?" whispered Alex. "Mr. P's. I had to go see him yesterday, and man! I don't think he's bathed since we arrived. It's like something died in there."

"Shhh!" said Jorge suddenly. He had leaped to his feet and was standing at the back of the shelter, his lit flashlight sweeping the tree line above.

"What is it?" asked Mr. Iverson, sounding groggy.

"Everybody get to the fire!" shouted Jorge. "Quickly!"

"But it's raining!" said Alex.

"Now!" Jorge yelled.

"Is that really necessary?" said Mr. Iverson, standing

and turning on the shelter's storm lantern.

The others turned to him, and everyone went very still, staring with horror.

"What?" asked Mr. Iverson.

Behind the science teacher, on the very edge of the lamplight, were pairs of yellow lights.

Eyes.

"Go," said Jorge in a low voice to the students. "Get to the fire and stay there. I will bring Mr. Iverson."

"What?" said Mr. Iverson. Then he did the thing they had all been hoping he wouldn't. He turned to see what they were looking at.

Mr. Iverson saw the gathering pouncels, and he panicked. He half jumped, half fell away from them. They reacted at once, leaping into the light, knifelike claws held out in front of them, mouths open and snarling. Mr. Iverson barely saw them. In his hurry he stumbled, turned his ankle, and fell, catching his head on the edge of the bench. The sound was sickening, a firm crack like the sound of a bat hitting a cricket ball. He lay motionless.

"Go!" roared Jorge.

Darwen, Rich, and Alex ran out into the rain and down the beach toward the fire. As they ran, the shingle became sand, and all they could see in the darkness was the blazing heap of wood, which roared and hissed at the rain like a volcano. Back in the station there was a crash, and Jorge's voice rang out in a wordless cry.

They heard another shout, and it seemed so much further away now that Darwen's heart sank. He didn't trust Jorge, but he liked Mr. Iverson a lot. If something bad happened to him, something he couldn't actually bring himself to imagine right now, he would never forgive himself. How many of the pouncels had there been? Five? At least that many, he thought. Maybe eight or more.

Another shout.

Darwen reached for a hefty-looking tree limb stuck deep in the heart of the blaze and pulled it out.

"What are you doing?" asked Rich.

"Going back," said Darwen.

The branch was hot in his hand, and it steamed as the rain hit it. He held it overhead and started back toward the shelter.

"Darwen, that's crazy!" shouted Rich. "There are too many of them."

Darwen didn't answer. He began to run so that he wouldn't change his mind, looking up at the blazing branch above his head. It was still burning, but the flames were small and bluish, not nearly as impressive as he had expected them to be. He slowed. Jorge's flashlight was slashing around the ranger station like a laser. There was another crash, like overturning furniture, and the light became still.

Darwen rushed to the scene, gratefully aware that Rich and Alex had brought burning brands of their own and were right at his heels.

The flashlight had rolled under the overturned table, but the lantern hanging from the roof beam was still lit. There was no sign of the pouncels. The two men were sprawled on the ground. Mr. Iverson was out cold. Jorge was crumpled in the corner, covered in blood.

Darwen ran to him instinctively and dropped to a crouch. "Jorge!" he screamed.

The guide's eyelids tightened, then opened. "I am not your enemy," he gasped between low, rasping breaths. "You have to trust me."

"Darwen!" shouted Rich.

It was a warning. Darwen turned, rising, and saw three of the pouncels, the largest he had seen, edging back into the shelter. He waved his branch at them, but the flames were virtually out. The pouncels hopped backward as the branch scattered sparks, but then they stalked closer again.

"Go back to the fire," muttered Jorge, his eyes closing once more. "You are safer there."

"No," said Darwen. He took a step toward one of the cat-faced creatures and lunged with the branch, but it dodged, then leaped in close, claws slashing.

Darwen shrank away, but he felt a gash open along his thigh, and he cried out. Two more pouncels had joined the other three.

"Go!" shouted Jorge again. He sounded weak but determined, and desperate though Darwen was, he knew the guide was right. They could do nothing here. He turned and fled back toward the beach.

Rich and Alex were in front of him now, and Darwen sensed their hesitation immediately. They were facing the fire, but they weren't running.

"What's the matter?" Darwen yelled, trying to see past them to the plastic storage boxes they had used as benches. "Run!"

But they didn't move, and as he took another step toward them, he saw why. Something moved between them and the sea, something quick and dangerous, silhouetted against the glow of the fire. Then another. And another. There were more pouncels on the beach. A whole pack of them.

Darwen glanced wildly to Alex and Rich. They had been cut off.

"I don't think hand-feeding them will work this time, Alex," said Rich.

"That way!" shouted Alex. "Up to the dig."

"Why?" gasped Darwen.

"Where else is there?" she replied.

She had a point. The beach wasn't safe. The shelter wasn't safe. The dig wouldn't give them any more protection, but it might buy them a little time and cover.

Alex started to run, swinging her still smoldering stick at the pouncels on the beach so that it glowed fiercely.

Out on the beach they could see the sky. Once they went up that path again, they would be in the altogether different darkness of the forest. Darwen caught a flash of movement in the darkness, and he flung his stick in that direction. It flared briefly in the wind and then landed on the beach in a shower of sparks.

They found the path, but only just. Alex's burning stick had gone out, and they had no lantern. It was only due to Rich's tiny pocket flashlight that they were able to pick their way through a darkness that was almost complete. If the pouncels chose to attack now, Darwen knew they wouldn't see them until it was too late. They slowed, faltering as they traced the trail inland, but they didn't reach the dig site. A couple of hundred yards before they got there, there was a flash of lightning, and Darwen stuttered to a halt. He had seen something to his left in the sudden bluish white, something odd that made the ground look pale. Thunder rolled overhead, and then the lightning came again, and this time Darwen was looking right at it.

No more than a few yards off the path was a circle of rainwater ringed with stone spheres that they hadn't noticed before. Darwen stared at it, and though the night was still warm, he felt cold. He also felt with uncanny certainty that he was being watched. He turned hastily around. The others had stopped and were waiting for him.

"Turn your flashlight off," Darwen hissed.

"What is it?" Rich whispered. There was a click, and the pencil-like beam of light went out.

"There's something on the path behind us," Darwen replied. He saw it only as a deeper blackness in the dark, but he knew it had not been there before. It was just the size and shape of a pouncel. One, maybe more, had tracked them.

He didn't know what to do. If only Mr. Peregrine had told him something, anything. Rich raised his hand with the tiny flashlight, aiming, but Darwen caught his wrist before he could turn it on. "That might provoke it," he said.

Rich lowered his hand, and they stared into the darkness.

The lightning came again, and Darwen saw the pouncel clear as day, but it was not poised to attack. It was not even looking at them. Instead it was huddled on the ground as if terrified, and it was staring directly up into the trees.

Slowly, with a swelling sense of dread, Darwen did the same, and as the lightning flickered again, he saw it, the pale and purplish sack-like body, pulsing up there, the massive trailing tentacles, the terrible beak-like mouth with the terrifying feelers. There was no question that this was the creature carved into the ancient stone at the dig site, the thing the adults had thought was an octopus. It was suspended up there, its body the size of a car, slick under a tangle of short hair, undulating sluggishly, wrapped around a tree and hanging in the dark like a nightmare.

Darwen wasn't sure which of them had cried out. He knew it hadn't been him, because though a part of him had wanted to scream, no sound would come, and he could do nothing but stand and stare in horrified silence.

The darkness was complete for five, maybe ten seconds. Darwen couldn't say for sure. But when the lightning came again, he saw that the creature had moved. The sky flickered like a faulty movie projector, and the great mass of the Insidious Bleck—for that was surely what it was—was unfurling its tentacles and reaching over the path with fluid, snakelike ease. It extended its tentacles, their pale undersides studded with suckers and hooks, their top sides bristling with hair. When it reached the next tree, it coiled one of its tentacles quickly and silently around it, and then the entire creature was hauling itself overhead, its great weight breaking off branches as it swung through the canopy. Its movement was easy and slow, so that an extraordinary possibility struck Darwen like a ray of hope in the darkness.

It hasn't seen us.

He hadn't moved a muscle since spotting it, and Darwen now found himself praying that Rich and Alex would make the same deduction. Out of the corner of his eye, however, he saw movement: a long, careful, loping stride that quickened suddenly. The pouncel was making a run for it.

Without pausing in its languid motion through the trees, without even clearly turning to see the pouncel at all, the Insidious Bleck dropped one long tentacle to the forest floor and snatched it up. The pouncel fought, lashing and scratching, but the Bleck's tentacle had the strength and studied deliberation of an elephant's trunk. It swept the howling pouncel upward and opened its appalling beak mouth wide to receive it.

The spell was finally broken, and Darwen was able to look away at the last second. Amid the pattering rain, drops of blood fell through the leaves. Darwen couldn't think. He couldn't plan or decide what was best or smartest. The horror of the thing was too great. Without an idea in his head, without even being able to see where he was going, he ran.

Somewhere high up in the forest, a tree creaked and groaned as the monster shifted its weight suddenly. A branch snapped, then another, and then there was a new rustling in the leaves that was louder and more violent than the storm.

It was coming after him.

THE INSIDIOUS BLECK

Darwen didn't even know which way he was facing. The lightning showed he was on the path, but he didn't know if he was going inland or back down to the beach. Not that it mattered. He was headed away from the creature in the treetops, and his sense of the thing behind him was as good as a compass.

There was movement beside him, and even though Darwen was running, he jumped and almost stumbled. It was Rich. "It's the thing from the carving!" he gasped.

"The thing that took Luis. It's going to take us too."

Darwen couldn't answer. He was sure the abomination in the trees was about to reach for him with one of those long, hairy tentacles and then sweep him up toward that horror of a mouth. He could almost feel it inches from his skin, his hair, and the thought worked on him with a revulsion he couldn't switch off. He ran. It was all he could do.

"Where's Alex?" asked Rich, fighting to keep up.

The question punched through the smothering fog of terror and stopped Darwen cold. He didn't know. He had no idea where *he* was, let alone where Alex might be. He dropped, rolling into the leafy underbrush off the path, giving no thought to snakes or insects. He looked up. Rich was clambering awkwardly over a tree limb and squatting beside him, but beyond him Darwen could see nothing. There were no stars, no streetlamp glow as he was used to at home, no moon. Overhead the sky was the faintest gray smear beyond the silhouettes of the trees. The wind dropped, and for a second all was perfectly still. And then the grayness seemed to shift, and a blackness moved over them like a blimp drifting against the clouds.

Darwen felt its presence like a foul smell, and he shuddered before he could stop himself. Rich clamped one large, sweaty palm over Darwen's forearm, and the two boys sat motionless as the creature in the trees moved with deliberate caution above them.

It knows we're here, Darwen thought. *But it doesn't know exactly where. It's waiting. Listening.*

His heart was racing, and he had bitten down on his lip so hard that he could taste blood in his mouth. He breathed through his nose, as still as the trees themselves, and he too listened.

There had been a noise. Faint and not up in the canopy but down on the forest floor. In the darkness Darwen had no idea how far away it had been. Ten yards? Twenty? It had been a stealthy sound. Another pouncel, perhaps. Or Alex.

Darwen turned as slowly and quietly as he could and stared into the blackness where he thought the sound had come from. Almost immediately, he heard it again. Louder now. Closer. Something coming quietly toward them across the ground. Rich's grip on his arm tightened. He had heard it too.

The lightning flashed, and for a moment Darwen saw the jungle, a clutter of underbrush and tree trunks reaching up into the sky, but he saw no animal or person, nothing that might have made the noise. The darkness came again, and thunder rolled like a series of distant explosions. And beneath it, lasting a fraction longer than the thunder, something moved through the leaf litter. Not footsteps. A consistent slithering sound . . .

The lightning came again. Darwen's first thought was that the forest had somehow grown denser, that new trees had sprouted around them. But the light lasted just long enough to see that some of what he had thought were tree trunks were purplish and matted with short bristling hair.

The monster was trailing its tentacles from above, sweeping the ground, searching for them.

Another flicker of lightning and Darwen had to clap a hand to his mouth. One of the great ropelike tentacles was less than a foot from his face. It hung quite still, but its tip, which bore a long, hook-like claw, writhed and pulsed like a maggot as it felt blindly for its prey. It inched toward them, and Darwen shrank inwardly, forcing himself not to kick the vile thing away.

And then he felt it. It had brushed the fabric of his T-shirt just above his shoulder. It stopped.

Darwen sat motionless and felt the tentacle grow almost thoughtfully still, and the entire world, in spite of the rain and the lightning, seemed to follow suit. For a second that felt like ten, nothing happened, and then the claw rotated a fraction, testing its hard tip against his shoulder. It pressed, then the pressure eased, and it moved more gently, almost caressing as it tried to figure out what it had found. It snaked down his chest, and he felt the hard bristles brush against his cheek as it moved. He could smell it too, an old and slightly rotten smell like wet earth or mulch. It was, he thought, the aroma of the grave.

The thought was still bright and horrible in his mind

when he felt the tentacle curl slightly as it moved down. It was starting to tighten. Exploration had turned into something else. It was going to take him like it had taken the others.

The realization gave him no choice. He leaped to his feet, spinning as he had seen Rich do when he was trying to break a tackle while playing American football. He turned against the curl of the tentacle, rotated halfway around, and broke into a run, pulling Rich after him.

Behind them he heard the tentacle writhe, grabbing wildly at the air, breaking branches as it whirled around, searching. Then it was sucked upward, and the entire creature was on the move up in the canopy, following them.

Somehow they had to find the path. If they could get to the beach, the monster wouldn't be able to reach them from the trees. But first they had to get there. Branches whipped at their face and arms as they blundered through the undergrowth. One lashed the side of Darwen's neck like a scalpel, but then he was out on the wide-open beach, free of the tree limbs through which the Bleck had moved.

"This way!" shouted Rich, who seemed to have had the same idea: get to the shore, and they might be safe. He snapped on his pocket flashlight, and though Darwen knew that would make them visible, he said nothing. He couldn't stand the darkness any longer, and they just had to get down to the sea.

The creature seemed to sense what they were doing. Branches fell from above as it tore through the canopy, and—just when Darwen thought nothing could add to his terror—it began to scream: a deafening shriek of fury that silenced the storm and every other beast in the jungle. Darwen's skin seemed to shrink like cellophane in a candle flame, and his hair stood on end. The appalling sound lasted several seconds, and Darwen felt his strength fade, as if the noise was draining the hope and courage out of him.

"Keep going," breathed Rich, lumbering into him from behind. "Don't stop."

Rich's words cleared his mind a little, and Darwen's feet began to pound the track again. Somewhere behind them they heard the groan and crack of a trunk splintering from the Bleck's weight, but they didn't pause. They ran harder than ever, and suddenly it seemed that the path, though just as windy, was sloping down.

"This is it!" shouted Rich, his flashlight waving erratically. "We're nearly there!"

Darwen found a little well of energy deep inside him, dipped into it, and accelerated into the path. They rounded one last overgrown corner, and a glorious sight met their eyes. Off to the left, no more than a couple of hundred yards away, they could see the orange glow of the fire.

Rich paused, checking behind them, and his flashlight found the Bleck's pale and pulsing body up in the treetops, its many glassy eyes staring, its tentacles spread wide, some gripping tree trunks, others poised to strike.

Darwen grabbed Rich by the back of his shirt and pulled, but the larger boy was too scared to move.

"Come on!" shouted Darwen. "Get to the fire!"

The Insidious Bleck opened its great beak-like jaws, and the mouthpart feelers around it flexed hungrily.

Rich didn't move.

There was something hypnotic about the slow unfurling of those tentacles, the way they stretched out toward them. . . .

"Now!" bellowed Darwen, and he kicked Rich hard in the shin.

Rich blinked, gave Darwen a startled look as if he had just woken up, and then, finally, started to move.

Not a moment too soon. A tentacle lashed the place where they had been.

Fortunately, they were already sprinting the final yards down to the sand. They made for the fire, vaulting over the plastic boxes of supplies, conscious as they got out from under the darkness of the trees that the rain had stopped and the clouds overhead were blowing away already. They ran on, relief washing over them with each step they took away from the trees.

"There you are!" said a voice from beside the fire. "What kept you?"

"Alex!" gasped Darwen. "Are we glad to see you!"

"I don't know," said Alex, "are you?"

"We thought . . . you were . . . out there," Rich managed as he doubled over, breathing hard. "The thing . . ."

"The Insidious Bleck!" said Darwen. "It's back there."

Alex gazed past them, her face serious.

"Not so much *back there*," she said, "as just *there*."

No, thought Darwen. *Not here. We're safe here*.

But she was right.

Crab-like, it came toward them from the tree line, half walking, half slithering on those awful tentacles, and on land it seemed more spider than octopus. In the firelight it looked hellish, a sprawling, throbbing horror. It was even bigger than Darwen had thought. Its tentacles could have wrapped around a bus—and crushed it.

"Get your bows!" said Alex.

The idea was so preposterous that even in his terror, Darwen stared at her.

"You got a better idea?" she said.

They picked up their bows and fumbled with the little stack of arrows they had made. They felt pathetically, comically inadequate.

The monster came toward them, upending the boxes so that one popped its lid and spewed its white powdery contents.

"It will be afraid of the fire," muttered Rich feverishly.

"It's not," said Alex as the monster clambered over the supplies.

"Well, it should be," Rich answered. So saying he drew back his bow, and Darwen saw that he had set the tip of the arrow alight. He fired. The burning arrow scudded through the darkness and found one of the monster's tentacles. It bellowed in rage, and its pincer-like mouth gaped at them, but it did not slow down.

"Good idea," said Alex. "Let's make it really angry."

"I wasn't aiming for it," said Rich. "I was aiming for the box! The one with no lid."

"The box?" said Darwen, not taking his eyes off the lumbering creature. "Why?"

"Just shoot it!"

Darwen didn't dare turn his back on the monster, so he thrust his arrow back in the direction of the fire and held it there without looking at it. When he put it in his bow, he saw that the tip was smoldering but not truly alight. Gripped with panic and feeling trapped between the beast and the flames, he fired anyway. The bow twanged absurdly, and the arrow buried itself in the sand. Rich fired again, and his arrow flew up and out of sight.

The monster slid closer, raising itself over the plastic box of white powder.

"Shoot the box?" said Alex, who was sighting down her wonky bow, a burning arrow poised to fire. "Really?"

"Really!" shouted Rich.

"Okay." She shrugged.

It was only feet from them now, and it showed no sign of slowing. Two of its tentacles were reaching for them.

"Now!" yelled Rich.

Alex fired.

What happened next took everyone by surprise. The arrow flew perfectly straight and clean, smooth as a javelin, right into the open box. The moment it made contact, there was an explosion of yellow flame considerably brighter than the fire at their backs. It roared up, engulfing the monster's body, surrounding it in a blaze so dazzling that they had to turn their eyes from it.

The Insidious Bleck roared again, not in anger, but in mad and desperate pain. It rocked backward, stumbling, its underside black and scorched. The hair on its body burst into short-lived flame, and the upper parts of its tentacles looked raw and shiny. It fell back, twisting in its agony, rolling in the sand.

And then it was retreating up the beach, groaning, limping into the darkness. Moments later, it was gone.

"What in Krispy Kreme heck fire was that?" said Alex, still kneeling like a statue, her bow extended.

"I told you," said Darwen. "It was the Insidious Bleck."

"Not that," said Alex. "The stuff in the box. What was that?"

"Nondairy creamer," said Rich. "I saw a show about it on TV. Supposed to be highly flammable."

"Er, I'd say so," said Alex. She considered her twisted bow proudly. "Couldn't hit the ocean from the edge of

the ocean, huh?"

"That shot defied the laws of physics," said Rich to Darwen.

"You can't underestimate the power of attitude," said Alex. "And style," she added. "And poise under pressure—"

"Okay, Alex," said Rich. "It was a good shot."

"That's all I needed to hear," she said. "And I guess your sciencey bit with the nondairy creamer didn't suck either."

"We're a team," said Rich, grinning.

A team, thought Darwen, *but not the Peregrine Pact.*

Mr. Peregrine had abandoned them.

"So," said Alex, "when the nondairy whatsit stuff went all kablooey, would you say you were right chuffed?"

"Something like that," said Rich. "We should check on Mr. Iverson and Jorge," he added, gazing toward the shelter. "You think it's safe?"

"I think that octo-spider nightmare scared off everything within a ten-mile radius," said Alex.

"Good enough," Rich declared.

The three of them set off across the beach to the ranger station.

The shelter was a confusion of shattered glass, broken plastic, and splintered wood. The two men were huddled in one corner, partially barricaded in with overturned tables and chairs, which Rich and Darwen set to pulling

away. Alex picked up Jorge's fallen flashlight and shone it as Mr. Iverson crawled out.

"Are you okay?" asked Rich.

"I'm fine," said Mr. Iverson, finding his glasses and putting them on. "Just a bit of a headache."

He didn't look fine. He looked scared and confused. But before Darwen could inquire further, Jorge emerged from the rubble, and he looked worse, pale and blood spattered. Rich rummaged through a first aid box and set to dressing a particularly nasty-looking gash across the man's forearm.

"It's okay," said Jorge, though he didn't resist when Rich started anointing and bandaging.

"What about you three?" asked Mr. Iverson, eying the cut on the back of Darwen's leg. It had stopped bleeding quickly and looked much worse than it was.

"We're fine," said Darwen. "Did you see—"

Jorge shot him a hard look, and Darwen tried a different approach. "What did all this?" he said, gesturing vaguely at the shattered remains of the ranger station.

Everyone was watching Mr. Iverson. He rubbed the back of his head thoughtfully. "I'm not entirely sure," he said, looking around him. "I assumed the storm had brought the roof in, but it doesn't look like it. I thought I saw . . ." He hesitated, shrugging, and everyone was quiet for a moment. "I'm not sure. A minor concussion, I guess. Jorge?"

"Very strong winds," said Jorge, nodding but not really looking at him. "I cut my arm on the edge of the table."

"Really?" said Mr. Iverson. It was a genuine question. The science teacher seemed thoroughly unsure of himself.

"Yes," said Jorge. "But the storm has gone now. We're safe."

Darwen found himself wondering, not for the first time, why it seemed so important to keep the truth from Mr. Iverson, who had always been kind and helpful. What difference would it make if there was one more person who knew that they were in danger from the inhabitants of another world? What possible harm could it do? It would be good to have an adult to confide in, particularly with things as they were with Mr. Peregrine. Then again, if Mr. Peregrine didn't believe him, what chance did he have of persuading Mr. Iverson, who knew nothing of Silbrica or its creatures?

No. He couldn't tell Mr. Iverson, and he didn't trust Jorge. He was on his own, as usual—or rather *they* were. He knew he could count on Rich and Alex. He gave them a nod to follow him.

"You're going back out there?" said Jorge, curious and concerned.

"Won't be long," said Darwen.

"Be careful," said Mr. Iverson.

"Always," said Darwen.

"Well?" said Rich as soon as they were out of earshot of the shelter. "You think Mr. Iverson remembers more than he's saying?"

"No," said Darwen. "But listen. The monster—the Insidious Bleck—ran away."

"Well, I'm not sure about *ran*," said Alex. "More like *limped*."

"What do you want to do?" asked Rich, eyeing Darwen keenly in the last light of the dying fire.

"We should follow it," said Darwen.

"I'm sorry," said Alex. "I think I have sand in my ears. We should *what now*?"

"It's the opportunity we've been hoping for," said Darwen.

"When that creamy stuff caught fire," said Alex, "did you, you know, *inhale* any of it? Because something certainly fried your brain."

"The monster is running away, right?" Darwen insisted. "It will go through the portal to wherever Scarlett keeps it. If we follow it, we'll find Luis and the others. I know where the pool with the stones around it is."

"And if we find ourselves welcomed with open tentacle-like arms?" Alex persisted.

"You saw it," said Rich. "It's hurt and scared. It won't be waiting to attack us now."

"Oh, right," said Alex, "make me feel sorry for it!"

Darwen and Rich stared at her.

"I know," she said, holding her hands up. "It's an animal, right? It's probably just hungry."

"That's what Mr. Peregrine's been saying, but I'm not so sure," said Darwen. "It ate the pouncel right away. But with us . . . it was different. Like it was trying to catch us to take us back."

"Fine," said Alex. "But I'm bringing my physics-defying bow and arrows."

"Deal," said Darwen.

Rich snapped on his flashlight.

"Lead the way," he said.

It took them only a few minutes to find the mirror pool ringed with stones, and that was moving slowly, their flashlights constantly scanning the surrounding trees for pouncels. They found no sign of life, however, and the jungle was oddly quiet after the storm. Darwen gazed at the perfectly round depression brimming with bright rainwater, the stones around its rim arranged with mathematical precision.

"What makes you think it's still online?" asked Rich. "Looks like a puddle to me."

Darwen took a step closer and leaned over the pool, dreading the sight of a beak and curled tentacles nestled within.

There was no sign of the Bleck. But there was no sign of anything else either. The water was not actually water—not to Darwen's eyes, at least—but what it was he couldn't say. It looked like mist, a pearly fog in which vague, greenish lights pulsed, but beyond that . . .

"Take my hands," he said.

They did so, uncertainly. Rich's palm was hot and sweaty, Alex's cool and dry. Neither of them looked sure about this, and their lack of resolve deepened when they could see what Darwen could.

"Nothing's there," Rich cautioned. "It looks like cloud. What if it puts us in the treetops of some Silbrican jungle full of God knows what?"

"We've waited a long time for this," Darwen implored. "Alex?"

"Ready," she said.

"Rich?"

There was a moment of silence, then Rich slowly blew the air from his lungs. "Dang," he said. "Okay."

"On three," said Darwen. "One. Two. Three."

They stepped into the pool.

Immediately they found themselves on a mist-wreathed staircase, broad and fashioned from wrought iron, like the footbridge in a Victorian railway station, but huge, at least fifty feet wide, and rising—bizarrely—out of dense jungle. The light had a curious greenish cast that seemed to come from the forest itself.

"Why are the stairs so wide when the portal is so small?" asked Alex.

"The portal is just the stones and water on the other side," said Darwen. "They can be positioned anywhere, making the portal big as you like."

"These aren't just stairs. Look at that," said Rich, pointing to a huge lever. "They pivot, see? Pull that, and the stairs become a ramp."

"What for?" asked Alex.

"Let's find out," said Darwen.

They went down the stairs, and the metal steps rang beneath their feet as they descended into the stiff, wet fog that rose from the jungle floor. As they got lower, strange plants loomed out of the mist—thick, glossy leaves the size of elephant ears, pagoda towers of crimson flowers, bulging and pendulous amber fruit. The air was thick with the smell of damp earth and fragrances sweet and sour that hung in clouds around the vegetation. There was no breeze, and the stifling heat of the jungle rose significantly as they reached the forest floor. The odd green light seemed to emanate from the plants themselves. They throbbed as if they were taking long, slow breaths that set their leaves aglow. There was an electric hum that might have been machinery and might have been insects, and though there was no wind, Darwen could hear creeping movement all around.

"Whoa," said Alex. "This is even junglier than the place we just left."

Despite his rising unease, Darwen gave her a look. "*Junglier?*" he breathed.

"More jungle-y," she said, and then, shrugging at Rich, "More rainforest-y."

Rich barely smiled as he inched forward, leaning to avoid a massive blossom whose heavy cream petals were etched with veins of a poisonous-looking purple. "There's a clearing," he said, moving so that the fog billowed around him.

Darwen and Alex followed warily and saw that he was right. Though crisscrossed with vines, the ground was open in a circle. There was nowhere else to go unless they forced their way into the seemingly impassable wall of shrubs, flowers, and trees that surrounded them.

"So what do we do?" asked Alex, who was tiptoeing into the circle.

"Careful," said Rich. "There could be anything—"

But before he could get the warning out, something shot from the ground at Alex's feet. She leaped backward, and Darwen grabbed her arm as a pair of vines about ten feet apart erupted from the earth and shot straight up. It was like watching a time-lapse film of plants growing. The vines were thick, ropelike tendrils that twined and reached in the air like fingers looking for purchase. Great leaves sprouted and hung as the stems rose higher and leaned in toward each other, beginning to intertwine.

"Looks like muscadine," said Rich. "Wild grape."

"After you've dumped about a thousand gallons of Miracle Grow on it," said Alex.

"It's a gate," declared Darwen.

And as he said it, the two united vines throbbed, and something coursed through them, running top to bottom, whereupon the arching space between them flickered with rippling turquoise energy that sparkled like a waterfall.

"Okay," said Darwen, stepping closer so that he could feel the light from the portal flickering over his skin.

"Wait," said Alex. "I wanna try something."

She began to pace the rest of the clearing's perimeter. As she walked, new vines burst from the ground, sped up, united, and pulsed with the strange power of the gates. By the time she had rejoined them, there were four new portals around the edge of the clearing.

"So which do we go through?" asked Rich.

"How would Scarlett get the Bleck to . . ." Darwen paused, stooping, then straightened up. "It's this one."

"Why that one?" asked Alex.

Darwen ran his hand down the side of one of the vines and showed them his fingers, which had come away black and greasy. Pinched between his forefinger and thumb was a scrap of burned skin sprouting the remains of a coarse bristle. He studied the ground, following an imaginary path from the vine gate to the great staircase. He hadn't seen it before, but by the throbbing, sickly light from this side, he could make out the broken stems of plants in a clear and direct line. Something big had dragged itself straight across the clearing to the portal behind him.

"It went through here," he said.

They looked at each other, their faces ghastly in the pea-green glow.

"Ready?" said Darwen.

"I wish you'd stop asking that," said Alex. "No. We're not ready. Never will be. But we're going anyway, okay?"

"Okay," echoed Darwen.

"Wait," said Rich. "Let me just check something." He stepped up close to the curtain of energy as if studying it, then, being careful not to touch Darwen with any part of his body, he brought his right hand up to the portal and made contact.

There was flash of emerald-white light, and Rich staggered back, shaking his fingers. His hair was standing on end, and there was a wisp of smoke that smelled faintly of electricity.

"That was smart," said Alex. "Time to hold hands with the mirroculist, I think."

Rich nodded, his eyes wide. "Good call," he said.

They joined hands and stepped through together.

It took less than a second for them to wish they hadn't.

It was the sound that struck them first: a deafening blare of drills and hammers, the rumble of heavy machinery, and the clang of metal. The smudged and brownish air was thick with the smell of welding torches, smoke, and oil, and after the brightness of the energy curtain, it took them a moment to see where they were.

Indoors, thought Darwen. *Not a jungle locus. Some kind of hangar or warehouse*.

He could feel flagstones beneath his feet. As he gaped

through the murk, his eyes stung and ran, but he made out shapes in pools of feeble yellow light: great iron hulks linked with girders and cables and studded with warning lamps, engines with riveted water tanks and tall funnels, and—strangest of all—a massive iron cage the size of a house, a cage whose bars flickered with electricity. Inside, huddled against the back wall, was the Insidious Bleck.

So his suspicion had been right. The Bleck was not acting alone.

But it wasn't its own master either.

Darwen stared, and as his eyes grew accustomed to the dim light, he could see that the warehouse was packed with items even stranger than the caged and tentacled beast. There were statues in gold and gaudy colors, booths and tents for sideshows and fairground games, a dusty carousel with painted horses and mystic symbols lettered in enticing paint. It felt like an abandoned carnival or circus, but then something else caught his eye: a long black metal tube, like a submarine, but on caterpillar tracks, like a tank. The tube had smoky windows.

Darwen didn't need to get up close to know that it contained child-sized seats and metal harnesses linked by wires to oversized batteries. It was a generator like the one he had destroyed in Moth's forest, and there would be children in it. But this one was on wheels and was pointed right at the archway through which they had just come. That meant only one thing.

They—whoever they were—planned to bring it through.

That was why the iron steps to the jungle portal became a ramp. Darwen looked around and saw massive bulldozers arranged like tanks and other pieces of machinery—including more generators—that they were still finishing.

And inside each one of them there would be children. Luis, Eduardo, and Calida, for sure, but also others whose names he could only learn after he got them out.

But that was easier said than done, because the warehouse wasn't just full of machines. It was alive with man-sized figures in overalls, their heads hooded with what looked like grotesque bronze-colored gas-masks.

Scrobblers.

They were a good hundred yards away, but there was no doubt in Darwen's mind: they were bigger and scarier than any he had seen before, and several of them were armed with huge, strange-looking weapons sprouting copper pipes and iron blast shields, but they were scrobblers all the same. Darwen watched them, and that was when he saw it. Right in the middle of all that weird carnival bric-a-brac, seated on a raised platform, was something that chilled Darwen's blood more than the scrobblers, more even than the terrible generator.

It was a glass case with what looked like a dummy seated inside. The figure was dressed in clown clothes and had orange hair and a little blue hat, but its staring eyes had a manic focus, and its gaping mouth was black, hollow, and lined with bright teeth.

"No," Darwen muttered.

"What?" Rich whispered.

"Just . . . don't look at it," said Darwen. "I have to get to that generator."

"But there are scrobblers everywhere!" hissed Alex.

"This is what we came for," said Darwen. "I have to."

And he took a step forward.

Instantly the mechanical clown kicked into sudden and horrible life. It lurched backward and forward, its movements jerky and unnatural, and as it did so, the laughter started, full voiced but recorded, as if coming from long ago.

Whatever else it was, the clown's laughter was a species of alarm. The scrobblers straightened up, turning, roaring with muffled anger as they spotted Darwen, Rich, and Alex.

One of them raised what looked like a cannon fixed by a metal arm to the harness it was wearing, pumped back a slide, and fired. There was a crack like thunder, a rush of smoke with a hot, flaming center, and something shot toward them. For a fraction of a second, Darwen thought madly of tentacles before realizing that it was in fact a tangle of steel cable and hooks: a net.

He dove to his right, and the steel trap missed him by a hair's breadth. It hit Rich and Alex, throwing them back and springing closed around them. The web tightened, and, with a squeal of metal, a winch mechanism on the scrobbler's back started to draw them toward it. Darwen caught a glimpse of Alex's face as they were pulled past him. Her eyes were wide with horror. Rich was crumpled, his eyes shut. He had been knocked unconscious by the impact.

Darwen sprang to his feet and ran after the metal net, not knowing what to do but sure he had to help. Other scrobblers had focused on him now, and one of them fired another of the harpoon traps. It careened over his head and snapped back again as it exhausted the slack with a sound like a whip cracking. He ducked as it cannoned back toward the scrobbler, then ran forward again, swallowing down the terror that he was actually moving *toward* the enemy. One of the scrobblers, its red eyes just visible through the glass of its gas mask, had picked up a heavy wrench in its massive fists and was swinging it menacingly, the muscles of its greenish arms rippling.

Darwen took one more stride, then flung himself headlong onto the net. He seized the cables but was almost thrown off as it sped back toward the scrobbler like a retractable tape measure. Alex was squirming inside, but Rich was motionless, and his eyes were still closed. Darwen scrambled for a release mechanism, but the tension of the cable kept the net shut tight.

"There's got to be some sort of quick-release catch!" shouted Alex over the cackling laughter of the clown. The scrobbler with the wrench took a long stride toward them.

Darwen looked wildly around. He had no more than ten seconds. Less if the one with the wrench decided to rush them rather than wait for the winch to do its work.

As the three of them were pulled closer, the net plowed through castoff cable and discarded tools. Darwen saw a metal implement and reached for it without knowing for sure what it was until he had it: a crowbar, long and heavy with a spike at one end.

He swung it at the clasp that fastened the net to the cable, missed, and tried again. The point slid off the iron, but Darwen had put all his weight into the strike, and he couldn't stop it from slamming into the stone floor beneath. Sparks sprayed from the tip of the crowbar for a moment, and then, with a terrible keening sound, the net's progress stopped so abruptly that Darwen was thrown forward.

The crowbar had gone through the net and lodged in a gap between the uneven flagstones. The pitch of the winch shifted up a register, whining dangerously, and Darwen rolled around to see the scrobbler batting at the controls with its massive, clawed hands as smoke issued from one side. Whatever the creature was trying to do didn't work, because it pitched suddenly forward onto its face.

With the net stuck, the winch was pulling the scrobbler toward them!

Darwen got to his knees and fumbled for the clasp where the crowbar was jammed into the ground. There was a single restraining bolt holding it to the net. He seized it and tried twisting the nut off the end, but his sweaty fingers slid, and it wouldn't move. The scrobbler on the end of the cable was getting closer, sliding on its back toward them as the one with the wrench gave chase.

Darwen gritted his teeth and tried again, sure his hands were bleeding, and suddenly the nut moved.

Darwen spun it off. Then he tugged at the bolt, ignoring the scrobblers that were almost on top of him now.

It came free in his hands, and several things happened at once. The scrobbler that had been winching toward them stopped abruptly as the cable tore free, and the scrobbler with the wrench tripped heavily over its companion. In the same instant, the net sprang open, and Alex emerged with impossible speed.

Rich, however, did not move.

Darwen pulled at him, but the boy was too heavy, too tangled up in the trap.

"We have to go!" shouted Alex.

More scrobblers were coming from all over the great smoky chamber. Dozens of them. One of them fired some version of the energy weapon that Darwen had seen at Halloween, and a great jet-like lightning tore across the room and slammed into the wall beside them like an artillery shell. There was a blaze of light so bright that for a moment Darwen couldn't see at all, could only feel Alex pulling at him. "Rich!" he shouted. "Wake up!"

But Rich didn't stir, and dimly, horribly, Darwen realized that Alex was right. He couldn't even let her go by herself. She needed him to open the portal.

The scrobbler with the wrench was back up and running. Others were only feet behind that one.

Wiping angry tears from his eyes, he muttered, "Sorry," and, "I'll come back," and then he sprang to his feet, shooting one last desperate look at the generator he had not reached. He ran back the way they had come, snatching at Alex's hand as he did so, the clown's laughter still ringing in his ears.

They crashed through the curtain of energy that led back to the jungle clearing, and Darwen stumbled in his haste. Alex's hand slipped from his just as they came through, and she tore across the circle to the other side, falling straight into one of the other vine-framed portals despite her attempts to stop herself. Darwen saw the arch in front of her, saw the flickering wall of light, and waited for her shout of pain as she bounced off.

But she made no sound. And instead of being thrown back as Rich had been, she rolled right through. The flickering curtain closed behind her, and Darwen could only stare in disbelief.

What on earth . . . ?

He stood up. Should he go after her or abandon her as he had abandoned Rich? The scrobblers would be following. He had no time to decide.

And then she was back, standing in the gateway looking astonished and scared. "Pouncels," she said. "Lots of them. Go!"

They ran along the path from the clearing and onto the wrought-iron staircase. As they reached it, they heard the crackle of a portal opening behind them, and the scrobbler with the wrench came barreling out into the green and glowing jungle.

"Go!" shouted Alex again.

The scrobbler turned its terrible gas-masked face and came after them.

Darwen ran up the stairs two at a time, reaching behind for Alex as he got to the top. She didn't wait to take his hand, however, and went straight through the portal. He followed, horror and confusion and panic fighting inside his head for dominance, and then he was out in the clammy night air of Caño Island again.

Darwen stopped, all of the terrible things that had happened breaking over him.

He had failed to get Luis. And they had left Rich behind.

"Darwen!" Alex screamed.

A gas mask was coming up through the portal. For a moment Darwen could see its hateful red eyes through the glass, the green-tinged skin and yellowing tusks beneath the brass and leather, but Darwen felt frozen, like he had left half of himself back in the warehouse with Rich.

"Darwen!" Alex shrieked.

And that was all it took.

Darwen came to life again, kicking the stone spheres out of position. There was a flicker and a pop. The scrobbler dropped out of sight, and the portal became dark, leaf-strewn earth once more.

The boat arrived for them shortly after dawn. The official word was that Rich had gotten lost in the storm, so while Darwen and Alex were ferried back to the mainland with a stunned Mr. Iverson and a taciturn Jorge to be fed and to have their wounds tended, a team of three local people who knew the rainforest best would comb the island for him. The journey back was spent in absolute silence, a silence that Darwen did not break until he found Mr. Peregrine in his odd-smelling tent. "They took him," he said in a flat, hollow voice. "The scrobblers took Rich."

"Scrobblers?" said Mr. Peregrine, his teacup poised at his lips, his injured hand still bandaged. "Are you sure?"

"We saw them," said Alex, coming up behind Darwen. "They nearly got us too."

"We had no choice," Darwen added, desolate but determined to explain this above all. "We had to leave him. But we're going back. We just need to figure out how." He had not discussed this with Alex, but he knew he didn't need to.

She just nodded, her face defiant.

"Scrobblers?" Mr. Peregrine repeated.

"And you know who they work for," said Alex.

"Well, historically," Mr. Peregrine began, but Darwen cut him off.

"Greyling," said Darwen. He said it without bitterness, without triumph, but he gave Mr. Peregrine a long, frank look until the teacher finally sat back.

"Greyling?" said Mr. Peregrine, incredulous. "Greyling was defeated. This has nothing to do with—"

"It does," said Darwen. "I saw the generators. It's him."

"Did you see him?" asked Mr. Peregrine.

Darwen shook his head, but at that moment they heard people on the track to the village: two local adults and their three small children loaded with bags going down to the beach. Scarlett had bought off another family.

"That's not all," said Darwen. "Gabriel marooned us on that island on purpose. Possibly with Jorge's help. We were supposed to be taken by the Bleck."

"Whatever is taking the children is just an animal," said Mr. Peregrine, smiling. "It's not working with anyone. I realize that you have had a terrible ordeal, but—"

"No," said Darwen, his eyes full of fire. "You don't. You weren't there. You didn't see. That's why I'm telling you." He paused, then continued more stoically, determined to get his point across. "You were right that it's not the Bleck that's primarily responsible. It appears to be what you say it is—an animal. But there's a kind of portal junction that connects several Silbrican jungle loci, and, with Scarlett's help, Greyling is using it to send the Bleck through to kidnap children. It doesn't eat them. It takes them for the generator." Darwen gave Mr. Peregrine a half second to let all of this sink in. "Once Greyling's figured out how to get machinery through the portals, they're going to bring the generators through. They will then have a power source in our world. Rich"—Darwen's voice fractured, and he had to clear his throat before continuing—"is probably already inside."

"And the pouncels?" asked Mr. Peregrine, his expression still guarded.

"They're irrelevant," answered Darwen automatically. "I think they're getting into our world by accident."

Mr. Peregrine stared at him for a long moment, then put his cup down and got to his feet.

"Oh, and I opened a portal," said Alex. "By myself. Not much of an upside, I'll grant you, but still. Kind of cool."

"You did what?" said Mr. Peregrine, staring at her.

"Opened a portal," said Alex. "Without touching Darwen or anything. Fell right through it into this weird-looking jungle where about twenty pouncels were hanging out. Got the heck out of there faster than green grass through a goose."

"But *how*?" asked Mr. Peregrine.

"Don't ask me," said Alex. "Guess the world now has two mirroculists. Count 'em, see?"

She pointed first at Darwen and then at herself.

"Maybe it's like an upgrade," she said. "If you spend a lot of time nearly getting killed over there, they let you in and out all by your lonesome."

More than anything else they had told him, more even than Rich's capture, this seemed to arrest Mr. Peregrine's attention.

Darwen was annoyed. "I'm telling you all this so you can help me when I go back," he said.

"I need to . . ." Mr. Peregrine began, but he still seemed preoccupied and was regarding Alex with a peculiar intensity. "I'll catch up with you later," he said, walking briskly off the platform and up toward the dining shelter.

"Okay . . ." said Alex as she watched him go. "You ever get the feeling someone's not telling us everything?"

"How about *anything*?" said Darwen.

"I can smell smoke," said Alex. "Why can I smell smoke?"

Darwen turned toward the dining shelter and saw an unwelcome figure in crisp khakis and a safari shirt on the path.

"There you are, Arkwright," said Mr. Sumners. "Lessons have begun. I suggest you bring your notebooks and pens."

Darwen stared at him. "Lessons?" he said. "Now?"

"Life at Hillside goes on," said the math teacher.

"We're not at Hillside," said Alex. "We're in the jungle, and one of our friends is missing."

"Hillside Academy," said Mr. Sumners, drawing himself up, "is a state of mind. We, ahhh, take it wherever we go. It is our guide, our compass, and our mode of being, all of which makes this"—he gestured at the trees around them—"a school, not a holiday resort. As for Mr. Haggerty, I am confident the locals will find him. It's not that large an island. Now, time for class."

He walked away, and Darwen, suddenly flooded with rage, took a step after him.

"Whoa there, tiger," said Alex, staying him with a hand. "We've got bigger fish to fry. Sumners is an insufferable loser, but the chances of him strapping us into a

machine that drains our life force to power his microwave are slim. Let's stay focused, yeah?"

Darwen couldn't argue with that. "We need to get ready," he said, pulling himself together. "We need a plan and a weapon."

"I'm thinking bows and arrows plus a vat of coffee creamer aren't gonna cut it," said Alex.

"Agreed," said Darwen. "But if Mr. P has a Silbrican rocket launcher in his tent, he hasn't mentioned it."

"Judging by the smell, I'd say he's more likely to be hoarding some very old cheese," said Alex. "And even if he has a weapon, I'm not convinced he'd give it to us."

"What do you mean?"

"Well, he's not exactly helped out a lot so far, has he?"

"He's the one who brought us here in the first place," said Darwen, looking away. "His mirror showed me Luis being abducted."

"That was handy, wasn't it?"

"What do you mean?" Darwen faltered. There was something in Alex's eyes that he hadn't seen before, some terrible thought that she couldn't put into words. "What?"

"Don't freak out on me, okay?" she said, her voice lowering. "But have you considered the possibility that Mr. Peregrine isn't being honest with us?"

"He's made some mistakes," admitted Darwen.

"What if they weren't mistakes?" Alex said.

Darwen stared at her, and for a moment everything around them, the cries of birds and monkeys, the wash of the ocean, the distant chatter of students, went away. "What are you saying?" he said.

He couldn't explain it, but something cold and terrible was welling up inside him, something worse than fear, and it brought tears to his eyes.

"We came here," said Alex, staring at the ground, "because Mr. P brought us. Then his portable portal took us to the very worst place possible, and we were lucky to get back alive."

"He said it malfunctioned."

"And you didn't believe him," she interrupted. "You thought it had been tampered with, that it was a trap to get us killed. What if it was? What if it was him who set it?"

Darwen turned away, his eyes swimming. "I know he's been skeptical," he said, unsure of why he was trying to defend Mr. Peregrine. Alex was saying no more than he had begun to think himself. She was just pushing it further. "But he sent the oven door that took me to Weazen."

"You don't even know that for sure," she said. "It was mailed to you. The one useful thing you've been given might not have come from him. Darwen, from day one you've told him that the kids were being taken by the Insidious Bleck, and from day one he said that it didn't exist. We've seen it. You say Scarlett is controlling the

Bleck, and he says she's not. Turns out, she is. You say she's working for Greyling, he says she's not. I think you're right. So either he doesn't know what he's talking about, or he's lying."

Darwen stared straight ahead, refusing to believe it.

Alex continued, her voice softer this time though no less commanding. "We escaped the Bleck. If we had relied on him, we'd be dead. Again."

"So he made a mistake."

"What if he didn't? What if he's working for—"

"NO!" shouted Darwen again, his hands coming up to his ears as if he could blot out her challenge, stop it from giving fire to all his own smoldering doubts. "He wouldn't. He's my friend. . . . My . . ."

Darwen's blood roared in his ears, but he kept his fists clenched to his sides.

"He's not," said Alex. "I know you want him to be, but he's not. And you are going to have to think real hard about how much he's helping, because if you just trust him blindly . . . I don't know. I see badness ahead."

"Why would he send us into a trap?" said Darwen quietly, as if his own voice was afraid of admitting the possibility. All of a sudden he remembered the blood he had seen on the note attached to the oven door.

"You're the mirroculist, Darwen, remember? You are what Greyling fears most: a person who can see right into what he's doing and can come in to stop him. You are the target. Rich and I are just . . . bystanders."

"Not if you're a mirroculist too," he replied.

"Don't think that hasn't occurred to me," she said.

"And they already have Rich," said Darwen, squeezing his eyes shut. "It's my fault. I have to . . ."

He started to walk.

"Where are you going?"

"To find Mr. Peregrine," said Darwen, not looking back.

"And do what?"

"I'm going to ask him which side he's on," said Darwen, still pressing forward.

"Oh, that's genius," said Alex, running up behind him. "Masterful spy work there. Ask him which side he's on, because if he wants us dead he's really gonna just tell you the truth."

"You have a better plan?"

"That's not a plan."

"A better idea, then," he said, turning to glower at her.

"Well, for one thing," she said, "I'm coming with you."

Darwen shrugged, and together they marched up the path toward the dining shelter. They were almost there when they realized something was going on. The quiet of the lesson had been broken by the sounds of voices and shifting benches. By the time Darwen and Alex could see properly, the students were streaming up past the washrooms and onto the trail into the jungle. There were teachers and camp workers with them, several of them running.

Darwen and Alex gave chase, conscious that the tang of wood smoke in the air was getting stronger. The group moved on through the trees, all the way up to where the end of the zip line was fixed to the final tower. It was immediately clear what had attracted the attention, and Darwen could only stare in amazement.

A huge circle at least fifty yards across had been cleared out of the jungle. Monumental trees had been pushed over, torched in pyres around the rim, and the underbrush had been scraped clean right down to the dirt. In the center was a ring of stone spheres and a shallow pool. Around the edge were bright yellow bulldozers marked with the logo of Sunbelt Vacation Properties.

The babble of excitement died as soon as the students saw what had happened. The forest, which had breathed and called and pulsed with life, was dead, ravaged, and smoking. The silence was deafening, and Darwen saw that even the teachers looked stunned and uncertain. Miss Martinez was sobbing quietly.

"Three cheers for progress!" shouted Nathan Cloten. "Hip, hip, hooray!"

Barry Fails joined in, but no one else did, and Naia Petrakis turned such a fierce look on them that they stopped, smirking.

Standing beside one of the yellow bulldozers, Mr. Peregrine and Jorge were talking earnestly. Darwen looked into the water at the edge of the circle and saw only his reflection, but there was no question that this was a portal. All that was needed was for the sun to come down, and then it would come online.

He left Alex, pushing his way through the crowd, but Jorge saw him coming.

"Stay back," Jorge ordered. "It is very dangerous here. Everyone needs to go back to the camp. Señor Delgado!" he called, and the man from the village pushed his way through the crowd. He was carrying a rifle, and there were other villagers with him, all armed. They stood around the circle of observers like guards, their backs to the devastation in the center. "No one is to come in this area."

Jorge turned and started walking out of the blasted clearing, Mr. Peregrine at his side. Darwen was about to head them off when a hand caught at his elbow. It was Alex.

"What?" he said.

"It's not just this," said Alex, and her eyes were shiny. "It's worse."

"What do you mean?" Darwen asked. "What's happened?"

"Two more kids have been taken," she said. "Gabriel and Chip."

Darwen stared at her.

"Are you sure?" he asked. "Gabriel? But he was working with Jorge! And Chip Whittley?"

She nodded.

Darwen marched toward Mr. Peregrine and Jorge so forcefully that both men stopped.

"What are you going to do?" he demanded. "To get them back. Rich and Gabriel. And Chip. What are you going to do?"

"I don't know what you mean," Jorge began.

"Yes, you do," said Darwen. "You know all about it. So do you," he added to Mr. Peregrine, "and so does Gabriel, who marooned us on the island for the Insidious Bleck."

Jorge opened his mouth to say something, but changed his mind. Instead he looked at Mr. Peregrine, who sighed. "We should probably talk," he said.

"In the office then," said Jorge, who looked irritated. "Now get these people away from here."

As the students were corralled and led, complaining, back to the dining shelter, Darwen and Alex slipped into the office by the kitchen and waited. Barry Fails saw them, but he just assumed they were in trouble and made faces. Mr. Sumners saw them, but his protests were cut off by Mr. Peregrine. Mr. Iverson saw them, and his eyes tightened with puzzlement and suspicion.

Darwen and Alex ignored them all, waiting.

At last Mr. Peregrine and Jorge entered the wooden

structure together and closed the door behind them. Jorge's eyes flicked to Mr. Peregrine, who just nodded.

"I am an emissary from the Guardian Council of Silbrica," said Jorge. "I was assigned to this territory a year ago and am the ranking official in matters concerning this region."

Darwen looked at Mr. Peregrine, but the old man was silent, his eyes downcast, his face somber. Whatever they were about to be told was not good news.

"You were brought here to find tears in the fabric of the barriers between worlds," Jorge continued. "You have failed in that task, and your mission is at an end. I suggest you rejoin your classmates—"

"What?" sputtered Darwen. "We did find them, and they're not tears, they're portals. People make them! There's one back there behind the camp!"

"That is all I am at liberty to say," said Jorge.

Mr. Peregrine coughed quietly and, when Jorge looked at him, nodded slowly once more.

"Very well," said Jorge. "The creature who calls herself Scarlett Oppertune has made an offer to the council through me. We, the camp and the villagers, are to leave this place for her development. The council has agreed to her terms."

Darwen's jaw dropped open. "You can't be serious!" he exclaimed.

"If we stay," Jorge said, "more children will be taken.

The Oppertune creature has plans."

"Greyling," said Darwen. "She works for Greyling."

"Greyling?" Jorge repeated, eyebrows raised. "No," he continued, shaking his head. "The situation is bad, but there is no reason to think—"

"Scarlett is Miss Murray," said Darwen. "I'm almost sure of it. I saw her transform, and inside she looks exactly like the eel thing that came out of Miss Murray. Let's not forget that she worked for Greyling last year. That's why she has a scrobbler army and generators."

"No," said Jorge. The half smile was gone now, and the look he shot Mr. Peregrine was impatient. "You should not encourage such fantasies, Octavius," he said. "I have told you this before. We already have two real problems. Let's not invent a third."

"Two problems?" asked Alex.

"I mean that things are bad enough with this Bleck creature loose and Miss Oppertune's demands without imagining that Greyling himself is somehow involved."

Darwen couldn't believe what he was hearing. "You don't have two problems," he said. "You don't even have three. You have one. Scarlett and the Bleck and Greyling are working together! The Bleck creature isn't loose at all: it's in a cage, and it's sent out specifically to take kids and bring them back for Greyling's generators."

"Nonsense," Jorge riposted. "Miss Oppertune intends to

establish a place for herself here. We have decided that we cannot fight her without considerable loss, and the council feels that if a portion of the world has to be given over to her, it is better that it is a place like this rather than—"

"Somewhere closer to home," Alex cut in. "Somewhere with richer people in it."

"It is not an ideal situation," said Jorge. "We have to make the best of a bad predicament. You will all be going back to Hillside tomorrow anyway."

"And you get what in return?" Darwen demanded.

"Scarlett will sign a treaty promising not to expand from this area," said Jorge.

Alex gave a caustic bark of laughter. "And you buy that?" she said. "Boy, you are cute, but you're dumb. This is just wrong."

Jorge began, "We have no reason to think—"

"She's right," Darwen cut him off, his voice as cold and hard as steel. "You're dumb. Scarlett wants this area because it's dotted with those stone spheres that she can use to open up portals anywhere she likes. All she has to do is collect them, put them wherever she wants, in whatever country she wants, add water, and invade. She's going to build a base here for her master, and then he's going to go wherever he feels like going, and you won't be able to stop him."

"Miss Oppertune is a businesswoman," said Jorge.

"We will be able to make a fair deal with her."

"She puts children in Greyling's machines!" Darwen exclaimed. "She takes them from their families and drains them, and you think you can *deal* with her?"

"You are confusing separate problems," said Jorge, "and imagining others. The council knows nothing of these generators you speak of."

"We've seen them," Darwen insisted.

"We have only your word for that," said Jorge. He seemed slightly embarrassed to have to call Darwen a liar to his face, but clearly he thought they could dance around it no longer.

There was a moment's silence.

"Mr. P?" Alex demanded. "You go along with this?"

"I serve the council, of course," observed Mr. Peregrine. "But . . ."

"Hold it," said Jorge. "You don't want to say anything else."

"Let him speak," said Darwen. "It's time he told us the truth."

Mr. Peregrine considered him, and Darwen thought he saw a flash of something in his eyes that was almost a smile. A fat, black fly had settled on his cheek just below his left eye, but he didn't seem to notice. "Truth," he said, musing. "Very well. I think that you, Darwen Arkwright, do not need the Guardian Council. I think they know that and are afraid. I think that you should open the portal behind the campsite—"

"Now wait a minute," sputtered Jorge.

"Open the portal," Mr. Peregrine persisted, "and see for yourself."

The old man's manner was quite different. His eyes were full of a strange intensity, and the flicker of a smile was now unmistakable. Still, though, his body hadn't moved a muscle, and the fly on his face was still there.

"Octavius," said Jorge to Mr. Peregrine, fuming, "we have known each other a long time, but you leave me no choice. I am relieving you of your authority."

"Which was to be expected," said Mr. Peregrine, finally moving so that the fly was dislodged and flew buzzing around the office. "The Guardians never did tolerate opposing positions very well."

"Come on, Alex," said Darwen. "I guess we'll have to stop him by ourselves."

"Darwen, I understand your feelings," said Jorge.

"You understand nothing," said Darwen, turning on him savagely. "You believe in nothing."

"If you interfere with the Guardians' wishes," said Jorge, "we will have to stop you."

"Yeah, pretty boy?" said Alex, stepping so close to where Jorge was sitting that her face was inches from his. "Bring it on."

Darwen and Alex had left the office full of defiance and determination. Five hours later, their plans and preparations made, that determination had not dulled.

"You okay?" Darwen asked Alex.

"I think so."

"We have a little over an hour until sunset," said Darwen. "I think you should go."

She nodded, but still looked uncertain.

"What if I can't—"

"You'll be fine," he said. "I trust you."

"Great." She frowned. "No pressure."

Darwen grinned and watched her leave before setting off on his own. She was making for the houses by the soccer field; he was heading into the jungle again.

Though the sky over the ocean was painted with the soft blue and gold of twilight, the forest itself was getting dark fast. Since Darwen had decided that he couldn't stick to the path all the way for fear of being seen, he had to pick his way through the trees, studying the leaves at his feet for signs of movement. No one had seen a bushmaster or fer-de-lance so far, and he prayed he wouldn't be the first, particularly not out here by himself in the gathering gloom. He tried not to think about the wandering pouncels.

It took him over half an hour to complete the journey, which was odd because he knew he would soon be covering the exact same distance in a matter of seconds. At one point he had pushed a little too far north and had only caught himself when he saw the trees thinning suddenly: it was the clearing. He waited, conscious of a man—Mr. Delgado, he thought—pacing the perimeter with a rifle. Again, Darwen crept west. He didn't swing back north until he knew he was well past the circle of yellow bulldozers.

How could anyone not be outraged?

Perhaps, as Rich said, they just didn't care. Hillside

looked after its own, and the people who lived here—worthy though they were of the kind of study you would apply to Latin or algebra—were anything but Hillside's own. For the students this was a trip into a different world. It might be a kind of theme park erected for their amusement, but as a place where people lived, it was no more real to them than Blackpool Pleasure Beach.

For a moment the image of the clown face came into Darwen's mind, and he heard its cycling laughter, but he pushed the memory away.

Even in daylight it would be hard to navigate through this part of the jungle. To the north and east, the ground rose steeply, but down here Darwen could see nothing beyond the trees surrounding him. Only when there was a gap in the canopy could he correct his course based on the metal cable high above the treetops, and as the light dropped still further, he would lose even that.

He checked his watch and picked up the pace.

The woods hummed with the chirp of insects, and once Darwen spotted a brilliant yellow-and-black frog, bright as plastic, sitting on a leaf. He kept his distance, knowing it was poisonous. Once, he heard movement in the undergrowth to his right and saw bushes shift as the creature—pig, coati, deer, or something predatory like a mountain lion—moved off. He was still watching for the animal when he realized he had found what he was looking for.

It was, simply, a tree. A big one that lanced up into the canopy like the mast of a ship. It was twined with ancient vines as thick as Darwen's waist. These had grown into the bark as they spiraled up, and at various heights on the trunk, steel cables had been bolted into place. Spikes were set into the tree all the way up in a kind of ladder.

Darwen took a long look up, wiped the sweat from his brow, and started to climb.

It was slow, precarious going, and by the time he reached the planked platform, the sun had set entirely. He moved cautiously, feeling his way around and clinging to the vast trunk. It was so dark that it hardly made a difference, but he kept his eyes focused on the tree itself, not turning outward until he felt absolutely secure.

He was at least a hundred feet up, gazing out over the dark jungle canopy. The zip line's twined steel cable ran up to the northwest and down, back over that distant clearing with its yellow bulldozers, to the camp. From here he could barely make out the space where the trees had been cut. It seemed very far below and miles away, though he knew he would cover the distance in under a minute once he got moving.

From his backpack he took out a harness that he had taken from the office that afternoon, and he stood on tiptoes to hook it over the cable. He was struggling with it when a whir of movement and a volley of sound exploded inches above his head. He jumped, lost his balance, and stumbled toward the edge of the platform as the toucan—fortunately that's all it was—rocketed into the dusk. He caught himself, but the harness slipped, hung tantalizingly on a stray branch, then fell all the way to the bottom.

Darwen swore, then checked his watch. Perhaps he would have time to climb back down. . . .

Darwen had barely completed the thought when a flicker, like lightning, flashed up from the forest floor in the distance behind the camp. He watched it change to a soft radiant glow, circular, in the middle of the clearing.

It was now or never. There was certainly no time to make a perilous climb back down the tree for the harness.

Fumbling with the dread of what he was about to do, Darwen unthreaded the belt from his pants and reached up. He looped the belt over the cable twice, threaded the end through the buckle, and twined what was left around his wrist. He tried a little jump to see if it would take his weight, and the belt slid a few inches down the zip line, leading Darwen to drop his feet to the platform in panic.

His hands and face were sweating. He could feel the cold trickle down his back, soaking his shirt. He felt the air beneath him stir and was reminded of just how far he had to fall, how much danger awaited him even if he succeeded.

He gritted his teeth and stepped off the platform into nothing.

He shot down the zip line, the wind rushing against his face, and almost immediately he could feel the leather of the belt getting hot. He tried to adjust it, but his weight was too great. He was also picking up speed.

He took his eyes off the belt, which he thought had started to smoke, and realized just how quickly he was going. Ahead and below he could make out the clearing, lit by the soft glow of the portal. And then he saw a flash and, a fraction of a second later, heard the crack of a rifle from the trees below.

They had spotted him.

He pulled his legs up, feeling the heat in the leather starting to burn his fingers, and looked down. The pool gazed up at him like an eye. He was still forty feet above it, but it had to be . . .

Now.

He untwisted the belt from his wrist, held for one last second, then let go.

He fell like a stone, pointing with his feet, hoping against hope that he would hit the target and not the ground, which would surely kill him. He dropped through the darkness, heard the singing path of another bullet speeding past him, and then entered the pearly glow of the portal.

There was no splash. There was only the sudden dazzling flare of energy, blinding him completely for a second, and then only chaos and pain.

It took a second for Darwen to realize what had happened. He had expected the shock in his legs and knees, but the shot to his right arm and forehead took him so completely by surprise that he almost blacked out. He opened his eyes, his head swimming, but he was still moving, falling, rolling down the wrought-iron stairs from the portal into the thick greenish fog of the jungle locus. He was holding something large and padded, like an oddly shaped leather couch that was falling with him, and it was that object that was protecting him from the hard metal edges of the steps. He had reached the bottom before he realized that the couch was actually nothing of the kind.

It was a massive toad. Or very nearly. It was like a toad, its skin warty and brownish, its eyes huge and bulging, its mouth wide and flat, but it was also like a scrobbler. It had paws like hands with long, horny nails, and it was longer than a toad so that it might stand upright. It also wore fragments of armor and equipment.

It hit the ground with a thud and rolled onto its back. For a moment Darwen lay on top of it, staring into the blank eyes of the appalling creature he had landed on. Then he was scrambling off, terrified, but the monster didn't move, and its huge brown fists were open. The collision had knocked it out.

Darwen looked hastily around. It seemed like this was the lone guard. The jungle clearing with its vine-framed portals looked exactly as it had when he had seen it last.

Darwen's eyes returned to the prone toad-man. It was wearing what looked like pieces of stained chain mail looped across its chest and around its long, powerful limbs, and its head was half-covered by a leather helmet to which metal plates had been fastened. It wore an oversized backpack covered in dials and switches, all sparking ominously, which seemed to disappear into the creature's neck somehow. Darwen nudged the helmet with his foot, and it moved enough to show that the tubes from the backpack fitted through brass valves right into the monster's throat. Darwen shuddered. With an effort he lifted one of the beast's massive muscular arms and revealed a belt holster. He peered again into its face to ensure that those dreadful bulbous eyes were still blank, then unfastened the holster's flap and drew out a kind of pistol.

It was so heavy it would take both hands to aim and fire, and it wasn't quite like any gun Darwen had ever seen before, with its brass barrel and the curious bulb of blue glass that stuck out just beside the heavy trigger.

He considered shoving it down the back of his jeans, but decided that was a pretty good way of accidentally blowing his legs off. He held it in front of him instead and crossed over to the portal he had entered with Alex and Rich, but had left only with Alex.

He knew what was inside, knew also that if he was spotted right away, he was as good as dead, gun or no gun, but he thought again of his friends, of Luis, the boy he had seen in the grip of the Bleck weeks ago, and of that awful generator that was going to roll into his own world. He had no choice.

He took a deep breath and stepped through.

Things had changed since Darwen's last visit to the warehouse locus. What had been dark and smoky was now full of hard, brittle light, and the air pulsed with the swirling, wheezy music of a carnival organ. The wheeled generator had been swung around and shunted up to the very archway by a huge armored bulldozer covered in pipes and gears, which made the Sunbelt Vacation machines look like toys. As soon as Darwen stepped in, he was up against the generator. This was a stroke of luck, as it meant he didn't have to try to cross the vast warehouse unseen. Before, the generator had been bare and cold black iron, but now it was roughly painted in candy-striped red and white, like a circus tent. He ducked behind one of the great sets of wheels and looked for an entrance hatch.

Lights glowed dimly along the generator's length, and Darwen guessed that the cables that trailed from it were powering everything in the warehouse, even as they prepared to unhook it for the short journey fifty feet up through the portal and into the jungle clearing a world away. Darwen didn't need to look through the portholes in the side to know where that power was coming from, but he was also sure that they couldn't get it through the gate. He didn't know why, but the scrobbler machines stopped working when taken through the stone-sphere portals. That was why Scarlett was using a living being like the Bleck, and it meant that he still had time.

He peered through a gap in the caterpillar tracks and saw that the rest of the great chamber was pulsing with activity. There were the awful, headless gnashers bounding about on their knuckles, dragging spools of cable and machine parts, their shark mouths gaping across their chests like savage gashes. There were scrobblers with tools and weapons, their gas masks slapped with bright paint so that they all had leering, rigid clown faces. There were more of the ugly toad-men, some squatting, their heads low, others making slow, grotesque hops around the machinery, their warty skin like underfilled leather sacks. They all wore the control-studded backpacks, all wired directly into their throats. All the way at the back, there was the Insidious Bleck, pulsing slowly in its cage, watched warily by a handful of scrobblers with energy weapons. If any of them spotted him, he was dead. Simple as that.

Cluttering the floor were discarded sideshow booths and fair rides. He could see a long counter with air rifles fastened to it and a mechanical parade of rubber-duck targets. There were the cuplike seats from a luminous green waltzer studded with oversized lightbulbs, red bumper cars stacked up with their rod-like antennae and the lurid entrance sign for a ghost train, hung with fake cobwebs. Above them all, its back turned toward Darwen and sitting dark, still, and silent in his glass box was the World-Famous Laughing Man.

Darwen tore his eyes away and scanned the room for Greyling, whom he had seen last year as a glowing, silvery man in a hooded cloak. There was no sign of him, and only one figure truly stood out: a glamorous woman in a carefully tailored suit of shocking pink. Scarlett Oppertune. She, it seemed, was in charge.

Darwen watched her pointing and ordering, sending the gnashers and scrobblers scrambling to do her bidding, and a deep anger welled up inside him. This was all her doing: the abandoned village, the shattered jungle, the kidnapped children, and whatever her master, Greyling, planned to do once he had his base established.

Darwen had to force himself to return his focus to the generator. Before anything else happened, he had to get the children out. He had been searching for Luis for weeks, for Eduardo and Calida, and now for Rich.

But how?

The underside of the machine was like a great iron pipe that had been bolted together in sections. Each nut was the size of Darwen's fist. No way in there.

He crept out, keeping the hulking torpedo shape of the generator between him and the scrobbler army and its high-heeled general. He climbed onto the tracked wheels and then up onto the generator itself. There were portholes along the side, and through them a yellowish radiance streamed out. Reluctantly, Darwen looked in.

There were ten seats, eight of them already occupied. He saw Calida, Luis, and other local children whose faces he didn't recognize, all strapped in place, with metal headpieces wired into the generator's circuitry. At the far end was Chip, slumped over as if asleep, and beside him . . .

"Rich," Darwen breathed.

From here it was impossible to say how many of the children were still alive.

There was one way in: a hatch with a red-painted wheel, like an air lock. Darwen set down the heavy pistol, got a hold of the wheel, and tried to turn it first one way, then the other, but it wouldn't move. He strained, sweating, until he thought his muscles would tear from his bones, but the wheel wouldn't budge.

He sank back, gasping, and in his exhaustion he failed to notice the pistol that had been balanced precariously on a ledge behind him. He nudged it, watched as it wobbled and fell as if in slow motion, then swung his hand to catch it, and only succeeded in losing his balance. He slipped off the generator and hit the ground hard, no more than a second after the pistol had clattered its way down among the valves and pipes.

And then the laughter started. It seemed to come from everywhere, the same cycling roar of hysteria, and over in the center of the warehouse, Darwen could see the mechanical clown turning toward him and rocking in his chair.

They had seen him.

Darwen hurled himself to the ground as the first uneven

salvo of energy-weapon fire came streaking toward him. It lit the air like lightning, cannoning off the iron apparatus around him with showers of sparks. Somewhere at his back a valve burst, and steam rushed out in a hot and angry hiss.

Scarlett Oppertune spun toward him, her face a mask of fury. She bellowed her orders to the scrobblers. "Don't shoot at him, you idiots! You'll damage the equipment. Bring him to me."

As the hulking figures started their ponderous advance—joined by one of the monstrous toad creatures, the elbows of its forelegs splayed out as it lumbered forward—Darwen made a choice.

He knew he couldn't get the generator hatch open by himself. He dropped to his knees, reaching under the pipes and dusty cables, fingers straining, searching. The nearest scrobbler was only ten yards away, and there was a gnasher loping in his shadow, its shark mouth gaping. Darwen felt something hard, snatched at it, and came up with the pistol in his hands. He aimed and pulled the trigger.

But nothing happened, and then Scarlett began to laugh, a low, throaty chuckle of real amusement.

The scrobbler, which had hesitated, came on again, quicker now. The toad was coming too, and much faster than Darwen had thought possible. It opened that massive horizontal slash of a mouth, and Darwen suddenly knew how it would catch him.

Its tongue.

He stared at the gun. Maybe it had broken when it fell, or wasn't loaded, or . . . wasn't turned on! There was a switch just above the trigger guard. He flicked it over, and the glass bulb on the side glowed blue and steady, the whole pistol shivering in his grasp. The energy throbbed inside it, and the weapon become distinctly live, hovering, shifting, as if eager to find a target. It took all of Darwen's strength to keep it pointed in front of him. Once again, this time wincing away from it as he did so, he squeezed the trigger.

The pistol leaped in his hands. What came out of the end was not like a bullet at all. Instead a stream of blue-white force shot from the end and held like a rope for as long as he held the trigger. It wasn't tight and hard like a laser, but wandered and sparked erratically, so that the scrobbler had to sprawl a good ten feet out of its line of fire to be safe. The toad creature behind wasn't so fortunate. It strayed into the energy stream and was blown backward off its feet. When it hit the ground, it lay motionless and smoking, its tongue lolling.

Darwen released the trigger, scared of the power he had unleashed but confident that he had created a useful standoff. Scarlett, who wasn't laughing anymore, had retreated behind a massive Egyptian sarcophagus with a gold death mask, and the scrobblers were lumbering behind cover all around the warehouse. Only the blind gnashers seemed uncertain, stock-still and testing the charged air with their probing tongues as the laughter of the mechanical clown rose in pitch and volume, drowning out the carnival music. Darwen had bought himself valuable seconds.

But to do what? He couldn't use the pistol to open the generator without killing everyone inside, and though the gun was still humming, it was less than it had been. He wouldn't get many more shots like that out of it. His eyes flashed desperately around the warehouse, with its gleaming sideshows and carousel animals. The scrobblers were starting to inch toward him again. A voice came from the great gold sarcophagus: Scarlett.

"Well, now, Mr. Arkwright," she said. "We've been expecting you. So nice to see you again. Well, not really, but we must observe the pleasantries. As I recall, you made life rather difficult for me back in Atlanta when you knew me as Miss Murray. I won't be permitting anything like that tonight. So, while you have made quite an entrance, I'm afraid it won't improve the manner of your exit. But you have my attention. So let's see if we can come to some kind of agreement that might help you avoid any unpleasantness."

Darwen looked up. *Some kind of agreement?*

"I mean," she continued, "we can do it by the book: you sit there shooting until your weapon runs out of energy, and then my trusty agents gather you up and feed you into the generator. Or"—she paused, savoring the possibility—"we can try something different."

"Like what?" Darwen shouted back, stalling.

"Okeydoke," she said, suddenly chipper, "how about this? How about you kick your little gun over to one of my gas-masked friends, and I'll get you a milk shake—chocolate, of course—and we can have a little chat about some alternative futures."

Milk shake?

"Like I'd trust you!" Darwen shouted back. "You'd kill me as soon as you had the chance."

"Trust?" She laughed. "Who's talking about trust? I may have been a teacher, but I'm also a businesswoman. I wouldn't expect you to take my offer without a decent incentive. Lay down your weapon, walk away from the generator, and we'll talk. I could certainly make it worth your while."

"Meaning what?" said Darwen.

"Meaning that the New Council might make room for the mirroculist," she said, her voice silky now. "You've been confused, that's all. Learn to see things from our perspective and, oh, Darwen! What wonders will be open to you."

New Council? Darwen thought. But that's not what he

said aloud. "Wonders?" he echoed, lowering the pistol a little in his hands.

"All the marvels of Silbrica," she purred. "Not the few tame loci your friend Mr. Peregrine has shown you, but whole worlds beyond your imagination! Stand with us, and you will be able to stride between them all without so much as a thought, and with them will come power! It must be so tiresome, all your potential wasted on the petty doings of school and homework and bullies, trudging from place to place, sitting in traffic, when you could be leaping from portal to portal. How tedious it must be for you! How lonely!"

Distantly, Darwen was aware of the continuing laughter of the clown, and he remembered taking his mother's hand all those years ago at the Pleasure Beach in Blackpool.

Lonely.

"You talk about trust, but you can't trust the old Guardians any more than you believe you can trust me," she went on. "You know that. The members of the old council were always liars and manipulators. What have they told you of their real purpose, I wonder? Not much. Enough lies and misdirection to keep their pet Squint at their side, but not nearly enough of what is really going on. Because, Darwen Arkwright, if a mirroculist like yourself could see the true picture, you would quickly snap Mr. Peregrine's leash, the rope of lies with which he keeps you tethered, and then you would really come into your own. You haven't begun to tap the kind of power you could wield. The old shopkeeper won't let you. But join us, and things could be very different.

"The Guardians will be replaced," Scarlett purred, and now she stepped out into the open again, moving to where a great red lever stuck out from a bank of valves and dials. "I could give you a seat on the council that will take their place. And then you could have anything you wanted. With me beside you, Darwen Arkwright, and my master at our head, who could stand in your way?"

Darwen felt a rush of something unexpected, a thrill of pleasurable anticipation. Power. He had never had it. He had a gift, but to be able to use it for whatever he wanted, not having to worry about other people . . .

"She speaks the truth."

The voice seemed to come from everywhere. It was calm and low, distant but crystal clear, and it unwound like smoke in Darwen's ears. He realized that the mechanical laughter that had been ringing through the building had stopped. He looked up. The clown's face had changed. It was still the same figure, but what had been hard and shiny was now pliable and soft, like flesh, and its eyes, which were open now, were somehow, unmistakably, alive.

Greyling.

Darwen knew him at once, even in the clown's impossible face.

"You recognize me," said the clown. "How gratifying."

"I knew it would be you in the end," said Darwen.

"Of course you did," said Greyling. There was something of the clown in his voice, a lilting playfulness that went through Darwen like fingernails on a blackboard. "Because you are clever. Because you are talented in ways those around you cannot begin to appreciate."

"What do you want with this place?" Darwen asked.

"The place is irrelevant," said the clown, its head lolling, "or it would be without these wonderful little stone spheres. They really are remarkable, Darwen. You know what gives them their power, of course? It's not the stone itself. It's the labor that went into making them. The care. The respect. They were produced by a people without the most basic of metal tools. Do you have any idea how much work that would take? The time? The craft? The *love*? There's power there, Darwen. We had to adjust our equipment, of course, fine-tune the frequency to make them resonate in just the right way, but the real power came from the stones themselves. They hold the memory of those who made them like the tracks of tears. Emotional residue, Darwen. Potent stuff. They have only one drawback, which you have kindly sidestepped for me."

Darwen frowned. "I haven't done anything for you."

"Actually," said Greyling, "you have. As you know, those wonderful little stone spheres can be used to open portals, but, as you have probably begun to realize, anything to do with Silbrica—especially the power bound to its portals—is tied to thought, to intention. If it wasn't, I would never have been able to get so much energy out of a few children's books and toys last year. The people who made the stone balls knew nothing of machinery, Darwen, and their respect for—even love of—the jungle and all that lived in it was almost boundless. Again, there's power there, and it lingers, but it's a particular kind of power, and it doesn't suit all things. Imagine my disappointment when I found that my wonderful machines all died as they tried to cross through the gates! It was very frustrating to have to rely on living creatures like the Bleck to do my work for me."

"So you can't bring the generator through after all!" said Darwen, practically shouting. "You've lost."

"You misunderstand me," said Greyling. "I cannot open the stone-sphere portals for my beautiful and terrible machines. Only the mirroculist can do that, because the mirroculist masters the portal from whichever side he is on, while my powers are limited to Silbrica only." He paused, like a magician savoring the moment before the magical reveal, and Darwen felt a swelling sense of dread. "That is why I brought you here," Greyling continued. "So that you could do for me the one thing I could not:

open a nice wide gateway for my scrobblers and their equipment, including, of course, their generators. I am immensely grateful."

Darwen stared at him, his confusion turning to dismay. His gaze flashed over the scrobblers, the armored bulldozers, and the generators, which sat as if biding their time, and the horrified realization finally hit him. He knew what they had been waiting for. He remembered the zip line, his long, slow fall through the portal . . .

No.

"Thanks to your spectacular entrance tonight," the clown continued, "I can now pronounce this portal open to whatever I want to send through it!"

As he spoke, Scarlett threw the great red lever beside her, and there was a hiss of static. Darwen turned back toward the sound and saw that the arch was now flooded with a blue radiance that came from beyond the portal.

"My lords, ladies, and gentlemen," Greyling sang out, like he was introducing a circus act, "thanks to our most honored guest, the world-famous mirroculist, Darwen Arkwright, the invasion of the human world has begun!"

Darwen stared at the portal, overwhelmed by a sense of despair so crushing that he could not speak. Everything he had done had been in vain. All his courage, his determination—it had been for nothing. He had thought he was a hero, a savior, but the whole time Greyling had been toying with him, luring him so that he would do the one thing Greyling could not do for himself.

He had failed. Worse, he had handed victory to the enemy.

"I had hoped," Greyling continued, "that you would have helped willingly, knowingly, rather than by stumbling accident, as it turns out you have, but I still believe that we might be partners in greatness. With a mirroculist of your talent at my side, what could we not achieve?"

There was a pause, and Scarlett's eyes flicked between them, watchful.

Then the clownish Greyling smiled. "Darwen," he said, "you have already opened my portal for me. Would you care to have done it as my friend or as my enemy? We may not have such an opportunity again, Darwen Arkwright. Join me."

"Why do you look like that?" asked Darwen.

Greyling seemed to hesitate.

"You know things about me," said Darwen, answering his own question. "About my past. You can change the way people see you, and you tapped into my memories somehow, looking for something that would make you seem . . . familiar, comforting. Something that would associate you with happy times in my life. But I think Alex was right. There's something in my head that's trying to send me a message. I don't know why, but when you chose the way you would appear to me, you got it wrong. I remembered Blackpool," he said, thinking it through, "because going to the Calloway lights had reminded me of going there with my parents. You found the right place, the right moment, but you chose something I always hated, something that scared me, and you know what I think? I think that—somehow—*I did that*. Without knowing, without even sensing you were doing it, some part of me made you choose the wrong image so that when the time came for me to choose, I would recognize you for what you are. And now that time has come, and I've made my choice."

Darwen stood up. He took a long, steadying breath, raised the pistol in two hands, and fired, clamping the trigger down, emptying the weapon.

The energy stream sent the strange fairground shadows leaping, as if the carousel horses had come to life and the clown had grown twenty feet. Then there was a fizz, a pop, and the gun died in Darwen's hands.

"Missed," said Scarlett, smiling her toothy politician's smile. "And now it's all empty."

She leaped toward him, something of the eel creature's speed in her uncanny approach, and in moments she was close enough to touch. Instinctively he reached for her face, clamping his hand to her mouth and holding on. It had worked once before. . . .

But she did not wince away in pain as she had at Halloween, and when he released her, the smile was back. "You didn't think we'd try again before we'd found a way around that little weakness, did you?" she said silkily. "Ironic, isn't it? You have opened the portal for us, and none of your little friends will be able to come and help you. Not without the mirroculist to hold their hands. You are going to regret not being a better shot, little boy."

"Who says I missed?" said Darwen, recovering his defiance. "I wasn't aiming at you."

She smiled, thinking this was a ruse, but then she heard the scrobblers streaming out of the shadows. She caught their panic and turned.

The cage door was still smoking where Darwen had hit the lock. It hung open. And in great undulating waves of its sinewy tentacles, the Insidious Bleck was coming out.

Darwen wasn't sure, but he thought it looked angry.

It moved with extraordinary speed, pulling itself from the wreckage of the cage and crawling on the elbows of its tentacles across the factory floor. It tossed aside a pair of scrobblers and a gnasher, one of which had tried to stick it with some kind of spear wired to the pack on the scrobbler's back: a cattle prod. The scrobbler was down, but the prod was still sparking, as if jammed in the "on" position. Scarlett had bolted into the cover of the fairground clutter, but the monster seemed uninterested in her. It was making for the portal, trying to get out.

Darwen ran toward it. Diving toward the prone scrobbler, he rolled into a crouch with the cattle prod pointed up at the Bleck. The cable reaching to the scrobbler's pack gave him just enough room to lunge once and find the underside of one of those bristle-covered tentacles. There was a sound like fish going into a deep fryer, and the Bleck screamed, shrinking away. Darwen waited to make sure it had seen him, then ran as hard and fast as he could back toward the generator. Again he dove, sliding into the dust beneath the machine, drawing his legs up tight as the Bleck came after him.

If it was patient, he thought, it would seek him out with its tentacles, probing until it found him, and then it would drag him out and lift him up to that awful beak. But it wasn't patient. It was furious. It had been kept penned for weeks, perhaps months, pushed and prodded and caged by creatures of malice and greed, and it was now blind with rage.

Which was what Darwen wanted.

The Bleck caught the generator in its immense tentacles and lifted the entire thing off him. In the sudden light, Darwen saw its furious eyes and, dimly, heard Scarlett scream with anger as it cast the generator aside. There was a crash that shook the warehouse and a series of popping explosions.

The room was filled with a terrible, high-pitched shrieking. It was Greyling, raging as he lurched back and forth in his chair.

A tentacle like a massive python caught Darwen and snatched him up into the air. His legs kicked, but his arms were bound fast to his sides. He could do nothing. He smelled the monster's breath and saw the pulsing feelers around its mouth reaching for him as the great, razor-sharp beak opened.

Then there was a flash, and the Bleck quivered. Its eyes widened, then dimmed. It collapsed, and Darwen found himself rolling free. Another flash. Scarlett Oppertune had taken one of the scrobbler's energy weapons and fired it directly into the Bleck's fleshy underside. Her face was a mask of fury and hatred. She shot again, and the monster twitched. Then again, and again, until the weapon would fire no more.

For a moment Darwen thought Scarlett had saved him on purpose, but one look at her told him that was not true. She had just been angry, furious with the creature that had finally refused to do her bidding. But she still wanted Darwen dead.

Scarlett turned to the generator, which was lying on its side, its rivets popped and its seams broken open, before her gaze again found Darwen. All the style and polish was gone from her face now, it was so twisted with bitterness and savagery. She aimed the weapon at Darwen and tried the trigger again, but it merely clicked. "Kill him!" she shouted at the dazed scrobblers. "Now!"

But as she gave the order, something remarkable happened.

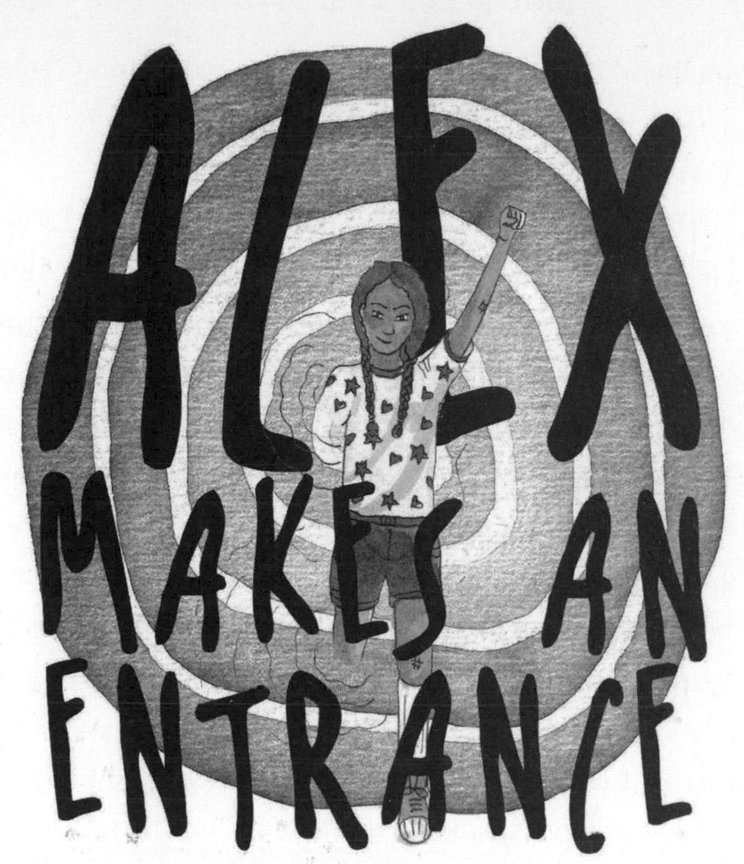

Alex stepped through the portal.

"Hey, Darwen," she said. "How's it going?"

"Been better," said Darwen.

"Two mirroculists!" exclaimed Scarlett, her eyes narrowing with disbelief. "How can there be two mirroculists?"

"Must be one of those buy-one-get-one-free deals," answered Alex. "Your lucky day. Not so lucky for Señor Delgado and his pals. They were on their way to help out here and really didn't see me coming."

"Rich and the others are in there," said Darwen, pointing at the ruptured generator. "Get them out."

"Oh, I don't think so," said Scarlett with a nasty grin. "It's time you learned some manners, young lady. You might have somehow slipped past those half-wit humans, but you are in my world now and that means—"

But before she finished her remark, her voice trailed off. She shaded her eyes and peered past Darwen toward the flickering portal.

"Oh," said Alex, who was stretching one hand back into the shimmering curtain of light. "You thought I came by myself? You really have to stop underestimating us."

Scarlett reached into her dainty purse and came up with a pistol, small but quite lethal. She raised it to shoot, and something hurtled past Darwen's head, hit Scarlett hard in the face, and sent her sprawling. At first Darwen thought it was one of the stone spheres, but then it bounced. Darwen had known that sound all his life.

A soccer ball.

He turned, and there were Felippe, Sarita, and Calida's mother. Last of all came Mr. Peregrine.

Darwen stared at the teacher, almost overwhelmed by a relief so sharp it brought tears to his eyes. Mr. Peregrine met his eyes and nodded once, smiling. Darwen nodded back, then he pointed at the generator and shouted, "Get them out of there!"

Scarlett was getting to her feet, but her unintended header had left her face warped and torn, and as she tried to adjust it, it ripped further. With a shout of frustration, she opened her mouth wide, and the great eel creature spilled slickly out, leaving the Scarlett suit crumpled on the ground.

"Do you have any idea how hard it is to grow those things?" she spit, turning on Darwen. Her voice was slightly slurred, as if her eel lips and tongue couldn't form the words properly, but the hard eyes were still Scarlett's. "You will pay for it with your sorry, pathetic little lives. Scrobblers!" she roared. "Once and for all. Wipe. Them. Out."

Darwen looked around. The scrobblers, which had scattered during the attack of the Bleck, were regrouping and checking their weapons. Two of the hulking toad things were hopping slowly forward, their immense mouths gaping. To Darwen's right, Mrs. Delgado was pulling the dazed and pale children from the wreckage of the generator. Rich and Chip were there, and Gabriel was unsteadily carrying the boy who Darwen had seen taken by the Bleck all those weeks ago: Luis. Gabriel was gazing into the boy's still face, his own face tear-streaked, and suddenly Darwen understood.

They were brothers.

That story Alex had told him about how Luis had a brother named Eduardo who had searched for him until he had collapsed of exhaustion was about Gabriel all along! But he hadn't been abducted by the Bleck. Somehow he had met Jorge, and the Guardians had put him to work.

But even as the truth registered, Darwen realized just how desperate their predicament was. There was just nowhere to go, and the scrobblers seemed to be everywhere. As Darwen glanced frantically about, the massive helmeted creatures began calmly sighting their weapons on the humans. They were all going to die.

"Get down!" Darwen yelled, running toward them.

They turned as if in a dream, looking for cover just as the first shots came. One of the toads flicked its tongue at them, and Darwen was horrified to see the thing extend at least twenty feet. It struck the side of the generator, slamming the metal pod with a surge of energy, and stuck there. In that moment a new threat presented itself: the toads could direct the power from their backpacks through their bodies.

The children and their would-be rescuers cowered behind the shattered generator as the scrobblers poured shot after deafening shot at them, and the machinery around crackled and exploded. Darwen hunkered down, scanning the anxious faces around him. Rich was rubbing his face as if trying to wake himself up, but there was no sign of Alex.

"What is going on?" said Chip, disoriented. All of his usual cockiness was gone, and he looked young and frightened. "Who are those men with the . . . faces?"

"I'll tell you later," said Darwen. "Just keep your head down."

It didn't seem like they—the humans—had any choices, and the scrobblers knew it. While one or two fired occasionally to keep them pinned down, the others were coming closer, some of them switching to wrenches and crowbars as they approached.

Rich was clenching and unclenching his fists as he tried to shake off the drowsiness of the generator. "If we can get over there," he said, "we might make it to the portal."

"Where?" said Mr. Peregrine, moving in the direction Rich had indicated.

"There!" shouted Rich. "I think I can make it. Get out of the way, and I'll draw their fire."

But before either of them could move, the boy Darwen was used to calling Gabriel stepped forward. He had something in his hand, a water bottle without a cap, and as Rich gaped, Gabriel jerked it in Mr. Peregrine's direction, splashing the teacher across the face.

"That wasn't very nice," said Mr. Peregrine in an odd voice, his bandaged hand to his cheek.

"Get out of the way," Rich began, but then Mr. Peregrine took his hand away from his face, and everyone stared. Where the water had hit him, his skin was falling away, dissolving, and beneath it all was black and shiny.

"Well, now," said Mr. Peregrine, with a strange, lopsided smile that seemed to split his face. "It seems the cat is out of the bag."

He pulled the bandage from his hand, and two of the fingers came with it, the flesh melting where it had gotten wet. The long, bloodless cut across his palm looked pale and greenish now, and the wound was wriggling with maggots that scattered and fell as something long and black poked through. The rod-like limb was slick and ended in a cruel hooked claw, which sliced the wound wide from the inside. First the hand, then the whole arm peeled back, the insides pale, sickly, and glistening like meat left out of the fridge.

"No!" gasped Rich.

"Mr. Peregrine" twisted sideways, using his good hand to grasp the splitting flesh, which now reached his shoulder. He tore it back, peeling his chest open so that the thing inside could clamber out in a thicket of shiny black limbs. As the insect form stepped out of the ruined flesh suit, it shook its head, and what was left of Mr. Peregrine slipped to the ground. In its place were composite eyes and a black and gaping insect mouth.

Darwen stared at the old man's deflated body on the ground, and for a moment he could not breathe. It wasn't horror. It was despair. Tears sprang to his eyes and all strength drained from him so that he swayed as if about to collapse.

Not Mr. Peregrine. Not Mr. Peregrine.

But even in his shock and misery, Darwen forced himself to look into the monstrous insect eyes, and he knew them.

Mr. Jenkins.

"Remember me?" said the insect in a harsh, brittle voice that stretched its dripping mouthparts. "I have looked forward to this."

And as Rich shrieked, the insect creature sprang at Darwen.

The others screamed, spilling out into the open as they fought to get away from the creature, out to where the scrobblers were waiting.

Darwen kicked and punched, but the Jenkins creature was too strong for him. It slammed him to the ground, its weight on his chest and its awful face inches from his throat. Its mouthparts moved, and its maw clicked open and closed in excitement.

Then it shuddered and rolled off, dislodged by a firm kick to its head. Rich. Darwen scrabbled to his feet. He staggered back and into something hard: one of the tank bulldozers.

There was a ladder fitted to one side. Darwen swung himself up and started throwing switches and pulling levers. A scrobbler fired at him, but the shot ricocheted off the armored plate just as the engine came roaring to life. If he could buy the others a minute, less, they might get out. He shoved another lever, and the great tracked juggernaut lurched forward.

The scrobblers scattered again. There was no steering wheel on the machine, just a pair of levers. Darwen pushed hard on the left one, and the bulldozer slewed to the side, crates exploding into splinters under its massive tracks. Scarlett was shouting and pointing, but even as Darwen shrank low in his seat to avoid another flashing energy shot, he saw his target. The hideous, lurching clown loomed over him, its face set, its mouth moving in commands he couldn't hear over the bellow of the engine. Darwen slammed both levers, and the bulldozer surged forward.

The clown turned to him at the last moment, its smooth amusement replaced with a deep, malicious hatred. It screamed once, and then the great plow of the bulldozer crashed through the glass case and into its body. Its head kicked backward, its body buckled and fell beneath the machine's deadly treads, and it was ground to powder.

Darwen saw the moment Greyling left. One minute the clown's eyes were alive and full of wrath, the next they were just painted glass again. The leader of the New Council was gone.

Darwen grabbed the levers to send the bulldozer toward the nearest group of scrobblers, turning to find the Jenkins insect on top of the bulldozer and poised to strike. He tried to dodge, but the insect claw caught him on the shoulder, and as he slumped backward, his shirt snagged on one of the levers. The machine leaped suddenly to the left and then locked itself in a slow, dizzying spin. A toad tongue shot through the air. Darwen leaned back as it missed his head by inches, but he felt the surge of electricity as it struck the bulldozer. The engine died in a puff of black smoke. Then he was being lifted bodily by those long, impossibly strong insect legs, and Mr. Jenkins dropped him heavily to the warehouse floor.

Wordlessly the scrobbler troops corralled the captives, the children shrinking from the blank stare of the bloated toads. Darwen looked hopelessly up. There was no way out.

The Scarlett eel glared at the shattered remains of the clown.

"You haven't killed him," she hissed, pivoting on her tail and gaping at him between words so that her pointed teeth showed like rows of knives. "But you will be punished anyway."

"What are you going to do?" snapped Darwen with all the defiance he could muster. "Kill me?"

"Of course," she said. "Last."

Darwen looked wildly around. His eyes found Rich, but he still couldn't see Alex. She must have been hit.

Well, he thought. *At least she was spared this.*

A strange silence had descended on the warehouse. Distantly there were the snaps and fizzes of broken machinery, but no one spoke, and even Mrs. Delgado's tears were silent. The scrobblers raised their weapons, gazing blankly through their masks, but even they did not bellow or snarl. Everyone knew. This would be an execution, not a battle.

One more moment of stillness and then . . . an electronic hiss from the portal.

There was Alex, standing half in, half out, silhouetted in the flickering light, holding the gateway open for . . . whom?

Not *whom—what*.

Darwen caught the movement, which was quick, stealthy, and animal.

No, he thought. *It couldn't be*.

Scarlett turned, puzzled, and for a second the scrobblers just stood there.

And then in a blur of fur and claws, they came: the pouncels from the jungle locus, led by one that was slightly smaller than the others and that moved with a limp. They streaked in, and the scrobblers fell back, firing, shrieking, and bellowing as the pouncels flew at them. One of the toads shot out its tongue and caught a pouncel, zapping it lifeless before it pulled it into its sickening mouth.

But then something like a rocket struck the toad, and it went down in a blaze of light and smoke.

Someone had come with the pouncels, and he was shooting back. It was Weazen—he was alive!—and he was picking off the enemy like a tiny otter-sized sharpshooter, blasting openings for the boiling mass of pouncels, which dragged the scrobblers and gnashers down in a wild, animal frenzy.

The thing that had been Scarlett Oppertune snapped its jaws, throwing the pouncels off, but there were too many of them, and they were too fast. Her hard little eyes found Darwen. She reached toward him, imploring, desperate, and without thinking he took a step toward her, extending his hand. She snatched at it, caught his fingers in her teeth, and held on, even as the pouncels pulled her backward. She didn't bite down, just gripped like she was holding on to a lifeline. Darwen felt Rich grab his free arm so that he wouldn't be sucked into the pouncels' snapping fury and saw realization flash through Scarlett's animal face: for her, it was over.

Her jaws relaxed a little, and Darwen felt her slipping away, but then her grip tightened again, her bright eyes snapped wide open, and, with her last ounce of strength, she pulled herself close enough to whisper into his face, releasing his hand as she spoke. "If you ever find him, ask him how he knew your name."

And then she was yanked backward, and the pouncels fell on her.

For a second Darwen stood where he was, stunned, dimly aware that Rich was dragging him back and away. Weazen sent a barrage of covering fire over their heads, and Darwen shrank back, Scarlett's words rolling around in his head.

Alex had stayed where she was, and Darwen, barely daring to glance back to the fight, led the children with Mrs. Delgado back to the portal and out. He paused only to see the Jenkins insect that had been chasing them being sucked backward into the surging throng of pouncels, where it fell, shrieking, and vanished.

Darwen hesitated, his eyes flashing around the great chamber, searching.

"Time to go, Darwen Arkwright," said Weazen, who appeared next to him, his blaster at the ready. "He's not here."

"I can't leave him!" said Darwen. Tears suddenly burned hot in his eyes, and he shouted at the top of his lungs, "Mr. Peregrine! Mr. Peregrine, where are you?"

He took a step into the warehouse, but Weazen caught his arm with one tiny but powerful claw. "It's not safe—the whole place is going to go up," he said, pulling at

Darwen so he had to stoop to look the little creature in his pale masked face. "He's not here."

Darwen's eyes fell on a painted hand—the last shattered remnant of the laughing clown—and then, as one of the pieces of equipment wired to the generator exploded with a burst of orange flame, he let Weazen pull him back toward the portal and out into his own world.

"How much does Chip remember?" asked Alex as she watched Rich and Darwen pack.

"Don't know," said Rich. "He's not talking—not to me, anyway. Looks kind of spooked."

"Like he's a butterfly that got hit with a book?" asked Alex.

"Kind of," said Rich.

"Good," said Alex. "Do you know how he ended up there in the first place?"

"The thing that called itself Mr. Peregrine took him," said Rich. "Whittley must have seen some stuff, but he was pretty out of it. We all were. In the generator you sort of lose track of who you are. I wouldn't be surprised if Chip's a bit hazy on what actually happened."

"Probably good," said Alex. "Though no one is going to be hazy about us going home without Mr. P."

There was a long silence.

Alex began, "You think he's—"

"No," Darwen cut in. "Scarlett—Miss Murray—said something about talking to him if I found him. I don't know how those flesh suit things work, but I don't think they are the bodies of the people they look like."

"So you think they're, like, cloned from living tissue or something?" Rich asked.

"I don't know," said Darwen.

"Like they keep the real person alive and grow the suit—or whatever it is—from the person?"

"I don't know."

"You think that's why the fake Mr. P smelled weird and didn't want to get wet?"

"Rich," said Darwen, giving him a hard look, "I really don't know."

"Rich is right, more or less," said a voice. They turned to find Jorge watching them cautiously.

"You," said Alex.

"Darwen," said Jorge, ignoring her tone. "Rich. Alex. I've come to say thank you. What you did last night was extremely . . . brave and, er, courageous."

Darwen nodded, but he didn't speak.

"The Guardian Council wishes to honor you," Jorge began, but Darwen cut him off.

"The Guardians told me to stay out of it," he said. "I acted against their orders."

"That's true," said Jorge, looking uncomfortable, "but given the outcome—your success—they are prepared to overlook the nature of your behaviors."

"Is that right?" said Darwen quietly, smiling.

"How nice of them," said Alex, whose face was stern.

"This honor," said Rich, "not some kind of cash prize, is it?"

Before Jorge could respond, Darwen spoke. "I won't be taking any of their honors," he said. "In fact, I don't think that the Guardian Council and I are going to be on speaking terms from now on."

Jorge's face clouded. "What do you mean? You are their mirroculist. You work on their instructions."

"Yeah?" said Darwen. "I'm not sure I like the kind of instructions I've been getting. I was told that the Guardians wanted to make a deal with Greyling. I was told to abandon the people who live here, the rainforest itself, even my friends. Now, I don't always know what the right thing to do is, but I know that some things are worth fighting for, and I never abandon my friends. So unless there's something else you have to say, you can be on your way."

For a moment it looked like Jorge was going to argue, but then he nodded simply, his face set. He half turned to leave, but stopped himself. "We think Mr. Peregrine is still alive," he said. "He seems to have been taken by Greyling two months ago in preparation for . . . everything. He knows a great deal that the enemy might find useful. Rescuing him is a priority for the Guardians. Whether you choose to work with the council on this is, of course, your decision."

He walked away, and the three students watched him go.

"He sent me the oven door," said Darwen.

"Mr. Peregrine?" said Alex.

"The real Mr. Peregrine," said Darwen, "not the Jenkins thing. It may have been the last thing he did before they took him. We have to get him back."

"Well, duh!" said Alex. "We're the Peregrine Pact, remember? Of course we're going to rescue him."

"With or without the council's help?" asked Rich.

"Not sure yet," said Darwen. "What have the students been told?"

"Melissa Young said that Mr. Peregrine had to go home early," said Rich. "Family emergency."

Darwen sighed. He had been morose all morning, and it wasn't just because they were heading back to regular classes and a comparatively cold Atlanta winter. His mind was full of questions, some of them so unsettling that he wasn't sure he wanted to know the answers.

"Look at him," said Alex to Rich, "like his goldfish died. You should be celebrating, man. You know what we pulled off last night? We stopped Greyling! We saved the jungle—"

"Rainforest," inserted Rich.

"You do that one more time," snapped Alex, "and I'll slap you till you squeal. Hand to God." She turned back to Darwen. "You listening? We turned the pouncels on Scarlett Murray or whatever we call her eel-headed self, and we saved a bunch of kids. You should be—"

"Right chuffed?" Darwen supplied.

"Exactly," said Alex. "Oh, and guess what?"

"What?" said Rich.

"Sarita told me that now that Scarlett's development plans have fallen through, some of the families are going to move back."

"I'm surprised you involved the local kids," said Darwen. "I thought you would keep it within the Peregrine Pact."

Alex shrugged. "It was their fight too," she said. "In some ways, more than ours."

"What do they say about what happened?" asked Darwen.

"They're sort of rolling with it," Alex said, frowning. "It's weird. They didn't know about the portals and stuff, but they aren't exactly surprised to find out that they were there and that there were monsters coming through them. I don't think they'll be bringing in the big-city reporters or anything. They'll just get on with their lives. Speaking of which," she added, turning to Rich, "you said they didn't have anything beyond the rainforest and their past. The shattered remnants of a once noble history, remember?"

"So?" said Rich.

"So it's not true," she said. "They have each other. They have family, which means more to them than anything. They showed that last night."

Darwen nodded. *Family*. He felt the word like a warm spot in a cold bed, and for a moment he was jealous of them.

"Anyway," said Rich, "if the reporters do come, there's nothing for them to see. The scrobbler engines never made it through. The portals don't work anymore. Whatever got destroyed in the warehouse last night, it messed up the gates. Even the circle of stones under the zip line closed up right after we came out of it."

"You know what this means," said Darwen softly.

"What?" said Rich.

"It might be just us. Rescuing Mr. Peregrine, protecting

Silbrica, defending our world against Greyling's invasion. We might have to do all of it by ourselves, without the Guardians' help, possibly even . . ."

His voice trailed off.

"Against them?" said Alex. "Not sure I like the sound of that."

"No," said Rich. "That would not be good."

Alex raised her eyebrows at the understatement.

"Hi, Chip," said Rich, cutting her off.

The tall, good-looking black boy was walking down from the dining shelter with his bags. He slowed, and his eyes narrowed as he saw them. He looked uncertain, suspicious.

"So," said Rich breezily. "Interesting trip, huh?"

Chip Whittley just stood there, looking at them. "Last night," he stammered. "That place. Where . . . ? What . . . ?"

Darwen tensed.

Fortunately the previous night wasn't the only thing on Chip's mind. Chip looked at them, then turned and stared at the ocean. At last his gaze fell on Alex, then dropped to the ground. "Listen," he said, his voice low. "About that butterfly . . ." The words dried up, and he stood rigid, his fists clenched, eyes staring at a tiny hermit crab in the grass.

"What about it?" said Alex.

Chip looked up, and Darwen was amazed to see that his eyes shone with unshed tears, but at the same moment there were sounds of people coming down the path. Nathan and

Barry, with Genevieve and Melissa at their heels.

Panic crossed Chip's face.

"What's going on here?" asked Nathan. "Saying good-bye to the jungle creatures, Chip?"

Chip blinked, and for the briefest moment, Darwen thought he saw a spasm of anguish in the boy's face before it set into its usual haughty confidence. "Something like that," he said, turning back to Nathan. "Come on. I want to get a good place in the boat."

Together they walked down to the beach, leaving Darwen, Rich, and Alex by the tent.

"So close," said Alex. "For a second there he was nearly human. Ah well."

"After what he went through," Rich exclaimed, "how can he just go back to being . . . like himself?"

"Easier this way," said Alex. "And besides, now I can go back to hating him. The trip has brought me clarity."

"That's not all you got out of this trip," said Rich grudgingly. "You're a mirroculist too. I still can't see through the mirrors, let alone open them, but you two . . ."

"Maybe it's just here," said Alex, shrugging. "Maybe something about those stones rubbed off on me. We'll have to test it when we get back. If all I can see through Darwen's oven door is Aunt Honoria's apple pie, then I guess I'm not a real mirroculist after all."

"You're just saying that so I won't feel left out," said Rich.

"Partly," said Alex. "And partly because I like saying 'apple pie.' Red beans and rice is all well and groovy, but I'm ready for some down-home cooking."

"You won't get it from Aunt Honoria," said Darwen, shouldering his backpack. "She doesn't cook."

"You think the pouncels got out before the place blew?" asked Alex.

"Weazen said most of them made it," said Darwen. "I take it the leader was the one you looked after?"

"And you said they were just animals," said Alex. "There's no *just* about it. Smart they were, and loyal. More than some people. Like Sasha. You reckon the Bleck knew what it was doing when it destroyed the generator?"

"I thought it was just mad," said Darwen, "but maybe there was more to it."

"And this Weazen character," said Rich, "he's a feisty little weasel, isn't he?"

"I wouldn't call him that if I were you," said Darwen.

"You think we'll see him again?" asked Rich.

"Definitely," said Alex. "We have to find Mr. P. We'll need whatever friends we still have."

Darwen nodded. It could not be a coincidence that he had not been able to reach Moth. Greyling must have sealed her locus so that he couldn't learn anything about what was happening from her. He would need to find a way in. "You think Weazen and the dellfeys will stand with us if it means going against the Guardians?" he asked.

"You really don't get loyalty, do you, Darwen?" said Alex. "Of course they'll stand with us. If you had a dog, you'd know."

Rich was gazing along the shore path toward the village. People were coming. Mrs. Delgado, holding her daughter's hand, and some of the village children. Sarita was with them, along with Felippe and his sister, Calida. Behind them were two boys, one whom they had called Gabriel—Eduardo—and his brother, Luis.

"We have come to say goodbye," said Sarita. "And thank you."

Mrs. Delgado stepped forward and took Darwen's hand. Into it she pressed a small stone sphere about the size of a baseball.

"What?" he said. "I can't take this. I appreciate it and everything, but it belongs to you. To your people."

As the woman continued to press it, nodding and smiling, Sarita spoke up. "It is not ancient," she said. "Some of the villagers still make the stone balls to mark special places. They make them the old way. It takes a very long time. She wants you to have it."

Darwen gazed at it. It was heavy and perfectly round.

"Thank you," he said. "It is beautiful."

Alex jabbered in Spanish, and the children laughed.

"What?" asked Rich and Darwen together.

"I was just thanking Felippe for that soccer shot to Scarlett's head. I think it would have scored from the half-way line."

Darwen and Rich shook Felippe's hand.

"Too bad we never got to have a rematch," said Darwen.

"Yes," said Felippe. He added something in Spanish, and the kids laughed again.

"He said they went easy on you the first time," said Alex.

Gabriel—Eduardo—stepped forward and offered Darwen his hand. "Can we speak in private?" he asked. He seemed older now, more confident and direct now that he had his true identity back.

Darwen flushed, then nodded. "Sure," he said.

Darwen and the two brothers walked down to the beach in silence. A scarlet macaw flew up from one of the palm trees, calling, and Darwen found that such things still amazed him.

"I am sorry that I did not trust you," said the boy formerly known as Gabriel. "Jorge told me that you might be dangerous, that you might not follow the Guardians' wishes, and that I should hide who he was from you." Eduardo paused, glancing down at his feet in shame. "I spied on you. I spilled the gasoline from the boat because he wanted to see what would come through the portals after dark. He wanted to see if you were right about the

Bleck and if there was evidence of Greyling. He didn't want to tell you about it, but he needed you there to open the portal if it appeared." He inhaled, his breath catching in his throat. "I did not know how much danger I had put you in. I am sorry."

"It's okay," said Darwen. Then a realization struck. "You wore that veil so that the local kids wouldn't recognize you, didn't you?"

Eduardo grinned and nodded, peeking at Luis for approval.

"I'll bet you had a lot of explaining to do last night," said Darwen.

"Not as much as you would think," said Eduardo. "They are just happy that we are back. When the creature disguised as Mr. Peregrine gave you the portal, I recognized it, and I knew where it would take you because I had been there. It was a place in Silbrica where Jorge used to communicate with the Guardians. It would have exposed him. I reset the device. I think that made it open up in the last place it was used. Since Mr. Peregrine was one of those flesh-suit things, that probably put you in danger too."

Darwen thought back to their nightmarish experience in the Jenkins house, but found himself shrugging. "It's okay," he said. "I would have probably just ended up in front of Greyling sooner. That's what that fake Mr. Peregrine would have wanted."

Eduardo nodded ruefully, and Darwen searched his face. "Tell me about how you became involved with the Guardians."

"Everything I did," said Eduardo, giving Darwen a level, piercing look, "I did to find my brother. I should have joined you, but I did not know that then. The Guardians came to me when I was lost, when the search for Luis had deprived me of my ability to think. They used me, but I had to trust them, because losing my brother was like losing a part of myself. It made me alone. You understand?"

Darwen nodded and looked down. He understood all too well.

Luis spoke up. "Thank you," he said simply.

He looked embarrassed, unsure of himself, and it struck Darwen as strange that this was the first time they had spoken.

"I remembered your face," said the boy, "from when the monster took me. When I was awake in the machine, when I could remember who I was, I thought of your face, and I thought you would come for me. I knew my brother would search for me too, so I had two. . . ." He sought for the word, then spoke quickly in Spanish.

Eduardo smiled and, clearly wishing he didn't have to say it, completed his brother's thought. "Heroes," he said.

"Heroes," Luis agreed.

Darwen smiled and—as much to change the subject as anything else—turned back to Eduardo. "Why were you with Chip?" he asked.

"The thing that said it was Mr. Peregrine was suspicious of me because I was always watching you and talking to Jorge," said Eduardo. "I think it knew who I was. It said it wanted to show me something, something about the village children who had been taken. I didn't trust him, but I had to see, so I took someone with me. I thought that if one of the Hillside students went missing, then you would go looking for him. It was . . . a mistake."

"Why Chip?"

Eduardo flushed, ashamed of himself. "Because I thought that whoever went with me might never get out," he said. He looked down and was about to say more when Alex yelled from the camp.

"They're leaving!" she called.

The three boys nodded, relieved to rejoin the others.

"We will meet again, Darwen Arkwright," said the boy they had called Gabriel. "I am sure of it."

"I'd like that," said Darwen.

They shook hands and said goodbye. Alex hugged everyone, then waved expansively as they walked back along the shore.

Darwen slipped the stone sphere into his backpack and said, "Okay. Is that everything?"

"Looks like," said Rich. "I guess they'll leave Mr. P's stuff here."

"I, for one, am not touching it," said Alex. "And stop calling him Mr. P."

"You'd rather I called him Mr. Jenkins?" said Rich.

"How about Swamp Thing?" said Alex. "Swampy for short. It suits his smell."

"Those people suits they wear," said Rich. "You think they have to fill them out with struts and wires and stuff, like you do when you stuff an animal?"

"When you *what*?" said Alex, giving him her beadiest stare.

"I have an uncle who's an amateur taxidermist. He had this raccoon that he hit with his truck one night—"

"Fascinating though this story is sure to be," Alex interjected, "I don't need more details about the insides of animals and the exploits of your hillbilly family."

"Who are you calling hillbillies?" Rich exclaimed.

And they were off, a squabble that lasted all the way to the boat, then back around the cove to the main village and halfway back to the airstrip.

Darwen gazed out of the jeep window as they forded a brown river, watching something that might have been a log and might have been a crocodile, and he grinned to himself. It had been an amazing trip, but he was ready for . . . home?

Well, Atlanta. The smile stayed on his lips, but faded

from his eyes. He couldn't keep thinking of his aunt's apartment like it was a hotel in some place he was visiting for a while. England was part of his past. He might never return now, and if he did, it would be as a different person. Because it wasn't just that he no longer had family there that would make a trip to Lancashire strange. He had changed. He knew it. What he had done last night would have been completely beyond him only a few months ago. Losing his parents and coming to America had torn him apart, but he had grown, strengthened in the process. His parents, he felt sure, would be proud of him.

He just wished they could see it.

Look, Dad, what I can do, he thought. *Look, Mum. It looks like a mirror, but I can go through it. I can fight monsters too. I even wiped the smile off that chuffin' clown from Blackpool.*

He wiped his eyes, grinning, and as he pictured the mayhem of those final moments in the warehouse, Scarlett's parting words came back to him.

Ask him how he knew your name.

For a moment he had thought she meant Greyling, but that wasn't right. Last night he had been thinking about rescuing Mr. Peregrine and had found himself remembering their first meeting in his shop just after Darwen had arrived in Atlanta. They had been talking about the shopkeeper's old clock, which said only if it was day or night and was accurate up to about twenty seconds. Darwen had said that he was sure that was good enough, but the shopkeeper had turned that odd look of his on him and said, "Never be sure about such things. A lot can happen in twenty seconds, Mr. Arkwright."

But Darwen had not told him his name.

It had struck him as odd at the time, but he had forgotten the moment entirely until last night. He was sure that was what Scarlett had meant, but how had she known about it, and why did she think it significant? And what did it mean that Alex had, at least for the time being, become what everyone said was impossible: a *second* mirroculist? He didn't know why he put those two questions together, but in his gut he knew they were connected, that if he could find out more about what it was to be a Squint, he would be able to answer both questions. When he found the real Mr. Peregrine—and he *would* find him—he would have a lot of questions for the old shopkeeper.

That would have to wait. For now there was the wearying journey, which seemed a lot less exciting in this direction, and then getting home and getting clean—properly clean—for the first time in a week, and getting truly dry, and sleeping in his own bed.

He smiled again. It might not be home, exactly, not yet, but there was a lot to be said for his aunt's Atlanta apartment.

"Now that I'm a mirroculist," said Alex, "I think I

should write a book about it. One day when I'm famous for saving the world, people will want to know all about my first experience as a Squint. I will call it *Alexandra O'Connor and the Insidious Bleck*."

"What about us?" said Rich.

"You're not a Squint," said Alex.

"Thanks. What about Darwen then?"

"*Darwen Arkwright and the Insidious Bleck*?" said Alex derisively. "That's terrible. Darwen is a ridiculous name. Sorry, but it is. No one is called Darwen. You have to give the reading public something they can relate to."

"I wonder why I can't open the portals," said Rich.

"Maybe it's a race thing," said Alex.

"What?"

"Hey, I'm just saying. I'm black. Darwen is half black."

"Why would race have anything to do with it?" said Rich.

"Maybe because the white folks have enough already, so we get this," said Alex.

"Right," said Rich, rolling his eyes. "Because you and Chip Whittley are really living at the poverty line."

They reached Hartsfield Jackson Airport in Atlanta in the late afternoon and were met not by Eileen, as Darwen had feared, but by Alex's mom and her baby sister, Kaitlin. They had been delegated to pick up Darwen and Rich, whose father would be coming to collect him from

Aunt Honoria's place later. They were all going there.

They said their goodbyes to the other students, then found their way to Mrs. O'Connor's car in the frigid parking deck, all the while telling her tales of what they had been doing in the jungle and all the things they had seen. Well, some of them. They left out anything to do with Silbrica, but that didn't seem to make their adventures any less exciting. Mrs. O'Connor hugged Alex to her at each mention of snakes and spiders and poison-dart frogs, punctuating each new detail with a cry of "Oh, my lord!"

They drove through Atlanta's traffic-jammed streets, and Darwen was surprised to find the massive city's tower blocks and freeways familiar, even comforting, after his spell in the jungle.

At their apartment building, Darwen, Rich, and Alex lugged the bags into the elevator under the watchful eye of Mrs. O'Connor and Kaitlin, and they rode up to the seventeenth floor. As they got higher, Darwen felt an unease similar to embarrassment or anxiety swelling like the pressure in his ears. In many ways, his aunt was still a stranger to him. He didn't want everyone watching his reunion with her. By the time he had dragged his bag out onto their floor, he was feeling distinctly uncomfortable and was beginning to wish Rich and Alex had gone straight home.

But as he reached their apartment door, something

remarkable happened. Darwen was muttering vaguely that his aunt didn't normally have company over, when he stopped short, sniffing the air.

It couldn't be.

It was a warm, rich smell of potato and onion cooked slowly with stewing beef, a hearty smell that took him right back into his best, most cherished memories.

Lancashire hotpot.

The door opened before he could knock, and there was Aunt Honoria, smiling, a little teary, and wearing—for the first time that Darwen had ever seen—an apron that was dusted with flour. She folded him into her arms and, forgetting the others entirely, Darwen embraced her.

"Welcome home," she said.

THE END

Acknowledgments

Special thanks to Professor John Hoopes and Anne Egitto for fielding questions about the archaeology of Costa Rica and the stone spheres. Thanks to Raven Wei, to my agent, Stacey Glick, to my editor at Razorbill, Gillian Levinson, and to my illustrator, Emily Osborne. Finally, thanks to my family, who keep me grounded in this world while helping me to invent others.